THREE BARGAINS

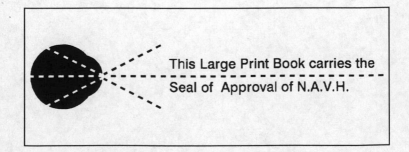

This Large Print Book carries the
Seal of Approval of N.A.V.H.

THREE BARGAINS

TANIA MALIK

THORNDIKE PRESS

A part of Gale, Cengage Learning

GALE
CENGAGE Learning·

Farmington Hills, Mich • San Francisco • New York • Waterville, Maine
Meriden, Conn • Mason, Ohio • Chicago

GALE
CENGAGE Learning®

LIBRARY OF CONGRESS CATALOGING-IN-PUBLICATION DATA

Malik, Tania.
  Three bargains / by Tania Malik. — Large print edition.
    pages ; cm. — (Thorndike Press large print reviewers' choice)
    ISBN 978-1-4104-7444-5 (hardcover) — ISBN 1-4104-7444-5 (hardcover)
  1. India—Fiction. 2. Fathers and sons—Fiction. 3. Social classes—Fiction. 4.
Large type books. I. Title.
PR9499.4.M356T47 2014b
823'.92—dc23   2014030679

Published in 2014 by arrangement with W. W. Norton & Company, Inc.

·Printed in Mexico
1 2 3 4 5 6 7 18 17 16 15 14

Dedicated to my parents,
Rita and Ranbir Gambhir

CHAPTER 1

Gorapur, 1983

Sawdust, soft and fine as Ma's best muslin duppata, tickled Madan's nose, making him sneeze. His father's grip on his hand tightened, as if the sudden movement would make Madan lose his footing on the timber mill's uneven brick floor. Madan flexed his fingers to make his father loosen his hold, but his father was using the tightness of his grip to navigate Madan through the obstacle course of whirring saws and hot clanging plywood presses. Everywhere, piles of logs lay in misshapen triangles. Madan felt his grimy kurta adhere to his skin, the sweltering temperature of the midafternoon intensified by the raging furnace in the center of the factory. Struggling to keep pace with his father's determined step, Madan faltered, and his father grunted impatiently.

"Keep up, you son of a bitch," his father said. "He's waiting for us."

By the time they reached the offices at the far end of the factory, Madan had lost sight of his mother and six-year-old sister sitting outside the high iron gate. Swati was asleep, curled up in Ma's lap, her sari's pallu protecting Swati from the sun and flies.

His father knocked on the glass half of the factory owner's office door. "Stay here till I call you. Okay?"

Madan jerked his head up and down in a gesture he hoped conveyed deference. His father's lips twisted into what Madan took for a smile, but it was not one of reassurance or welcome. If his father could, he would pack the family back on the train to their village, continue to send them money intermittently and visit them only when he wanted. But now they were here, and his father was adjusting to this development as if he'd discovered that someone had taken a piss in his morning cup of tea. The smile hovered around his father's lips but Madan didn't bother returning it. He knew to fear the capriciousness of that smile, how it teased and promised many things yet was easily tempted away by a quarter liter of desi tahra.

He nodded again but his father, responding to the call of "Aaho!," disappeared into the office.

Placing his back to the office wall, Madan looked out onto the factory floor. Men, black as the cawing crows above and shiny with sweat, worked in groups around large machines. They glanced curiously at him. He turned and faced the wall. It was yellow and chalky, with ridges and bumps, and when Madan rubbed his hands against it, they came off covered with a delicate white dust.

The door opened suddenly and his father's hand reached out, catching him by the collar and pulling him to the other side of the wall.

He kept his head bowed. He dared not raise it. Through the opening at the bottom of the large desk he saw two monstrous feet, dried and cracked like parched earth. Broad-strapped leather sandals, each with a big brass buckle in the center, glinted up at Madan.

"This is my boy," his father said.

"Come here," he heard.

His father pushed him forward. "Say salaam to saab."

Madan lifted his head and his first thought, even before he could articulate the "Salaam . . ." was if Avtaar Singh stood up, he would surely go through the roof. He loomed over Madan and his shiny wooden

9

desk, in a striped blue short-sleeve shirt hanging loose over his trousers, his hair swept away from his face and cropped short to the fold of his shirt's collar. A thick, hooded mustache dominated his otherwise clean-shaven face, and the deep blackness of his eyes twinkled with the reflection of the bright overhead tube lights.

"What's your name, boy?" The sound boomed in his ear like the thundering train he'd just got off. Madan lowered his gaze to the watch ticking on Avtaar Singh's wrist, his only adornment besides the deep red mauli string looped tightly around the other wrist.

"Madan."

Avtaar Singh swiveled his chair toward him. Madan had never seen a chair do that, let alone have tiny wheels under its legs. It looked like a ride at the fair.

A hefty hand cupped his chin. Though the hand wasn't packed with heavy muscle, every action seemed generated from some explosive power source. "And how old are you, Madan?"

"Eleven . . . twelve," he stammered.

"Eleven or twelve, boy?"

"Twelve . . . saab."

Avtaar Singh fixed his gaze on Madan, and Madan tried to glance toward his father but the tight grip on his chin wouldn't let him.

"What is that?" Avtaar Singh asked, and Madan flinched. He followed Avtaar Singh's gaze to the top buttons of his kurta. A folded comic book peeked out of his collar. Madan felt the smooth paper disengage from his sticky skin as his body cooled down in the air-conditioned room. He'd stuck it in there before they'd left the village.

"Show it to me." Releasing Madan's chin, Avtaar Singh held out his hand.

Madan reached into his shirt and unfolded the comic, handing it to him. He watched Avtaar Singh scan the comic book.

"But . . . this is in English?" Avtaar Singh looked from Madan to his father. For a moment Madan thought Avtaar Singh's bulging eyes looked comical. But just for a moment. Avtaar Singh shook the flimsy pages at his father, saying again, "Did you know this is English?"

Madan, relieved that his chin was finally free, also looked to his father for an explanation.

"Saab." His father laughed, but it sounded like an abrupt cough. "In the village . . . there was a crazy army-wallah, saab. Some retired colonel. He tried to teach the children English. My wife told me Madan used

11

to wait for him every day to come and teach. But what are we people going to do with this fancy-type language? Children . . . they don't understand. Don't worry, saab. I've got him a job at Prem Dhaba, serving tea, earn a little money for the family . . ." His father trailed off when he saw Avtaar Singh wasn't listening.

This was the first Madan had heard of a job, but before he could begin to daydream about what he would buy with the money earned, Avtaar Singh asked, "Can you read this, boy?"

Madan glanced at his father. He didn't want to get into trouble, and the look on his father's face promised a belt on his back.

"Don't look there. I'm talking to you."

Madan forced himself to look at Avtaar Singh. Slowly, he nodded.

Avtaar Singh's finger moved along the title. "Start."

" 'Amar . . . Chitra . . . Katha,' " Madan read. " 'Pan-cha-tantra.' "He was not sure if he was saying it right. " 'The Brahmin, the Goat, and Other Stories,' " he finished quickly.

"And this?" Avtaar Singh opened the comic and pointed again before Madan could catch his breath.

" 'How . . . could . . . the villiager . . . villager . . . pl-ay such a . . . treeck . . .' "

Avtaar Singh brusquely whipped the comic book away before Madan finished. He folded it back up and handed it to Madan, but did not let go right away. Unsure what to do, Madan held the comic by the other end.

"Can you read this, Prabhu?" Avtaar Singh asked his father.

"No . . . no, saab," Madan heard his father's quiet reply, sounding distant and inconsequential. Madan wanted to go to the toilet, but he willed himself not to tremble or look in his father's direction.

Avtaar Singh finally released his hold on the comic and Madan scrambled back to his father.

"So, Prabhu, now your family is here, I want no more excuses. I want to see hard work, that's what I pay for." Avtaar Singh appeared more preoccupied with the papers on his desk.

"Yes, saab."

"Where's your woman?"

"She's outside, saab."

"Send her to the kitchen tomorrow. I'll tell memsaab and she'll work out her pay."

"Thank you, saab."

It was time to go. As his father swung open the door, ushering Madan out, Avtaar Singh spoke once again, still not looking up.

13

"Prabhu, bring the boy in next week. He'll go to school. To my Gorapur Academy. I will take care of it. No dhaba work for this boy."

They stood paralyzed within the doorframe, his father's fingers digging into the nape of his neck. Madan glanced up to remind his father of whose neck was in his pinching grip, and caught the whiplash of anger across his father's face, the sharp intake of breath and then the quiet, "Yes, thank you, saab." The door swung shut behind them.

CHAPTER 2

Madan watched Swati's sleeping face bump along on his father's shoulder. He trailed behind his parents as they kept to the dirt sides of the road. Trucks and cars whizzed by with a ferocity that blew sand in his eyes and made his head spin.

"It's a good-size room," he heard his father say to his mother. "The servants' quarters are behind the main house. There are two more rooms for the other servants."

From the train Madan saw the Yamuna River curving around the eastern end of Gorapur, but the rest of the town seemed to have forfeited this grace, erupting haphazardly through the fields of millet and rice, a checkerboard of green and concrete. They had made their way to Avtaar Singh's factory down wide thoroughfares constricted with houses and storefronts with no beginning and no end. Walking back now, they skirted deep green paddy fields and pyramids of flaxen hayricks between eucalyptus trees. In ponds crusted with algae and scum, brown-feathered dabchicks and their young bobbed attentively along.

Ever since they'd left the village, his mother chanted, "Ram, Ram," and Madan wished she would stop. He was tired and thirsty. His feet throbbed, and he was tempted to sit down right there and cry. Avtaar Singh's words whirred like crickets in his mind. He knew his father didn't want him to talk but he had to ask this one question. He didn't know how he could go another step without knowing.

"Bapu," he said. "Remember that man — will he make me go to school?"

His father stopped suddenly, making Madan run into him. He grabbed Madan's arm.

"Aah, Bapu!" Madan protested, but his father ignored his yelp of pain.

"You listen to me and remember this. Don't put so much faith in the words of these types of people, these saabs. They like to put high and big ideas in our minds. Then, when they lose interest, your fall from such height will leave every bone in your body broken."

"Bapu, I don't want to —"

But his father pushed him on ahead. Rubbing his arm where the force of his father's grip still stung, he kept on walking, avoiding his mother's reproachful gaze, ashamed about breaking his promise to refrain from agitating his father in any way. He was not sure how long they walked but he dared not complain about his chafed toes or his legs shaking with weariness.

After a while, Swati awoke and his father said, "Your grandfather is waiting to see you both." Madan hadn't seen Bapu's father since he was much younger, but knew that his grandfather had moved in with Bapu after retiring from his job in a ball bearing factory.

When Madan saw the walls surrounding Avtaar Singh's house, the vastness of the structure did not surprise him. It should be that way for a man as immense as Avtaar Singh. They stood at an intersection, and his father pointed to the gravel driveway visible through the bars of a latticed front gate and to the creamy white stucco house beyond. From their vantage point, a line of windows was visible through the tapering tips of the Ashoka trees abutting the outer wall. There was some intermittent traffic, a car or a lorry. They seemed to travel a long way before they came to the end of the property. Across the road was a grassy field, and a stout cement marker emerging from the ground stating DELHI 200 KMS, but apart from that, nothing but Avtaar Singh's house occupied this stretch of land.

When Ma made a move toward the gate, his father said, "No, no. This way for us."

He turned left, leading them into the narrower street running along the outer wall. They passed a rickshaw stand, fruit and vegetable stalls, carts piled high with spicy dried channa and puffed rice poured into twisted cones of old newspaper for a quick snack. At the end of the road, a dhaba with a corrugated tin awning gave welcome shade to its hungry customers. Madan saw a boy, not much older than himself, running between the worn wooden benches and taking orders for food and tea. From a distance, the boy could have been Madan, all flailing limbs and skin the color of turned earth. Was this where Bapu was planning to send him?

Toward the end of the outer wall was an opening with a low rusted gate. His father shepherded them through. They were at the back of the main house now. A cement courtyard led to three adjoining rooms. On one side was a communal toilet and bathing area with a plastic bucket. A second opening provided access to the main house.

His father shouted, "We're here!"

Out of the darkness of a room at the far end, his grandfather emerged leaning heavily on his curved cane. Ma went up to touch her father-in-law's feet and Madan did the same.

"How they've grown," his grandfather said to their mother, beaming down at Swati and Madan, his loose lips flopping and smacking against each other, but he made no move toward them and instead seemed distracted as he twirled around on his cane.

"There they are." Picking out a set of teeth from a glass of water, Madan's grandfather shoved them into his mouth with a snap.

His mother began to survey the room, removing the bundle with their few belongings from atop her head with a sigh of relief. Bapu left to get some food and Madan watched his grandfather shuffle after him, calling, "Don't forget my beedi. You ran off today without getting me even one, so don't forget now, ha?"

Madan and Swati took off their rubber slippers and ran around the room in circles. The cool concrete soothed and tickled their burning soles, making them giggle. In the corner was a charpai, which, Madan could tell from the acrid smell of beedi emanating from the dirty white sheet, was where his grandfather slept. A small stove attached to a red gas tank sat on the floor on the other side of the door. The rest of the room was open and clear, strewn here and there with Bapu's things. Madan knew it wouldn't remain that way for long. Ma would fill it up with what they needed; she had a way of doing that without much effort.

"Ma, I want . . ." The rest of Swati's sentence disappeared in Madan's and their mother's uncontained laughter. It was a running joke among the three of them, how Swati, ever since she could talk, would begin everything with, "I want . . ." as if she had emerged from the womb needing more than they or life could give her.

Most times, it was ridiculous things that caught her eye — a runaway kite in the sky, a flower of uncommon hue in a far-off field, a knock-kneed horse clopping by. Sweet as a stick of sugarcane, she would gaze up like a dog asking for a pat from its master as she made her guileless request, the thick sweep of her lashes enough to make one catch one's breath in wonder, her tight braids angling her ears forward as if anxious to hear her verdict. When explained to her, she accepted the impossibility of her many requests with a touch of disappointment, but with overriding equanimity, never fussing, deferring with a sideways tilt of her head to their greater authority. "I-want Swati . . ." Madan and Ma affectionately called her, and she too played along, as amused by her own self as they were.

"I want water," Swati said, a practical appeal in this instance. Madan shared another smile with his mother. It was such a relief to be in Gorapur finally, to be with Bapu whatever his opinion on the matter, to be laughing like they had not for so long. Ma took the cover off a large earthen pot and poured water into the two steel tumblers stacked next to it.

"Here." She handed Madan a tumbler as well. "It's nice and cold."

Swati glugged the water down and stepped outside to gawk at their grandfather mumbling at the compound's exit. His mother sighed. "Don't mind your father. He's a man whose life doesn't seem to move ahead without some sort of trouble." Then, casually, "What was that about the saab and school?"

He told her about the man with the great mustache and the chair that spun in circles and how he said that Madan would go to school.

"But Ma," he said, anxious to share what else he had learned, "Bapu said he's got me a job at a dhaba. I'll bring money for you, Ma."

She rose from the floor, wincing as she stretched her legs.

"I'm so happy we got this place, this . . . room," she said. "But it's only one room. That's all your father will ever get us and I'm grateful for it. But an education . . . an education is a way to get a house full of rooms and food to quiet your stomach and clothes that don't fall off your back."

His mother dipped a corner of her sari in the remaining water in the tumbler, wiping his dirt-streaked face. "Just don't upset your bapu," she said.

He looked down at his feet, the toenails framed with dirt, feeling the lingering touch of her roughened hands on his face. Since Bapu had gotten this job in Gorapur, Ma had been pleading with him to bring them here. "My place is by your side," Madan would hear her whisper to his father when he visited. What she feared was the way people looked at her, the men, who smirked and asked where her husband was, or made remarks about what Bapu was doing in Gorapur. "He's fucking every whore in town, like this," they said, jerking their hips like someone was biting their backside. "Why don't you enjoy with us too?"

When someone tried to break down the family's door one night, rattling the wooden planks hard enough to loosen the hinges, they'd slipped out the back window and hidden in the fields all night. "I want my shawl," Swati had said, trembling at Madan's side as they crouched among the dewy stalks. He had shushed her harshly, trying to keep her quiet, burning inside with his own helplessness, shamed by his own fear. The next morning, Ma threw their belongings into a sheet and hauled them to the train station. She used the last of their money to call Bapu.

"You'll understand someday," she said to Madan. "But without a husband, I'm nothing to this world. Without him, I have no value."

"Fucker, son of a bitch, son of a bitch!"

Rubbing the sleep out of his eyes, Madan squatted next to his grandfather, staring up at him. Sitting on a worn-out rattan chair, its seat sagging with his familiar weight, his grandfather leaned one hand on his cane, the other flailing toward the entryway to the servants' quarters. "Son of a bitch," his grandfather repeated like a windup toy monkey that wouldn't stop beating its cymbals.

Madan giggled. He knew what the words meant but he couldn't understand why his grandfather was spitting them at his father's now-vanished back.

"Shut up right now, old man, or I'll wring your neck!" Bahadur, who occupied the adjacent room, had had enough. "Do I have to hear such language first thing in the morning?" he said through their common wall to Madan's mother.

Ma came out shaking her head and shushing his grandfather. "Keep quiet. I'll send Madan to get your beedis." She held on to her father-in-law's shaking shoulders and tried to still him, but he escaped her grip with a jerk of his head. Madan giggled again.

"Take this," said his mother, shoving a one-rupee note in Madan's hand and giving him an exasperated look. "You know where to go?"

He nodded. Yesterday, as if loath to watch his family gobble down the rotis he'd brought for dinner, his father had announced he needed to go out for a while. "Why don't you take Madan with you?" his mother suggested. Satiated but exhausted, Madan hoped his father would refuse, but he realized Ma wanted to show his father that his son could be of help, an asset perhaps his father had overlooked until now.

So he'd stuffed the remainder of the roti into his mouth, pushed it down with a deep glug of water and was ready by the door by the time his father grunted his assent. He would make sure his father would wonder what he ever did without them.

Madan had walked quietly along as they headed toward the main market, past the dhaba dealing with the evening tea rush. Questions still bubbled in him but he thought it best to talk only when spoken to in case he said something that would set his father off again.

Though far enough not to disturb their quieter neighborhood, the market appeared before them faster than Madan had expected. Their road ended in a T-junction and to all sides of him the market unfolded. Madan's heart lurched as his father dragged him into the pandemonium.

"Madan-beta, this is a world far away from the bleating goats and mustard fields. Here there are people who bleat pitifully to your father." He laughed heartily at the play on his own words.

The market circulated around a central chowk, splitting hurry-scurry into different directions. Dodging three-wheelers weaving perilously onto the unpaved roadside, Madan scooted under heaps of sugarcane loaded on wooden carts while keeping an eye out for piles of horse droppings, the cacophony of blaring horns drowning out his father's words.

When they passed Sunrise General Goods, his father said, "In here for sure!"

Assorted household items and nonperishable foodstuffs crammed the shelves of the narrow store, and from behind the laminate counter a small, squat man jumped out.

"Prabhu-ji, I did not expect to see you today," he said, his smile appearing and disappearing as he rushed up to pump Madan's father's hand. He rushed back to the till and, taking out a handful of notes, said, "This is all I have right now."

His father threw his head back and laughed. "I've only brought my son, Sharma-ji. I'm showing him around."

Mr. Sharma reached into a large glass jar on his countertop, filling Madan's pocket with small hard sweets dusted with sugar, and hastily stuffing a white plastic bag with Parle-G biscuits, Rin soap and a bag of chappati flour.

"This is my son," his father said at Komal Cloth Shop, Dhingra Motor Garage, Mamta Shooz, and Select Wine and Beer Shop. "This is my son," he said at Shami Petrol Pump, Jindal Watches, Arya Tires, and

Touch N' Feel Flower Shop. At all the different places, people squeezed his cheeks and looked happy to see them.

"Everyone knows Bapu," Madan had told his mother on their return, emptying his pockets of all the coins and candy as if to prove Bapu's influence and importance. His mother, shaking out a bedsheet, told him to share with Swati. He gave a few sweets to Swati and put the rest back in his pocket, cramming sweets into his mouth every moment he was alone.

His grandfather's head kept twitching and trembling and Madan wanted to ask Ma why his head danced like that, but he hitched up his shorts and sprinted out, the money she had given him clutched tightly in his hand.

At Bittu's Paan Stand, he shoved his way through the tangle of legs and loudly asked for the beedis, holding the money up like an ultimatum.

"Oh-ho, who's this little commander?" asked one of the customers, making space for Madan. He placed his hand on Madan's head, roughing up his hair.

"This is Prabhu's boy," said the paan-wallah as Madan pushed the offensive hand away. "His family has come from the vil-

27

lage." He paused. "They're staying at Avtaar Singh's."

"Really?" said the customer, shaking his head and reclaiming his space around the stand as Madan's hand closed around the conical beedi packet. "I guess even pigs need to have shelter sometimes, ha?" he said with a smirk. The paan-wallah indicated with a flick of his eye that Madan was still there. He needn't have bothered. Madan reminded the customer with a sharp kick to the shins before flying back down the road, the wind stroking the back of his bare legs, his feet thudding unerringly on his empire of tar and mud.

"What took you so long?" asked his mother on his breathless return. "No, no! Don't give him the whole packet. Here . . ." She took a couple of beedis out and placed them on his grandfather's wrinkled, out-stretched palm. "Now wash up quickly. I have to go to the main house. You and your sister are coming with me."

"Bitch, where're you going? To clean people's shit? Our ancestors were warriors and she wants to clean people's shit."

Madan's grandfather's words followed them out as they walked through the back lawns, past the guava and mango trees and down to the two-story house looming up ahead. The backsides of air-conditioning units jutted out almost obscenely from some windows and a few of the ground-floor doors opened onto half-box verandas. On the expansive terrace above, a woman swept between the water tanks and potted plants.

"Ignore him," said his mother, noticing Madan's curious glances back to their quarters. "He says these things. He can't seem to help himself. One day someone's going to slit his throat. Now I need you both to behave." Her tone was sharp and firm.

Madan flashed an encouraging smile. He sympathized with the underlying desperation of her request; to have her own income, from which she would siphon some portion for their needs before it went to his father, would go a long way to easing the constant lines across her forehead.

They waited on the sun-heated stone patio outside the kitchen door. He kept Swati from troubling their mother by letting her win games of pitthu with the pebbles she had gathered in her skirt. When she tired of that, he made her laugh by juggling the pebbles and comically pretending to collapse from pain when he missed and they bounced off his foot. They played guessing games and he repeated her favorite stories

29

of the bird with two heads and the girl who married a snake.

Finally, after the sun's rays sharpened enough to slice their fields of vision in two, one of the servants beckoned. "Minnu memsaab will see you now."

Leaving their slippers slick with sweat outside, they entered the cool, air-conditioned maze of rooms. Traipsing through long corridors and wide spaces crowded with chairs and sofas, and past a gleaming dining table, they came to a stop when they could no longer feel the smooth, hard marble, but soft, cushy carpet instead. Madan and Swati rubbed their feet back and forth in wonder.

"Hi, Gagan, its Minnu, listen . . . this pandit, Bansi Lal? He wants us to do a havan tomorrow. He's told Avtaar it will help the Darjeeling deal . . ."

As Minnu memsaab talked into the black handset about her plans for the ritual of prayers and offerings, Madan's gaze wandered around the square room that was at least two times bigger than their own. There were so many places to sit; he wondered how many people lived in the house. Sparkling glass bowls and statuettes of animals and people in different poses covered the small oval tables flanking the memsaab's chair. A picture above memsaab's head, of a lady by a river pouring water from an earthenware jug, looked like it was encircled with gold.

"You are Durga?"

"Yes, memsaab," said his mother. Madan tore his eyes away from the large television at the end of the room to gape at the woman sitting on a chair that looked like it could fit three people in a row. Was this a woman? He had never seen a lady with hair so short that her neck and ears were exposed, but he knew she must be a woman because his mother kept calling her "memsaab." She wore a green and gold salwar kameez, its flowery embroidery stretched tautly across her ample frame like a leering smile.

"So, your man said you cook well," memsaab was saying. "What do you make?"

His mother began listing her attributes, and Swati pulled on Madan's shirt and pointed. "I want that," she said under her breath.

Cushioned in the memsaab's sizable arm was a small dog, with fluffy hair like a cloud of purest white surrounding its face. Memsaab murmured and stroked the dog's back, twirling a strand of its fur around a finger crowned by a magenta-colored nail. The dog yapped shrilly and squirmed in her protective grip. "What's wrong, baby? What's wrong? Tell Mama," she cooed, ignoring Madan's mother's ramblings.

"Now, look," she interrupted. Everyone, including the dog, shut up. "I need someone reliable. I do not like excuses." She paused, and his mother nodded. "I have two girls, they need looking after. See that their uniforms are ready for school every day, their lunch . . . that sort of thing. Also, the cleaning. These people — they just cannot do dusting properly! I have a sweepress, but you have to make sure she does not do half a job. And do you make any chicken dishes? Saab likes his meat . . . And who are these?" she asked abruptly.

"This is Madan, and this is Swati." His mother pushed them forward.

"This is Prince." Minnu memsaab patted the dog and it bared its teeth at them.

"What's your name again . . . Madan? Come close and put your hand out."

Madan approached slowly, his hand outstretched, allowing Prince a sniff.

"Are you a careful boy?" she asked, and Madan nodded, though he was not sure what she meant. "I need someone to walk Prince. That other idiot is too rough with him. Every evening he needs fresh air." They stared dumbly at her, not knowing what was expected of them.

"You can go to the kitchen now. Bahadur will show you where to start." She turned Prince around and kissed his wet nose.

They began filing out. Then Madan realized that memsaab may have finished with them, but his mother had not finished with memsaab.

"Memsaab," his mother said, and Minnu memsaab looked up in surprise.

"I wanted to ask . . . what I wanted to say is that saab had said yesterday that he'd send Madan to school?"

Minnu memsaab gave a big sigh and massaged her temple with a magenta-tipped finger. "Saab and his charity cases," she murmured loudly. "Look, I don't know about saab and what he said. Ask your husband to remind him." She picked up the phone, dismissing them with a whir of the dial.

CHAPTER 3

Swati stuck her tongue out and Madan grinned. "It's really red now," he said.

He took the chuski from her, licking it quickly. The market buzzed and their father hummed softly as he walked ahead. The glare of the sun, always strongest just before it set, bathed the crowds jostling to return to their homes in halos of amber light. Many held handkerchiefs and hands to their noses, shielding their senses against the sickly sweet smell of bagasse wafting down from the sugar factory. The factory's smokestacks, like two fingers, were the highest structure in the town, but Madan and Swati's father assured them that of all the factories that fed off the land — sugar, paper, cotton and even the mustard oil factory — none could outdo the majestic span of Avtaar Singh's timber mill.

Madan and Swati concentrated on licking every drop of the sticky rose-flavored syrup dribbling down their arms as the cone of crushed ice melted in their hands. It was so good that Madan told Swati they should not waste a drop of it.

Their mother would not be back anytime soon. Her day ended when the family at the main house had eaten and didn't need anything more for the night. Madan hoped his mother would bring home leftovers for their dinner.

The food, Madan and Swati agreed, was an unexpected bonus of their move to Gorapur. There was always plenty once Minnu memsaab indicated to Ma that the memsaab's family did not want any more. Most afternoons, Madan and Swati would wait by the kitchen, sitting cross-legged on the stone patio, as Ma passed out stainless steel plates heaped with tender chunks of paneer or the thickest paranthas, which left their fingers greasy with ghee. On very hot days, they drank freshly churned lassi, cold out of the fridge. They shared the surplus food with Bahadur, and with Avtaar Singh's main driver, Ganesh, both of whom lived in the other rooms that made up the servants' quarters. But since they were bachelors and needed only enough for themselves, there was always plenty of food left over for Madan's family.

"Here, you finish it," Madan said, passing the slushy ice cone to Swati. Right then, in a burst of black fumes and dust, a motorcycle skidded alongside, forcing them to jump out of the way.

"Prabhu, there you are!" the man astride the throbbing machine yelled. "Avtaar Singh's looking for you. He needs you right now. Did you leave early or what?"

"Yes," Madan's father shouted over the revving machine. "He said it was all right for me to go."

"Okay, okay, that does not matter now. He's calling you. A situation's come up and he needs your expertise." The man grinned and winked conspiratorially at Madan and Swati.

"I'll meet you there," said Madan's father. "Let me drop my children home."

Avtaar Singh's messenger did not look pleased, and Madan understood that he didn't want to return without his father riding behind him, but the man nodded and sped off.

"I was having so much fun," Swati whispered to Madan as they hurried the short distance home. Madan nodded sympathetically. He didn't want to return to their quarters either. For most of the days since their arrival in Gorapur, he and Swati had whiled away hour after hour playing marbles and gilli danda.

"But I can play with my new doll," she continued, at once happier at this prospect. The doll was not truly new. It had been discarded by one of Avtaar Singh's daughters, and Ma had brought it home a few days ago. The doll's chubby arms and legs, molded in smooth, creamy plastic, had entranced Swati, and she kept its naked body wrapped in one of her shirts for warmth. Madan fashioned a little cradle for it out of an empty shoe box, lining it with old newspapers and hooking a wire hanger lengthwise through either end as a handle. Swati's barely contained excitement as she watched the cradle come together made Madan laugh. She'd jumped up and down when it was done, declaring that she'd sleep in it, if it were big enough.

But Madan was in no mood to entertain his sister right now. Their father dropped them off at the entrance to the servants' quarters, shouting to their grandfather to keep an eye on them. When he whistled down a cycle-rickshaw to take him to the factory, a half-formed idea propelled Madan to say to Swati, "Go inside. I'll see you later." He ran off, leaving her gaping after him.

37

■ ■ ■ ■

"Is he coming too?" Madan heard the rickshaw-wallah ask his father before turning onto the main road. It was about time, thought Madan; he could not have kept up much longer. When his father looked down to see him huffing and puffing a little way behind, Madan put on his finest smile.

"What're you doing?" asked his father.

"Bapu, I don't want to stay here. Please, take me with you."

"You're going to delay me," he said as the rickshaw slowed down. He pulled Madan up by his arm and Madan settled in next to him.

Paying the driver outside the entrance to the factory, his father said, "You better keep quiet and stay out of the way." He caught Madan reading the sign arching over the gate, AVTAAR SINGH AND SONS TIMBER, LTD.

"When Avtaar Singh was married and took over full control from his father, he renamed the factory," his father explained. "Avtaar Singh was optimistic. But even he doesn't always get what he wants."

A scream echoed through the empty factory, followed by shouts. "What's happen-

38

ing, Bapu?" Madan resisted the urge to grab his father's hand.

"Nothing, nothing. This won't take too long."

Madan had not been back to the factory since that first day, and now, seeing the quieted machines glow in the yellow light of the one hanging bulb, he quickened his step to keep up with his father. The shouts and scuffles were clearer as they moved deeper into the darkness. Madan wanted to ask if the sound was of someone crying, but he did not want to remind his father of his presence.

The light spilling out of Avtaar Singh's office illuminated the area outside. Madan's father entered on Avtaar Singh's command and as the door swung shut he heard Avtaar Singh say, "Is that your son again, Prabhu?"

Madan stood still and stiff outside, hoping that he had not got his father into trouble. Just when he thought it was safe to shift his weight, the door opened again.

"Go inside," said his father. "Saab says you should wait there. I'll be back soon."

He held the door open with his body and Madan inched his way forward. It banged shut and he turned around to see his father was gone.

Every detail he consigned to his mind

about Avtaar Singh seemed magnified at this second meeting. He towered over his desk, more immense, his mustache more plentiful and his eyebrows two bristly lines over eyes that searched Madan like he was the keeper of some unknown treasure.

Avtaar Singh swiveled in his chair from behind his desk. "Come in, come in. How're you liking Gorapur, boy?"

Not waiting for an answer, he continued, "Pandit-ji, I want you to meet this boy. Say hello to Pandit Bansi Lal." With a wave of his hand, he indicated the elderly man sitting on a faded blue sofa along the side of the room.

Madan turned to the man in the crisp white kurta and flowing dhoti. He joined his hands together and bobbed a quick, "Ram, Ram." The balding man continued to look toward Avtaar Singh, as though Madan's entrance were an imaginary puff of wind.

"This is Pandit Bansi Lal," Avtaar Singh announced. "If you want to live in Gorapur, better take his blessings. We all fear the special connection our pandit-ji has with the Almighty!"

Avtaar Singh's laugh boomed through the room and Pandit Bansi Lal closed his eyes, murmuring, "Hari Om." Madan stood

40

stranded in the middle of the room, between the two men.

"Sit, sit," said Avtaar Singh, and Madan gratefully slid to the floor beside the sofa, the pandit's feet an arm's length away.

"This is Prabhu's boy," Avtaar Singh was saying. "Can you believe it? When I first laid eyes on him, I couldn't imagine he was from that man. I have not seen the wife yet, but the boy doesn't look at all like that ugly goonda."

Pandit Bansi Lal was using his pinkie finger to intimately explore each of his nostrils, examining his nail every time it emerged from the orifice.

Unsure how to react to the two men, Madan focused his attention on a large photograph garlanded with jasmine flowers on the wall behind Avtaar Singh. This must be Avtaar Singh's father. His gaze wandered to the other picture on the facing wall, of a long bumpy-shaped object crisscrossed with lines, pins inserted here and there. After staring at it for a long moment, Madan realized that in his nervousness he had failed to recognize the map of India.

"You know, Pandit-ji, sometimes one has a feeling," Avtaar Singh went on. He leaned back in his chair, his arms behind his head. "From when I myself was very young I

41

learned that what I feel here" — he rubbed his lower belly — "works out for the best here" — he pointed to his head.

"When I first saw this boy . . . there was just something . . . something." Feature by feature, he scrutinized Madan, then sighed, deep and loud. "Sometimes I think it's foolishness . . . but you . . . I've heard you talk about it before, Pandit-ji."

Pandit Bansi Lal's eyes flickered in Madan's direction.

"You tell us of other lives we may have lived. People we may have known, who we may have battled with or cheated or . . . loved. Who will call on us in this life, with familiarity?"

Madan and Pandit Bansi Lal exchanged an involuntary glance, both perplexed by Avtaar Singh's stream of thought.

"For once I think you may have said something of use to me, Pandit-ji." Avtaar Singh was animated again, a grin spreading across his face. "You know me. When I come to a decision, when some idea gets ahold of me, I find it hard to shake. So, what do you think?"

"About what? This servant boy?" Pandit Bansi Lal said, unable to keep the surprise from his voice.

"Who is servant and who is master? Who

decided this, Pandit-ji? Your God? When you said you needed a new temple, that God would be pleased with one that rivaled Lakshmi Narayan Temple, I spent lakhs to build it. You took payment for each prayer I sent to him. I paid thousands and thousands for pujas and havans. I needed one thing, and for that I gave plenty, whatever you asked. Why, Pandit-ji, it's like you're my banker for God. So tell me, why does he not give me a good return on my investment?"

"You're in a mood today, Avtaar Singh. God has been kind to you, count your blessings. You have two beautiful daughters and Gorapur would be a village of dung houses if not for you. And look at Minnu-ji. I just saw her yesterday, so pious, and beautiful with her new haircut."

"Yes, yes." Avtaar Singh became pensive again. "That fucking Princess Diana haircut."

"Boys like these are as plentiful as seeds in a pomegranate, Avtaar Singh. You want a charity case, I will bring you a deserving one. This boy is nothing." To Madan, Pandit Bansi Lal's shrill, rising tone sounded like Swati's when she whined about something.

"I give you enough money as it is," Avtaar Singh said. "I do not need you to bring out

43

some poor soul as another avenue to milk me."

"Avtaar Singh, what are you saying? I've only done what you wanted me to do. This boy" — he grimaced — "is as good as any other." Pandit Bansi Lal glared at Madan like he was a fly buzzing too close to his daal.

"Of course, you know best," Pandit Bansi Lal added. Madan felt a cold, bony hand encircle his upper arm and shake it. He looked up into the priest's eyes, which were now directing God's fury at him.

"Go and touch saab's feet, boy. You're lucky such a great man noticed you."

How long until his father returned? All these words shooting overhead confused him. And on top of that, this pandit was angry. If Ma heard he had upset a man of God he would get a red backside, and he hadn't even done anything.

"Go and touch saab's feet," Pandit Bansi Lal repeated, pulling Madan off the floor and smiling at Avtaar Singh, his grip on Madan's arm getting more and more painful. He shoved Madan toward the desk, but before Madan could bend down, Avtaar Singh stopped him. He pulled up a chair. "Sit here," he said.

Madan tentatively placed his bottom on

44

the seat.

"Be comfortable," encouraged Avtaar Singh. "Do you like pinnis?"

Avtaar Singh reached across the desk to an uncovered rectangular box and offered one to Madan. Lying in the waxy paper lining were two rows of the roundest, fattest pinnis he had ever seen, tawny brown, sugar glistening on their surface and almonds peeking out like nuggets of gold.

Madan nodded, though he could not recall if he'd ever had one. Avtaar Singh shook the box again in an impatient offering, but before Madan could reach for one, the door swung open and his father entered, dragging another man in with him.

Seeing his father's stupefied stare when he saw Madan sitting next to Avtaar Singh, on a chair, no less, he tried to smile to show that it was not his idea.

The blubbering of the man hauled into the room by the collar of his shirt broke the momentary silence and diverted both their attentions.

Avtaar Singh leaned back in his chair again. "Mistry, Mistry, what were you thinking?" he addressed the man, whose mouth was a smear of liquid red. There were gashes and cuts all over his exposed arms, and his shirt hung raggedly. "You were here for a short while but we thought you were one of us, Pandit-ji and I."

Realizing that Pandit Bansi Lal was sitting on the sofa, Mistry launched himself out of Madan's father's grip and prostrated himself in front of the priest. Unable to see clearly through his puffy, swollen eyes, he lay on the cold floor a little off-center to Pandit Bansi Lal's feet, and when he spoke it looked like he was pleading with the sofa.

"Have mercy, Pandit-ji. You are a man of God, have mercy."

Pandit Bansi Lal grunted with distaste and looked away. "It's not in my hands," he said, his eyes sliding from Avtaar Singh to Madan. "It's Avtaar Singh-ji's decision."

"Mistry, let us not waste any more time and any more of your blood," Avtaar Singh said. "You've wasted enough time by trying to disappear. Now, Pandit Bansi Lal gave you the money, and not a small amount. You promised to get him that land in Jind. Land that you said belonged to your family." Avtaar Singh paused. His eyes skimmed over to Madan, giving him a tight smile in acknowledgment of Madan's intense gaze.

Then, as though amazed by a sudden turn of events, Avtaar Singh continued, "Pandit-ji went there a few days ago to find no such land exists. What is there is already owned

by some other people! How can that be?
Can you tell me?"

Avtaar Singh closed his eyes and pinched
the bridge of his nose. Then he looked at
Mistry with the fondness he had bestowed
on Madan a moment ago.

"How I wish Pandit-ji had consulted me
on this land deal before he went off on his
own." His voice became firmer, and Madan
drank in the love, disappointment and
surprise flitting across Avtaar Singh's face.
"But he did it without consulting me. He
wanted to strike out on his own. He used
his own money. He forgot that to benefit us
all we need to support one another."

Everyone turned to look at Pandit-ji, and
even Mistry, now awkwardly up on his
elbows, looked at the priest with reproach.

"Now what I wish to know is where did
Pandit-ji get all that money?" The silence
lengthened till a bubble of blood popped
near Mistry's mouth.

"But wait . . . no. Pandit-ji is like my
father and I will not question my father
about the depth of his pockets, even though
they've been filled mostly by me. No —"
Avtaar Singh exhaled, shrugging his shoulders as though apologizing for his words.
"The bond between Pandit-ji and me will
outlast all of you and all your children. To

47

cheat Pandit Bansi Lal is to cheat me. So, we need that money back, Mistry. Fifty thousand is no small amount."

Avtaar Singh gave a discreet nod. Madan watched his father pull Mistry around and slap him hard. Flecks of blood flew into the air. Madan recoiled, though he was too far for it to reach him.

"Prabhu, Prabhu," Avtaar Singh chastised gently, "all this blood, let him talk at least."

Removing the piece of cloth hanging around his neck, Madan's father wiped Mistry's mouth.

"Speak freely," Avtaar Singh said.

Madan could feel the expectation in the room and knew that Mistry would speak, for there was no other way for him to leave this room.

"My . . . my brother lives near Budha Khera Village —"

Before he could complete his sentence, Avtaar Singh said to Prabhu, "Take him out and get all the details."

Madan watched his father tow the man out, his slack legs dragging behind him.

In the remnant silence Madan squirmed in his chair, and the movement seemed to bring Avtaar Singh back to the present, and to Pandit Bansi Lal, who stood up and rearranged his white dhoti around his legs.

"That is a lot of money, Pandit-ji," said Avtaar Singh.

"Oh, Avtaar Singh, there will be much good done with this money. Yes, of course, I was thinking . . . yes, I will build a small ashram, where people can have a peaceful place to be near God."

He gathered his sling bag and Madan sensed he was anxious to leave the room. "I'm so grateful. You've done a big thing for us. Tomorrow I will do five thousand and one satyanarayan pujas for you and your family . . ." He was nearly at the door now.

"You're right, Pandit-ji, to think of doing some good with the money." Avtaar Singh swung his chair toward Madan.

"This boy" — he placed a hand on Madan's shoulder — "can read English, Pandit-ji. Lived in the village all his life, but picked up English." Pandit Bansi Lal gave a disbelieving laugh.

"It's true," Avtaar Singh said. "I've seen it myself. Shall he read something for you?"

"No, no . . . of course not. If you say so, it must be true." Pandit Bansi Lal's hand was on the door now, ready to push it open.

"You know that school I started a few years ago, Gorapur Academy near Ambala Road?" Avtaar Singh said. "You know it, you are there for Children's Day every year," Avtaar Singh went on calmly, as though he were not speaking to the pandit's back. "We need a student like this, someone who will make a name for Gorapur, who will make us known not only in Haryana but all over the country. We should be famous for more than your temple. I've been thinking of adding senior classes, renovating the auditorium." Avtaar Singh smiled at Madan. "And now this young man will be going there soon. Fifty thousand would be a good donation toward his education and would help the school. Ashrams, Pandit-ji, can wait."

Pandit Bansi Lal turned around to face them, turned again to the door and then back, struggling with the folds of his pristine dhoti. His eyes bore down on Madan and he recoiled as if a mangy jackal had appeared before him. If there was anything else Pandit Bansi Lal was going to say, it did not see the light of that room. "You are right as always," was all that escaped his tightly compressed lips, and without another glance, he took his leave.

Madan tilted back in his chair. He felt like he had run a hundred times to the market and back.

"Did all that scare you?" Avtaar Singh

eyed him, holding the forgotten box of pinnis under Madan's nose again. Madan did
not look down at the box, but at Avtaar
Singh.

The world was full of trembling men.
There were the men who trembled in front
of his father and then all of them who came
here and trembled before this man, even
when he smiled at them. This man who sat
beside him, their knees almost touching,
and his head attentively inclined toward
him.

He picked up a pinni, kept his eyes on
Avtaar Singh and shook his head resolutely.
"No," he said, and did not add *saab* to that.

"Take another," said Avtaar Singh, and
Madan had a pinni in one hand and another
almost to his mouth when his father came
back.

"We got all the information. Looks like
most of the money is still there. What should
we do about him?" said his father.

"He will end up in a hospital if we let him
go?"

"Yes, there will be unnecessary questions . . ."

"Better to finish this business once and
for all. Who does he have at home? Anyone
to follow up with the police?"

"Nobody. He's quite useless. We will take

care of the brother tonight, what can anyone say? The inspector can handle any questions . . . if they come up."

"Do it," said Avtaar Singh.

Madan's father turned to leave, but not before Madan caught the hard stare as he took in the sight of them still sitting side by side at the desk.

"Eat, eat," said Avtaar Singh. Madan bit into the dense sugary flour, chewing slowly, each bite heavy and satisfying. *I will never eat anything as rich as this pinni,* he thought.

He smiled up at Avtaar Singh reading some papers on his desk and settled back in his chair. As he worked his way through both pinnis, he didn't let the faint noises from the other side of the door, of his father at work and a man gurgling away his last breath, interrupt the warm sweetness enveloping him.

CHAPTER 4

Ma and Madan quickly gathered some money, and slipped on their shoes. Ma had taken a few hours away from work so they could go to the market to buy Madan's school uniform. Madan was due to start school on the Monday of the coming week.

His father had heard of their planned shopping trip for the school uniform and cursed out Madan's mother. "You think you know better or I know better? I have a job already lined up for him," he shouted, storming out of the quarters.

"Ma, I don't have to go to school," Madan said, shaken by his father's outburst.

But his mother was determined. "Your father will calm down once he gets used to the idea," she tried to assure Madan. "If you do well, then maybe saab sends Swati to school."

Huddled by the stove, Swati shook her head vehemently, her braids bouncing off her shoulders. "Na-baba-na. I don't want Bapu to be angry with me too."

Madan might have snapped a harsh retort at Swati, he didn't need reminding of their father's bruising hand or dark temper, but the door to their room clattered open, and his father came weaving back into the room, making a beeline for their mother.

"What're you trying to do, you witch? You want your son to rise higher than me?" His hands cut through the air. "I will give him one, and he will rise right up to the sky."

The bottle in his hand slipped and crashed to the floor. He looked at it in surprise, like he had forgotten he was holding it. "He's not going," he roared. "There's no need for school. I never went to school."

Ma started swabbing the floor and said, "He's your son too."

A decisive kick got Ma in the ribs, toppling her over into the tawny pool of spilled drink and shards of glass. Madan wanted to go help her, but fear and Swati cemented to his side kept him in the corner. Unfazed, his mother got up. She wiped her hands, dabbing her dampened sari with a kitchen rag. Before Bapu's swinging hand got her under the chin, she grabbed his cocked fist, massaging the coiled mess of taut, protruding veins, whispering to him until his roar tapered down to a drunken mutter.

"Go out with your sister," she said to Madan without looking at them.

In a fading shaft of sunlight, their grandfather mumbled softly, his head twisted to the side as if whispering to his shoulder. Swati and Madan waited, as they knew to do, with their backs against the door. Madan wanted to stay close in case Ma needed him. When the grunting and groaning started, Swati slipped her hand into Madan's, squeezing tight until their father emerged, stretching and yawning.

Flopping down on a vacant chair, Bapu pulled Swati close into the crook of this arm and asked to see her doll. "Such a beautiful thing," he said, stroking the doll's plastic cheek, "like my beautiful girl."

There was a dull thump as the doll fell to the ground, landing on its side with its glassy eyes wide open. Their father drew Swati in tighter, pressing her stomach hard against his knee. He traced the rise of Swati's cheek with his thumb, progressing down past the sweep of her neck to the delicate spread of her collarbones. Standing by his grandfather's chair, Madan saw her squint to hold back the gathering tears.

"When did this rosebud become such a big girl, ha?" their father asked no one in particular. Swati stood stiff and dutiful. Bapu's long fingers brushed the top button of her cotton shirt. In the village when the men catcalled at Madan's mother, it was not so much the whole leering mob, but the one man at the back silently following the sway of Ma's hips with a slitted gaze who terrified Madan and made his bones rattle with fright. Recognizing the same glint in his father's eyes, Madan desperately looked around for a distraction. He reached out and pinched his half-dozing grandfather, who startled awake and fell off his chair, screaming and caterwauling a torrent of abuse.

His father turned on Madan. A blow to his head narrowed Madan's vision to a pin-prick. A subsequent kick to his backside sent him spiraling into their room.

Lighting the stove for the evening meal, his mother told him that they would get his school things the next day.

"Call Swati in to help you," was all he managed to say through the pain, as she began to peel the potatoes.

The bus dropped him off in front of the school gate but Madan, in his new navy shorts and light blue shirt, hesitated outside. The occasion seemed too momentous to simply stroll in. Children of all ages streamed past him into the sandy front courtyard and toward the long building at the back. A large sign near the roofline proclaimed GORAPUR ACADEMY, SOON TO BE AFFILIATED TO CBSE, NEW DELHI.

All those years of following Colonel Bhatnagar around, nipping at his heels like the stray dogs that followed the scent of the chappati scraps hidden in the colonel's pockets, of exacting promises from the colonel to return to teach English this day and the next and of curling his tongue around strange words like, "they" and "them" and "mother" and "around." All that time spent waiting for the colonel each evening after regular village school, even after most of the other boys had long since stopped. Why did he do it?

"See that vulture?" Colonel Bhatnagar would say, pointing with his walking stick to the circling, redheaded, scraggly bird in the sky. "It can fly anywhere, and as high as it wants. That's what you can do with this English language. It can free you from this village, and take you wherever you want, Madan."

It was such a fantastic notion. The idea gripped Madan with a fervor he was unable to explain to anyone — not to his mother

57

or to the boys who rolled their eyes at him and called him Prime Minister. Not that he would ever leave Ma and Swati, he told himself, but just that he could say those words was enough.

He studied the school name again: GORA-PUR ACADEMY.

Below the billboard, painted directly onto the wall, was another sign, its bold script confined in a rectangular border. COME TO LEARN, Madan read, his lips moving with the words. Hands curled into fists by his side, he took a deep breath and stepped inside the gate.

In the front room hung a photo of Avtaar Singh shaking hands with a man in a suit, who turned out to be the principal. "Yes, yes, Madan Kumar. We were told to expect you," the principal said, guiding Madan through a quiet corridor into a classroom. "Young man, Avtaar Singh-ji has high hopes for you," he said, handing Madan off to the teacher.

That was his last coherent moment of the day. First, there was Master-ji, the teacher who spoke so fast that Madan had a hard time keeping up with the instructions he barked out all day. Repeat after me, he instructed. Repeat louder, he said. And if he caught them looking anywhere but at the blackboard, they got a rap on the knuckles with the ruler that seemed affixed to his hand like an extra long finger.

Then, while Madan watched some boys play cricket at break time, someone sneaked up from behind and tried to pull down his shorts. He caught his shorts in time, before they got low enough to be embarrassing. But the girls on the creaking swings, their pigtails flying in the air, saw this much and laughed. It made Madan burn to find out who had done it. He would thrash them until their own parents wouldn't even recognize them.

Tired and hungry, his feet hot and swollen in his new black shoes, he took the bus home and was washing his face when Swati came running into the quarters. "Ma wants you."

But it was Minnu memsaab, who recalled she wanted Madan to walk Prince. Leashing the dog, he proceeded down the gravel driveway that looped around a tinkling fountain and cut through the front lawns, where Minnu memsaab savored her evening tea. "Bye-bye, my Prince." Minnu memsaab blew kisses their way, her cup of tea sloshing precariously. Prince ignored her, pulling on his leash, urging Madan toward the gate.

A boy squatted outside the gate, flipping

old bottle caps. Madan had seen him before, and figured he was Rani's son. Rani came to sweep the house every morning and evening, her sari permanently hitched to midcalf. She swept all the houses in this area. This was her turf.

The boy didn't look up when Madan passed, and since Minnu memsaab told him to stay away from the main road and market, Madan wound his way through the side streets under the shade of gulmohar trees. The houses here were not of the usual tenement variety scattered all over town, and he could see arched entryways and stuccoed colonnades through their gates. A man on a bicycle pedaled by with toy guns, dolls and miniature kitchen sets in clear plastic packets hanging from a cardboard display affixed to the handlebars. He rung his bell hopefully up and down the street but no children emerged from behind the shuttered gates.

Madan kept his head down and walked on, keeping himself between Prince and any car that passed, like memsaab had directed. Prince was eager, hardly ever lifting his nose from the ground, sniffing every tree and lamppost. He was particularly attracted to the brackish water in the drains running alongside the roads and his tail wagged with eagerness anytime he lurched in their direction. Once Prince squatted and then disdainfully walked away from his pile of muck, they turned around and headed back to the house.

"Kasmankhana!" Minnu memsaab swore. "What have you done?" She held Prince up by his middle, the small dog flopping down on either side of her hand, and twirled him around in a half circle. Prince yapped every time she lifted up a paw.

Madan thought he should look contrite. He should apologize. Only he was not sure what was wrong.

"What has this boy done to you, my Princey? Oh, look at him." She placed Prince back down on the lawn, his leash hanging off his collar, and pinned Madan down with an arrow-like stare. "Don't you have any sense?"

Madan couldn't understand why memsaab was so furious.

"This silly boy! What has he done to you?" she wailed again to Prince, then shoved the leash back in Madan's hand. "Oof-ho! Take this and do something!"

Madan held on to the leash, his mind still a blank, and this incensed memsaab even more.

"Do I have to do everything? Bahadur!

Bahadur! Have all the servants gone and died, or what? Where are you all?" Her screech reverberated down the lawn, and Bahadur, Madan's mother and Rani came running out of the house from different directions. Seeing them all pelting toward her, memsaab shouted, "Don't you two have any other work to do?" Rani and his mother turned around and went back in.

"Bahadur, look what this boy has done to Prince. The ladies will be here for my kitty party tomorrow. Look at this!" She held out an accusing finger at Prince's paw. It wasn't white as cream anymore. Prince's constitutional had left him with socks of brown caked mud.

Bahadur scooped Prince up and Madan followed meekly to the stone patio behind the kitchen, where Bahadur filled a large basin from the spout sticking out of the wall. Madan squatted next to him. "Don't feel bad," Bahadur said over the drumming of the water. "No one told you."

"I don't understand. I did exactly what she said."

Bahadur placed the squirming animal in the water and began lathering his legs with a bar of soap. "I don't know how to explain this to you, but you're not supposed to get him dirty."

"But he got dirty when we walked," Madan gushed in defense. "She said to stay away from the main road. The back roads are no different . . ."

"Okay, here's the trick," Bahadur said. "He's a small dog, so we're lucky. You walk out of the front gate with him on the leash and as soon as you are out, pick him up. Take a few rounds, he wiggles, you set him down. If he goes, you know, does his business, well and good, otherwise pick him up again until he wiggles again."

"But then he's not . . . walking?" Madan said, sure that Bahadur was playing a trick.

"That's what the other guy used to do." Bahadur and Madan turned around at the sound of the voice. The boy who had been flipping bottle caps by the gate came in, squatting beside Madan. "You know royalty," the boy said, grinning. "They need their walk, but can't get dirty."

"Do you know Jaggu, Rani's son?" Bahadur asked Madan, as Prince tried to leap out of the basin. Both Madan and Jaggu leaned forward to help hold Prince down. The dog would have none of it. He squirmed, jiggled and yapped. Madan was not sure who laughed first, but a few minutes later they were all wiping tears out of their eyes, not sure if it was the flying soap

63

suds or the bedraggled dog making their eyes water.

"I saw you at school today," Jaggu said, once the last of the giggles subsided.

"You go to Gorapur Academy too?"

Jaggu nodded, and Madan realized that he was wearing the same navy shorts and light blue shirt, only they weren't new, but faded to a tired gray.

"The great Avtaar Singh is making sure we're all able to balance his checkbooks." Jaggu joined his hands in mock thanks and looked up at the sky. Madan giggled again but at the same time he looked around. He thought Jaggu was brave to make fun of Avtaar Singh.

Bahadur didn't look too happy about it either. "Stop it," he said. "Get out of here, both of you. I will take care of this."

"My apologies, my guru." Jaggu joined his hands again and bowed to Bahadur until his forehead touched the ground and his bottom stuck up in the air. Madan caught Bahadur's eye and they began laughing again. Jaggu straightened up, looking pleased. He held his hand out to Madan. "Come," he said. "You and I have the world to conquer."

Madan grabbed his hand, and they ran out, Jaggu singing his own made-up ditty over and over again, *"The dog is Prince and I'm the pauper."*

In the servants' quarters, Madan's grandfather lay on his charpai shoved against the wall outside the doorway of the family's room. His grandfather had pulled the old rope bed out the day after their arrival. "I will sleep under the stars," he had insisted, and now spent all his time on the bed among his jumbled sheets, talking to anyone who passed by, puffing away on one of the two daily beedis Ma restricted him to, only getting up to use the toilet. "Our learned Valmiki has returned with a friend," he said as they went to sit by the entryway. Madan hoped his grandfather wouldn't get into one of his funny moods again. Once he had hurled a string of swear words at the retreating back of Minnu memsaab when she came looking for Ma. Later, Ma probably got an earful from memsaab.

Jaggu's left shoulder twitched as they sat down. "I've been going to school now and then, not sure if I want to go on," he said, flicking an imaginary fly from his shoulder. "But it's not too bad. It gives me something to do instead of following my mother from house to house all day. Everyone's talking about you at school, you know."

"About me?"

"Everyone knows Avtaar Singh asked the principal to take you, even though the year had already started, and of course he had to agree. This is the first time Avtaar Singh asked the principal to take a particular student since he opened the school."

"Oh?"

"Aha, Avtaar Singh promised the principal that he would not interfere in the school, but when Avtaar Singh asks for something now, what is the little principal going to do — say no?"

"How did you get in?"

Jaggu waved his hand about. "This school was built for all of us who could not pay fees for any of those other schools, the ones that all the saab's children go to. Some time ago, Avtaar Singh was having a bad time in his business. Pandit Bansi Lal, as usual, told him he should do a pilgrimage to a temple in Manali, where the pandit's own teacher lives. He threw in something about helping children there, and said then Avtaar Singh's bad luck will go away. I'm sure Avtaar Singh must've given a big donation in Manali. But he did his bit for children here, in Gorapur, also."

When Madan didn't respond, Jaggu went on, "Bet Pandit Bansi Lal is double sorry now."

"Pandit Bansi Lal? Why?"

"We also heard that Avtaar Singh made Pandit Bansi Lal give money to the school so you could join. Is that true?"

"I don't know." Madan was unsure how much to divulge about the night at the factory.

"My mother's probably looking for me," Jaggu said after a while. "You know, the thing with your shorts . . . at school . . . don't feel bad. Those kids are just jealous."

Still embarrassed about the whole thing, Madan didn't respond and they were quiet again. Jaggu kept fidgeting, and under his breath he hummed a song from a recent movie Madan had often heard on the radio.

Sure enough, Jaggu turned to him and asked, "Have you seen *Do Aur Do Paanch*?"

Madan shook his head.

"No? You missed something. I laughed so much I nearly had to change my pants."

"I've been to the cinema hall one time."

"What?" Jaggu stared at him for a second. "Do you have any money?"

Madan had nothing on him and Jaggu was crestfallen.

"Too bad. Otherwise I would've taken you to the cinema hall. We could sneak in, but I'm already in trouble for doing that. The bastard owner is on the lookout for me. I see one film a week. More if I can. On the screen, there's always something going on, some action, some commotion. They don't even have time for a shit. So I too am full of action. I'm learning karate —"

"Where? With who?"

"Right now I'm teaching myself. And I'm working on my talents. I can hear a dialogue and I remember it. I hear a song and I can sing it back to you word for word." He belted out a few lines.

Madan didn't have the heart to tell him that he did not recognize the song, or that Jaggu could not carry a tune.

But Jaggu was ahead of him. "My voice is a little rough, but that's okay. My real talent is in my emotion. My heart, it is full of emotion. You want to see me cry?"

Madan nodded, fascinated. Jaggu scrunched his eyes, he squinted into the sun, he contorted his face.

"See?" He pointed to his eyes. They were moist. "Any scene you want me to do — my mother is dying, my love is dying, my friend is dying, my dog is dying, I can bring the tears out.

"You want to see me in a comedy scene?" Jaggu acted out a few scenes for Madan, action, romance, drama from his favorite movies, ones Madan had heard about but never seen.

Soon Rani came calling for her son. "Oh, Jaggu, at least let someone know where you are so I'm not searching everywhere for you. I'm tired enough as it is."

Jaggu jumped up and bowed. "Sorry, my esteemed mother." He stretched his words out, and when she smiled, he was satisfied. "Will you take Prince for a walk tomorrow?" he asked Madan.

Madan shrugged.

"What am I saying?" Jaggu slapped his forehead. "I'll see you at school tomorrow, won't I?"

"Yes, I'll be there," Madan said, watching Jaggu till he went around the bend, following his mother to the next house that needed cleaning.

He should have asked Jaggu if he knew who had pulled the stunt with his shorts. He would ask tomorrow. He curled up next to his grandfather, who had fallen asleep sitting up, his back against the wall, his mouth wide open. The sheets bunched untidily around him smelled of his grandfather, unwashed and musky. They smelled of beedi smoke.

Madan thought about getting up and

looking for Swati, who must be at the main house with his mother, but he was too tired. The streetlights came on, and his stomach groaned with hunger.

"Who is it? Who is it?" His grandfather awoke, grabbing and thrashing. "Motherfucking robber comes to empty my bag. Motherfucker, motherfucker."

"Dada-ji, it's me. Madan." He caught his grandfather's hand.

"Madan, is that you? Thank god, I thought it was a robber. Has your mother come back yet?"

Madan shook his head. "Are you hungry? I can get something for you."

"No, no," his grandfather said. He was quiet for a while then. "My toes hurt," he said, and got up to stretch.

"You mean your foot?"

"No, no. My toes." He pointed down and wiggled them. "You know where she keeps the beedis; get your poor grandfather one."

"Dada-ji." Madan tried to look strict but was too tired to follow through. "Okay, one last one."

He went inside, and from behind one of Ma's jars took out a beedi from its packet and went back out. His grandfather lit it and, taking a deep breath, said, "God bless you and give you a long life."

Madan resumed his place next to his grandfather.

"Have you seen your father?"

Madan shook his head. None of them had seen him for the last few days, and his mother hoped aloud that he was working a job, perhaps sleeping at the factory because he did not want to come home to the crowded room. But she was beginning to worry.

Cracking his toes, his grandfather exhaled an acrid stream of smoke. "Even as a child your father couldn't find happiness in anything. I bought him a watch once. It had a golden face, leather straps, tick-tock, he was so happy. Then a few days later, I see him whacking it against a rock. It's not making time pass faster, he said. Idiot, I said, it tells you the time, but he wanted to be the master of time." His grandfather flicked the ashes, but not far enough, and they landed on the sheet.

"It was the same with everything. He would cry for ice cream and then complain it was too cold. A girl he would lust after, who he couldn't live without, would turn out a whore."

His grandfather farted, lifting a buttock away from Madan. "I used to say, 'Watch out, he empties himself of happiness too

71

fast.' It's your grandmother's fault, of course. She gave him visions of grandeur, giving him the name of God. I tell him that everywhere I go I meet someone named Prabhu. Prabhu here and Prabhu there. Don't think you're so special."

"Where do you go, Dada-ji?" Madan asked. He had never seen his grandfather step a foot out of these quarters. His grandfather grunted and leaned back again.

Soon they heard footsteps and Swati came into the courtyard of the servants' quarters with a tall stainless-steel tiffin-box. She helped their mother at the house, doing small chores mainly for Avtaar Singh's twin daughters. "Madan-bhaiya," she said, her slender fingers working her scalp, her head bobbing back and forth, "I want that — makes your hair smells like flowers after a bath."

Other things on the list she wanted were pink lipstick, a doll with yellow hair and long legs, miniature clothes that went with the doll, pillows to rest her head on, colorful hair clips that snapped shut with a click. Leaning forward, she regaled Madan with her findings, lowering her voice as if she were furtively plotting a takeover of the main house for shampoo. Madan knew all he had to do was hear her out. To Swati, listing these things held the same joy as acquiring them.

She skipped into their room and fetched three steel plates, spreading them out on the ground in front of the bed. She unloaded the bowls of steaming hot food from the tiffin-box compartments.

"Teeth, where are my teeth?" their grandfather asked.

Swati retrieved the dentures from under the bed, picking them out of the glass of water. "Open," she said, one hand cupping their grandfather's chin. He let her slip them in.

They began to eat and Swati said, "That man was asking Ma about your day at school." She hunched her shoulders and flexed her arms in front of her chest to convey the strength and size of Avtaar Singh. "He also asked if she'd seen Bapu."

So Avtaar Singh hadn't seen him around either. Ma would be more worried now that Avtaar Singh had mentioned it. Maybe this was going to be Madan's first and last day of school. He pushed his plate away, his appetite gone.

"Don't worry about your father," his grandfather grunted through mouthfuls of aloo baingan. "Children should not worry about their parents."

Madan wished his mother was back from the main house. He wanted to find out what she said to Avtaar Singh to explain his father's disappearance, and also tell her about the kids who laughed at him and the teacher who sounded like a loudspeaker. Swati began clearing away the dirty dishes. His grandfather shuffled off to rinse his hands at the water pump.

"Your father will be back," his grandfather said. "No one else in the world can stand him." He laughed and hit his chest to release a captive burp.

Madan was not so sure. "He's emptied himself of his happiness with us, Dada-ji," he said.

CHAPTER 5

"Wake up. Please, wake up." Swati shook Madan.

"What? What is it?" Half up on his elbows, the sleeping mat stuck to his back, Madan turned in the direction of Swati's voice.

"There're some men outside," Swati said, her eyes wide with fear.

Madan heard muffled voices through the slightly open door. "They're asking for Bapu," Swati whispered. Wrapping his covers around her, he went to the door, peeking through the slender opening. His grandfather was in quite a state.

"Is this any time for decent people to be out? I ask you . . . bastard!" his grandfather yelped. "I ask you, I ask you . . . bastard!"

"We aren't here for trouble," a calm voice said from the entrance by the outer wall.

"Forget him, forget him, he's an old man," he heard his mother say.

His grandfather came trundling past, flapping his arms. "This is the time to sleep . . . bastard, disturbing . . . bastard . . . I ask you, is this the time to sleep?"

"Get him under control," said the man's voice again.

"Look, I'll tell my man you were here. Go, please," his mother said. "We don't want any trouble."

Ma sounded frantic. Pushing the door open, Madan stepped out. In the pool of the streetlight, he made out two men. They looked like they were out for a celebration; both wore crisply pressed pants and the one speaking to Ma had a scarf tied jauntily around his neck. The man behind him used a palm-sized switchblade to clean under his nails.

Madan went out to his grandfather and guided him back to his bed, helping him lie down. "Only want to sleep, I ask you . . . bastard, I ask you . . . bastard," his grandfather mumbled before quieting down and turning toward the wall.

"Tell Prabhu we were here, he knows where to find us. Tell him," the man added, "that big debts need big repayments."

"I will, I will," Madan's mother said, "but now go, go. If the big saab knows you're here, then we'll all be in trouble."

The man's gaze traveled up and down the

length of Ma's body, lingering on her bosom. Madan started forward, but Ma's hand stopped him. The man smirked, not lifting his eyes off her. He yawned and then said, "Prabhu, of all people, should know the consequences of unsettled debts." Both men turned and left, but Ma and Madan didn't move until the sound of their footsteps faded.

They returned to their room, past his grandfather hunched in his sheets, now fast asleep. Inside, Madan asked, "Why are they looking for Bapu, Ma?"

His mother turned around and gripped his shoulders. "Listen, don't tell anyone about this."

"Who'll I tell, Ma?"

"If Avtaar Singh finds out such goondas were at our door . . . his door . . . we'll be on the streets in no time. Thank god Bahadur and Ganesh didn't come out of their rooms."

"But Ma . . . that man, he was looking at you like . . . like . . ."

"That's nothing! What do you think will happen to us if we're on the streets?" She twisted the end of the sari in her hand, a helpless gesture that irritated Madan.

"Where is he?" his mother muttered to herself. "Why won't he come back? Hai

Ram, without him, who'll protect us?"

He tried to reassure himself as much as her. "Ma, he'll come back. He brought us here. Got us all of this . . ." He gestured around the room.

"And his vices will make it disappear like this." She snapped her fingers. "Where will we go if Avtaar Singh throws us out? What will we do without your father? You might survive somewhere, but think of your sister. What will happen to a young girl like her?"

She took out an incense stick and lit it in front of a picture of Ram and Sita pasted to the wall. Her chest heaved and she rubbed it, breathing hard.

"You're scaring Swati," Madan said. He went to his sister and put his arm around her. They lay down on their mats. Swati sidled next to Madan until she was right alongside him. Soon they fell asleep to Ma's prayers going on into the night.

The bell rang and Madan and Jaggu made their way to class. They had met by the school gate, Jaggu waving and whooping when he saw Madan. They walked through the sandy courtyard into the long building of the school, past the picture of Avtaar Singh and to their classroom, where Master-ji was waiting, ruler in hand.

"Take your seats quickly, quickly," he bellowed. "I don't have all day for you children."

As the day progressed, Madan found it harder to concentrate, his mind on the visitors from the night before and his father's mysterious whereabouts. He found himself staring down at his open notebook as the teacher's voice droned on. The blank lines ran from end to end and he wondered when he would get a chance to write on them. He yearned to fill in those lines, to alter the austere white paper so it would be more than a blank sheet.

He reached for his pencil, his hand hovering over the notebook, considering what he would write. A resounding crack reverberated through the room. The sound came from his hand that a second ago held the pencil, which was now on the floor in two jagged pieces. Pain shot up his arm and made his eyes water.

"What do you think you're doing?" Master-ji towered above him, the ruler raised once again. "Have I given permission to write yet?"

Tears pooled in Madan's eyes. He blinked rapidly like his grandfather did when trying to control an onslaught of jerks and spasms. He shook his head in apology and forced his eyes to dry up under Master-ji's livid stare.

"What were you thinking?" Jaggu shook his head as they walked to the bus stop at the end of the school day. Madan shrugged, not wanting to explain what had come over him.

They hopped on the bus, stepping on toes as they made their way down the crowded aisle.

"Is this any way to ride? Smelling people's armpits?" Jaggu asked, sitting down in an unoccupied seat near the back of the bus. Madan grabbed on to the overhead rail.

"Now, in an Ambassador, like Avtaar Singh's girls — that's the way. Sitting in a car with the windows up, inhaling only your own breath again and again." Jaggu grinned up at Madan. "Don't you think?"

Madan nodded. Avtaar Singh's twins, Rimpy and Dimpy, darted in and out of their gleaming gold car all day, the darkened windows sealing them in and away from the rest of the world as they went to school and visited friends.

The bus swung sideways and came to a stop. They hurriedly disembarked before it lurched away. They walked past the corner dump, its low walls barely containing the piles of garbage that spilled out, providing a family of pigs with a sumptuous feast.

"I don't know if I'll be coming back to school," Madan said before he could stop himself.

"Ha? Why?"

He had not meant to say anything, but since Jaggu asked, he spoke hurriedly, eager to say everything aloud so it was more than bewildering images in his head — about his father and the visit of the men the night before, of Ma and her fears that they would find themselves without a job or a home, and particularly without Bapu.

"Those men sound like they're from the Jalnaur gang," Jaggu said at last, stepping into the entrance of the servants' compound. "They do it all — cards, hashish, women. If your father is mixed up with them, that's not good."

"How do you know about this gang?"

"I've walked every road of this town since I was this big" — he pointed to his knee. "I think my mother's swept every house at some time." He shrugged. "I pick up on things; I keep my ears clean and open.

"Your mother's right to worry about Avtaar Singh finding out about your father," Jaggu continued. "Gambling and women! And the Jalnaur gang on top of that. Avtaar Singh wouldn't like it. He does many things, but he doesn't like that sort of drama."

"Do you think my bapu will come back?"

"He may, he may not. You never know with fathers. Mine left when I was two, and he never came back." Jaggu held up his palms to show the inevitability of it all.

"Fathers," he said, bending to sip straight from the water pump spout and encouraging Madan to do the same, "are strange, a puzzle, and I for one have never understood them."

His father did return, four days later. Four days in which Madan and Jaggu went back and forth to school, Madan incessantly discussing his father's possible whereabouts.

Returning from taking Prince out, the tiny animal cosseted in the crook of his arm, he knew his father had returned by how his grandfather and Swati sat huddled on the bed outside. Swati gently massaged his grandfather's shoulders as his neck convulsed erratically.

Madan rushed in to find his father lying on his mat, his back to the door.

"Bapu?" His father didn't move. "Bapu?" He took a step toward him. The familiar rank smell of alcohol hit Madan like a solid wall, making him gag. The sound got a grunt out of his father, and he turned around.

His gaze settled on Madan covering his nose with his hand.

His father squinted. "Who are you?" he said, before turning over again and falling back to sleep.

"You know," said Avtaar Singh, "you started off as my best man. I usually don't misread people, but you may have fooled me."

Madan stared at the back of his father's bent head, his uncombed hair sticking out in all directions. His father stood in front of the same great desk, hands clasped in front of him, his mumbled apologies worsening Avtaar Singh's mood. Madan wished to be anywhere but here, but when his father awoke, he had dragged Madan with him to the factory as if hoping Madan's presence would appease Avtaar Singh in some way. "What?" his father had rasped when Madan resisted. "How come you don't want to come with me now? Otherwise you're always keen to go and sit with him."

"But," Avtaar Singh continued now, "Minnu memsaab is very pleased with your woman's work, she's done a good job with the house, is a good cook, and so I'm hesitant to let you . . . your family go."

Avtaar Singh swung his chair from side to side. "But what is the meaning of this? Disappearing for days. Work half done. You promised this would end when your family came here."

He stopped the motion of his chair by slapping his hand on the desk. Madan and his father jumped. "How many chances have I given you?" His father shifted his weight but gave no answer. "This is the last time we repeat this scene, Prabhu." He waved them away. "Do your collections first, they haven't been done for these few days. Let's start with that and then we shall see."

The machines sounded even louder in the factory once they'd left the quiet office, but before they got too far Avtaar Singh called Madan back.

He held on to Madan's arm, pulling him closer to his chair. "All through life you learn, from the people around you, what to do and what not to do. A forest is made of many trees, it's always best to choose the strongest one to lean against. You understand?"

Madan nodded quickly. He was keen to leave, sure that Avtaar Singh's calling him back must have further upset his father.

Avtaar Singh patted Madan on the cheek. His hand lingered there for a moment, he seemed unwilling to lift it off and allow Madan to leave, but he said, "Good. Go now and see to Prabhu . . ." He checked himself. "Your . . . father."

Madan accompanied his father on his rounds but Avtaar Singh's words troubled him. He considered his father again, watched his hands dart out as he collected and counted the money shopkeepers and businessmen owed Avtaar Singh, money they had taken to start their businesses and money they still gave to ensure their businesses kept running. Try as he might, he couldn't shake the notion that the man before him seemed no more than a roadside reed, easily crushed under the weight of any passing bullock cart.

"He built the town, so I guess he deserves some recompense," his father sneered, slipping another roll of notes in his pocket. "Though of course if they're doing well they have to give more, otherwise they still have to fork over the standard rate that Avtaar Singh sets when they start out."

Back at the servants' quarters, Madan counted the collections and rolled the notes into neat bundles. Swati twirled around the courtyard and Bapu sat on the charpai, watching her through the hazy smoke of his beedi. Swati's long skirt billowed around her slim ankles and she sang a rhyme to her doll about the shy moon hiding from the morning sun.

"So much money, Bapu," Madan said. With the final count done, he walked out with his father, who was to deposit the collections back at the factory.

Once outside his father said, "Wait a minute." He took out the wad of notes from his pocket and separated more than a few hundred-rupee notes, returning the rest.

"Bapu, what're you doing? Avtaar Singh . . . said not to . . . Bapu?"

His father had to stay out of trouble with Avtaar Singh. There would be no more chances — not for his father and not for the rest of them either. Madan dived for the money slipped casually into his father's other pocket, but his father held him back with one hand.

"Don't worry," his father said. "I have Avtaar Singh's number — I'll slip a few of these to Nathu and he'll cover for me. Your bapu needs to take care of some of his own business right now." Madan struggled against his grip and he shoved him back against the wall. "What're you?" his father asked. "His accountant?" He went off down the street in the other direction, away from the factory.

■ ■ ■ ■

In the days following, Madan's father appeared and disappeared with the changing angle of the sun. He was with them when he had nowhere else to go, no money to collect, no one to drink with or no games to play in the back rooms of towns far enough for him to be gone for days at a time. Madan couldn't fathom how his father explained his absences to Avtaar Singh or how long this Nathu would cover for him. Sometimes the Jalnaur gang visited late at night and there were hurried conversations outside. Once, his father returned from these meetings with a bleeding lip.

"Don't let this end badly," his mother beseeched Madan, and prevailed on him to keep Bapu in town and in their sight. Madan made every effort to accompany his father wherever he could. He made sure Bapu's shaving water was hot in the morning and pressed his legs when he was tired in the evening. With Jaggu's help, he ensured there was enough of his father's favorite Jagadhari No. 1 whiskey at hand to keep him fast asleep and unmoving at night. And when his father's backhand would send him sliding across the room, he would fight the dread seeping through his bones, and bounce back and begin again.

"Arre baba, how many times have I said it?" Minnu memsaab came bustling in behind Madan as he placed two glasses of cold milk on the center table in the drawing room, bits of chocolate Bournvita floating on the surface like defiant mites. Madan had stirred and stirred, but the powdered chocolate refused to dissolve into the milk. "Coaster, baba, use the coaster."

Minnu memsaab had never said it, at least to Madan, and Rimpy giggled. Madan replaced the glasses on his tray, found the coasters, and served the girls once again. Though similar in shape and size — they reminded Madan of balls of squishy dough — the twins were easy to tell apart. The girl who always spoke first was Rimpy and the one who agreed with what she said was always Dimpy.

"Yuck, I hate milk," Rimpy said.

"I hate it too," Dimpy said, though her glass was already half empty.

"Mama, can't we have Campa Cola? Milk is so disgusting." Madan waited near the door, knowing they would soon need something else. They would make him go for more sugar and then more Bournvita and then cream biscuits, unable to settle on anything that pleased them.

"No, no, no, girls," Minnu memsaab said. "Milk is good for your skin and health."

Rimpy made a face and Dimpy copied her and they laughed, spilling milk on their skirts. "Madan, napkin!" He scurried to the side table for the napkin box.

He wished he were out with Jaggu. They could have been fishing in the canal, playing cricket or watching a movie if it was Jaggu's choice, though Madan had come to enjoy the cinema too. He found these evenings when he was required to work in the house interminable, except of course when the girls watched TV.

"Madan," Rimpy said after their mother left the room. She smiled sly and slow, and Dimpy held a hand to her mouth, holding back a giggle. "We heard a story today, at the temple. About the legend of Shiva and Parvati and . . . Madan. Do you know who he is? Do you know what your name means?"

Madan knew where they were heading. He was going to be the target of a joke he would not understand or find amusing, and that would delight them even more. His mother had told him they were twelve years old like him, but he was sure she had misunderstood, for they acted much younger.

"Do you know who 'Madan' is?" Rimpy repeated. Madan shook his head.

"Madan is . . ." They couldn't contain themselves. "The God of Love! Madan . . . with his bow of sugarcane and arrows decorated with flowers. You know, riding his parrot chariot, helping gods and people fall in love?"

They laughed so hard Madan was afraid they might burst like overfilled balloons. He kept his face blank. He had no opinion on the meaning of his name one way or the other.

But the girls thought it hilarious. They mocked a swoon. "Who're you going to shoot your arrows of love at, Madan? Who're the girls you have your eye on? Is there a girl at your school?"

When Madan didn't answer, they went on, "Or that old woman who sells roasted corn, with her funny eyes?" Dimpy crossed hers. "You're always there, near her stand." He didn't bother to point out that the old lady's stand was next to his bus stop.

"Oh, Madan, you make me as hot as the coals on which I roast this corn." Rimpy fanned herself with a magazine. Dimpy clapped in approval.

A commotion from the back of the house hushed them. Minnu memsaab was shouting for his mother. "Durga! Oh, Durga! Go check on your father-in-law, he's going crazy. I tell you, I won't have this. Why can't you people control yourselves?"

His mother came running down from the upper floor and Madan joined her as they both ran toward the kitchen and out the back. They could hear his grandfather's raised voice, cursing and shouting.

"Son of a pig . . . leave her . . . no, leave her . . . son of a pig . . . help! Who is there to help?"

At the quarters, they came upon his grandfather struggling with his father, who was carrying Swati in his arms. "Let go, old man," his father said as he tried to loosen Madan's grandfather's grip on his waist. Swati swung from side to side as they struggled.

"What's happening?" Madan's mother asked.

"I'm taking Swati out, that's all." His father panted as he freed himself.

"Don't let him go, Durga," his grandfather wept, pawing the ground. "He's made a deal with that man . . . for Swati." Outside, Madan caught a glimpse of a man revving the engine of a green car with a missing back light.

"What? What d'you mean?" Madan asked as his father hurried toward the gate.

"No!" his mother screamed. "Please, I beg of you, we'll manage whatever the problem is. We'll manage," she repeated. She lunged for her husband and caught the corner of his shirt, but he twisted her arm, making her release him.

"I'm doing us a favor," he roared. "In a few years you'll be the one paying dowry to her groom. Right now I've found someone willing to pay me! You should be grateful you have a husband who's so smart about the future!"

"But she's just a child," his mother sobbed, down on her knees, hands folded, pleading. "Just six," she kept repeating, "Just six."

His father left with Swati huddled in his arms as Ma screamed, "At least fear God!"

But his father had made a deal. And right now twenty thousand rupees danced in front of his eyes like the women of Grindlay Road.

"Madan, do something," she shrieked, turning to him.

"Bapu," he said, his legs trembling, his voice barely audible from his constricted throat. He ran after his father. His father swung around to face him, and Swati's arm reached out.

"Madan-bhaiya?" she said, her eyes glazed with confusion.

He tried to grab her hand but his father thrust her into the car, leaping in after her. "Go! Go!" he shouted to the driver. Madan pushed in after them. His father's flailing kicks caught him in the groin, sending him sprawling onto the road. The door slammed shut and the car shot forward. Madan scrambled after them, running till his side hurt. It wasn't until the car disappeared behind the fumes and traffic that he realized he would not be able to catch up to them.

His mother was still on her knees with her head in her hands, gasping for air as she wept when he returned home. His grand father had crawled under his bed.

"What'll we do?" His mother looked up at him. "Madan, I don't . . . what'll we do?"

Madan reached under the bed and helped his grandfather out. He went inside and got a glass of water for his mother. He forced her to drink when she pushed it away. When she was done, he pulled her up and wiped her tears with the edge of her sari.

"We'll go to Avtaar Singh," he said.

They met Avtaar Singh in the dining room,

93

the mutton curry and rice prepared by Ma a short while ago steaming in front of him.

"I heard," Avtaar Singh said. Madan and his mother stood before him with heads bent.

If only he had leaned forward a little more, Madan thought, he could have grabbed hold of Swati's hand. He should have run faster, maybe he could have caught up with the car. Or blocked his father from leaving the compound. Take me, he should have said. But that plea would have been of no use. He held no value to his father.

Somewhere, Prince yapped and the sound of voices floated into the room from another part of the house. Madan's bent head began to feel heavy. How far until his head bowed low enough to touch the floor? The patterned marble swam into focus and it did not seem too far to fall.

With great difficulty, he lifted his head slightly. Rimpy and Dimpy passed by the dining room window, chatting, their heads thrown back with laughter. There were some fathers who would never give you cause to bow your head in front of anyone. And there were some who would leave you like a skinless goat hanging from the tree outside the butcher's shop.

"A girl as young as that, he must have got

a good price," Avtaar Singh said, mixing the curry into the rice.

"Anything you can do, saab." Madan's mother sobbed. "You can take my pay; we will work for free for as long as you want . . . we just want our girl back."

"Selling a child, even for marriage, is illegal. We may need to involve the police. Are you ready for that?"

His mother sniveled, but Madan's head snapped up.

"He can go to jail, saab," he said, as his mother choked back a surprised cry. "Or you can do whatever you want with him."

Avtaar Singh stopped chewing and considered Madan. He wiped his mouth with a napkin and smiled.

"Durga, go get me some onions and a bowl of curd to go with this." He sat back and waited, his gaze fixed on Madan.

His mother stopped crying, her eyes darting from Madan to Avtaar Singh. "Go," he said again in the way that made men quake. "I will talk with Madan."

Madan heard her back out of the room, the door shut and Avtaar Singh said, "There should be no secrets between us, Madan. My trust and my support can be very beneficial to you, and your family. I know what I know about your father. But" — he paused — "what are you willing to tell me about him?"

"Ma needs . . . she wants to keep her job." Madan said first.

"That's fine," said Avtaar Singh.

Madan held out his hand, and Avtaar Singh looked at it, surprised. Madan wanted to let Avtaar Singh know he was serious. There was no one else who could help them find Swati, and if he was going to expose Bapu's treacheries, he wanted some gesture from Avtaar Singh that he would not go back on his word.

"What's this?" Avtaar Singh said. Madan swallowed but kept his hand extended. He hoped Avtaar Singh wouldn't think it childish or take offense, but to seal this bargain between them, Madan had nothing else to offer but a handshake.

"Such a gesture is not really needed with me," Avtaar Singh said, giving Madan's hand a firm solemn shake nonetheless, "but I hope, boy, that this will be the first of many dealings between us."

Madan couldn't imagine what else he would ever possess that Avtaar Singh would need, but for now he was overflowing with information. He told Avtaar Singh about skimming the money from the collections, and Nathu who covered it up, the Jalnaur

96

gang and the gambling debts, and the drinking that made his father so happy yet so sad.

It didn't take very long. The list of his father's sins was short but ran deep. Avtaar Singh was quiet once Madan finished. The door opened and his mother came in, placing the bowls on the table.

"We will find her," said Avtaar Singh to his mother. "I'll send someone right away."

She fell to Avtaar Singh's feet. "God bless you, saab. For the rest of my life I will pray for you every day, for all your wishes to come true. God bless you."

Avtaar Singh waved her away. "Save your prayers, Durga." He smiled over her head at Madan. "Madan has given me what I need."

They waited. Unable to endure his grandfather's big rolling tears and his mother's stifling despair, Madan hung out about town with Jaggu, or spent time throwing stones into the muddy waters of Western Gorapur Canal. In the evenings, he went to the factory gate, waiting for Avtaar Singh's men to emerge. We'll come to you when we have something to report, they said, you don't have to come every day. But Madan found he couldn't stop.

A long week later, as farmers plowed the last stubble of basmati to make room for the winter wheat, there was a knock on their door past eleven at night. "Durga? Durga? They found your girl. Saab said to take you to the hospital."

Tumbling off their mats, hurriedly fixing their clothes, Ma and Madan opened the door to Avtaar Singh's driver, Ganesh. "Saab said to take you to the hospital. The car is ready."

"Hospital? Hospital? What happened? Why the hospital? Why didn't they bring her home?" Following Ganesh out, Madan's mother tripped over her sari. Madan grabbed her elbow to keep her from falling but she shrugged him off.

Only the streetlights warmed the darkness. Reaching to open the car, Ganesh turned around. "You are a good woman," he said, "and I'm sorry for your girl."

"What do you mean?" Madan asked Ganesh. "Have you seen her?"

"All I saw was blood. You need to be prepared."

Outside the hospital, Madan saw a few of Avtaar Singh's men loitering about, and after dropping them off at the entrance, Ganesh went to join them. "I'll be here in case you need me," he said.

In the waiting area, another of Avtaar Singh's men was talking with a nurse. He beckoned them over. He was a young man, with eyes a strange shade of milky light green. He introduced himself as Feroze.

"This is the girl's family," Feroze told the nurse. "They're from Avtaar Singh's house."

Like Ganesh before him, he said, "I am outside if you need me." They followed the nurse down a long corridor, the subdued lights casting a sickly glow on the white-washed walls. The empty corridors echoed with their footsteps and Ma's constant keening. As they neared the door to Swati's room, Madan felt his breath leave him. His muscles seized up as if to prevent him from going any farther. The nurse opened the door, putting a finger to her lips, then they were in the room.

"We are waiting for the doctor," the nurse said. "Avtaar Singh-ji called him personally."

The bed in the center of the room looked like no more than a pile of white sheets. Ma let out a shriek, throwing herself on the bed, pushing the sheets aside as if she were trying to dig Swati out of a deep well. Madan could not see Swati on the bed. Tears burned in his eyes for this horrible trick played on them, bringing them here and promising them Swati.

"Stop!" The nurse pulled his mother away,

and now Madan glimpsed his sister, uncovered by Ma, a thin line etched into the dip of the bed. A nurse cleaned her face with cotton balls that turned quickly from white to black, but they did not erase the odd dark tint of her skin or the black, puffy holes of her eyes. A kitten-like mew escaped when the nurse dabbed at her swollen, chapped lips.

A smell rose from her, of rotting apples, cloying and acidic, with an underlying whiff of shit and dirt. She wore a ragged T-shirt, crusted with blood. It fell off her shoulders and reached past her knees. It was a man's T-shirt.

His mother had slipped to the floor. Gazing sightlessly up at the bed, she beat on her chest with her fists and wailed silently. Tears flowed down her cheeks.

The doctor came in, patted Ma on the back and said he needed to examine Swati. Then he would talk to them. The nurse hustled them out, placing them on the bench outside the room. After the nurse left, Ma slid down to the floor again. She resumed her silent crying. Madan left her there and walked down to the end of the corridor. A row of windows looked out into a yard. He wanted to kick them all in, one by one.

When the doctor came back out, Ma scooted forward from her place on the floor and grabbed his feet. "My child, Doctor-saab?"

He pulled Ma up by her arm. "Stand up, woman," he said. "If you can't manage yourself, how will you manage your girl?" He was no longer the calm, steady man who had entered the room. "Do you know who did this?" he asked, his pen clicking an angry tap-tap on the clipboard.

Madan's mother whined and hit her head with her hands. Madan didn't say anything. The doctor looked over his glasses at them. "The nurse cleaned her up for now," he said, "but she will need many stitches, maybe an operation. To repair her." He paused as if giving them a chance to ask a question, but Madan couldn't think of anything. "In a case like this I usually have to inform the police, but Avtaar Singh has stopped me."

"My girl, Doctor-saab. Her life is in your hands." Madan's mother attempted again to reach the doctor's feet, but ended up hanging off his knees. Madan pulled his mother off the doctor, and she swayed limply in his grasp.

"Go wait with your child," said the doctor. "I'm going to check on an operating

101

theater."

His mother went inside, but Madan couldn't go in just yet. He ran down the corridor, catching up with the doctor by the doors. "Doctor-saab?" The doctor didn't hear him, or ignored him, so he said a little louder, "Doctor-saab, please."

"What is it?"

"Saab, what is wrong? Why the operation?"

"What does it matter, boy? You won't understand. But be assured we will do our best."

"No, Doctor." Madan couldn't let it go. "Please." He wanted to know the details, know what the doctor had seen and construed and diagnosed. He needed to hear it, to understand what exactly she had forfeited, what she could not reclaim ever again.

"I have to call for another doctor. I may need help." The doctor made as if to move on, but Madan grabbed onto his sleeve.

The doctor looked from his sleeve to Madan. "What do you people do for Avtaar Singh?"

"My mother, she is the maidservant." He willed the doctor to overlook his too-short pants reaching to his ankles and his faded checked shirt, and just tell him.

"Well, listen carefully, boy," the doctor said after a moment. "Whoever did this to her? This man? Because she is so small, everything is torn. You understand what I mean?" Madan could only nod.

"This area" — he pointed to between Madan's legs — "is like when you grind the meat for keema."

Orderlies rolled a stretcher past them, the patient in a nest of wires and tubes. They moved aside to let them pass, but the doctor continued without a break, as if anxious to unburden himself.

"And you got the smell? That means an infection. There are rope marks on her wrists and ankles and she went to the bathroom on herself many times. It's not so good for her wounds." He paused, allowing Madan to take this in. "Do you know her blood type?"

Madan shook his head.

"Of course you don't," said the doctor. "She's lost a lot of blood. I need to check if we have the type of blood she needs. If she is torn all the way to her stomach, it's even more serious."

He patted Madan on the shoulder and left quickly. Madan returned to the room. Swati was now out of the old T-shirt and in a clean blue hospital shift. Their mother was sitting by the bed, her head resting by Swati's hand. The nurse was applying an ointment to the bottom of Swati's feet.

She noticed Madan watching her. "Cigarette burns," the nurse said. "Poor girl, maybe she tried to run."

The sky turned blue and gold by the time the doctors finished with Swati. They had stitched her up, trussed her in bandages and pumped her full of medicines and antibiotics. There were no damaging intrusions to her stomach or bowels. Lucky, the doctors claimed, she escaped the fate of other young girls like her who were doomed to defecating in a bag for the rest of their lives. Her luck, in Madan's opinion, was probably because the man's cock was too small.

He brought his mother some bread and tea. She waited on the bench. Sitting beside her, he was glad to see she had washed her face and retied her hair.

"Any word from Avtaar Singh?" she asked. They spoke quietly.

"No. But he is not going to take your work away. He agreed to that."

"And what did you agree to?" Her cup clattered down on the plate. "You agreed to make me a widow?"

Doubting he had heard her correctly,

Madan opened his mouth to speak, but she said, "My one child is like this" — she gestured to Swati on the other side of the wall — "and the other one turns me into one of those cursed women. People will fear even my shadow."

Madan stared at this mother, daring her to face him, but she kept her eyes on her cup of tea. "What did you want me to do?" he whispered harshly to the back of her head. "Didn't you want Swati back?"

Ma moaned, doubling over. How could she say this to him with Swati in this state? She'd gone mad. Mad. Without Avtaar Singh's reach and resources they would never have found Swati. She knew that. And Avtaar Singh wouldn't help them for nothing.

He grabbed her arm, squeezing until she cried out in pain. He wanted her to take it back. Not make him responsible for her too. Already he couldn't bear what he had let happen to his sister. She shook her head and cried into her sari. He couldn't stand to be near her. "Widow or not, you're cursed either way," he said, letting her arm go in disgust.

He slammed the door on his way out. He didn't care if this was a hospital.

CHAPTER 6

The cheers from the crowd of kids echoed and bounced around the two boys tussling on the playground. Madan watched his own fist swing in a perfect arc and land near the mouth of the boy he had pinned to the ground. He observed with surprise how easily the skin and hard teeth yielded to the punch. The boy, Raju, coughed and spit a mixture of blood and saliva at Madan. Wiping his face on his sleeve, Madan hit the boy again.

He had been walking across the playground with Jaggu when Raju made some comment. Madan couldn't remember if it was about Swati or his father or if Raju perhaps said something else altogether. He saw the contorted grin, saw the lips move and then Madan was grinding Raju's face into the sand.

He needed to see Raju's blood to silence the bomb going off in his head. The girls and boys surrounding them whooped and hollered, but the noise was like the whir of an airplane far above. Holding Raju down with one hand, he reached out to Jaggu with the other. "Give it to me!" he yelled to Jaggu, who was trying to pull Madan off.

"No," said Jaggu, "are you crazy?"

Madan lunged at him. Reaching under Jaggu's trousers leg, he removed Jaggu's latest acquisition hidden away in his sock. He flicked the switchblade open with a jerk of his wrist and the blade shot out. The knife felt light in Madan's hand. He held it to Raju's neck, but Jaggu's strangled sound of protest made him move it lower down. The kids fell silent.

He positioned the blade right under Raju's collarbone and drew a thin long line, a half-moon from one shoulder to the other. *Shouldn't this be more difficult?* he thought. *To cause damage to someone like this?* The blood appeared dark and fast. Liberated from the confines of Raju's body, it trickled down, quickly absorbed by the sandy ground. Raju screamed, though it probably hurt just as much to make the sound through his lips, now as soft as mango pulp.

Madan sat back and watched the blood flow, the sight of it finally quieting the rage in his heart. He felt the same freedom. He could breathe again.

The principal dragged Madan and Jaggu to the factory. The workers snickered as he pulled the boys by their ears to Avtaar Singh's office. "I was promised," he huffed, "there would be no such behavior in the school. I was assured I wouldn't be running a school of goondas."

He entered the office, leaving Madan and Jaggu to wait outside. Jaggu hopped around like he had to piss. "Why did you have to use the knife?" he went on. "Just break a few teeth, that's enough."

After the principal left, Avtaar Singh swiveled in his chair and studied them for a few long moments. Jaggu fidgeted. His mouth kept opening like he wanted to say something, but the words disappeared before they hit the air.

Madan stared straight ahead. *What can Avtaar Singh do?* he thought. *Let him do anything to me, I don't care.* But at the same time he stiffened his legs and held the muscles tightly in place to stop from trembling.

"Who is this?" Avtaar Singh's voice startled them both.

The words tumbled out of Jaggu, though Avtaar Singh had asked Madan. "I'm his

108

friend, saab."

After what had happened, Madan couldn't believe Jaggu was admitting to being his friend.

"My name is Jaggu . . . Jaggu," he stammered. "Rani's son," he continued, and then shut up, realizing he probably should not have mentioned his mother's name, in case she got into trouble too.

"Rani?" Avtaar Singh frowned. "You mean the sweeper woman?"

Jaggu barely nodded.

"God help me!" Avtaar Singh bellowed, and a factory worker came running in.

"Did you call, saab?"

"No, no," said Avtaar Singh waving him away. "But it seems the world thinks I've nothing better to do with my time than chastise the servants' children."

The factory worker backed out looking confused, but Jaggu sensed an opportunity.

"Yes, yes, saab, you're quite right." He bowed twice in quick succession and pulled on Madan's arm. They began to back away. "We don't want to bother you. We'll go. Saab cannot be disturbed," he explained to Madan as though Madan were a small child.

"Wait." Avtaar Singh's voice stopped them at the door. "Come back here." They shuffled back to the desk and Madan couldn't hide his trembling anymore. "Where did you get the knife?"

"You know, saab." Jaggu spread his hands out. "I go here, I go there, and there are some people —"

"Okay, okay," Avtaar Singh interrupted. "I see you're a man of the streets. Go wait outside. I want to talk to your friend here."

Jaggu scrambled out, giving Madan a quick, rueful glance. Madan's stomach rumbled. In all the commotion, he'd missed the lunch his mother had packed. Thinking of his mother made his stomach twist even more. She'd been acting like nothing had ever happened at the hospital, but the way she burrowed into herself, talking to him only when necessary, made Madan wary.

"Saab," he said, "sorry, saab." He looked down at the floor, ashamed of his scruffy shirt, his raw knuckles, his blood-splattered shoes.

Avtaar Singh tilted his head back. "He said something about your family?"

Madan nodded.

"Then why are you sorry?"

Madan had no answer. He kept his eyes downcast but his mind was frantic. Whatever Raju had said, it was as though he had murmured a spell, cast an enchantment over Madan. His body hummed, but every minute standing here was eclipsing that feeling very quickly.

He heard Avtaar Singh's sigh and then he bade Madan to his side, handing Madan a tissue from the box on his desk. Wiping his face, Madan realized that tears had scored through the streaks of dirt.

"Would you do the same if it happened again?"

Madan was about to say no. The word sprang to his lips, but when he glanced up at Avtaar Singh, he knew he could not lie.

"Madan, Madan." Avtaar Singh took Madan's hand in his own, his touch soft as he rubbed the dried blood. It came off in flakes. "In life we need to beat up people now and then." Avtaar Singh leaned in close as though whispering a secret in his ear. "Sometimes to get our way, sometimes people don't listen and you need to make them see sense. And sometimes . . . to make them feel what we feel." Madan's hand was still lost in Avtaar Singh's own gigantic, fleshy palm. "They will try to do the same to you. But whose fist wins?"

Their breathing matched in rhythm. Madan blinked when Avtaar Singh blinked; he shifted only when he sensed movement from the man in front of him.

"You've been to an akhara? Seen the wrestlers?"

Madan nodded. A village may not have regular electric power but it will have a wrestling gym, and his village had two. And who hadn't heard tales of the great Haryanvi pehlwan, Master Chandgi Ram?

"Every move the wrestler makes has a purpose, whether it's a twitch of his arm, a shifting of his weight — even when he's not moving — there's a reason. Each motion has a consequence in his favor or he'll not initiate it. If you fight, it should have a purpose, otherwise you're just wasting time. Do you understand?" No answer was required. When this man spoke, you accepted and you followed. Madan knew that much.

"Now." Avtaar Singh tapped the edge of the table. "We're finally going to add more classes to Gorapur Academy. We're getting more teachers. I would be very pleased if you were in the first batch to graduate from there."

With his hand in Avtaar Singh's, Madan had no hesitations. He would have set his feet on fire right now if Avtaar Singh asked. "I will do it, saab," Madan said. "Whatever you want, whatever you say."

Avtaar Singh laughed. "You've made this promise, boy. Before I could stop you." He patted Madan's hand and released his hold. "It will not be forgotten."

Knowing he was dismissed, Madan moved toward the door.

"Wait." Avtaar Singh stopped him. His laughter was gone. "What d'you think of my factory? You've been here a few times?"

"It's very big, saab," he said. "It's grand."

"Do you think you'd like to spend some time with us here?"

Madan nodded his head vigorously.

"This work is hard, and demanding. This is not a place for boys who are soft in any way." He looked Madan over, from top to bottom. "Also, you're a fighter, ha?"

"Yes, saab." But he felt unsure of this admittance, as if he had not fully understood the scope of the question.

For his part, Avtaar Singh looked like he was concentrating on some difficult problem, trying to work out a complicated equation for which the answer lay beyond his grasp.

"Tell Ganesh to bring the car around," he commanded at last. "I'm going to take you somewhere. And . . . tell your friend to come too."

Where? What? Baffled by these rapidly changing events, he nevertheless pulled himself together and rushed to comply with

Avtaar Singh's directive. "Yes, saab!"

The front bench seat of the Ambassador, high and springy and stretching continuously from driver to passenger door, allowed Madan enough space to sit between the driver Ganesh and Jaggu, who was bouncing up and down, happy to have appropriated the window seat.

"Jaggu," Madan whispered, aware of Ganesh sitting next to him listening in on them. "You could have been in trouble because of me . . ."

"What trouble? I'd have got us out somehow." Jaggu tried to laugh, but it came out like a relieved yip. "Weren't we like Veeru and Jai in *Sholay*? You must've seen *Sholay*, at least, everyone's seen that movie. But I'm Veeru, okay? Because I don't want to die in the end."

Ganesh harrumphed from his side of the car.

"Listen," Madan said, interrupting Jaggu's starring-role fantasy. "Avtaar Singh said we could come here after school, to the factory. He'll put us on the payroll."

"Us? You mean you and me?"

Madan nodded.

"How come . . . how did . . . ?" Jaggu shook his head in disbelief. "Well," he said, bemused by this twist of fate. "Money in my pocket. Do you think I'll be able to get a new knife?"

The back door slammed shut, and Avtaar Singh said, "Take us to Guru Gianchand's akhara."

Jaggu cocked a questioning eyebrow at Madan. *Why are we going to the wrestling gym?* Madan was equally puzzled. The sound of Ganesh's soft knowing chortle swiftly robbed the two boys of any pleasure of being in the car and going for a ride. Jaggu stopped his fiddling and became very still, his hand reaching out for Madan's.

They approached the akhara from off the main highway. The place had an air of remoteness, as if too far to hear a songbird's call. A low stone wall surrounded a large rectangular pit of red earth. Men dressed in loincloths emerged from a cavernous building with its corrugated roof, its outer walls adorned with a gallery of faded murals of the wrestlers' patron god, Hanuman. The wrestlers stretched and did push-ups; some oiled their bodies and slapped their forearms and chests.

When they spotted Avtaar Singh, the wrestlers immediately rushed up to him, touching his feet and welcoming him. They talked all at once, but fell silent when Avtaar

Singh spoke, and occasionally they turned to look at Madan and Jaggu standing off to the side near a mud-splattered buffalo tethered to a pipal tree.

The ground was being prepared for competition, ghee and mustard oil mixed into the mud to tame dust clouds, and turmeric sprinkled over the ground's surface to disinfect any wounds the wrestlers may happen to suffer. Finally, as a heavy wooden block was dragged across the pit, packing the earth down to a level plane, Avtaar Singh called to Madan and Jaggu.

"Waheguru," said Jaggu, remembering God, "what is happening?"

Madan and Jaggu reluctantly scooted to the edge of the group. The men parted, giving them a clear pathway straight to Avtaar Singh, who stood respectfully next to a man in a white kurta and brown trousers, with lines down his face that said he was old, but his hair was dyed tar-black.

"Everyone has to learn from someone," Avtaar Singh said to Madan, "and this is my guru, Guru Gianchand-ji."

Madan realized suddenly that Jaggu wasn't with him anymore, but he knew why Jaggu had finally abandoned his side. This was too much.

The guru-ji squinted down at Madan. If

116

he could, Madan would have turned and run all the way back to his village. He trained his sight on Avtaar Singh's feet encased in leather sandals, and held his place. The guru-ji shouted a name out into the crowd and the men melted away, but someone grabbed Madan, lifted him away from Avtaar Singh and he was back in the shade of the pipal tree, and a man with a chest as tight as a drum was removing Madan's shirt and slathering his body with oil.

"Are you ready?" the wrestler asked Madan.

Though the oil was warming his muscles, Madan shivered. "I don't know . . . I've never . . . I don't know how . . ." Avtaar Singh had been so nice to him a short while ago. He couldn't understand it. What did Avtaar Singh want? Why was he doing this?

The wrestler knocked Madan on the head, and he reeled, finding his balance with some difficulty. Though it was not the hardest knock he had ever received, it still hurt, and it shut him up.

"Just try to remain standing," said the wrestler.

The square pit seemed like the largest desert in the world. In only his shorts, Madan could feel the last rays of the evening

117

sun trained on his back. There must be some misunderstanding. He frantically searched the crowds for Avtaar Singh. He could sort out this confusion, and give the order to pluck Madan out of the ring and return him to the sidelines, where he belonged.

The boy circling before Madan in a blue loincloth was not much older than Madan, and of a similar height and build. He seemed to have been born in this place. Just then, Madan saw Avtaar Singh lounging on a cane chair at the edge of the arena, the corners of his shirt fluttering in the breeze over his sharply creased trousers. With his head tilted back and arms draped lazily on the chair's sides, he looked as if he were here to watch the clouds float by.

Madan blinked, swallowing the hot lump of coal burning a hole down his throat. The mist of tears in his eyes cleared. There was no escape from this pit.

He brought his attention and focus back to his opponent. All he could hear was his breath whistling through him. The boy touched the ground reverently, sizing Madan up. Before Madan could do the same, the boy was upon Madan. Welded by their intertwined arms, they vigorously grasped each other's shoulders, forming a

118

bridge of limbs. Madan dug his heels into the sand and held on, unwilling to release his first solid hold. The crowd called out encouragement or advice from the fringes.

In a few moments his leg muscles were on fire with the strain of bearing down on his opponent. All he had to do was get this boy on the ground. But it seemed that the boy would take advantage of any small movement, the slightest tremor, and it would end the other way around. The grappling continued. Then the boy slipped under and over Madan, and onto Madan's back. Madan couldn't believe it. How had the boy managed it? Hunched over with the boy's weight, he swayed but remained on his feet. From the corner of his eye he could see a snippet of Avtaar Singh's shirt fabric, a flash of his mustache.

"Aargh!" Madan shouted, launching the boy off his back and in Avtaar Singh's direction. He would show Avtaar Singh that no one put Madan Kumar on his back. The boy landed with a thump and the audience broke out in a scattered applause. Avtaar Singh's head was turned. He was talking reverently to his guru-ji. He appeared not to have seen Madan's move.

The boy bounced back up. All of a sudden the ground disappeared beneath

Madan. The boy had flipped him with such ferocity that the crowd expelled an involuntary groan.

He rolled away, but the boy flew through the air, landing on top of him. Madan pushed off from the ground, lifting them both up, and wrangled into a position where they were grappling side to side, each trying to find an opening to finish the other off. If he'd had but a moment to think before the match, he would have come up with some strategy, some tactic recalled from the many bouts he had seen from the sidelines of the akhara in his village. But there was no time to think now.

The boy untangled himself from Madan and Madan was barely able to take a breath when they were standing up again, arms interlocked, head butting against head. The crowd grew restless, but Madan's only hope seemed to be in never giving up his position. The other boy, however, had other ideas, and in a spectacular cluster of moves, he grabbed Madan's hand and, pivoting on one foot, kicked his other foot up and around, hooking Madan behind the knee. In a thud of bodies, they fell to earth. The boy sprawled over Madan, crushing him into the dust.

Rolling in the mud to cool off his sweat-slicked body, the boy rose up from the ground to great applause. People flowed into the pit. Madan stared up at the blue-gray sky, grit covering his tongue and the skin of his face, arms, legs and back, stinging like a million needle pricks. No one noticed as he got up with some difficulty and slinked back to the shade of the tree, collapsing next to the wall.

"You weren't that bad." Jaggu appeared at his side, slipping two hard-boiled eggs rolled up in a chappati into his hand and placing a steel tumbler of cold almond milk by his feet. Madan attacked the food and drink eagerly. "There's more in the kitchen if you want," said Jaggu.

He squatted down next to Madan and scanned the scene before him, his gaze alighting on the tall silhouette of Avtaar Singh. "It's strange," Jaggu said. "He gives you a job, makes sure you get into school, helps your family, always wants to talk to you. Gorapur was never a boring place, but everything has certainly become more interesting since you arrived."

Madan scarfed down the last bite and licked the crumbs off his fingers. "Avtaar Singh used to be a pehlwan here," he said, feeling the need to change the subject. "That's his guru-ji."

121

The guru-ji noticed their attention and came to join them. He seemed much friendlier, and chatted fondly about his akhara, about Avtaar Singh.

"He wrestled for a few years when he was young," the guru-ji shared. "His father was a very stern man. Didn't approve of him coming here, of this lifestyle of training and abstinence and sacrifice. Every day, arguments with his father. 'Only pigs roll in the mud,' his father used to come and shout from the wall. Avtaar . . . while he thrived in the akhara's discipline, his father's strictness choked him, for some reason. He'd come every morning at five before school to train, and would grapple all day if you asked him. After school, he was here again, exercising, training and competing."

"Why did he stop?" asked Jaggu. "No one tells Avtaar Singh what to do."

"Young man, you always listen to your father." The guru-ji laid a stern look on Jaggu, but dispensed of it as he looked out onto his akhara again. "He loved it deeply, but the akhara is too small a place for a man like him. Don't you think? Like any first love, it was not enough. He could win every Bharat Kesri, Rustom-e-Hind and Maha Bharat Kesri, but these awards would not be enough for him. Perhaps his father was the wiser one, and recognized this much before all of us."

Madan was beginning to see why Avtaar Singh paid respect to his guru-ji apart from his status as a teacher. The man spoke astutely.

A crowd made up of old men from nearby farms and younger ones returning from work accumulated at the wall. Motorcycles were propped against the few trees, bicycles flung down to land where they may. Young boys in tattered shorts mock-wrestled. The chanting of prayers offered to Lord Hanuman floated wispily over the throng.

"We're having a few bouts of kushti in honor of Avtaar Singh," said the guru-ji. "Time to show Avtaar Singh a real match," he said with a laugh.

Madan moved in closer to Avtaar Singh's chair as the wrestling began. He noticed that Avtaar Singh did not smile or add to the mayhem of catcalls, but his whole body seemed to speak in many tongues to the spectacle before him.

After the matches, the men returned to their training, and Jaggu poked Madan in the ribs. "Saab is calling you."

Standing before Avtaar Singh once again, Madan hung his head and mumbled, "I'm sorry, saab." He was exhausted.

"For what, now?"

"For losing, saab."

Avtaar Singh looked down on him, appraising the worth of his dirty clothes and his blistered and peeling skin. His hand lifted like he was going to lay it comfortingly on Madan's shoulder or ruffle his hair, but he paused and said, "You know why that boy was fighting?"

Madan shook his head.

"To save face is the obvious reason — he couldn't lose to a fresh apple like you. But if he didn't win, he wouldn't get to eat. Why were you fighting?"

He couldn't think why. He had thought Avtaar Singh wanted him to, but Avtaar Singh had given him no such order.

"So soon you forgot what I told you," said Avtaar Singh. "You must always have a purpose. Your opponent can be anyone, but to win, it's not who or what you're fighting against, as much as what you're fighting for."

Instead of feeling chastised, Madan wanted to fall against the pillar of Avtaar Singh's leg and cry in relief. No longer could he feel his cold shirt plastered to his back by sweat and oil or his aching muscles or dejected heart. He wanted to rush back into the ring and defeat the strongest pehlwan. *I'll never forget, saab,* he said to himself, imprinting it in his mind.

"Come," Avtaar Singh said, calling Madan to accompany him for a walk in the green paddy fields beyond the wall.

Floating between the rice stalks, dabchicks dipped their beaks into the cool water. "Look at that." Avtaar Singh pointed with delight, as if he hadn't seen these common birds in the rushes many times before.

"How's your sister?" Avtaar Singh asked.

Madan wished for any other topic but this. It felt too harsh and too soon to steal away the elation pulsing through him.

"Still in hospital."

They turned around to look at the akhara. The dusty, sweaty men were moving shadows against the sun, the gathered crowd dispersing, analyzing the evening's bouts, each with their own opinions on how the play should have gone down.

"Saab?"

Avtaar Singh's attention shifted to Madan. "Saab, my father, saab? Did you find him yet?"

"Soon," Avtaar Singh said, his words measured. "Do you want to know when we find him?"

Madan was scared to say yes or no, unsure where either answer would lead.

"Then what do you want to know, boy?"

Questions like these made his head hurt. He wrapped his arms around himself. Though there was farm and town rolling away behind the akhara, from where they stood the arena could be at the edge of the world.

"There are no rules in the akhara," Avtaar Singh said. "No time limits. You fight till you win. That is it. Yes, you need strength and skill, you need to know every move and countermove. But you fight, until you win."

He took Madan's hand in his own and they traveled slowly back, each with his own thoughts, not yet shoulder to shoulder, but leaning on one another.

Exercise books, stationery, sports equipment, toys and more toys filled the shelves and the floor of the toy shop, brimming onto the sidewalk. Every passing gust of wind deposited another layer of dust, especially on the bicycles and strollers hanging off the sign outside. The shopkeeper kept an eye on Madan as he tried to find room to wriggle deeper into the confines of the overstocked store.

Madan couldn't decide what to get Swati. Maybe a chalkboard set? For her to draw on. Or a cooking play set? He settled on another doll, a blond baby with its own baby bottle, and then made his way home, his shopping bags full. Ma should be back from the hospital by now. These days, he was taking care of his grandfather, with Ma busy at the hospital when she was not at work. A few more days, the doctor had said, and then they could bring Swati home.

The entrance to the servants' quarters came into view and he saw a pair of Avtaar Singh's men waiting. They straightened as he approached, greeting him with their eyes. "You are wanted by saab, at the factory."

Why? He was going to ask but the saliva fled his tongue, and his arms and legs began to tremble with the weight of his bags. "I . . . I'll put this inside," he stammered. They moved aside, allowing him to enter. In their room, his mother prayed before pictures of her gods, Ram, Sita, Lakshman and Hanuman. Lately Ganesh and Kali Ma had joined the confederacy pasted on the wall.

"Ma?" Didn't she hear him come in? "Those men are here."

"I know," she said. She didn't turn around.

"Ma, they got Bapu. Avtaar Singh is calling me."

He didn't know what to do. Should he go? He had to go. He couldn't disobey Avtaar

127

Singh. But he was unsure if he wanted to see his father. Why wouldn't his mother say something?

"Ma." She still refused to look. "What should I do? I'll do whatever you say."

He reached out to pull at her sari, make her turn his way, look at him instead of those stupid pictures. *Leave your gods,* he wanted to say. *They never saved Swati and they won't save Bapu. Just tell me what you want me to do.*

He heard the men rustling outside. They would come looking for him soon. His mother mumbled prayers under her breath, each incantation adding to the spiraling anger in the pit of his stomach.

"Fucking woman," he shouted, unable to bear it any longer. "Only prayers all the time."

He stalked out of the room, but before he reached the men, he turned around. "Ma —" If she forbade him from going, he would defy even Avtaar Singh.

But she had shut the door.

They walked Madan to the massive steel furnace in the center of the factory. In the prism of heat surrounding the furnace, men milled about in an informal circle. The rest of the factory was deserted. There was a sharp tang of motor oil and hot metal in the air. Pushed to the center of the group, he looked up to see Feroze, the man from the hospital with the faint green eyes.

Someone went to get Avtaar Singh. When he emerged from his office, the men moved to attention. Madan could tell that they were not used to Avtaar Singh being present at such occasions.

"So, boy, how is the work going?"

Madan startled at the mundane question. "Good . . . very good, saab."

"And school?"

He bowed his head. He couldn't speak anymore, nothing would come out.

Feroze and the other men laughed. "Saab, why did you call him here? This lizard's pussy is going to throw up all over our shoes."

Avtaar Singh silenced them with a look. "Come here," he said, pulling Madan to his side, sheltering him from the heat and the cluster of hard, staring eyes. "Do you want to leave? You're free to go if you want."

Madan heard Feroze titter in the crowd. He moved closer into Avtaar Singh. "No, saab," he said. "I don't want to go." The furnace roared behind him.

At Avtaar Singh's signal, two of the men disappeared, returning shortly with a sack between them.

"Look," said Avtaar Singh. Madan turned to see what they had placed on the floor. It wasn't a sack. His trembling ceased; he suddenly began to feel mellow, like he was swimming underwater.

Released from Avtaar Singh's side, he approached the man quivering on the floor like he was cold, and well he should be. He looked stripped clean of any cover of skin and hair. Mesmerized, Madan peered at the face, trying to discern any movement. The eyes opened and fixed on him, glazed and unblinking. A mangled stump reached out as if pleading for a hand up.

Madan could feel the men's eyes on him, wondering what he would do. If he'd be shocked, horrified, cry like a baby. Moving past their curious gazes, he regarded Avtaar Singh. These men did not know about that day in the dining room, and the deal he'd made with Avtaar Singh. Madan knew then where those disclosures would lead. Thinking of it now, he grasped that he revealed something about himself that would terrify anybody else but Avtaar Singh.

Looking up at Avtaar Singh prevailing over them with a hint of a smile, he understood why Avtaar Singh had summoned him to the factory. This wasn't a place for confusion with consequences, for trying to divine intent and meaning, or for regret. It was Madan's rightful placc, more than any of these men's. At Avtaar Singh's side, everything became clear and uncomplicated.

A low, plaintive moan drew his attention back to the floor.

"Son . . ." The stump rocked back and forth.

A plank of wood not four feet in length lay within reach. It was in Madan's hand now. He swung it up in the air and slammed down. Chunks of flesh flew by him, splattered on his face, slithered down his legs. But he heaved the plank up and brought it down, again and again.

"Don't — call — me — son." Sweat stung his eyes, and blood misted the air, yet he pounded on. With every strike, the lump on the floor jerked up and down.

The men, caught by surprise at first, sniggered and clapped each other on the back. "Look . . . look at the little cocksucker. Jumping up and down like a hijra."

Moments later, Feroze stilled his hand. "Enough," he heard Avtaar Singh say. "He's gone."

The plank slipped out of his bloody grip. Sawdust cushioned its return to the floor.

Someone undid the hutchlike opening to

the furnace. Waves of heat billowed out. The men swarmed around the broken body and Madan stood back to give them room. They gathered the mass of flesh, pushing forward through the heat. The legs went in first; there was a sound of bones popping. Then a last shove to the shattered skull.

He didn't notice when the men dispersed. They left him staring into the roiling flames, roaring and flaring up as if inviting him in as well. After a while, he felt someone beside him.

"At least you got to consign him to a fire," Feroze said. "Never got to do that last rite to my bastard father."

Feroze slipped a bottle into his hand. "Here," he said. Madan lifted the bottle to his lips. He was thirsty. The sip did not cool his parched throat but instead warmed him up. He took another big sip, splashing some of the toddy on his clothes.

"Slowly, slowly," Feroze said, closing the hutch door of the furnace.

Feroze disappeared too, leaving him with the bottle of toddy. Madan took another long sip. A light spilled out of the window of Avtaar Singh's office. He wasn't sure if Avtaar Singh was in or had gone home. He went and stood outside Avtaar Singh's door. He didn't know what to do with himself.

The door whooshed open, and Avtaar Singh stood in the light.

"Where've you been?" Avtaar Singh said as if he had been wondering where he was. "Come in."

Tentatively, Madan stepped into the office. He was a mess, and reeked of perspiration, blood and the rank fumes of the toddy. A whiff of himself brought up a bit of his long-forgotten meal, and he swallowed hard to push the bile back down.

Avtaar Singh went to his desk and Madan stumbled after him.

Removing a hand towel hanging from the desk's drawer handle which he usually spread on his lap when he ate lunch, Avtaar Singh soaked it through with water from the drinking jug.

"Come here," he said to Madan. He took the toddy bottle from Madan's hand and tossed it into the bin.

"Who gave you this?" he asked, but it was a rhetorical question. Avtaar Singh knew.

Steadying Madan by the shoulder, Avtaar Singh began to wipe him down, gently cleaning his face and behind his ears, swabbing the back of his neck and running the towel down his arms. The towel changed color as Avtaar Singh attended to Madan. Intermittently, he rinsed the towel out, beginning afresh, tending to Madan's hands, carefully scouring the blood and gore from under his nails and between his fingers. Madan could feel Avtaar Singh's breath, warming his cleaned skin as he lifted Madan's T-shirt, sponging his chest and under his arms, then attending to the mop of Madan's hair, fussing over each strand, coaxing the blood and tissue matter off until his dampened hairs stood on end. Avtaar Singh's touch was tender, as if he sensed the tension in Madan's muscles and did not want to add to the soreness and the ringing pain.

He bent down and ran the towel over Madan's legs. Pulling his scummy rubber slippers off, Avtaar Singh placed Madan's foot on his knee and scrubbed the dirt off Madan's rough sole and the underside of his foot. A dirty imprint remained on Avtaar Singh's trousers.

Madan wanted to tell him to stop. It was ill-fitting for a man of Avtaar Singh's stature to do such a thing. Even his father had never ministered to Madan like this. His father had never cared to bend low enough to count Madan's toes.

Madan's breath caught in his throat as he remembered the events that had occurred outside the door. He tried now to connect the man who would come bellowing into their quarters and the scrap of pounded bones and flesh scraped off the factory floor. Were they the same? Would he go home and find him resurrected from the ashes, sitting on the chair with a bottle between his legs, sour and angry, waiting to exact some kind of retribution?

Madan's legs trembled, and he did not know at first if it was with fright or from exhaustion. He placed a hand on Avtaar Singh's shoulder to balance himself. He could feel the strength in the sinew, tendons and tissue rippling with life under his palms. He knew then his legs shook with nothing but relief. A tear leaked out and ran unbidden down his cheek. Avtaar Singh wiped it away too.

"These tears are too precious." He held Madan's chin and dabbed at the corners of his eyes. "Don't waste them."

Avtaar Singh stood back and scrutinized Madan from top to bottom. Satisfied, he threw the dirty towel in the corner of the office.

Madan looked at his arms and legs. He was glistening. Avtaar Singh had wiped every trace of his father off him.

CHAPTER 7

Stepping into Sunrise General Goods,
Madan glanced around the empty store
looking for the proprietor, Sharma-ji. He
heard thumping overhead and looked up to
see Sharma-ji perched halfway up a ladder,
a dust cloth in hand.

There were two clear divisions to Sharma-
ji's store. The items in the glass cases under
the countertops were of Indian origin:
packets of Parle-G glucose biscuits in waxy
yellow wrappings, Swati's favorite Britannia
chocolate cream cookies, packets of bhujia
and chewra and other salty delights —
"domestic goods," as Sharma-ji called them.
On the shelves above were the goods from
abroad consisting of whatever could fit in a
suitcase: Kraft cheese tins, Pepsi cans, Her-
shey's chocolate syrup and tins of Del
Monte sweet corn.

Madan had once asked Sharma-ji who
wanted tins of corn when fields of maize as

golden as the pictures on those tins surrounded Gorapur. "There's always someone," Sharma-ji said, "some poor sucker who wants to show off or taste something outlandish." While waiting for this person to materialize, the bright green labels bleached to white, remaining unsold and unmoving as if they had staked their claim to that area of shelving.

Sharma-ji flapped his dust cloth at Madan and began to descend, his short legs negotiating one rung at a time. "Ah, Mr. Madan, I knew you would come today."

"It's the same day every month, Sharma-ji," said Madan.

"Yes, yes," Sharma-ji replied, reaching behind the counter and taking out a roll of notes. He looked up at Madan as he handed him the money. "It seems like it was only yesterday you were this high . . . here with your father . . . now look at you. Tell me again, how old are you?"

Madan smiled down at Sharma-ji. "Seventeen . . . nearly eighteen."

He unrolled the money and began to count it. He knew it would all be there, but still he counted it in front of the man. That way, in case there was a discrepancy he could take care of it there and then. "Even if you know they'll not cheat, why let them

137

feel too comfortable?" Avtaar Singh would say. "The moment they feel at ease, they might think of doing something you don't want them to do."

Madan listened with half an ear as Sharma-ji talked on. Why did Sharma-ji always launch into the retelling of Madan's first time at the store? Did he want to remind Madan that he knew his father, or was he trying to find common ground, some empathy for their shared experience at the hands of his father?

The money all counted, Madan added it to the other rolls in his pocket. "Thank you, Sharma-ji," he said, leaving the man in mid-sentence.

"Wait, wait. I know you're a busy man these days." Sharma-ji darted around randomly, gathering up sundries and supplies.

"Please don't, Sharma-ji," Madan said. Swallowing his irritation, he quickly exited the store. Sharma-ji should know better by now — Madan would never take anything more or anything less than was due to him.

At Bittu's Paan Stand, Madan reached through the smoke curling up from the burning incense stick and over the jars of gulkand and betel nuts and took out a pack of Gold Flakes. He flipped open the cover, tapping out one cigarette. The pan-wallah struck a match and lit it. "Put it on my account Bittu-bhai," he said.

"Oh, Madan-babu! Madan-babu!"

Madan turned in the direction of the supplicating tone. Shuffling up to Madan was the crooked figure of 1984, his arm cradling a shehnai, the double-reed wood instrument scuffed and stained from years of rough use. His right arm stayed by his side, straight and stiff, as if in a splint.

Bittu shooed him away. "Motherfucker, get out of here." 1984 did a small backward dance, but kept his eyes on Madan, grinning, waiting, jiggling the shehnai in his good hand.

"It's fine," said Madan. "Give me two more." He tucked the cigarettes into the breast pocket of 1984's shirt.

"Salaam, saab. Thank you, saab." 1984 bobbed up and down, following Madan through the market.

Madan hurried on, nodding absently at passersby who wished him, "Ram, Ram." There was no time to stop and chat. All they wanted was his support in approaching Avtaar Singh for assistance to ask for money for their daughter's wedding or to acquire a contract for a government tender.

With his lurching gait, 1984 kept up

behind Madan. No one could recall 1984's real name, and even 1984 claimed he couldn't remember. When asked where he used to live or who he was born to, 1984 just chuckled. He had come to their notice after the riots following Indira Gandhi's assassination, when, in towns like Gorapur, with their volatile mixture of Sikhs and Hindus, vengeful mobs pulsed down the streets, some with a torch in one hand, ax in the other.

Rounded up in a colony on the southeast side of town, 1984 was part of a group of Sikhs dragged out of their homes and cars by their turbans. The mob shoved car tires around their waists, doused them with petrol, and set them on fire. Their women screamed, their babies cried, but mobs of any kind don't listen. Rubber melts quickly, adhering to the skin, and in intense bursts of flames, those men were pools of grist and bubbling rubber.

1984 ran to the canal when the mob moved on. They had used too big a tire on him, a truck tire on his scrawny frame, and he held it up till they were gone, slipping out of the ring of fire before it consumed him like the rest of his neighbors.

"God saved me, Madan-babu," he said.

"God causes the problem and then saves

you from it. Like a policeman who steals so he'll have a job. You're a fool, 1984."

Madan's derision didn't affect 1984. He salaamed and grinned, and asked for a bread pakora, his favorite food. The flames had licked his face and the puckered skin widened his eyes, his mouth was perpetually open and lopsided. His arm was the biggest casualty, fused to his side by scar tissue or, as 1984 reckoned, by melted rubber. The market was his home now. He followed people around, spreading news and gossip, earning money playing his old shehnai badly and shrilly with one useful hand, known only to everyone by the year he sprang into the town's stream of consciousness.

Madan was in the office when Avtaar Singh received news of the mob's onslaught on his town, when he handed out missives to his men to go and control the streets of Gorapur — to do what the police were unable or unwilling to do. For those few days, as the town descended into an eerie calm and Madan served Avtaar Singh endless cups of tea, he waited and watched to see if Avtaar Singh would reveal to Madan what to think about the frightening events outside their door — for even in all the fear and confusion people still had opinions and took

141

sides. Avtaar Singh's ancestors were Sikhs, but through marriage and time, his faith had become twofold, the temple on Tuesdays and the gurdwara one morning each week.

Yet, as he followed a pensive Avtaar Singh from home to factory and back again, he realized that Avtaar Singh had no side but his own. These few years later — now that the razed buildings had been rebuilt and the hustle and bustle had returned — 1984 stood as the solitary reminder to Avtaar Singh of that time when the reins of the town briefly slipped from his tight grip. 1984 knew this better than anyone. That was why he would not follow Madan past the borders of the crowded market. His true survival, 1984 knew, depended on his staying away from the factory and out of Avtaar Singh's sight.

The fat brown dragonflies hovering over the open yard were the first to welcome anyone entering the timber factory. Madan and Jaggu had spent many afternoons pondering over why they droned over the arid factory floor, when a few meters away, surrounding the entire factory, were waterlogged fields of rice.

Stopping to drop off his collections with

the accountant, Mr. D'Silva, he wound his way to Avtaar Singh's office. Madan could walk the factory blindfolded, steer through the workers, machines and trucks trundling through, by the smell, the noise and the heat.

Nearby, the blade of a peeler screeched as it met a log of eucalyptus. Almost as if the blade were undressing the hapless log, it shaved off layers of bark into sheets as thin as paper. Madan picked his way through the debris obscuring the brick floor; already he felt the sawdust settle on him like a fine veil. Workers in scruffy white vests slathered a formaldehyde and urea glue mix onto dried sheets of bark. The toxic glue made the resulting plywood board resistant to termites. Overhead, tentacles of pipes crisscrossed the ceiling, dispersing the heat generated by the furnace to the pressing and bonding machines.

The massive furnace was no more than part of the landscape of the factory now. Ma had never asked about his father, had never shown any inclination to know what had happened to him, though there were instances when she caused Madan some disquiet, when he caught her scanning him with a look that was unseeing, yet sharp as a talon. Other than that, she had settled into her changed situation. She stopped applying the vibrant slash of sindoor to her hair and quietly donned the plainer clothes of a widow. Every year during the dark fortnight of Shradh, she joined the throngs offering prayers at the temple to cleanse the sins committed by the dead. Madan never accompanied her, nor did she ever ask.

She did not have much to complain about — a place to live, her work, hard but respectable, and money in the bank. He suggested to her in passing that she open a bank account. "Me? Your old mother, have an account like a big lady?" The idea took her by surprise yet pleased her, and she nagged him until he accompanied her to Punjab National Bank.

She cherished her bank passbook. Her finger tracing each line of deposits, she asked Madan again and again to tally up the totals. "Maybe the bank people made a mistake," she said, but he knew she wanted to hear the total amount out loud. "We'll need it for your sister's wedding," she said to him. Madan did not have the heart to remind her that it would take more than a good dowry to find a man to marry Swati.

Madan knocked and entered, in a quick second taking in everyone who was in

144

Avtaar Singh's office. One could tell the time of day by the occupants who happened to be in there.

During the day, Avtaar Singh was busy with the running of the factory — vendors, buyers, tree farmers coming and going. But in the evening, a different type of mood overtook him. Then Feroze with his cloudy green eyes and pockmarked face, Gopal with his nunchucks, Harish and his psoriasis, the flaky, peeling skin bugging Avtaar Singh no end, and their cohorts, mainly wrestlers from the akhara, would come by. They would discuss everything from politics to the latest film star visiting Chandigarh for a live show. Madan was neither part of the day crowd nor one of the evening visitors. He was everywhere. He was where Avtaar Singh wanted him to be.

"There he is," said Avtaar Singh, and the men squirmed, making room for Madan. He pulled up a chair and sat near Avtaar Singh, who patted him on the shoulder. There was a snort from the corner of the room. Madan recognized it as Pandit Bansi Lal's.

"Look who's here today," Avtaar Singh said to Madan, indicating the man sitting next to Pandit Bansi Lal on the sofa. Madan acknowledged Ved Prakash, the legislative assembly member from their area, who usually visited Avtaar Singh when he was under pressure to follow through on one of his many election promises. He would come to Avtaar Singh to see what he had permission to do and how best to do it. The elections were coming up and Madan assumed that Ved Prakash was probably hoping for a repeat of the landslide victory Avtaar Singh had orchestrated for him the last time around. Descending on the polling booths on election day, Avtaar Singh's men had no trouble persuading the arriving voters that it was better to go back home. Then, while Feroze and the others held the election officials at bay and the police kept watch outside the polling booths, Madan and Jaggu, electrified with their inclusion in the electoral process, stuffed the boxes with bunches of ballots premarked in favor of Ved Prakash.

There was much celebrating after Ved Prakash's win, especially by the politician himself, who promptly announced to everyone present that he would name any future sons after Avtaar Singh. No one paid much heed to the inebriated sixty-four-year-old politician's rhetoric, since he was already a father to four grown children. But nine months later, as promised, he produced a son who was duly named after Avtaar Singh, and it went down on Ved Prakash's curriculum vitae as one of the only promises to his constituents he had ever fulfilled on his own volition.

"Ved Prakash comes with interesting news," said Avtaar Singh. "You know the land near Jobal? It seems Kishan Sood's son has returned from Bombay and he wants his father's land."

"No one owns that land," Ved Prakash cried out as if he couldn't help himself.

"All land is owned by someone," said Avtaar Singh impatiently to the politician. "If you had taken care of this with the father we would not have to deal with the son now."

A large swath of fertile agricultural land encompassed the Jobal area and, as with much of such land directly around Gorapur, farmers paid a yearly fee to Avtaar Singh in exchange for tilling the land. Aware of only the rudimentary facts of the land's murky provenance, Madan nevertheless knew this parcel of earth held a mythic importance to Avtaar Singh, for tucked in a small corner was Guru Gianchand's akhara.

"Many years ago I wanted to buy the land where the akhara sits so I could gift it to Guru Gianchand," Avtaar Singh explained.

147

"That bastard Sood would not sell. Offered him cash, offered him land on the other side near Jagadhari. It was like he wanted to start a fight with me. So I accommodated, and took that land and the rest of his property around it. Ved Prakash told Sood he was going to claim the land for the government . . . What did you say it was for?" he asked

"Hydroelectric power plant," whispered Ved Prakash.

"And my boys went to his house and gave Sood a more personal message from my side. He disappeared from town with his family after that."

"It was the subdivisional magistrate," said Ved Prakash. "He was supposed to issue the papers in your name. If I ever see that motherfucker again . . ."

"This is a small thing," said Pandit Bansi Lal, consoling his friend. "Avtaar Singh will take care of it."

"I shouldn't be taking care of small things!" Avtaar Singh banged his hand against the desk. "All you had to do was to arrange for the title in my name."

Though Madan was enjoying Pandit Bansi Lal's discomfort, he was anxious to share the information he had recently gleaned from his friends at Monty's Taxi Stand.

"They were talking about a visitor staying at Dawn Guesthouse," he told Avtaar Singh. "The man wanted a taxi to the financial commissioner's office."

"Ha?" Ved Prakash perked up. "Why? What does that mean?"

"Arre! He doesn't know anything," Pandit Bansi Lal consoled the worried politician. "He's just a child. Don't worry about what he says."

"I —" Madan spat out, half rising from his chair. Avtaar Singh's firm squeeze on his shoulder silenced him. Swallowing his resentment, he turned to Avtaar Singh, but refused to meet his eye. He understood why people like Ved Prakash associated with someone like Pandit Bansi Lal, but he could not understand why Avtaar Singh entertained the pandit, no matter how long their association or Avtaar Singh's religious convictions.

"Pandit-ji," said Avtaar Singh, "I give more credit to Madan's word than anyone else's in this room. I've told you this before."

Though he knew he shouldn't, Madan shot Pandit Bansi Lal a smug look. Avtaar Singh tut-tutted, but Pandit Bansi Lal got up, whipping his cotton wrap around him. "Avtaar Singh-ji, this is the respect I get after all my years of service to your family?

149

This is how an old friend is treated? Because of this . . . of this — I am going," he said with finality. "Ved Prakash-ji, if you want to stay, then stay, but I will not . . ."

"What?" said Ved Prakash, looking over-whelmed and confused by the words firing like loaded cannonballs through the room.

"Sit," said Avtaar Singh. "Sit, Pandit-ji. Why do you get upset so easily? No one means any disrespect. If you feel Madan has insulted you in some way, he will apologize."

Madan felt the focused gaze of Ved Pra-kash, Pandit Bansi Lal and Avtaar Singh on him while the other men in the room looked on.

Avtaar Singh looked pointedly at Madan, so he said, "Sorry," under his breath and at the same time Pandit Bansi Lal said, "Really, I'm above these little things but sometimes . . . sometimes —" he sat back down like he had said all he wanted to say.

"Good," said Avtaar Singh. "Financial commissioner's office means he's going to file a complaint. He could name all of us." His gaze flitted over the worried men on the sofa and then came to rest on Madan.

Madan had come to learn that Avtaar Singh was a man who was never alone. Whether it was by design or because of his busy life, his men or his factory workers, his wife, his children, his friends or someone or other from the town orbited around him at all times.

And then there was Madan.

Madan, whom Avtaar Singh called for every morning when he took his first sip of tea and whom Avtaar Singh demanded stay on his right side and on his left, whichever way he happened to turn, until he was back in his bed at the end of the day.

Madan looked around Avtaar Singh's office at the strong-armed men, the high-ranking politician, the influential pandit. After they took their leave, and the machines shuddered to silence and the crickets began their own musical labors, he would be back here with Avtaar Singh.

Madan would pour him a glass of Chivas Regal and get himself a Campa Cola, for he never drank alcohol in front of Avtaar Singh, and they would discuss the pros and cons of all sorts of business matters. Avtaar Singh would talk about land or real estate he wanted to acquire, or ask Madan about school and studies, and these days they were thrashing out the details on the new factory Avtaar Singh wanted to open.

When Avtaar Singh was done, they would drive home with the windows rolled down, Avtaar Singh sitting up front with him, the

151

deserted streets making it seem like there was no one else alive but them.

Madan sat among these men here, went out on jobs with them, but now and again he saw flickers of confusion when Avtaar Singh solicited his opinion, giving it consideration before making a decision. It made them wary of him and unsure of his position among them.

When he had brought this up with Avtaar Singh, he was told, "You and I have to be sure of no one but each other," answering and ending any further concerns about the matter on Madan's part.

Madan knew what Avtaar Singh needed from him. "I'll take care of it, saab," he said.

Everyone started filing out and as Madan got up, Pandit Bansi Lal addressed Ved Prakash. "See what I told you? Avtaar Singh-ji will take care of it, he takes care of all of us . . . even those who should've long ago been dumped at some roadside truck stop." He murmured the last part so no one but Madan, passing by him, heard.

Madan contemplated turning back and confronting the pandit. But it would elicit the same lecture from Avtaar Singh. *He's only an old pandit, set in his thoughts and ways,* Avtaar Singh would say. *What can he do to you? You're the one who is young; you need to control your temper.*

He saw that Pandit Bansi Lal was at Avtaar Singh's side, conversing rapidly, and for now it seemed best to go ahead and join the men outside.

He left a message for Jaggu to meet him later at home, and they all piled into the car and headed for Dawn Guesthouse. Earlier that day, Jaggu seemed excited about something. "Wait until tonight," he had told Madan, when Madan caught him whispering with Feroze.

Now Feroze was sitting next to him, humming, and when he caught Madan looking at him he said, "So you're meeting Jaggu tonight?"

"Yes, that's the plan," said Madan.

Feroze laughed and Madan noticed Gopal and Harish grinning as well. "What? What's going on tonight?"

"Nothing, nothing," said Feroze, refusing to meet Madan's eye and smiling all the while.

Dhiru Sood was finishing a cup of tea in the front lawn of the guesthouse. When Madan and the boys entered, he looked up curiously from his newspaper, and it was not until they were standing before him that comprehension dawned on the young fellow.

He stood up with a start, and reached down as if to touch his toes. It was then that Madan noticed the small boy playing by his father's feet. Dhiru Sood picked up his son and turned toward the house. On the front steps a girl in a red frock played with some dolls. Dhiru Sood ushered the boy up the stairs and shouted to someone to take the children and lock the door. Witnessing the flurried activity brought on by their presence, a mixture of anger and weariness overcame Madan. Dhiru Sood's father must have enlightened his son about the consequences of pursuing the ownership of their land and to the dangers that awaited him in Gorapur. And here was Dhiru Sood bringing his whole family along like they were going on holiday somewhere.

"So many people for me?" Dhiru Sood said. There was a time to be sarcastic, but Madan wasn't sure for Dhiru Sood's sake if this was the time.

"Get in the car," said Feroze.

"Why don't we talk here?" Dhiru Sood asked. But they pushed him out through the gate to the waiting car.

Dhiru Sood tried to hold back a tremble and look friendly when they shoved him into the middle of a storage shed made of hastily erected brick walls and a tin roof in the middle of some placid fields. Sacks of grain piled in high mounds at the entrance hid them from prying eyes. They had debated where to take Dhiru Sood, but their favorite spot on the canal was too far and no one wanted to drive back to the factory, so the shed ended up being their chosen spot.

"Boys, you have to understand. I have the title papers; the law is on my side. This is not done," Dhiru Sood said, his tremble sabotaging his show of bluster. "Let's go home, and I will not tell anyone about this." He folded his hands, asking for clemency. "This is just a misunderstanding."

"What about the going to the commissioner's office? Ha? Just a misunderstanding, ha?" Feroze said, punching Dhiru Sood on the side of his head.

"Please, I have small children," Dhiru Sood pleaded. "I don't want any trouble. I am happy to reimburse Avtaar Singh for the land. Please tell him I am ready to offer him anything he needs. In fact, why don't you take me to him and I'll tell him myself?"

Madan had had enough of this man. If Dhiru Sood knew that Avtaar Singh would come after him, then why had he gone forward? Wasting everyone's time with unnecessary meetings and actions. And why did they always mention their children? Like having children was a defense against bad judgment.

He popped Dhiru Sood right in the mouth and the men cheered because not only did it shut him up but two teeth fell to the floor. Someone punched him in the gut and Dhiru Sood tried to talk again but went limp, collapsing to the floor. They began to kick him, rocking Dhiru Sood with the ferocity of their attack.

"Please . . ." begged Dhiru Sood.

"Let's do this quickly," Madan said. He wanted to be done and out with Jaggu. The men paused, their panting filling the shed, and looked to Madan. He knew they were waiting for him but he couldn't lift his hand to ask for a knife or a gun. Under his heel, he could feel the beat of Dhiru Sood's heart but all he could see was the small boy clinging to his legs, the braids of the little girl swinging in the air when her mother swept her up and away.

A racket at the entryway forced their attention to Gopal, who had dashed out to the car and returned with a big grin and a plastic bucket swinging in his hands. Something inside the bucket was slamming against its sides and emitting an alarming growl.

"Stand back," Gopal said, placing the bucket down in line with Dhiru Sood, who was trying to rise but for the shaking of his legs and the agony of his beating. The bucket moved on the floor from the force of the crazed animal inside. Carefully, Gopal kicked the bucket to its side, aiming its mouth at Dhiru Sood. The lid fell off and out shot what looked to Madan like a large grayish yellow rat.

"Fucker," said Feroze, raising his voice above the din, "where did you get a mongoose?"

Gopal pointed to the charging animal. "Look . . . it's sick." He tapped his own head and beamed at them.

At Gopal's announcement, Madan and the other men hustled to the far end of the room, away from the rabid mongoose furiously racing in a straight line toward Dhiru Sood.

Dhiru Sood's vision cleared and he managed to scoot a few inches back before the mongoose launched up and on him, and snapped at his shoulder. Letting out a bloodcurdling scream, he wrenched the creature off and scrambled to his feet, losing control of his bowels and filling the shed with a stomach-turning stench. Before Madan or the others could move, Dhiru Sood and the mongoose had escaped out the other end of the shed into the fields, one screaming, the other gnashing its teeth.

"Fuck," said Gopal, "now what?"

Feroze was already at the doorway, taking aim. The screaming stopped right after the first shot, and the men applauded when in the dying light of the evening they saw Dhiru Sood stop and then crumple far in the fields.

"Should we go check?" said Feroze after a moment.

Gopal had thought to bring a mongoose but not a flashlight, and the men demurred, unwilling to venture out into the darkening fields where a rabid mongoose ran loose among the king cobras and Russell's vipers.

Madan massaged his own shoulder, unable to comprehend the turn his thoughts were taking. From the arch of the doorway, he numbly watched and waited for any movement from Dhiru Sood, while inside his mind was on fire. Dhiru Sood's boy had not wanted to let go of his father, blinking up at Madan as he hung on, his arms flapping in the air as he tried to reach out and maintain contact with his father's leg when he was pulled away. It should take more than a blink of an eye, more than just one shot, to lose a father.

After making a show of his displeasure at Gopal's antics, which had almost botched up their assignment for that evening, he gave a long-suffering sigh and, hoping the men would not think it too strange, said, "Let's go. He's not moving. If not now, then in five minutes he'll surely be gone."

The men were surprised but relieved. They were anxious to get on with their plans for the evening. "I'll explain to Avtaar Singh if he asks," Madan said, setting their minds to rest.

He had to stop himself from physically pushing the men back into the car, and willed them to drive fast back to the factory. A half hour later Madan was tearing back down the same road on a borrowed motorcycle, headed to the storage shed. His plan seemed possible and impossible at the same time. He gunned the throttle and cursed himself, cursed Dhiru Sood and swore at the men and their petty games, but was grateful for the distraction that had given Madan a way out. Feroze was a decent shot, but to shoot a running man in the waning light could have affected his aim. Madan hoped it was something else that had caused Dhiru Sood to fall.

Collecting a couple of empty gunnysacks from the shed, he followed the straight line of the flashlight. Dhiru Sood had made a heroic attempt at escape from both the mongoose and the men, and had fallen many yards away from the shed. Madan used the flashlight to check his wounds. The bite didn't seem too deep, but it was the animal's saliva that could be just as dangerous. An injury on Dhiru Sood's left side had clotted into a dried mass but seemed no more than a flesh wound. Still, it made Madan reassess his opinion of Feroze's shooting skills.

Dhiru Sood let out a frightened squawk when he saw Madan leaning over him but Madan had no time to explain. Cautiously, so as to avoid contact with the possibly infected saliva or splattered blood, he wrapped Dhiru Sood in the large, rough gunnysacks and, leveraging his own weight, pulled Dhiru Sood up. He half dragged, half carried him back to the motorcycle while wishing he wouldn't make so much noise but Dhiru Sood would not stop crying, moaning or gulping for air.

With Dhiru Sood up front and leaning against his chest, and the gunnysacks between them, Madan gunned the motorcycle all the way to Dr. Kidwai's. The doctor was finishing up his dinner and he motioned Madan to his adjacent clinic, expressing surprise that Madan had brought a victim and not one of their own, as was usually the case. Covered in sweat and grime, and unable to understand his own actions, Madan contrived to tell the doctor about the bite and the shot. The efficient doctor knew not to ask too many questions and bandaged, medicated and dispatched Dhiru Sood with the first of his series of anti-rabies shots.

Dhiru Sood then managed to sit behind Madan on the motorcycle, breathing shallowly and groaning with every bump in the road. "You're lucky this time," said Madan, helping Dhiru Sood up the steps of the darkened guesthouse. "Why did you return to Gorapur? You should've known this would happen."

"In my father's time, yes," wheezed Dhiru Sood. "But it's a lot of land, worth a lot of money, and I hoped by now things would have changed."

"Nothing changes here." Madan was furious at the man's naïveté. "This is not a big city like Bombay. Here there is only Avtaar Singh." He placed Dhiru Sood gingerly on the guesthouse's steps. "What do you do in Bombay?"

"I've a jewelry shop. Diamonds, mainly."

"Even in Bombay that's safer business than what you were planning here. Take your family and leave tonight. Don't come back or it will end how it was meant to end today. Do you understand?"

Dhiru Sood nodded, and Madan turned to leave.

"Why did you come back for me?"

A dim, tentative light had come on inside the house. Madan could hear the slow creak of an opening door.

"For your children," he said to Dhiru Sood.

The mosquitoes sizzled and fried to dust on the streetlights as Madan waited for Jaggu. Ma was busy at the main house and his grandfather cursed in his sleep beside him. Swati washed dishes by the hand pump. Madan watched as she pumped the water with one hand, rinsing each soapy plate with the other. The hem of her salwar's long shirt was soaked.

What had he done? How had he done it? Even now, he couldn't fathom the course of the day's events. He walked up and down the courtyard, trying to control the spasms of fear ricocheting through him. If he mulled over his actions any longer, he would have to go over and finish Dhiru Sood right now.

"Are you going out tonight, Madan-bhaiya?" Swati asked.

She spoke softly and Madan had to strain to hear her, but this was how it was with Swati.

"Yes, with Jaggu."

She had weaved the jasmine garland he had brought for her into her long braid and as she moved, a sweet whiff teased the air. He wondered why she had asked. Swati never went anywhere.

Her gait had something to do with her confinement. She hobbled as if walking on pins and needles, and could not go too far. "Give her time," was the doctor's advice when they had brought her home, "she is young."

During her long recovery their room became a mini-hospital: medicines took over the spice shelf; balls of cotton, soaked through with disinfectant, filled up the garbage bins. Her body healed as best it could, otherwise it was as if an ax had come swinging down that day and silenced her forever. Night after night she lay huddled in the corner, wanting nothing, needing nothing, her fragmented gaze staring out into the room, wordlessly asking for what they could not give her.

She feared every footstep outside their door, keeping her head down or cowering when anyone happened to come by. For a while, she cut herself, small slits at the back of her legs as if she wanted to shift the pain from one part of her to another. Often Madan would awake to find her staring at him, like she was asleep with her eyes open.

Eventually it was Swati who began the task of putting her broken self back together. She started sitting outside with their grandfather, forced a word out here and there. Yet, as hard as she tried, it was as if one piece of the puzzle that was Swati always slipped away, floated beyond her grasp, leaving her, as she approached her teenage years, like a girl they were sure they knew, but could not recognize.

They tried sending her to school, thinking that being around other children might help. Madan had dropped her off at her class but was unable to find her at break time. She had wandered off, and Bittu-bhai, the paan-wallah, found her near his house, dirty and distraught. Their mother wouldn't stop crying and when Madan questioned Swati, she said she had been feeling sleepy and went looking for her sleeping mat.

They tried school again, but it was no use

164

— they would find her halfway home before the first bell rang. And so they left her where she was happiest, here in the servants' quarters, singing to her dolls, taking care of their grandfather and helping at the main house.

"Girls do not need an education," their mother said, comforting no one but herself.

Madan stepped out now and saw Jaggu turning the corner. He watched as Jaggu walked down the street, his spindly legs snapping ahead of him, his arms swinging to his shoulder and back down to his side, each step a frenetic dance.

No wonder he's so thin, Madan thought, *with all that constant activity.*

Jaggu grinned when he saw Madan and Madan wondered what plans Jaggu had in store for them that night. Mostly they would go to the canal to drink or sometimes would watch a late-night show at Manika Cinema Hall. There was nothing Jaggu loved more than the movies.

"Whatever your problem," he would explain to anyone who would listen, "you're moody, you're feeling sick, you have some misfortune, in the darkness there's always an answer. Take my personal guarantee. There'll be a song to lift your spirits or understand your despair. There's always something beautiful to look at. It's like drinking a strong medicine. It'll take care of you, and make you forget where you hurt."

Jaggu loved not only the dishum-dishum as the hero beat the villain to pulp but he also loved the romance, the beautiful dewy heroines wooed so perfectly through song and dance. He would exit each movie singing — the songs already part of his repertoire — and usually someone from the factory would see them and cuff him playfully behind the ear.

Tonight Madan was in no mood for the movies. He was glad to see a bottle peeking out from under Jaggu's shirt. "Ready?" Jaggu asked.

"I've been ready for a long time," said Madan, taking the bottle and tipping it to his mouth. "You got the good stuff today." He flipped the bottle over to read the Presidents Premium whiskey label. Taking another swig, he passed the bottle to Jaggu, trying to hide the uncontrollable shaking of his hand. As much as he wanted to, he couldn't tell Jaggu about what he had done. No one could know. He told Jaggu instead about Pandit Bansi Lal's comments in the factory from earlier in the day.

"A man of God, but his dealings are more like the devil's," agreed Jaggu of the pandit.

The bottle was half empty before Madan realized they were heading away from the canal and the movie hall. "Where are we going?"

"You'll see," said Jaggu. "It's my early birthday present to you."

"What? What's all this going on? I just want to sit somewhere and finish this bottle."

Madan peered at the name of the street. The darkness and the alcohol made it hard to read, and Jaggu was pulling him away, saying, "Don't worry. This will be a night to remember, I tell you, come quick!"

Madan made out strains of music and laughter in the distance. They walked toward a house at the end of the street. "Here it is," said Jaggu, peering at the number. "Come on, they're expecting us."

Madan was not sure he liked this feeling of suspense, but he wanted nothing more than to forget the doubt and dread pressing down on him. Jaggu pushed open the door and someone called out. Madan turned to see Feroze lying on the divan. A woman wearing only a petticoat and blouse, her untied hair spilling over her shoulders, sat on his lap and fed him sips from a tumbler.

"Oh, there is our hero!" Feroze got up and the woman fell to the side. He threw his arm around Madan's shoulder.

"Champa, bitch, where are you?" Feroze bellowed. "Look what I've got for you today!"

From the adjoining room another woman came bustling in, a grease-stained apron over her salwar kameez. "Look," said Feroze, pushing Madan and Jaggu forward. "Today we have some new and fresh members, Champa." He tottered, leaning too close to her. "Only your best cunts will do. No overused maal."

Champa ignored him and looked at the two boys. "That's all right," she said. "But no one gives for free."

"We've got money," said Jaggu, taking out a wad of notes from his pocket. Madan looked at him in surprise and Jaggu winked. "I've been saving up."

Champa looked disinterestedly at the money and called a string of names. The girls poured out like ants from an anthill, pushing and shoving each other. Beside him, Madan heard Jaggu make a short noise, like a yelp.

"You're asking for money?" Feroze asked. He had returned to the divan and his woman. "Do you know who this is?" He gestured at Madan. "This is Madan Kumar, Champa."

168

"Ah," said Champa, her eyes alighting on Madan once again. "Avtaar Singh's boy."

"I just work in the factory," said Madan, and Feroze sputtered, choking on his drink. There was truth in that. He spent a lot of time unloading logs and hauling boards. Madan looked around the cramped room. It smelled and looked like he imagined it would — of stale liquor and smoke that had seeped into the walls and furnishings, of longing and lust.

"So, how about this one?" Champa asked. She pulled a girl forward and Jaggu nodded at once, enthusiastically. Madan gave him a quizzical look and Jaggu said, "We've been talking about this for so long, I can't wait any longer."

Champa laughed, revealing betel-stained teeth. Even this was as Madan had imagined it.

"So, how about for you?" Madan and Champa considered the girls together, and though Madan looked at each girl carefully, he could not make his mind work sufficiently well enough to make a decision.

"I'll take him," a voice came from the end of the room, and a girl detached herself from the group. "By the time he chooses, I'll be bent over with age," she said, her fingers trailing the breadth of his chest and the muscles of his shoulders, making appreciating sounds all the while.

"Roopa is a good one," Champa said. "What say you?"

Madan nodded and Roopa took his hand, leading him away to the other side of the house. She closed the door and Madan looked uncertainly at the bed covered with a beige sheet. A battered dressing table was the only other furniture in the room.

"So," said Roopa. She was undoing her hair, letting it fall free over her shoulders. "Sometimes men like to catch my hair and twist it when they come. You can do that if you want."

Madan watched her unwrap her sari, dropping it to the floor. Her breasts fell out of her blouse, exposing the tops of her nipples. Madan gasped and she smiled, undoing the hooks of the blouse and letting it fall to the floor. She came toward him and Madan backed up until the edge of the bed stopped him, and he sat down. She lifted his hands, placing them on her breasts. Madan squeezed and she said with a giggle, "Gently."

"Now, first we need to get these off." She bent down and unbuckled his jeans. "If it is your first time it can happen too soon, and then your pants will get dirty." He lay back

170

and in one movement she removed his shoes, jeans and underwear.

"Ah," she said when she saw him. "Who knew today would be my lucky day? And look at that, you are so ready too."

Madan was ready. He could feel the tightening and straining as he pulled her on top of him. She hitched up her petticoat and took him in quickly, moving fast and sure. He felt a mixture of the familiar and the strange, the wetness, the heat, the sticky tightness.

"See, how quick?" she said.

Roopa hopped off, and pulling her petticoat down she sat herself back on the bed next to Madan. Twisting and tucking loose strands of hair behind her ears, she admired her reflection in the dressing table's mirror. Still on his back, Madan stared up at the blank ceiling, spent and unwilling to move. Roopa hummed and waited.

She turned to him after a bit. "You'll need me again tonight, don't you think?"

Madan moved his head in acquiescence.

"Wait one minute," she said.

She stepped out of the room. Madan waited a moment, then went up to the door, wedging it open with his foot. Through the slender gap he saw Roopa conferring with the portly Champa. They whispered furtively, and he heard Avtaar Singh's name. When she returned, he was back on the bed.

"You got me for the night," she said. "Or for how long you like."

"Good," Madan said. He pushed her down on her back, pulled off her petticoat, and as she spread her legs, he grabbed her hair and wrapped it around his hand.

CHAPTER 8

Madan steered the car between the tongas, stray cows, bicycles and pedestrians littering the narrow roads of Gorapur. People hopped out of the way as the white Contessa weaved through them. They raised their hands in salute though they could not tell through the tinted windows whether Avtaar Singh was in the car or not. He was there today, his register books open on his lap, files taking over the rest of the backseat.

Madan shifted gears gently. Avtaar Singh was the first and only person in the Gorapur area to acquire a Contessa, the luxury car recently introduced into the North Indian market. Everyone in the factory clapped when the car first drove onto the factory grounds, delivered straight from Delhi. No one but politicians and film stars in shiny magazines drove Contessas. The local edition of the *Tribune* had featured the car, with its power steering and air-conditioning making the news.

"What happened to the Siliguri delivery?" Avtaar Singh shut the notebook and picked up a file.

"They said next week," Madan said. "Axle problem near Patna."

Avtaar Singh grunted and went back to his papers. In the rearview mirror, Madan's eyes skimmed over his face. Avtaar Singh would smooth out his mustache and then hold the end of the pen to his temple, twirling it there as he read. Madan waited for this sequence of actions that were so familiar and, when they were completed, his gaze slid back to the road.

When they drove by Dawn Guesthouse, Madan no longer felt the sharp stab of panic every time he thought of Dhiru Sood, who had come and gone so quickly, as if he had never appeared in Gorapur. And with preparations for college on his mind, Madan had scant attention to waste on Dhiru Sood anymore.

"When do your results come out?" Avtaar Singh asked, their eyes meeting in the rearview mirror as the grounds of Gorapur Academy, emptied for the summer, came into view.

"In a few weeks, saab."

"Nearly time for college, then, who would have thought?" Avtaar Singh looked out the window, stalks of sugarcane on either side of the road walling them in. "How time flies, Madan, how fast it goes by."

The driveway's gravel crunched under the Contessa, and Madan pulled around the fountain to the front entrance of the house. The marble entryway shimmered in the late afternoon sun. Such a grand house, Madan thought, with its wide portico, tall white Georgian columns and windows like a hundred blinking eyes. He took pride that there was none other like it in Gorapur.

"The girls' results should be out soon too," Avtaar Singh said as he got out of the car and Madan began to collect his briefcase and papers. Avtaar Singh leaned over and smoothed the top of the Contessa. "Each generation we go ahead of our fathers, don't we?"

"Saab?"

"My father spent his life chopping trees. I drive in a Contessa, and my children will probably fly in airplanes, and their children in rocket ships. You'll be the first to go to college. It's more than your father could ever dream of." Madan followed Avtaar Singh up the stairs. Avtaar Singh talked of Madan's father lightly and without hesitation. "What'll your children do, Madan, I wonder?"

Madan gave him a bland smile, like he did when elders talked of things he couldn't imagine.

Music from a film song seeped out from the room and Madan, glancing at his watch, knew that his grandfather and Swati would be watching *Chitrahaar.* Washing his hands at the pump, he splashed water on his face, and realized he was humming the well-known tune.

The antenna on the roof swung slightly as the wind rushed past. Inside, he heard them groan as the reception weakened, then caught again. He had bought the TV for his mother with his earnings some time ago, though, being so busy, she hardly watched it. But Swati and their grandfather had their favorite programs charted out. They planned their meals around what would air when, and waited and discussed their shows like bookies discussing the odds of their bets.

At exactly eight-thirty, the TV went off and they came out. His grandfather shuffled to his bed and Madan took a beedi out of his pocket, lit it and passed it on to him.

"You want to eat, Madan-bhaiya?" asked Swati.

"First look in that bag," he said, pointing to a plastic bag slumped by the bed. Swati hobbled over, pulling it open, flashing one of her rare smiles. "Velvet," she said, looking amazed as if it were a bag full of the most priceless of gems. "He finally had velvet."

Madan smiled and sat back. He had stopped at Fair and Lovely Tailors for the scraps of leftover cloth that Swati would spend hours sewing together. Not making a dress or a tablecloth or anything they would be able to use. She randomly sewed the pieces together into fantastic shapes, sometimes small as a fingertip and other times large as an irregularly shaped bedspread.

Squinting as she threaded needle after needle, she sewed scrap to scrap, her tiny hands stitching and marrying one bit of cloth to another, the finished piece making sense only to her. They never knew what to say about her fanciful creations, so they marveled at her tiny stitches running neat and straight, like little sparrows in a line.

Swati rubbed the scraps of purple velvet to her face. A few days ago, as she diligently worked on one of her pieces, she had hoped that sooner or later the tailor would have velvet. Madan didn't ask why. That she expressed a need for anything, even a scrap of throwaway material, was enough for him. Swati showed the cloth to their grandfather, and he laughed as she stroked it against his face too.

Their mother came back a little while later. They rolled out their sleeping mats and she admired the velvet scraps, glancing at the box in the corner piled high with Swati's creations.

Madan went out to check on his grandfather before they turned out the lights. He was sitting up in bed, and from the next room Bahadur's snores escaped through his closed door.

"Everything good, Dada-ji?"

When Swati returned from the hospital, his grandfather had railed against his father and clawed at his own body, tearing off his clothes and running naked out onto the street, his scrawny arms and legs bent crooked, the shriveled folds of skin swinging like ruffled chicken feathers. "I don't deserve to live for giving life to such a demon," his grandfather had bawled when Madan and Jaggu brought him back. "I have no shame anymore. If I had any pride, it's all gone."

He had refused to live with them anymore.

"You don't have to keep me; there is no need for me." But eventually he stayed when he realized it was Swati who needed him most of all.

Their grandfather had diminished in size over the years; soon he would be no bigger than Swati. Outside a dog howled and he jerked and shivered. "Fuck . . . mother . . . fuck . . . motherfucking dog," he finally squeezed out.

Madan nudged him down and covered his twitching frame with a sheet. "Someone's died," said his grandfather. "He's howling . . . motherfucker's howling . . . to let the world know."

Inside, Swati was already fast asleep, threads caught in her hair. Madan watched for a moment. Though he worried about her, he couldn't be around her for too long. The sight of her always left him aching.

His mother collected the scraps of cloth strewn around the room, putting them back in the bag. "I want to go see Pandit Bansi Lal again," she said.

Madan sighed. They had been over this before. "Pandit Bansi Lal can't do anything," he said.

"There must be some puja he can do for us. If he wants more money we can manage from somewhere."

It isn't about money, he wanted to scream. But he said, "You've done more than enough of that already."

"But Pandit Bansi Lal —"

"His prayers are no different from yours or any of his pujaris. Besides, his pujas cost much more than we have."

His mother sat down on her mat, staring blankly at the dark TV screen.

"I'll think of something," he said, more tersely than he had intended.

Lying down, he heard Ma mumbling her prayers. At the temple, the pujaris of Pandit Bansi Lal, who scurried and fed like rats on their god-fearing worshippers, had recommended many sets of pujas for Swati's well-being. His mother paid for the pujas, gave food and clothing to the pujaris and did whatever they said. Though it had been tough to afford, Madan let her indulge in these rituals. They all wanted to feel like they were doing something about Swati. Once someone told Madan about a psychologist in Karnal and Madan hoped for more practical help, but on further investigation the man had not been a doctor but a professor at the college, and nothing came of it.

Ma ended her prayers with a long sigh, and now there was no sound but the ceiling fan whirring a creaky tune above him. His mother wanted to appeal to a higher power for Swati, but Pandit Bansi Lal was no trustworthy messenger. If this God of theirs listened to men like Pandit Bansi Lal, then in all fairness he should certainly listen to her prayers too.

Anyway, Pandit Bansi Lal would never access whatever special connections he had with God for Madan or his family. Every time they were in each other's company, and it was regularly, since Avtaar Singh had other dealings besides those of a religious nature with him, the pandit looked pained and uncomfortable, as if Madan were an illegal squatter in Pandit Bansi Lal's own house.

"Snakes have no shit hole, all the crap stays inside," his grandfather once said in those early years, when he had come across Madan sobbing in the corner of their room after Pandit Bansi Lal had used his walking stick to admonish him for dropping his prayer thali. Madan never told Avtaar Singh about that beating, and though now he had no fear of the man, he steered clear of the Pandit as much as possible.

The dog continued to howl into the night and Madan forced his eyes shut, dreaming of a snakelike Pandit Bansi Lal coiled around his neck, squeezing slowly, while Madan begged to be finished off with one venomous strike.

In the accountant's office, Madan shut the last ledger and placed it on Mr. D'Silva's desk. Every morning Madan attended the timber auction at Lakad Mandi, bidding for quintals of poplar and eucalyptus. While poplar's price depended on its grading — a good-quality log might cost more up-front but yield more too — the mottled-bark eucalyptus was not as fussy, and he learned to look for logs that Mother Nature favored with near-perfect cylindrical proportions. That would mean less wastage when peeled down to its pale underbark.

For the rest of the day he helped in the office, reconciling orders and helping Mr. D'Silva with the accounts.

"All done?" Mr. D'Silva asked, flipping through the ledger. "You're getting faster and faster."

Madan thought about what he could do next. It was too hot to work on the factory floor and unless there was a problem, there was no need for him to go out there. He took out the book he had started that morning.

"What're you reading?" asked Mr. D'Silva,

peering over his glasses.

"Noble House," said Madan, holding the book cover up so he could see. Embossed on the paperback's stark white cover was a cracked bronze pendant with Chinese inscriptions.

Mr. D'Silva answered the curt ring of the phone. "Put it away, saab wants you," he said.

Avtaar Singh was on the phone when Madan entered. "He's here now, I'll send him over."

Placing the phone down, he said, "I need you to drive memsaab and the girls. Do you remember Trilok-bhai's house? On the way to Hathni Kund?"

"I think so." Madan recalled going there once; the house was out of the town limits of Gorapur, but still fell under its administrative jurisdiction.

"If Ganesh is outside, take directions from him, but it's easy to find, no other house is as big in that area. And Madan," he said as Madan stepped out, "take the Contessa."

The twins were waiting when he drove up. "Come on, Mama, hurry up, he's here!" they shouted into the house. Minnu memsaab came out a while later, adjusting earrings so big and round that they hid most of her ears.

The twins chattered like monkeys and Madan, his thoughts on his book, tuned them out. Presently they shed the clamor and tumult of the town, and as the Contessa traveled silently through fields of mustard and rice, the occupants of the car fell into a dreamy silence.

All the land west of Gorapur as far as one could see — farmland, forest, villages — belonged to Trilok-bhai. Madan first met the stout landowner in the factory and the man often came into town with his wife for social occasions at Avtaar Singh's house. Though Trilok-bhai was older than Avtaar Singh by a few years, they shared an easy friendship, for Trilok-bhai's focus was on the running of his lands, and he did not interfere with Avtaar Singh's ventures in Gorapur. It was during election time that Trilok-bhai's interest in Gorapur stirred, and he and Avtaar Singh usually supported the same candidate. They had to ensure that whoever took office would be amiable and open to running things their way and not the way of the distant government in Chandigarh.

If people talked about Trilok-bhai, it was because of his three sons. The girls from the villages and the deer in the forests ran and hid when the boys came thundering through in their jeep. They were well known to hunt them with equal enthusiasm. Madan often ran into the boys when they were in town causing a commotion. As long as you matched them joke for joke, one dirtier than the next, and admired their well-oiled hunting rifles, they had no dispute with you.

"There it is!" said Rimpy as the house came into view, its odd shape reminiscent of one of Swati's sewn creations. The house had stood in this location for generations, even longer than Avtaar Singh's family had been in Gorapur.

"Finally, Minnu, you come out to the country to see us!" said Trilok-bhai's wife, Neeta, who was waiting out front. Her bangles clinked as she hugged the girls and guided them toward the house. Madan looked around for a shady spot to park the car. They would stay for lunch and evening tea, so he had a few hours of reading time.

"Auntie, where's Neha?" Dimpy asked as they walked in.

It had been about twenty minutes. In his book, Ian Dunross, the new tai-pan, was about to discover who was behind the hostile takeover bid of his company, Noble House, when a movement at the front of the house caught Madan's attention. The twins and Neeta memsaab had come back out, and stood on the front steps.

He got out and went to them in case the girls needed something. Neeta memsaab looked agitated. "She knew you were coming," she said. "She loved it when you girls visited her in Delhi. Remember all the shopping we did at South Extension?"

The twins nodded. "I don't understand this girl." Neeta memsaab turned in the direction of the fields, looking perturbed.

"It's okay, Auntie, we'll go with Madan and find her," Rimpy said.

"No, no." Neeta memsaab threw back her shoulders. "You girls don't go out in this heat. We'll send your servant boy." She nodded toward Madan standing at the foot of the stairs.

Rimpy and Dimpy glanced uncomfortably at each other. They did not look at Madan but let their gazes wander to the side. Madan did not flinch; he kept his attention on Neeta memsaab, wishing the twins would stop looking so awkward. He did not eat on the same plates, let alone at the same table. Whatever he did for them, whatever he shared with them, no matter how much he was part of their daily lives, when the doors shut at the end of the day he went to the back of their house, to another world and another family.

"Just follow the path." Neeta memsaab pointed to the trails slicing into the fields surrounding the house. "You'll come across her at some point. Check one of the lookout towers." She turned back toward the house.

"It's Neeta Auntie's daughter, Neha," said Rimpy, realizing that no one had told him who he should be looking for.

"He'll find her," Neeta memsaab said from the doorway. "You girls come back in. I've made fresh nimbu pani, its icy cold and sweet, just how you like it."

Rimpy ran back up, and Dimpy, throwing Madan an apologetic look, followed her twin.

Madan tossed his book in the car and locked it, following the path Neeta memsaab pointed out. The hip-high stalks of corn allowed an uninterrupted view of the area, but there was no sign of anyone. He wiped his brow with the sleeve of his T-shirt. He hadn't even known that Trilok-bhai had a daughter, and now he was out hunting for this girl, who for some odd reason had decided to take an excursion on this burning hot day. She was probably "bored" like the twins always claimed to be, but at least he didn't have to waste his time searching for them all over the countryside.

He walked on, swatting at gnats that

greeted him. Soon the fields petered out and a clump of trees provided shade. The grove ended suddenly and he was back in the fields. It was quiet, even the hawks hunted in silence up above. He couldn't imagine some girl having walked all the way out here by herself. This may be her father's land, but it was foolhardy to be out this far alone; anything could happen and there was no one around to hear her screams. He turned back, looking for another path. Spotting a lookout tower not too far away, he decided to check there.

The wooden tower had a few rungs missing from its ladder but the platform above seemed sturdy enough. Madan looked up and around and thought he saw something glinting in the sunlight.

He tested one of the rungs before climbing up to the platform. The moment he swung up and onto it, he saw the girl curled in a shady corner, her head resting on a small backpack, her face hidden under her arm. Her scuffed and grass-stained jeans made him wonder how long she had been out. *Maybe she's hurt,* he thought, and then decided she was probably asleep.

He stood there, not knowing what to do. Should he call out to her and wake her up? He moved closer, but before he could say anything she said, "Were you sent to get me?"

"Yes," he said, "your mother wants you back at the house."

Her arm slid slowly off her face and she got up in one fluid movement, lifting her arms to capture her flyaway hair and twisting it into a knot at the nape of her neck. Her shirt lifted a little as she did this, and Madan turned his gaze to the small lake in the distance.

When he looked back at her she was holding her backpack out to him. He took it and she smiled. "Thanks," she said, startling him enough that he looked straight at her. No one had actually thanked him before; not the twins or their family, and he never expected them to either.

Flecks of copper lit the muddy darkness of her eyes and for an instant he thought it was a reflection of the yellow flowers sprinkled in the fields. She lowered her lids, and when she looked back up, the twinkling specks beckoned once again.

He turned abruptly to the ladder, in part to clear the sudden light-headed feeling that came upon him. Too much sun; he was getting dehydrated. He climbed down and then looked up to make sure she was following. She was nearly to the ground when she lost her footing on a missing rung and slid the next few rungs down. Madan dropped the backpack and caught her firmly by the waist before she fell too far.

She found a sure footing, yet he didn't let go, his arms feeling heavy and lethargic like he had been unloading trucks all day. He was reluctant to move them ever again. She turned slowly and put her hands on his shoulder. He lifted her up, placing her gently on the ground.

"Careful," he said, and then felt silly about the warning, as she had already slipped.

They walked back on the same path he had taken earlier, Madan a few steps behind, the backpack thumping against his side. Her hair came undone again and it swung long and straight as she picked her way forward, her hands gliding over the tops of the stalks.

Her mother was outside; she had probably spotted them walking back. She was angry. As they stepped onto the driveway, she grabbed Neha's arm and pulled her up the stairs. "Look at you! Filthy." Still holding her arm, her mother began to dust her jeans and T-shirt. Neha squirmed as she tried to avoid her mother's quick slaps. Finally, her mother ran her fingers through Neha's unraveled hair and twisted it tightly away from her face. Neha's hands went up to her head as a tiny cry of pain escaped.

"Go clean up. I want you in the drawing room looking presentable in five minutes. Don't embarrass me in front of these people." Neeta memsaab pushed her into the house, leaving Madan outside still holding the backpack.

A few seconds later the door swung open and Neha rushed out, extending her arm for the bag. He handed it to her; she looked distracted and didn't say anything. Madan returned to the car, felt under the seat for his bottle of water and took a long, cold drink. He opened his book, letting it claim his attention.

Then, sliding onto the page, obscuring the words and making him reread the same sentence over and over again, came the memory of those eyes speckled with copper and the smile that had lifted him off the ground, if only for a moment.

CHAPTER 9

The grounds of Gorapur Academy were quiet in the weak early morning sun, and some students clamored around the notice board in front of the principal's office. "There it is," said Madan, pointing to Jaggu's name. His own name had been easier to spot; it was on the top of the list.

"Second division," said Jaggu, surprised. He'd only agreed to stay on in school to give Madan company. Getting an education was a bonus.

At the factory, Avtaar Singh sent for a big box of ladoos. "Listen," his voice boomed across the factory floor, bringing work to a stop. "First division, again," he said, his arm around Madan's shoulder. "Remember when he came here with short pants and not a whisker above his lips?" His eyes swept the floor. "You fools will still be here years from now, gray hair and all, but the world will say, 'He is the son of Gorapur,' and each and every one of you will be made proud."

The speech was a variation of the one Avtaar Singh gave every year at this time, when Madan's results came out. It never failed to rouse the factory workers, and they clapped, even those who were new and did not understand why Madan was the focus of all this attention. Madan distributed the ladoos, fresh and fragrant, to the workers, accepting their congratulations.

"I heard, I heard," said a voice behind him. Pandit Bansi Lal picked his way between the machines in his white kurta and dhoti; a long saffron scarf draped around his neck and shoulders reached his knees. Jaggu followed, carrying his walking stick and making funny faces behind the pandit's back, imitating his shuffling stride.

Avtaar Singh spotted Pandit Bansi Lal too. "Welcome, Pandit-ji, you've come at a most fortunate time. Madan, give Pandit-ji the biggest ladoo in the box."

Madan bent to touch Pandit Bansi Lal's feet and the pandit laid a cold hand on his head in blessing. He proffered the box to Pandit Bansi Lal, who sniffed at it and, seeing Avtaar Singh's attention elsewhere, delicately picked a small crumb, touching it to his lips.

"Om," said Pandit Bansi Lal, slapping his own chest as if there were no other way to get the name of God out of him. Avtaar Singh swept them all into his office and Pandit Bansi Lal collapsed into his favorite corner of the sofa, where he could rest an arm on one side and wave the other one around.

"You're truly a great man, Avtaar Singh-ji. In the final act, when we're judged by our actions, your bountiful spirit will get its rewards. I've said it many times, that this boy should be kissing your feet." Pandit Bansi Lal dispensed his wisdom like playing cards. "You've changed his life! Like Lord Krishna who counseled Arjun on the Kurukshetra battlefield not too far from here, you have transformed this boy too."

Madan wanted to poke Pandit Bansi Lal's eyes out with the incense sticks burning under the portrait of Avtaar Singh's father. He hated when the priest talked about him like he was invisible.

"Like Lord Krishna?" Avtaar Singh laughed. "That's too much, Pandit-ji. You're the one who is too kind. But look at him again — he's not a boy anymore," he said as the phone rang.

"Yes." Pandit Bansi Lal turned to consider Madan. "And a black pot remains black no matter how many layers of silver paint you decorate it with." He tried to stare Madan down. Not wanting to give him the satisfaction, Madan began to excuse himself to Avtaar Singh, but there was a knock on the door.

"Ah, Mr. Kishore! Come in, come in," said Avtaar Singh, ending his phone call and getting up to greet the man in the safari suit.

"So glad to finally meet you, Avtaar Singh-ji," Mr. Kishore said as they shook hands. "I came straight from the train station."

"Come," said Avtaar Singh. "Meet Pandit Bansi Lal. He's here to show me the astrological charts for my new factory. We're looking for an auspicious day to begin. This is Madan," he said. "Madan, this is Mr. Kishore of Sapna Builders."

Madan recognized the name as one of their buyers; he folded his hands in greeting.

"Good to meet you, young man," Mr. Kishore said. "You never mentioned your son before, Avtaar Singh-ji."

Mr. Kishore beamed at the three of them but they were frozen in place, Pandit Bansi Lal's little finger halfway up his nostril, Avtaar Singh's hand on Madan's shoulder. The silence went on for an awkward moment until Pandit Bansi Lal said, "Avtaar Singh has no son."

"Oh!" Mr. Kishore looked confused. "I'm sorry . . ."

"Yes . . . well," Avtaar Singh murmured, the sound forced, as though he'd been punched in the stomach. Madan felt the weight of his hand on his shoulder as he leaned on him for support.

"Well . . ." said Avtaar Singh again.

"He's only the maidservant's son," said Pandit Bansi Lal, defying either of them to refute the truth.

Mr. Kishore looked even more uncomfortable, but the pandit's words seemed to bring Avtaar Singh out of the mist. Collecting himself, he walked determinedly around to his chair. "Sit, please, Mr. Kishore. What can we get you?" Avtaar Singh picked up the phone and called for tea while Madan slipped from the room. There would come a day when even Avtaar Singh would not be able to protect Pandit Bansi Lal's neck from Madan's bare hands.

Later, Madan ran into Feroze and Harish from the evening gang. They were early, probably running a quick errand, and Madan was offering them the last of the ladoos when Avtaar Singh came out of his office looking for his driver, Ganesh.

"Saab," said Feroze, indicating the bathrooms. "You know." Ganesh's ongoing struggle with piles was common knowledge.

"Oh," said Avtaar Singh. "He was supposed to drive us this evening to Trilok-bhai's house for dinner, but memsaab and the girls want to go now. When he returns tell him to pick them up at home. I'll need one of you," he said, pointing to Feroze and Harish, "to drive me there tonight. Madan needs a day off."

"No, saab, no need. I can take them right now," Madan said, the words out of his mouth before he realized he was speaking. They all looked at him with surprise.

"No, no," Avtaar Singh said. "Today you go have fun. I'm sure you and your friends have all sorts of celebrations planned for this evening."

Turning to him, the men grinned, but Madan found he could not stop himself. "Nothing really planned, saab. I can take them now and Ganesh can bring you later."

"No, no," said Avtaar Singh again, but Madan saw him hesitate. He knew Avtaar Singh would rather Madan or Ganesh do the driving than these men who forgot the cars were not guided missiles. "You know, the girls want to keep going there, now that Trilok-bhai's daughter is back; they're all the same age," Avtaar Singh said, more to himself than to Madan.

Madan did not want to give him a chance to think about it longer. He spoke quickly and firmly. "I'll go home right away. I have to tell my mother about my results too. I can do my celebrating tomorrow."

At last, Avtaar Singh agreed, looking relieved. Before he returned to his office, he called Madan to the side. Taking out a couple hundred-rupee notes from his wallet, he gave them to Madan.

"For your celebration tomorrow," he said.

"No, saab, I need only your blessings." Madan pushed the money back, but Avtaar Singh was firm.

"You have those always. This is for fun."

Madan nodded, touching Avtaar Singh's feet before leaving.

"What?" Jaggu would not let it go. "But I got this case of ThunderBolt, Madan. A whole case of beer, and what about . . ." He searched for a way to persuade Madan. "We were thinking about going to the canal or a movie and . . ."

Madan placed his hand on Jaggu's shoulder and made an effort to look contrite. "I know. I'm sorry. But Avtaar Singh wanted me to take them, no one else." He bit his lip on the lie. "You know how he is about his daughters."

"Oh . . . okay," said Jaggu, his brow furrowing. "But today? One day he could not use someone else?"

Madan shrugged. "What do you want me to do? I can't say no when he asks, can I?"

"No, you can't," Jaggu agreed.

"We can do all this tomorrow," Madan promised. "And we can even go to that movie you wanted to see. What's the name?"

"Maine Pyar Kiya," said Jaggu. "What a love story, what songs . . ." His voice trailed off. Madan looked away from Jaggu's piercing disappointment.

Ignoring the thread of guilt knotting tighter in his stomach, Madan patted Jaggu's shoulder again and moved with quick precision to the front of the house.

As Madan unloaded the fruit baskets Minnu memsaab brought along, he noticed a familiar jeep parked in the corner. Trilokbhai's sons must be home. He placed the huge baskets of fruit by the two ladies sitting out under the veranda's fan. Neeta memsaab said, "Really Minnu, you shouldn't do all this. I'm just happy that the twins are here. Your girls will be a good influence on Neha."

Minnu memsaab took a long sip of her cola, the ice clinking as she drank. "Don't worry, Neeta, even Sunita Rampal of Fine Paper and Pulp — you know her — she said the other day what a good example Rimpy and Dimpy set for all the girls. I don't know why you sent Neha away in the first place. With girls you need to keep them close and under tight control."

Neeta memsaab sighed, but Madan didn't hear her reply as he walked to the car.

After what seemed like hours, Madan checked his watch. Less than an hour had passed. He got up and stretched. It was quiet out front. The twins were so excited on their way here that they rushed into the house on their arrival, as if Trilok-bhai's daughter were a visiting pop star.

Madan walked around to the kitchen. One of the servants poured him some tea. He stood there looking out at the endless fields, sipping slowly and methodically.

"You've come from town?" asked the cook. He rolled and flipped chapattis on the tava, while on the stove several pots boiled and simmered.

"My saab's daughters have come to visit. I didn't know Trilok-bhai had a daughter. I just found out," he said.

Scooping a handful of chopped onions,

the cook threw them into the pot nearest to him. When the hissing and sizzling subsided, he said, "She used to go to school in Delhi, but it seems there was a problem."

They talked about common acquaintances in Gorapur and soon lunch was served, first to those inside and then to those waiting outside.

Madan went back to the car after lunch. He was dozing off when a commotion snapped him awake. Everyone was outside and Rimpy and Dimpy were calling to him.

Trilok-bhai's sons came down the steps and shook Madan's hand, acknowledging their association. The three older brothers, Rohan, Mohan and Sohan, appeared as a single unit. Something had keyed them up and Rimpy was eager to share.

"Madan, we're going to Maneswar Forest for hunting," she said. "Wow, this will be so great."

"Nothing as delicious as deer pickle," said Mohan, smacking his lips.

"I want to ride in the jeep," said Dimpy, and Sohan next to her grinned and swung his rifle onto his shoulder. She tossed her head back and giggled. Rohan was revving up the jeep. He backed up, turned it around and the other two brothers jumped in.

Madan looked from one twin to the other,

but thankfully Minnu memsaab came down to join them and said, "You girls ride with Madan if you want to go."

"But Mama!" said Rimpy. Minnu memsaab's expression forbade any argument.

Minnu memsaab went back up, smiling at Neeta. "The girls should ride with Madan," she said. "That way they'll have two cars if someone wants to come back. He's Avtaar's boy from the factory. We've had him since he was a child, very responsible. He'll take care of them."

Neeta memsaab nodded in agreement. She poked her head into the doorway and shouted, "Neha!"

It was like water had frozen to ice in his throat. He couldn't breathe. Dimpy was saying something to him and he nodded, not listening to what she said, his eyes fixed on the door.

She walked by the two women at the top of the steps, her navy backpack, with its red stripe like a slash of sindoor hanging at her side.

"Have a good time, all you girls," her mother said.

"Sure, Ma." Neha's gaze fell on Madan and she smiled. "You again," she said.

He didn't say anything, couldn't. The twins were calling her to the car, "Let's go," and her brothers were shouting from their jeep to hurry up. One of the other servants placed bottled water, soft drinks and snacks in the car's trunk, and before Madan knew it, he was in the driver's seat, maneuvering out of the driveway, following the jeep and trying to keep from glancing to the rearview mirror.

Maneswar was less than an hour away, but the narrow one-lane road slowed their progress to the lush forest.

Rimpy leaned forward and asked Madan to insert a cassette into the player. Right away the twins were singing along, miming the words to a popular English song. Madan had had front-row seats to this show many times before.

He stole a quick glance at Neha sitting between them. She was nodding to the beat, smiling and laughing with the twins. When Dimpy held out her fist like a microphone, Neha good-naturedly injected the main refrain from the song, belting out *"faith"* at the appropriate moment.

When there was a lull in the music, Neha said, "So . . . Madan?"

Madan nodded, and the twins quieted down, turning their attention to her.

"Madan, I hear you work at the factory?"

"Yes," he said, happy she was talking to

him, not stopping to wonder why she was asking the question.

"So do you feel that it's fair that you and your fellow workers do all the work, and yet it is Avtaar Uncle who reaps the ultimate benefit? Don't you feel you should have the same rights as the man you serve, that you should get the same rewards?"

"Huh?" said Rimpy. Madan himself nearly let go of the wheel to turn around in surprise, unsure if he'd heard her correctly.

"Don't worry," she continued, not skipping a beat, "it may look like our country is losing its socialist leanings, but change is inevitable. Sooner or later the struggle for all of us will come to a head. How long can the moneyed few suck the blood from the hardworking majority? Karl Marx said, 'The history of existing society is the history of class struggles.' It will happen, Madan, sooner or later."

"What the hell are you talking about, Neha?" Rimpy said. "This is why Trilok Uncle brought you back from Delhi, isn't it? We heard you got mixed up in some political stuff, rallies and all that."

"I didn't get *mixed up,* Rimpy. I saw the injustices that the upper classes perpetuate and I chose to take action. It was the Youth Communist Party," she said.

Madan was sure these were too many words for the twins to take in, but Neha wasn't done yet.

"More than ever there is a need to end the class differences in our country. The clear answer to this is the end of private property. The profit of labor should be shared by all, not limited to a handful."

"Madan is not like that," said Dimpy, belatedly. "He works with Papa and he takes care of us. He's been with us forever."

"What do you say, Madan?" Neha asked.

There was much Madan wanted to say, and it had nothing to do with Karl Marx. For now he said, "I'm satisfied with my work and grateful to be working with Avtaar Singh saab."

"See?" said Rimpy. "And by the way, isn't your father the owner of all these lands we just passed?"

"Exactly!" said Dimpy, though she still looked like she had run into a glass door.

"My father and your father are among those who will realize that no more can they live off the hard work of those less fortunate; they will all suffer the same fate."

"Okay, okay, enough," said Dimpy, already looking exhausted. "We're here."

The jeep in front honked and Madan turned to follow it off the road. They got to the border of the forest and parked in a clearing. In the distance, the roar of the Yamuna River echoed back at them.

Madan opened the trunk to take out the picnic blanket, the drinks and snacks. The twins went over to the boys, squealing over the rifles and the ammunition lying around the jeep. Neha appeared at Madan's side and helped unload the picnic from the car.

Now that he had her to himself, for this moment at least, he felt the need to say something. She said something disagreeable about Avtaar Singh but he couldn't remember what exactly, so he said, "I've never met anyone who has such strong beliefs . . . about communism, I mean."

She looked up at him in surprise. It was unusual. He was sure that when she spoke to any of the other workers, they gave her the same answer of being happy with their lot and left it at that.

"Not in these parts," she said, recovering quickly. "But it'll change soon."

"I don't know," said Madan, catching himself. What was he doing, offering a rebuttal, when the last thing he wanted to do was disagree with her? But it was too late. She looked at him curiously.

"I don't know," he said again. "You're supposing that we're all unhappy, but that's

206

not so. I'd rather work for someone, rise or fall on my own merit, than work for some bureaucrats who wouldn't allow me to be my own boss one day, if I want to be."

He couldn't tell from her expression whether she was offended or pleased, so he continued. "Besides, I know the full form of KGB and I don't know if I want those sort of people in my country."

"Really?" Her smile was dazzling. "What is it?"

"Komitet Gosudarstvennoy Bezopasnosti," he reeled off, thanks to all those spy novels he devoured.

Her eyes opened wide. She laughed, the flecks of copper dancing with her delight.

"What's going on?" Her eldest brother, Rohan, came up to them and his gaze shifted from his sister to Madan. Neha at once looked somber and went to join the girls on the picnic blanket. Rohan gave Madan a probing look before joining her.

They talked and bantered while they ate. Madan leaned against the car and waited, trying not to let his gaze linger on her. He shouldn't have said anything. Why couldn't he have kept his mouth shut instead of starting a conversation? He should have let it go. After all, who knew about these girls, what they might take offense to?

207

"Ready?" The brothers shouldered their rifles once done with the picnic, and the twins twittered like baby birds.

"This is so exciting," said Rimpy.

"Too much," agreed Dimpy.

"Okay, girls," said Rohan. "Follow us quietly and obey whatever we say; hunting is serious business."

Neha made a derisive sound but the twins nodded, entranced.

"Madan, you follow us," ordered Sohan. "We'll need help carrying back whatever we get."

He off-loaded the extra rounds of ammunition on Madan; they had enough to kill not only all the deer in the forest but all the fish in the river as well.

They walked through groves of trees, the leaves crunching and stirring underfoot. The brothers stopped now and again, dramatically indicating that everyone should get down and be quiet, but it led to nothing.

"This is stupid," said Neha, and the twins shushed her. After a while, they missed one deer and had not done much else than walk in circles. They stopped to catch their breath, and in that moment of silence they heard a distinct sound behind the bushes, not too far away.

Again, one of the brothers flailed his arms

around to tell them to remain quiet and watch. Rohan and Mohan raised their rifles and advanced slowly, separating as they approached so they could catch their quarry in the cross fire, whether it ran left or right.

Though they all expected the shots, when they rang out, the twins shrieked. The forest shook and mynahs and parrots flew out into the cloudless sky. Everyone but Madan ran forward. He was in no mood to see some helpless creature taking its last breath. But suddenly a scream rent the air, and Madan, realizing it was one of the twins, ran forward too.

First, he saw the trees right in front splattered and dripping with blood, and then, as everyone swarmed around, he saw a man lying prostrate on the ground, his legs bent at an odd angle.

The whites of his open eyes still looked wet and slick with life, but he was not moving. Madan knelt down, checking the man's pulse. He looked like one of those poor travelers along the river; all he had on was a faded cotton dhoti, wound around his lower half, covering him from stomach to knees. Madan looked around, and sure enough, a walking stick lay nearby. The man was probably resting here, perhaps awoken from his nap.

The brothers were certainly good shots; they both got him, one from either side. Rohan kicked the corpse.

"What are you doing? What are you doing?" Neha dropped down beside the body, pushing her brother away.

"What? It's just some old man," said one of the brothers.

" 'Just some old man'?" she lashed out.

"Relax," said Mohan. "These people are all over the area. That's what you get for living in a place for animals — you get shot like one."

Madan felt a throbbing begin at the base of his skull, and he was glad Neha spoke; the sound of her voice calmed him down. "What're you going to do about this?" she asked her brothers.

"Calm down, sis," said Rohan this time. "Madan will take care of it. He knows just what to do. Familiar territory, eh, Madan?"

Madan wanted to strangle him as Neha's eyes, filling with tears, shifted their gaze to Madan.

"Are you going to call the police?" she asked, confused. She was cradling the man's head in her hands now.

Madan wished he could give her another answer, but the police wouldn't want to be bothered with this and he knew, ultimately,

Avtaar Singh would want him to clear this matter up quietly, with the least amount of fuss. It was his responsibility, more so as Avtaar Singh's daughters were here, too. Remembering the twins, he looked for them. They were huddled together off to the side.

"I'm sorry," said Madan, and Neha gave a small cry as she understood more than what he was saying. "Can you take them back to the car?" He tilted his head toward the twins. "Will you be able to find the way?"

Neha nodded. She laid the man's head back on the carpet of leaves and went to the twins. They began to walk back to the car.

"The river isn't too far," said Madan. He grasped the man under his shoulders and Sohan took the man's feet. They headed in the direction of the roar of the river, while Rohan and Mohan hauled the rifles, following them to the Yamuna.

Though it was quiet around the banks of the river, Madan placed the body down and went ahead to make sure no one was there. When he returned, they picked up the body again, moving to where the waves lapped the shore. On Madan's cue, he and Sohan swung the body in a short arc, launching it far into the churning river. It didn't take long. The currents were strong and hurried, and the body turned over and under in a matter of minutes.

They walked back, the brothers talking and joking. "He'll be grateful we put him in the Yamuna. A holy river, he'll go straight to heaven," they said.

The twins were in the car, and the brothers waved to them and jumped in the jeep. "Straight home for dinner, I'm starving," said Rohan.

Neha was pacing outside the car. Madan approached gingerly, not sure what to expect. "You were kind to him," she said. "He had that." Madan didn't say anything. He opened the car door for her. "We live by their rules," she said, waving at the departing jeep, but Madan knew she also meant her father and Avtaar Singh. "That's all I'm saying. We're helpless."

The drive home was quiet. With the heat of the summer, the days were longer, but night appeared unexpectedly, like a hand blotting out the sun. With no streetlights on the country roads, Madan drove carefully, the halos from the headlights sweeping the darkened road and keeping them steadily on solid tar.

"You know who is often seen in this area?" Neha's voice came sudden and strong from the back.

When no one answered, she said, "The truck drivers tell this story of a woman who waves them down for a ride. She's beautiful, but when they pick her up, they discover she's a churail, because her feet are turned around, her toes facing back. And once she lays her eyes on you, it's too late. After, they are usually visited by terrible bad luck, terrible disease, floods in their village, the death of their child."

Dimpy shivered and they all glanced out. It was pitch-black on the other side of their windows, concealing behind its dark screen a woman with turned feet, her sari flapping in the wind as she waved them down.

At the house, the jeep was already parked in the corner, and next to it the Contessa. Avtaar Singh was here. The twins rushed into the house, but Neha got out slowly. Madan came around to empty out the trunk and when he inserted the key he found Neha standing beside him.

"What did you do?" she asked.

"The river," said Madan. "It's the easiest way." If the twins had asked, he would never have told them.

She sighed and looked down at her shoes. "There was so much blood. Is there . . . is there always so much blood?"

Her impression of him, whatever it was,

had changed now. He refused to allow the realization to concern him — what did it matter?

"Someone once told me, after my first . . . encounter . . . 'Blood is so common, everyone has blood, so why cry over it when it's spilled?' "

She made a choked sound. But what else could he say to her? He had nothing else. She fidgeted as if struggling with a decision, and then, taking a deep breath, gave a small smile. It comforted him, coaxing a half smile out of him too.

They heard the door creak as Avtaar Singh came out.

"Everything okay?" Avtaar Singh asked as she passed by him.

"Yes, Uncle. I was collecting my things."

Avtaar Singh walked up to Madan. "They told us what happened. Good you were there to take care of it. These boys cannot afford any more attention. There comes a time when even the police cannot turn a blind eye anymore. Anyway, Trilok-bhai will be in our debt now. Good, good." He smoothed out his mustache.

Always assessing the situation from all angles; tweaking it so he gained in the end. Madan concurred, relieved to be back with that familiar philosophy and with Avtaar

Singh's stalwart reasoning.

"Remember, you have the day off tomorrow." Avtaar Singh wagged his finger at Madan. "No excuses. I don't want to see you," he shouted from the doorway, following Neha into the house.

CHAPTER 10

It was early, the sun but a promise in the haze, when Madan got to the factory after his time off. A few of the overnight workers were stirring, but the giant machines, usually deafening with their clatter, were quiet. The familiar aroma — a cocktail of kerosene, smoke from nearby cooking fires and fresh wood shavings — made him want to embrace every bit of the factory.

The night watchman, looking heavy-eyed, saluted as he walked by. Madan made a mental note to check on him some night in case he was sleeping on the job.

"What are you doing here so early?" The car door slammed and Avtaar Singh emerged from the Contessa, Ganesh yawning in the front. Madan didn't know what to say. He was worn out, seized by an excruciating restlessness that filled the space of his days. He could hardly sleep, and found trouble following any conversation.

Thankfully, Avtaar Singh didn't wait for an answer.

"Let's have tea," Avtaar Singh said, heading straight for his office.

Madan wanted to run up and hold him close, inhale that sophisticated cologne so out of place in these crude settings and have Avtaar Singh reassure him that nothing had changed, that it never would. Avtaar Singh always knew what to say.

Madan sent the watchman to the dhaba down the street with a couple of rupees and the tall glass tumbler kept especially for Avtaar Singh's tea, for while he enjoyed the foamy sweet dhaba tea, Avtaar Singh did not trust the cleanliness of the glasses the dhaba used.

When the tea arrived, Madan placed it on Avtaar Singh's desk, retrieving from the side console the box of Marie biscuits. He lit the incense stick under the portrait of Avtaar Singh's father and then took his seat across from him.

"So, what're you doing here so early?" he asked again.

"Nothing, saab. Couldn't sleep."

"Some problem with collections? With the boys?"

"No, nothing like that."

"Hmm," said Avtaar Singh, taking a sip.

"I was thinking . . ." Avtaar Singh leaned back in his chair and closed his eyes. Madan waited.

Avtaar Singh sighed and opened his eyes. "What was I saying?"

"You were thinking of something, saab."

"Yes, yes. You know Rimpy, Dimpy. They want to go out of town for a while . . . Mussoorie or someplace like that."

Madan nodded. The twins had brought up the idea of a trip to Mussoorie with him as well, saying, "We want to go somewhere. Gorapur has nothing, only movies and buffaloes." Madan had left the confines of Gorapur a few times when driving Avtaar Singh to nearby towns for work and once to Delhi, and it was never more than overnight. Leaving Gorapur always left him drained and on edge, impatient to return. He was happiest here, and never saw the sense or the reason for wanting to spend time in places with unfamiliar bends in the roads and people who did not know who you were.

"Anyway," said Avtaar Singh. "I've been thinking about it. Memsaab would like to go as well, they all want a change." He gave a disbelieving laugh and Madan smiled too. Neither could imagine being dissatisfied enough with Gorapur to leave, even for a

218

short time.

"Let them go," continued Avtaar Singh. "It will be much cooler up in the hills away from the heat, and it's true the girls haven't had much of a holiday this time. But what I wanted to ask is, would you go with them?"

Madan wished that Avtaar Singh would give the order, tell Madan to do what he needed. Yet he had asked, giving Madan a choice that really did not exist, for he could not refuse Avtaar Singh. He didn't really want to go; the thought of spending even a few days with memsaab and the two girls was not appealing.

"Memsaab asked that you go, so if the girls want to do sightseeing you can take them around. I know you don't like leaving Gorapur, but maybe it'll be a good break for you before college starts."

Madan, at least, had the illusion of it being his own decision. Avtaar Singh extended that formality to no one else.

"Whatever you say, saab. When do they plan to leave?"

"Soon, soon," said Avtaar Singh. "Oh, and there will be two cars going — ours and Trilok-bhai's. His wife and daughter are going as well. They made these plans the other night. Trilok-bhai has a house near Mussoorie, so once they call up there to make it

219

ready, in two, three days' time I think . . ."

Avtaar Singh went on talking, but Madan heard no more, and before he knew it he was back home, telling his mother that he was going away for a few days.

Mussoorie. One road led up to it from the valley below, curving and snaking precariously up the mountainside, requiring all of Madan's attention. Honking cars, overloaded trucks and shepherds herding goats all fought for space on a narrow road that ended abruptly by spilling into a large square that signaled the entry to the hill town.

Minnu and Neeta memsaab were in one car with Trilok-bhai's driver, Bhola, an elderly man who, like all the rest of the help, had been with their family for as long as anyone remembered. In the other car were Madan and all the girls. Rimpy and Dimpy had wanted it like this so that they could talk and listen to their own music.

"No serious talk, okay, Neha?" Rimpy said when they stopped to pick her up.

"Agreed," Neha said. "From what I've heard so far, my views aren't shared by all." She met Madan's eyes as she handed him her bag and smiled.

Heaven's End, Trilok-bhai's family bungalow, was a few kilometers away from the town of Mussoorie. The mothers decided to stop in town to pick up groceries before proceeding on. Shops crowded the square, and in the middle stood a statue of Mahatma Gandhi caught in midstride, his walking stick in front as always.

"It's cold," said Dimpy, shoving her hands deep into her jacket pockets.

"If you're cold, think how he must be feeling," said Neha, nodding toward the half-clothed statue of Gandhi in his dhoti as small as a loincloth. In tandem, the twins glanced at Gandhi and then began to laugh, and even Madan, overhearing them from the other side of the car, allowed himself a smile.

They drove into Heaven's End as the sun descended over the snowcapped peaks in the distance, bathing the old colonial bungalow in a buttery light. After the daylong drive, they were glad to be out of the cramped cars and decided to leave any exploring for the next day.

Trilok-bhai's caretaker, who doubled as a cook, seemed glad for the company. Madan tried stifling his yawns as the old men continued to converse after dinner, but then excused himself. He thought sleep would come easily — he was tired after driving all day — but hours later, he tossed and turned.

It was no use. He pulled on his jacket and shoes and stepped outside. Moonlight flooded the hillside, bright enough to make his way around. The caretaker and Bhola were fast asleep in their rooms.

An expansive, well-manicured lawn surrounded the house in the front, but at its end the mountain reclaimed its space and the land fell away down a steep hillside. A short railing marked the beginning of the descent. Madan stood over it, looking into the shadows below.

"Careful," said a voice behind him.

He didn't move at first, giving himself time to breathe. He turned around and said, "You shouldn't be out here."

She came to the railing, peeking over as he had a moment ago. Her hair fell forward, draping her cheek, and he shoved his hand in his pockets to keep from reaching out to touch it.

She leaned against the railing, and he backed away as though to protect himself against a blow. "You shouldn't be out here," he repeated, the words hanging like a silent scream in the air.

"Yet here I am," she said.

She slid down and sat on the grass, her back against the rail.

"Sit with me . . . Madan," she said.

Madan looked up at the silent, slumbering house. *Come back,* it said. *Walk away. You've always listened to reason. Walk away and it will be okay.* Then he looked down at her and the house shut up like someone had cut out its tongue.

He slid down and they sat side by side, legs stretched out in front of them.

"Yes, memsaab," he said.

"Don't call me that," she said

He didn't look at her. "You may not agree with my thinking, but you don't have to rub it in by calling me memsaab," she said.

After a while he said, "Why did someone like you get into all that anyway?"

"Someone like me?" She laughed. "You mean the daughter of the great Trilok-bhai?"

When he nodded stiffly, she said, "I'm sorry. It's not funny, he was really upset."

And then she began to laugh, doubling over and wiping her eyes. Madan glanced toward the house, sure someone could hear.

"I'm sorry. I hated going to school in Delhi. My father thought the usual — convent-school-educated girl would make a good match. Sent me to live with my chacha. I begged in the beginning to come back home. But he refused to listen. And then, when I found friends and people I liked and everything finally became bearable, it upset him, so he dragged me back to Gorapur, and now I'm here . . . sitting with you."

"And that's funny," said Madan.

She stopped at once. "No, no. It's because now I really want to be here . . . right here."

A girl from school had invited Neha to a meeting of the Youth Communist Party when she saw her reading a paper on "Communism in Plato's *Republic*," she told Madan. At her first meeting — Madan sensed her excitement — these people, they made so much sense, talking about equality and a workers' state. The meetings took place during the day at a nearby college's cafeteria. She gave her attendance at school and then slipped out with the other girl. It was easy; the school never thought girls from such good families would attempt leaving the grounds, so there wasn't much security. And it was wonderful — meeting, talking, believing in something so strongly that you could see no other way. They even held a few protests.

Then one day her uncle and aunt came to school to pick her up earlier than usual. No one could find her, and when she returned it seemed like the entire Indian army was standing outside. Trilok-bhai let her finish school, but as soon as it let out she was back in Gorapur.

"Now she . . . my mother . . . they all keep a watch on me like I'm the Koh-i-Noor diamond. They thought I was escaping school to meet up with some boy."

"And . . . there was no one?" Madan asked.

"There were quite a few boys who were members of the YCP, the Youth Communist Party. But no." She sighed. "All I did was go back and forth — school, home, home, school. Here were people who argued and debated and thought hard and fought for their point of view, coming and going as they pleased. My parents, my brothers, still don't believe I went to all this trouble to get to know other people besides them, to have thoughts besides theirs."

"In that regard," said Madan, "I don't think that is where the country is headed."

"The death of Nehru's socialism and an open economy? You think that will work here?"

He nodded. "We all want to be our own boss. Isn't that what we say, 'Roti, kapda aur makan'? But we want to be the boss of our own basic necessities and have the freedom to multiply them without anyone

225

— the government or anyone else — setting any limits."

"You sound like Avtaar Uncle," she said. She laughed again and then shivered. The temperature had dropped, and as much as they wanted to talk more, it was freezing.

Reluctantly they got up. "Good night, Madan," she said, and held out her hand. He considered it for a moment and then took her hand in his own.

"Sleep well, memsaab," he said.

After breakfast, the twins were raring to go. "We'll meet you later," said Minnu memsaab, "just take them out somewhere."

The morning was clear and crisp but Madan found it hard to keep his eyes on the road. He was tempted to go on looking at Neha.

In town, they headed to Camel's Back Road, where Madan procured horses for them to ride along the curving lane, the blue-green deodar trees perfuming the air with their cedarlike aroma. Flocks of chestnut-feathered bulbuls rustled in the branches, and trails of mist lingered around the lichen-dusted tombstones clinging to the hillside at the old British cemetery.

"It's so beautiful out here," said Dimpy as the girls pointed out things that caught their interest along the way. The horses lumbered on, used to traversing this path all day. The twins and Neha rode a little way ahead while Madan hung back, but she turned around now and then, catching his eye.

The twins mapped out their activities for the rest of their day and, after their ride, they took the cable car up to Gun Hill, where one of the touts persuaded the twins to dress up in costumes of the tribal hill women for a photograph against the panoramic backdrop of the mountains. Neha chose to dress as a British colonial soldier in a khaki safari suit with a handlebar mustache that drooped past her jawline. She stood between the twins adorned in glittery imitation finery, her ancient rifle held up as if she were ready to pillage the local villagers.

They walked the Mall, the main thoroughfare, browsing in tiny boutiques, warming up with chicken corn soup and mutton momos, then back to purchasing more knickknacks from the Tibetan shops. The twins would often shop like this, buying everything in sight and never using most of it.

"The original capitalists," Neha whispered to Madan, swishing past him, her hand brushing against his as she followed the twins into another store.

That night she was waiting at the railing when Madan got there. "This spot is easily visible from the house," he said, giving her the chance to reconsider and head back.

But she said, "Come with me. I haven't been here for a few years, but if I remember correctly . . ." She led him back toward the house. He was sure someone would see them, but before they got too close, she turned, heading away from the cliff. Wooden steps took them down to a terraced garden. Unlike the gardens on top, it was unruly and overgrown. Tucked into a corner was a circular gazebo. They stepped into it; fallen leaves littered the cement floor and soft moss crept up the pillars.

"I don't think anyone's been down here for ages," said Neha.

"Doesn't your family come up here much?"

Neha sat down and patted the spot next to her. "Not much, my father's too busy. My brothers come up here sometimes, with their friends. They have big parties. There is hunting in the area but they don't have the same freedom. Here it's someone else's turf." Though not too far apart in age from her brothers, she did not share any of their interests and was not close to any of them. "Sometimes I used to wonder, in Delhi, whether I'd recognize them if they passed me on the street."

When she asked about him, he found it difficult to say much. About his mother, he simply said that she worked in the house. And about Avtaar Singh, he told how Avtaar Singh had made sure Madan went to school, and how he helped now in the office with the orders and books.

"You'll like this," he said. "We stopped chopping down trees from the forests some years ago and now buy them from the farms, especially poplar and eucalyptus, which grows like a crop — we call it *social* forestry."

She punched him playfully in the arm as he laughed. He told her what he was unable to articulate to anyone yet, that he believed that Avtaar Singh was going to give him the new factory to run, after he completed college. "If it weren't for Avtaar Singh . . ." He shook his head and trailed off. If it weren't for Avtaar Singh he would not have much of a life at all.

A true account of himself was not possible without telling her about Jaggu too. Their ties were stronger than those of brothers. He told of how he made a protesting Jaggu study for every exam and now he would be going to college too.

Madan glanced at his watch. "We better go back."

"Next time I'm going to bring a blanket or something to sit on," she said, and then continued about Jaggu. "It's wonderful you have a friend like that, we always need those."

She got up, stretching and dusting the back of her jeans. "Are you my friend, Madan?"

He got up too. She was standing still, facing him. The trees swished restlessly, and below them the lights of the town glowed like splatters of paint against the dark hillside. He reached out, pulling her toward him, the space between them insignificant.

This was nothing to do with friendship. Friends met out in the open, not secretly in the dark of the night. "No," he said.

Her lips were soft, cold. They pressed against the half wall of the gazebo. He felt her hands on his shoulders and the dense structure of her bones unyielding through layers of clothes and skin. When they broke apart, he waited, watching her closely to see her reaction. She zipped up her jacket and walked out wordlessly, and he, not knowing what to do, followed her back up to the house.

■ ■ ■

In the morning, Minnu memsaab called for him. Everyone was in the dining room finishing up with breakfast. Neha was reading the newspaper, her back to him. She didn't turn when he entered, but he was conscious of the slight firming of her posture as she became aware of his presence.

They were going for a day trip to Kempty Falls. Minnu memsaab got up from the table and began to explain how to organize the cars, pointing out the picnic baskets by the door and giving him a message from Avtaar Singh. He listened with half an ear.

Suddenly Dimpy's voice rang out, "Where were you last night, Neha? I got up and you weren't in the room."

Everyone fell silent. Madan saw Neha hesitate for a moment as she turned the page. "I don't know . . . bathroom, maybe?" she said.

"But I went to the bathroom," persisted Dimpy, "and you weren't there."

An awkward hush permeated the room, but Neha didn't pause this time. "Must be when I went to the kitchen to get a bite. I was hungry."

She went back to her paper and Rimpy

began talking about how she was hungry last night as well but it was too cold to get out of bed. Minnu memsaab resumed her instructions to Madan, but not before he saw Neeta memsaab's eyes roll over Neha with a worried look.

"I can't believe this is our last day," wailed Dimpy on their way back from Kempty Falls. Neha and Madan exchanged glances in the mirror. "This was my favorite day," said Dimpy. "The waterfall was spectacular."

"You said yesterday was your favorite day," said Rimpy. They began to discuss the highlights of their trip, soliciting Neha's and Madan's opinions now and then. Madan couldn't think beyond the present, he had already forgotten what they had seen and done.

That night he waited in the gazebo. When he heard the creak of the wooden stairs and she stepped into the circular dome, he was actually surprised. She was holding a rolled-up blanket in her arm.

"I thought you wouldn't come," he said.

The blanket dropped to the floor and they kissed as if hours and hours had not passed since the last kiss. Neha shrugged off her jacket. The floor must be cold, he thought, as her back touched it, but the thought was short-lived. Their limbs tangled like the branches of the ancient trees above them; his hands were under her T-shirt, his fingers splayed along the grooves of her rib cage. Who sighed first? Whose hand first fiddled with the clasps of their jeans? The curve of her hip rose to meet his, robbing him of every sane thought, and he succumbed without hesitation.

When their trembling subsided, they pulled on their clothes and Madan retrieved the blanket, folding it around them. They leaned against the wall. He stroked her shoulders, her arms, twisted strands of her hair in his fingers. He couldn't resist the urge to feel every inch of her.

"What's going to happen when we go back to Gorapur?" she asked.

Do we have to go back? he wanted to ask, but he knew the answer to that question better than she did.

"Madan?"

"I'll think of something." If there was one thing Avtaar Singh had taught him, it was to find a way where none seemed to exist.

When it was time to return to the house they sensed the reluctance in each other. There was no choice, though, but to leave the moonlit gazebo. Madan turned back to look at it one last time before he reached the top of the stairs and then the moss-covered refuge crept back into its little corner of the hillside.

They seemed to have more bags than when they'd arrived, thought Madan as he loaded the car the next morning. He fitted another paper bag into the back corner of the trunk and when he closed it up, Neha was standing by the open car door.

They stood smiling at each other, unwilling to look away, when Madan sensed the presence of someone else. Rimpy was standing by Neha and looking from one to the other. Abruptly, Neha got in the car and Rimpy followed, slamming the door shut.

From the house, Dimpy came running down the steps. "I'll remember this place forever and ever!" She rolled down her window and waved to the silent snowy peaks as Madan slowly followed the other car out of the gate and away from Heaven's End.

CHAPTER 11

Their long bristly tails waving like flags, the monkeys screeched and showered Madan with leaves as he walked down the brick path to the temple. He had no offerings they could pilfer off him as they did to unsuspecting worshippers, stealing fruit and sweets brought to pacify or beg the gods. Anyway, he wasn't here for any of those reasons. He was here to pick up Pandit Bansi Lal. Today was Avtaar Singh's birthday and, as always, the day started with a havan, the massive prayer ceremony that Minnu memsaab orchestrated on this day every year.

Before ascending the grand marble staircase leading to the main temple floor, he removed his shoes, placing them in one of the compartments in the shelves outside the temple, safe from the greedy monkeys. He walked around the main cupola, barely glancing at the statues of Ram and Sita with their hands raised in blessing, and went around to Pandit Bansi Lal's private quarters.

Silagaon Temple, much like Gorapur Academy, was another consequence of Avtaar Singh's philanthropic excesses. He financed its domes and spires of pink sandstone, its latticed marble columns, and its idols covered with flakes of gold. He'd procured the land on which the temple stood, paying off various government beauraucrats to acquire the property belonging to the state government. In the matters of the Almighty, Avtaar Singh did not hold back.

Madan met one of Pandit Bansi Lal's assistants, who led him to the pandit's rooms.

Pandit Bansi Lal sat on his charpai holding court, a few of his pujaris in chairs and on mats around him. Madan stood by the door as the assistant whispered in his ear about Madan's arrival. Neither with a twitch of his eyebrow nor a turn of his head did Pandit Bansi Lal acknowledge Madan's presence, talking on and on to the others in the room without interruption. This went on for over ten minutes before Madan walked out. The pandit knew he was here and where to find him. He wasn't going to wait at the door like a browbeaten dog.

Sitting back in the car, he slammed the door shut harder than intended. It wasn't really about Pandit Bansi Lal.

Two weeks had passed since their return from Mussoorie with no sign or sight of her, and every memory had become a deafening reverberation making each thought, each small action, a concentrated effort.

"What's the matter with you lately?" asked Jaggu. He concluded that Madan's unrest was due to his longing for college to start and though Jaggu was off the mark, the thought of college gave Madan an idea. He grasped on to the hope that she would be there at the havan today, and in some way he would be able to tell her of his plans.

From the corner of his eye he saw Pandit Bansi Lal approach the car and stand by the back passenger door. He knew the pandit was waiting for him to hop out and open the door. He didn't move and Pandit Bansi Lal waited. Even Avtaar Singh would open his own door. Finally, after a few minutes Madan opened the door, only because he didn't want the pandit to be late for Avtaar Singh's havan.

Quiet at first, Pandit Bansi Lal uttered an, "Om," drawing out the word till it was tight as a stretched elastic band. He began to recite the Hanuman Chalisa, his voice rising and falling as he chanted, *"O God . . . fully aware of the deficiency of my intelligence, I concentrate my attention on Pavan Kumar and humbly ask for strength, intelligence and true knowledge to relieve me of all my blemishes . . ."* He chanted on and on all the way to the house.

The driveway was noisy and crowded as if the market had relocated to the front of the house. Caterers, waiters and tent-wallahs careened and jostled into one another while carting their supplies back and forth. A large white marquee covered most of the front lawn, its canvas walls billowing in the gentle warm wind. Under the tent, white cotton sheets covered the grassy lawn, and red cushions lay scattered all around. On the fringes, pedestal fans whirred to and fro. At the head of all this, a square fire pit was being set up for the prayer ceremony and an overstuffed cushion was placed near it for Pandit Bansi Lal. Tables and chairs would replace all this when it was time for lunch.

Madan parked the car and once again Pandit Bansi Lal waited for him to open the door. As Pandit Bansi Lal lumbered up the stairs into the house, he said to no one in particular, "It would benefit some people to read the Hanuman Chalisa at least one hundred times in succession — they will at-

238

tain much-needed peace of mind." And he was in the house before Madan had a chance to say anything.

He went around to the kitchen, which was relatively quiet. All the cooking and preparations were taking place outside on the stone patio, where the caterers had set up makeshift stoves and tavas. Already simmering in the blackened vats and cauldrons were some of Avtaar Singh's favorite vegetarian dishes, for there could be no chicken or meat served during a havan. He stopped to watch as someone stirred the sarson ka saag, the dark green mustard leaves releasing a fragrant aroma wafting as far as the servants' compound.

Inside the kitchen, Swati prepared a large pot of tea, his mother giving instructions as she kneaded the dough. "Serve the tea," she said to Swati, "and then give the girls their breakfast."

A girl he recognized from his class at Gorapur Academy also helped in the kitchen today. He could not remember her name, but he knew her father, who worked at the factory.

"Can I get you anything, Madan-bhaiya?" asked Swati, when he stepped in.

"There's no time for that!" said his mother, shooing Swati out with the tea tray.

"Go, go, go! You know Pandit-ji can't be kept waiting."

Swati hurried out and he leaned against the counter. The girl smiled coyly up at him, her long braid swinging as she dried the dripping plates. Madan barely noticed. The world was spinning around him, yet inside he felt an impenetrable stillness. Butter sizzled and melted around the parantha on the tava, and his mother wiped her hands on the towel, giving the smiling girl a stern look.

"So what can I get you? Eat something. Have you eaten yet?" his mother asked, frowning and peering closely at him. Today, even the customary terseness which had invaded the tone of her voice in any conversation with Madan since his father's passing didn't rankle.

Madan began to assure her he was fine, but she was on to her next task. He stepped out of the kitchen and ran into Bhola, Trilok-bhai's driver. Was she already here and he was distracted by other useless things? He greeted Bhola and continued quickly on, pretending not to notice that the old driver wanted to talk. Out front, Jaggu called to him from the other side of the driveway. He was directing the arriving cars and drivers to the parking area on the far side of the house, out of sight of the guests.

Perfumed, well-dressed men and women filled the tent, chatting and finding places to sit. Ladies covered their heads with duppatas for the prayers, while men used white handkerchiefs. Pandit Bansi Lal sat near the fire pit with Avtaar Singh, who was in a raw-silk kurta of gold and taupe, and a bejeweled Minnu memsaab. It looked like Pandit Bansi Lal was about to begin. Madan searched frantically. He had a full view of the inside of the tent from his vantage point by the stairs.

He saw Trilok-bhai standing next to Neeta memsaab, his paunch almost obscuring his wife. Neha was not with them. Soon the throng began to settle and part, and then there she was. He hadn't seen her in a salwar kameez before, and it took a moment for his gaze to settle on her. She turned, looking out of the tent to the front of the house, their eyes meeting across the sitting crowd. A blast from the fan whipped her hair into her face and as she brushed the strands away, she smiled at him, and Madan smiled back. Then Rimpy appeared, pulling Neha to where Dimpy and their other friends sat, and she followed Neha's gaze to the front and to Madan. He turned at once and went to Jaggu, his only thought to see Neha alone.

As it turned out, it wasn't hard. Once the prayers ended, he was at the front steps with Jaggu, who was talking about all the food they would get to eat that day, now at the house and later at the factory. On Avtaar Singh's birthday all of Gorapur went to bed with full stomachs. The guests were rising and stretching, their legs cramped from sitting cross-legged for the past hour. They chatted and waited for the caterers to set up lunch. Neha paused in front of them at the bottom of the stairs, her eyes flicking quickly to Jaggu.

"Hello," she said, her tone formal, unsure.

Madan nodded and grinned, even though he knew he should appear indifferent.

"I am going inside, it's so hot out here," she said.

"Yes," said Madan. "There are guest rooms through the corridor past the kitchen, just near the back."

She nodded, and he followed her with his eyes until she went inside.

"These rich memsaabs can't even take a bit of sun," said Jaggu. "She was friendly, though, smiling at you like that."

"She knows me from the Mussoorie trip," he said, his mind racing ahead. "Listen,

Jaggu, can you do me a favor?"

"What?"

"Just ask Avtaar Singh when Pandit Bansi Lal is ready to go. Then can you drive him back to the temple?"

"Why?" said Jaggu. Madan wished for once that Jaggu would just get on with things instead of asking so many questions.

"You know . . ." he said. "He was on my case again on the way here. I don't want to be around him. It's not good for my health."

Jaggu laughed, understanding at once. "Okay, okay," he said, but did not move.

Madan looked at Jaggu pointedly.

"Oh, you mean I ask now?" Jaggu said.

"Yes," said Madan. "Pandit-ji will be the first to eat and the first to leave."

He watched as Jaggu headed toward the tent, and then raced around to the back. The house would be empty except for a few elderly people who preferred sitting inside where it was cooler, and they would be in the main drawing room. He rushed through the kitchen, glad his mother wasn't there. He hadn't thought about what he would say if he ran into her. In the corridor, he saw Neha and called to her. She came running, he took her hand and they hurried back out of the kitchen. He did a quick look around. Only the caterers were there now, and they

243

were busy, but anyone they knew could come up at any moment.

He was never so glad for the size of the house. There were plenty of nooks and corners to hide behind, and he knew them all. Still holding her hand, he led her away from the kitchen, around to the back, where the verandas opened out into the gardens. How many times had he and the twins played hide-and-seek back here? He'd taught them to make slingshots with the Y-shaped branch ends of the mango trees that now provided a spotty screen. He pulled her into a corner where the house's wall joined a veranda.

Time had sweetened the taste of her lips, the tenderness of her touch. He felt compelled to run his hands over her again.

"Stop, stop," she said finally. "Is that all we're going to do?" She giggled into his neck.

"I can't stop," he said as she pushed him, playfully, but not enough to move him away.

"Listen," he said into her hair. "Are you going to the same college with Rimpy and Dimpy?" The twins were going to the girls' college in Gorapur.

She nodded. "Why?"

It came to him all of a sudden. She had to continue her education somewhere, and even Trilok-bhai would not be so paranoid as to have her tutored at home. Now that she was back under his roof, Trilok-bhai would assume she was under his control. That's how men like Avtaar Singh and Trilok-bhai thought — in absolutes.

"We can meet when college starts," he said. "We'll have to figure out when you can get out. You used to do it at your old school."

"Yes, but that was different," she said, mulling over his idea. "But it's not impossible. I'll have to see how things work here."

He'd already thought of that too. He knew the girls' college. There was a guard in the front gate but that was not the only way in and out. All she need do was call him at the factory, whenever she got the phone to herself at home, and let him know what time she could get out the next day. He might get some good-natured ribbing if anyone perchance picked up his phone, but no one would know it was her. He would meet her outside, by the delivery gate.

She shivered. "Don't worry," he said. "It'll work."

"My father was furious the last time," she said. "I was locked in my room for over a week and my mother had to beg him to let me come out to eat at the dining table.

But . . ." She pulled his head down and he had his answer.

She looked past his shoulder to the end of the property. "What's there?"

He knew without turning. It was the wall that separated the servants' quarters. He wondered why she asked. She had the same area at her house.

"All lasting change begins with a revolution," she said, dreamily staring past the high walls into the world beyond.

"And what big rebellion are you planning?" He playfully kissed her neck, breathing in her floral perfume.

"I'm not joking." She leaned away from him. Her hands trailed up his arm. The activity at the front of the house faded to an indistinct buzz. "I feel like I can't breathe," she said.

"Sorry," he said, trying to give her space, but she didn't let him move away.

"No, that's not what I meant." Pushing a strand of hair behind her ear, she looked up at him, he thought with shyness or hesitation, but there was no hint of docility when she spoke. "There's this town I heard about, in the south, in Kerela. It started as an experiment by a group of people. It's a place where electricity never goes, and you can drink clean water out of the taps, and see

246

the doctor for free, and everyone works together and lives peacefully."

"Sounds like a paradise," he said. "Though usually with these places there's some guru or leader who seduces all the women and spends his followers' money on a fleet of Rolls-Royces for himself."

"There's no leader in this town," she said impatiently. "It has nothing to do with spirituality or religion or any hierarchy. Everyone is the same. There's no place for ego or status. And you don't work for yourself or your bank account. Your labor or skill is your contribution to the community, and the community looks after you." She paused as if waiting to judge Madan's reaction and then said, "It's a place where we wouldn't have to hide in a corner like this, and there are no walls separating you from anyone."

He was unsure whether to take her seriously. "What are you saying? You want to leave Gorapur?" His mind reeled with the thought. He tried to kiss her again, to distract her. They had a few treasured moments and he did not want to spend it debating social reforms.

"I want to be with you, but is this it? Is this all we'll ever have?" She didn't make an effort to keep her voice low, letting it rise with her emotions. "Why do we keep our plans so small? If I can slip out of school, we can slip out of this miserable town. Why are we staying here? Bending to this one's rules and that one's command. I can't go on like this. It's our life. We should choose how we live. It's a right we all deserve."

He cupped her face in his hands and tilted her gaze up toward him. Her eyes were bright. There was a small furrow on her brow, a line of distress he could not smooth away with a joke or a kiss, and it made him sad. Already he was dreading the few moments from now when she would leave to return to her family.

"I always thought I'd find a way to get there myself. Find out where it is and disappear one day. Now we can go together. Think about it. No fear, Madan. No nonsense with things that do not matter to us," she said.

He couldn't admit it to her, but his thoughts had turned to Avtaar Singh. Madan had never needed or wanted an alternative to Gorapur before. "Go anywhere, but there's no place like Gorapur," Avtaar Singh always said, and Madan always agreed. Here, in the shadow of Avtaar Singh's house, it suddenly seemed an empty declaration, an advertisement in the paper

248

that promised one thing and delivered another.

"Try to get out of college first and we can talk more then," he said. He needed time to think. What kind of man would he be in a world where there was no Avtaar Singh?

She smiled, and pulled him to her by the collar of his shirt, returning his kisses with a long one of her own.

"I'd better go back," she said. "They'll begin to wonder."

"One more minute," he whispered.

"Madan?" Jaggu's voice rang out from behind the trees and they barely managed to jump apart as he turned the corner and stood before them.

They all stared at each other for a moment. In a flash Neha ran past Jaggu, but he hardly noticed. He was staring at Madan like a truck full of logs had rolled down on him.

"What?"

"Jaggu —"

"You're going to get us all killed!" Jaggu didn't blink. He stared at Madan, frozen in place.

"No, Jaggu, listen —"

But Jaggu held up his hand, halting Madan's move toward him. Jaggu leaned against the wall, struggling for air.

"Are you crazy? What's going on? You've gone crazy," he said, his arms flailing like he was the one going mad.

"Calm down, Jaggu, listen to me."

"Listen to you? He's going to kill us . . . we're fucking gone . . . we're gone . . . they won't even find a fingernail."

"No one is going to kill you or . . . anyone," Madan said, fear briefly igniting in his gut. "How did you know I was here?"

"One of the caterers. He said he saw you go back here with a girl. I thought he was joking. I was tempted to put my fist to his ear." Jaggu shook his head, giving a small laugh that sounded more like the cry of someone choking on his own blood.

After a while he wrestled himself under control. He straightened up. "What are you thinking? Do you even know what you're doing?"

"Listen, Jaggu, you don't have to get involved. Go back and forget about all of this. For me," Madan sighed, "it's too late."

Jaggu snorted disbelievingly, and turned like he was going to leave. He kicked the ground, shaking his head. Madan watched as he muttered to himself.

After a few moments, he turned to Madan. "I can't believe . . . I just . . . how can you?" His voice cracked and he fell silent.

Jaggu took a deep breath. "You'll need one sensible person in all this madness," he said. "I've come this far. What would I do without you now? Where's the fun in that?"

Relief coursed through Madan and he hugged Jaggu.

"I need a drink," said Jaggu, still trembling.

"What about Pandit Bansi Lal?"

"Oh, one of the guests was going back in that direction and said they would take him. Avtaar Singh said he would see us later, in the factory."

They headed to the servants' compound, filling a couple of plates with food. Madan's grandfather was napping and they went inside the room, where it was cooler. Jaggu retrieved a bottle of homemade rum from his bag.

They ate and drank, the story coming out between mouthfuls until it was time to go to the factory. "Why can't anything be easy with you?" marveled Jaggu as they cleaned up.

Outside, Madan's grandfather awoke, mumbling to himself in his tangled sheets. "What's all the excitement?"

Madan helped him sit up and left the remainder of the rum bottle with his grandfather. It would keep him occupied while

251

Swati and Ma were busy up front, and the old man would enjoy the treat.

"Off again?" his grandfather muttered, more to the speckled pigeons perched regally on the outer wall than to Jaggu and Madan exiting the compound gate. "Who'll be with me, ha? Who'll be with me when Shiva does his tandava and the world splits in half? Fuckers."

The heat of summer finally scaled high enough to peak, and when it broke, the monsoons rolled over Gorapur. Everywhere umbrellas blossomed and then were whipped into the air by petulant winds. Except for the children who splashed in warm puddles, everyone stayed indoors. Drains overflowed and streets flooded, but for Madan the sheets of rain offered a watery shield behind which everything was possible.

Within the first few weeks of college beginning for both of them, Neha called. Madan slipped out, reaching the back gate of her college as she was tugging it open. He had borrowed a motorcycle from Feroze and they drove off, the puddles and misty rain washing away their trails as they headed out to the canal, farther down from where he usually met up with Jaggu, away from the bridges crossing over churning waters and the buffaloes standing unblinking in its muddy streams.

If the rains flooded the banks of the canal they headed to the high-walled back booths of Karim's Kebab Palace on the west side of town, isolated and smoky and far removed from the rest of the world. And if they could manage a longer time, to a room at the Barking Deer Inn, a rotund complex, some distance from Gorapur on the highway to Sirsa.

The future overshadowed all their conversations. There was hope and excitement when she talked about the places where they would go when they got away. Their lives would spin off into the unknown, but where they ended up would be far better than the provincial alleyways of Gorapur.

She did not know the name of the town she had told him about, and had no luck locating it on any map or book available in Gorapur. But Madan had made some discreet inquiries. There was a place that matched her description. A two-day train journey and four hours on a bus would take them away from these rented rooms and remote hangouts.

"I can teach art there," Neha said, "or I can take a course. I hear education is free.

I've always wanted to study philosophy. And I want to learn another language, maybe German or French. What about you?" she asked Madan, the roughened bed sheets of the Barking Deer Inn tangled in their legs. "What will you do?"

To choose of his own will was a luxury he never thought would be his. To her amusement, he could not make up his mind. "I'll decide when we get there," he said.

Jaggu covered for him on those days, taking notes in college and good-naturedly complaining that he did not sign up for all this studying. Madan cheered him up with jokes and trips to the cinema hall.

With the change of seasons the rain clouds lightened and the temperatures gradually fell, the colder nights and clear, sparkling days a precursor to the oncoming winter.

"You know what next week is?" Neha asked, tracing the outline of his hand with her fingers. The kitchen doors of Karim's Kebab Palace swung open and a babble of voices poured out. A server walked by with a tray of paper-thin rumali rotis drooping off its edge. Madan waited till it quieted down again.

"What?"

"Karva Chauth. And I'm going to keep the fast . . . for you. For your long life."

"For me?" No one ever did anything just for him.

"And the best part is that Rimpy and Dimpy are going to keep the fast as well. It was decided that we'll come to their house on Karva Chauth evening. Since we can only eat after we see the moon and then the face of the person we're fasting for, it worked out perfectly for me."

"They agreed to fasting all day?" He couldn't imagine the twins not eating for a whole day.

"The real credit goes to Pandit Bansi Lal. He said that even though Karva Chauth was a fast for married women, we girls should fast as well, to pray for good husbands. I said it was a great idea and he persuaded Rimpy and Dimpy. I don't think they realize how hard it will be."

He shook his head in amazement. For once Pandit Bansi Lal was of use.

Neha slid out of the booth, kissed him quickly and ran out, pausing at the drooping banyan tree by the road. On a circular cement platform built around the tree's base was a statue of the goddess Devi Mata on her tiger, her numerous arms swinging in all directions. Smears of vermillion dotted Devi Mata's forehead like bursts of fireworks, and offerings of coins, food and strings of marigolds lay by her feet. It was just like one of the many temples that sprouted unbidden under the trees around town.

Neha joined her hands and bowed her head at the shrine before hopping onto his motorcycle. She beckoned Madan to her, the copper specks glinting in the afternoon sun.

Where else was there to go? As Avtaar Singh would say when they played teen patti to pass the time: When all the cards have been dealt in your favor, there is no risk and all reward.

"Madan, go look again. It must be out by now."

For the twins, keeping the fast was indeed much more of a hardship than they had anticipated. The moon, as it usually did on Karva Chauth, was hiding, refusing to show its face this one evening when everyone would worship him instead of the sun.

Madan had already gone out a couple of times to see if the moon was visible from anywhere. "It'll be out in half an hour. The newspaper said moonrise is eight o'clock," he said.

"Half an hour more," Dimpy repeated, moaning and clutching her stomach.

"That stupid Bansi Lal," said Rimpy, hunger loosening her tongue.

"Shh . . ." said Neha. She was sitting on the steps while the twins fidgeted next to her. "He's just inside, he might hear you."

Everyone was inside. Trilok-bhai and Avtaar Singh returned early from work, as their wives would break their fasts after feeding their husbands. Pandit Bansi Lal, who could not pass up the opportunity of ingratiating himself with the two most important families in town, was lolling about on the sofa until called upon to bless everyone. Neha's brothers had already eaten, refusing to wait for the women to break their fast.

The twins went inside, and Neha stood, dusting her lehenga. All the women were dressed up, their finery akin to that of brides, in lehengas of gold and green, pink and maroon, tinkling bangles on their arms. Madan thought Neha never looked more beautiful.

Half an hour later, as promised, he and Jaggu spotted the moon. The front door swung open and the twins came rushing out.

"You saw it?"

He nodded from the bottom of the steps and they shouted to everyone inside, "Come on! Come on!"

Both families collected at the stop of the steps. "It's over there," Madan said to Avtaar Singh. "Behind the trees. If you walk to the end of the driveway you can see it."

They proceeded onward. As Neha stepped down, she missed a step, stumbling, but Avtaar Singh caught her elbow, breaking her fall.

"Let's go quickly," he said. "This girl needs to eat something."

Neha returned his kind smile. "Just a little light-headed, Uncle," she said.

"She's looking so pale," said Neeta memsaab, coming over to take Neha's hand. "Not eating anything these days . . ."

Neha kept her head down and walked past Madan. They returned quickly, the prayers rushed, as everyone was hungry. The group repeated their actions in reverse, going back up the steps, chatting. Rohan, Mohan and Sohan complimented Minnu memsaab on all the delicious food they had just enjoyed. Avtaar Singh hung back to tell Madan and Jaggu that they could go home. "I don't think we need anything else," he said. Suddenly someone shouted from the top of the steps.

Everyone stopped. Those by the door turned around, and Avtaar Singh, Madan and Jaggu looked up. Neha leaned over the wall of the front veranda, her body heaving and shaking as if racked by spasms. She abruptly straightened, and then crumpled to the floor, while Rimpy looked over her helplessly.

Rohan ran over, gathered Neha in his arms and carried her into the house. Food forgotten, everyone followed behind them. Madan and Jaggu stood in the driveway looking at each other.

Avtaar Singh came out a minute later and threw the car keys at Madan. "Go and get Dr. Kidwai," he said. Madan and Jaggu raced for the car.

"Don't worry, just not used to fasting," Jaggu said. Madan nodded, his mind blank.

When they returned with Dr. Kidwai, Trilok-bhai ushered the doctor to one of the rooms adjoining the drawing room. Neeta memsaab's voice floated out before the doors shut. People littered the drawing room, every sofa and every chair occupied by someone. Pandit Bansi Lal recited prayers, encouraging Sohan sitting next to him to join in, but Sohan ignored him, keeping his eyes on Trilok-bhai. Madan and Jaggu waited by the open doorway.

The twins were discussing with their mother if Durga could arrange two plates for them when there was a cry from the room. The doors opened and Neeta mem-saab came out, Dr. Kidwai behind her.

"What is it?" Trilok-bhai rose, his voice echoing in the room. Everyone's attention fell on him. "What is it?" he said again to his wife, who hid her face in her dupatta, her shoulders heaving.

"I'm very sorry." Dr. Kidwai glanced from one family to the other. "Trilok-bhai, maybe we can talk —"

"Speak," said Trilok-bhai, firm and impatient.

"It's a delicate matter," said Dr. Kidwai, "and I have to do a blood test to be sure . . ." He stopped, as if not sure if he should go on.

"What?" said Rohan. "Speak," he said, imitating his father.

"Well," said Dr. Kidwai, clearing his throat. "It seems that Neha is expecting . . . with child," he clarified, his gaze tentatively sweeping the room.

Trilok-bhai's roar overpowered his wife's strangled cry. "What are you talking about, Doctor?"

"Like I said," Dr. Kidwai wiped his brow. "It seems she's about halfway along, but I can only be sure after I do my . . . tests." His all-knowing doctor's voice wavered.

Madan heard Jaggu breathing behind him,

and Trilok-bhai's roar of disbelief. He heard the doctor's words but his ears seemed packed with sawdust. He shook his head to clear them. Music floated in from somewhere, and from the kitchen came the sound of dishes being washed.

Trilok-bhai barged into the bedroom, dragging Neha out by her arm. She tried to stand as her father hauled her into the drawing room. She stumbled, tripping on the long skirt of her lehenga. Trilok-bhai pulled her into the drawing room on her knees.

"What is this?" he demanded. "Is it true?"

"Please, Papa," she said. Her eyes were red and swollen.

Madan made a move toward her, but Jaggu's hand shot out, stopping him. "You'll make it worse," he whispered.

Trilok-bhai was shaking her now. "Is this true?" he demanded again. He turned around. "How could we not know?"

"In these cases, when girls are so thin, first-time pregnancy can be hard to tell," Dr. Kidwai offered.

"Trilok-bhai," Avtaar Singh said, composed as always, assessing, planning. He went to Neha, picking her up and seating her on the sofa. "Let's think about this calmly, let's talk to Neha and find out —"

"Calm? Calm? You want me to be calm,

261

Avtaar Singh? You wouldn't say this if it was one of your girls. My reputation, the name of my family, will be dragged through the mud. How will we ever show our faces in Gorapur again? This girl has ruined us, ruined us."

"Now, now," said Avtaar Singh, "we are friends here. No one has to know. Let's look at this calmly," he tried once more, but Trilok-bhai was shaking Neha again.

"Who did this?" he said. "Who did this?"

Neha hid her face in her hands, moaning and curling into herself, away from everyone's questioning eyes.

"It's Madan." Rimpy's voice rang out. From far away, Madan thought he heard angels scream as they fell into the fires of hell.

"Madan?" said Trilok-bhai. "Who is Madan?"

"Him," said Rimpy, pointing to the doorway. "There's been something going on. Now it makes sense . . . it's him. I know it." She turned to Avtaar Singh. "It's him, Papa, it's him!"

Dimpy said, "No, Rimpy," but it was so soft they barely heard her.

Neha gave a choked cry and ran back toward the bedroom. Trilok-bhai caught her by her hair and pulled. She collapsed on the brightly patterned carpet, her sobs revealing the truth to everyone. In the corner chair, Pandit Bansi Lal perked up, his beady eyes surveying the room.

Madan looked down at this feet; he could not feel them. When he looked up, Avtaar Singh's gaze was on him.

"Is this true?" Avtaar Singh asked.

Before Madan could answer, Mohan punched him, and he reeled back as his mouth filled with blood. It took two more punches before Jaggu managed to get Mohan off.

"Stop," said Avtaar Singh, before the other brothers made a move.

"A fucking servant. The bastard, I'm going to kill him," said Rohan.

"Stop," said Avtaar Singh. Even now he had the power to make people listen. "Take him back to the quarters," he ordered Jaggu.

"Saab," Madan said. "You are my father. I would do anything for you. Please, whatever you do, don't turn away from me."

Avtaar Singh watched, silent and unmoving, as a patch of red soaked the front of Madan's shirt. Madan struggled as Jaggu dragged him away. And Avtaar Singh turned his back, shutting the door.

When Swati saw Madan and Jaggu entering the room, she dropped her sewing

263

needle and rushed up to them.

"Wet some towels, we need to clean him up," said Jaggu. She ran out to the water pump.

"This face is not going to look as handsome tomorrow," said Jaggu, after he and Swati mopped up most of the blood and applied iodine to Madan's split lip and the gash on his head.

The door swung open, banging against the wall.

"What have you done? What have you done?" His mother fell on him, shaking his shoulders and screeching like someone had twisted a knife in her stomach.

Jaggu pulled her away. "It's not all his fault, Mata-ji. It's not just him."

She turned on Jaggu. "It's always the man," she spat out. "Does he even think of his mother? His . . . his . . ." — she reached out, pulling a crying Swati to her — "his sister? He has ruined everything. What are we going to do now? All my hard work —"

She collapsed on the floor, holding her head, stuffing the end of her sari into her mouth to stop from screaming.

"What happened at the house?" Jaggu asked

"Memsaab came to the kitchen and spoke to me," she cried, tears running down to her neck. "I knew this day would come." She shrieked, throwing her hands in the air.

Through his partial vision, Madan watched his mother cry and pound the floor. A bone-deep disgust and rage overtook him. He thought of Neha crumpled on the floor, and Avtaar Singh, and now his mother.

"Shut up," he said to his mother. "Shut up with your crying."

"You've left me with nothing but tears," she screamed.

Outside his grandfather asked, "What's going on? Will someone tell me what's going on?"

Except for Swati and his grandfather, no one slept that night. In the early hours, Jaggu went to get some tea and said he would find out what was going on. "It's too quiet."

Madan barely heard him. He was trying to work out a way to see Neha. If he could see her, if they could talk, he could tell her he was not going to give her up; together they could make everyone see sense.

The vegetable seller's cart trundled outside and the world stirred. Soon Bahadur came around. "Memsaab wants to see you, Durga," he said. She left, without looking at Madan.

Jaggu came running in right after. "You've got to get out," he said.

"What?" said Madan.

"You've got to get out, they're coming for you."

"Who?"

"Feroze, Gopal, all of them. They're headed here."

"It can't be," said Madan. Had not promises been made? "I have to go to him."

"It's too late. I know it's too much for you to believe now," said Jaggu. "But he's washed his hands of you. He can't overlook this; he can't let you go without suffering any consequences. There's nothing you can say to him."

Madan wasn't listening. "If the men are on their way here, then no one is there," he said.

He ran out, Jaggu following him, arriving at the factory as the morning's work began. Startled workers looked up as they ran past, into Avtaar Singh's office.

"Saab," Madan said. The door shut behind them. Avtaar Singh didn't look perturbed. His foamy tea rippled in the tall tumbler in front of him. The incense under the photo of his father perfumed the room.

"Did you know about this?" Avtaar Singh spoke directly to Jaggu.

"He knew nothing," said Madan, "no one knew anything, not my family, no one. Please, saab, listen to me —"

Avtaar Singh held up his hand. "You know I don't like to be obliged to anyone. You've put me in an extremely awkward position with Trilok-bhai — this is what he wants and I've agreed, besides which . . ." Avtaar Singh hesitated. He took a sip of tea and swallowed hard, grimacing as if it burned his throat. He struggled to speak. He looked down at his papers. "There are some rivers you do not cross. It's better you go, quietly, without any fuss," he said.

"Saab —"

Avtaar Singh stood up suddenly, the papers on his desk flying. "Don't speak to me! I trusted you like a son. With my family, with my business, with everything . . . with more than everything. You were a pitiful, sniveling shit of a boy who would've ended up as dirt under someone's shoe if it wasn't for me. It could've had been anyone. This boy . . ." He jabbed his finger in Jaggu's direction. "Or any other wretch out there. But I chose you. You. And this is what I get? You were worthless when I first met you, and despite all my efforts, you are worthless to me now."

He caught himself, and as suddenly as he

had erupted, he calmed down and took his seat again. "This is the end, it's time you go."

Behind them, the door opened and Feroze, Gopal and Harish entered.

"Madan, come, now, let's go without any trouble," said Feroze.

Jaggu threw himself at Avtaar Singh's feet. "Saab, please, saab, he's made a mistake, a foolish mistake . . . such a big punishment for this? You know him better than anyone. Forgive this one mistake, saab. I beg you, we'll do anything. Madan, come, ask for saab's forgiveness . . ."

Madan couldn't move. He watched Avtaar Singh extract his foot from Jaggu's grasp, ignoring his entreaties, keeping his head bent over his papers, continuing with his work as though alone in the room. Feroze and Harish pulled Madan out of the office, while Gopal held on to a struggling Jaggu. Madan heard Jaggu screaming for them to let him go, not to hurt him.

Soon Jaggu's shouts faded, and Madan was rolling in dust. "Thought he was too smart," Feroze said, kicking Madan in the ribs. "Like his father, he's no more than a hair on my ass. What a fucking dog."

Madan heard the lapping of water against a wall. From his side, from his head, from his stomach, the pain was relentless. He tried to roll himself into a ball to fend off the unflagging assault but he couldn't tell if his body was responding to him or not.

A final strike blotted out all sound and sight.

Madan heard the insistent honking like a rocket shooting through his head. He opened his eyes. Slowly he focused and Jaggu came into view.

"We're at the bus station," said Jaggu. Madan sat up groggily. Pools of light illuminated the green and yellow buses lined in a row, and all around people got on or disembarked. Travelers scrambled to retrieve their luggage thrown down from the tops of the buses.

Madan felt numb, like he was drunk. His clothes clung to him, steamy and damp. They gave off a muddy, fishy odor. He reached up to his face but Jaggu said, "Don't. It's better you don't know right now."

Madan looked at him questioningly. "They took you to the back area of the canal's reservoir," Jaggu said. "I followed them."

Jaggu had made it to the canal as they rolled Madan into the water. "After I dragged you to the bank, I couldn't believe you were breathing, but I didn't know how to move you." Jaggu had seen an unsteady beam of light heading toward the canal and thought the men were back, but a car came careening through the trees. "It was 1984. That crippled fucker. He'd broken into someone's car. He won't tell me how he knew, but we managed to bring you here."

Jaggu pointed to the food stalls by the parking lot not too far away. Through his swollen eyes, Madan made out 1984 chewing on a bread pakora, grinning back at them.

"Why are we here?" Madan asked, the words coming out in a painful, raspy burst.

"I've a cousin in Panipat. I've called him and he said he will take you in. I haven't told him much, but this is all I could think of right now."

Panipat? Madan's mind was still in the drawing room with Neha sobbing on the floor. "I have to see her."

"Do you understand you just got the gift of your life?" Jaggu was impatient. "What about your family? Think about them."

But Madan looked stubbornly in the distance. Jaggu said, "Look, go to Panipat now. It's only a few hours away. Whatever I find out, I'll let you know. But for now, it's better . . . you know . . . it's better you leave town."

"What about my mother?"

"It seems Minnu memsaab said that your mother, Swati and dada-ji could stay. A good servant is hard to find." He gave a harsh laugh. "I think memsaab can't imagine life without your mother. When I went to collect some of your clothes, I told your mother you're with me." He pointed to the duffel bag on the ground beside him. "Madan, she's upset, but you can't come around to the house. Everyone else thinks that you're . . . you know . . ." He drew his finger across his throat.

Madan nodded. He couldn't think about that right now. "And your cousin?" he asked.

"He has a carpet business. He's actually a second cousin on my mother's side. He will give you a room."

Jaggu had thought of everything.

"And what about you?"

"I'm safe for now, and so is my mother. He believed you when you said I didn't know anything, but I don't think I can go back to the factory. He'll have a hard enough time adjusting to seeing your mother at his house every day."

Madan watched buses pull in and out. "You can come with me," he said.

271

Jaggu shook his head. "If I disappear with you, then I'm guilty. My mother is here."

A blaring honk from the bus warned it was going to depart. Boarding the bus, Madan said to Jaggu, "How did I get so lucky to get a friend like you?"

"You certainly made some deal with Waheguru in your last life," said Jaggu, and he waved and waved as Madan's bus pulled out, the sun peeking over the fields of sugarcane.

CHAPTER 12

The nights were never silent here. Unlike Gorapur, which fell into a deep slumber for at least a few hours, Panipat throbbed constantly throughout the night, trucks and lorries plying its roadways to the northern towns. As he did every night, Madan silently counted the days, the weeks, he had been away. He'd never been out of Gorapur for this long. His face had healed and the bruises had faded, but the pain would not go away.

When can I come back? When can I return? he asked Jaggu again and again on the phone, needing Jaggu to believe, to concur more than anything else that he could come home. He knew of nowhere else he could live.

In turn, Jaggu cajoled him to stay for a few days more. Now more than three months had passed.

"What're you going to do?" Jaggu asked

during one of their calls. "Walk up to her house and knock on the door? All you'll get is a bullet in your heart."

There was actually very little news of Neha. Like Madan, she'd vanished into the dust swirling around the town. Gorapur was rife with rumors about Madan as well, but no one connected the two. Mostly everyone thought Neha was back in Delhi, and that Madan had been sent away for work or Avtaar Singh had set him up somewhere — he was running a new business or factory in another town.

But Madan didn't want to talk to Jaggu about rumors, he wanted news.

"You've got to forget her," said Jaggu. "We have to plan what you're going to do next."

There was no such choice. He would go over and over different scenarios with Jaggu. It's good, he would say to Jaggu, that I'm here for now. It'll make Avtaar Singh realize how much he misses me. Avtaar Singh must already be regretting his decisions. Jaggu gave a disbelieving laugh. "When has Avtaar Singh ever regretted anything?" he reminded Madan, but it did not stop him.

Avtaar Singh would be happy to see Madan alive. He would take him back. He would speak for him to Neha's family. With Avtaar Singh's blessing, they could get married and take a loan. He didn't know much about babies, but they had family to help. Once everyone understood how they felt about each other . . . yes, they were young, but it was not impossible. Avtaar Singh would guide him; he would make Trilok-bhai understand.

And if not, all Madan had to do was find out where she was — they could live anywhere. "It's such a big country, where will they look for us?" He could take care of her, take care of them; getting a job was not a problem. It was simply a question of making contact with her and getting away.

"You can't shift the gears your way," Jaggu said. "No one says your name here now, it's like you never existed."

Every morning when the shutters rolled up in a welcoming clatter at All World Carpets, Harbans, clapping and rubbing his hands together, would say, "Today we'll make some good sales, ha, Madan?"

Jaggu's cousin, Harbans, had been kind and generous to Madan ever since he'd picked him up at the bus station. Madan saw in Harban's face how bad he must have looked; no wonder everyone on the crowded bus had given him a wide berth. But Harbans did not say much. He took Madan to a doctor's office, where they fixed Madan's nose as best they could, taped his ribs, applied salves on his raw, bloody wounds, and then Harbans took him to his home, a place above his carpet shop, where his wife fed him. They showed him around the showroom downstairs. Rugs piled in flattened plateaus or grouped in rolls crowded the room. A bed was set up for him in the tiny office.

Assisting Harbans in the shop, Madan soon discovered that there was not an overwhelming local demand for hand-knotted wool carpets. Most people preferred the machine-made polyester. And unless it was pious ladies visiting the prayer halls of Shri Ram Sharnam Temple, most people did not turn off the busy highway to enter the town founded by the kingly brothers of the *Mahabharata*. Lost in the warren of lanes, old forts stayed forgotten, and markers of epic battles waited unseen. In the center of town, horse-drawn carts clopped under the floral arch of an ancient Mughal gate, its thick stone walls squeezed in on either side by precariously constructed multistory buildings of more recent origin, as it continued to witness the commerce and the bustle of the market.

Though All World Carpets was near

enough to the highway, the competition from the other carpet shops and hand-loom stores up and down the street meant that Madan and Harbans sat silently most days, watching an unwitting fly try to escape the confines of the store, buzzing near the doorway but never finding its way out.

Harbans perked up when a tourist passed through, his sales pitch repeated word for word to each potential customer. "Madan, show the one with the horses," Harbans would say, and Madan would unfurl the rug, a hunting scene, a beautiful garden, or some fruit in a bowl woven into its woolen yarn.

"No two pieces are the same," Harbans said to a finely dressed lady or suited man. "With hand knotting you have a unique carpet, each weaver makes his own piece different."

Madan's mind often drifted off as Harbans delved deeper into his sales pitch. If he closed his eyes, he could feel the sawdust beneath his feet instead of silky-smooth carpet. Yet at other times he struggled to recall the way the pipal trees bent in the wind as they pointed to the factory, or the look on his grandfather's face when Swati fed him. Shaking himself out of his reverie, he forced himself into the present, before panic set in.

Today, when the phone rang around lunch, it startled both Madan and Harbans, who were in their deep yet separate contemplations. To Madan's surprise, it was Jaggu.

Jaggu's occasional calls were usually in the evenings after he finished his shift at Dhingra Motor Garage. For a second Madan thought it could be his mother. They had not spoken since he'd left Gorapur, and Jaggu said the same thing he said about everything, give her time.

"Madan," Jaggu said when Harbans handed him the phone. "I'm telling you this, but it's because I won't feel right not to tell you. You just listen, okay?"

"What's going on?"

"It seems like Neha's been at her house all this time. But not for long."

"Why? Where're they taking her?"

"To Karnal, to Sheetal Family Hospital. She's ready any day now . . . to have the baby."

"How'd you hear all this?"

"It was Bhola, their driver. He brought their car in today. The old guy was quite upset. Said he had overheard her brothers saying that you were gone. You'd always been so respectful to him, he couldn't believe that they would have, you know . . .

to a nice boy like you. And he told me she and her mother were going to Karnal at the end of this week."

Madan was silent. Finally some news, finally the hands on the clock ticked forward.

"I don't know what you're going to do with this information . . . no, there's nothing you can do, should do." When Madan didn't say anything, Jaggu panicked. "Madan, you're going to go there, aren't you? I shouldn't have said anything. You ass, we saved your life for nothing, or what? She'll still be with her family, you know, it's not like she's there alone."

A hospital with lots of people who did not know him, did not know his face. Except her mother. There was a way. To Jaggu he said, "You're right, what can I do?"

But he was already on the move.

He told Harbans he was leaving, and thanked him and his wife for all their care. They were circumspect. People came and people went. Relatives always asked for favors; he had stayed longer than most, but they all knew it was temporary.

The old walled city of Karnal was a short bus ride from Panipat. It took longer to find Sheetal Family Hospital on the outskirts, far enough for discretion. He sat in a small dhaba across the road from the hospital's entrance. The gate stayed open all day, cars belonging to patients and doctors going in and out. While scoping out the grounds the day before, he walked through the parking lot to the garden, which was empty. For a while he sat on a bench by the garden pond, the floating green scum mirroring his own idleness. He watched a car pull up and a family tumble out, everyone clucking around a moaning woman as they wheeled her in.

Today he walked up to the front when one such car pulled up. It was a big family, with a husband and, from what he could make out, a mother and mother-in-law, plus a younger sister or daughter and an elderly gentleman. In the confusion, he strolled in with the family.

There was a check-in desk to the side of the reception area. While the husband spoke to the clerk, Madan walked through the double doors that led to a clean white hallway, bright lights illuminating the sign-board. Arrows pointed toward the patients' rooms and the operating wings.

He proceeded toward a bank of rooms, peeking into an empty one. There was a well-made bed and a TV perched in the corner wall. Orderlies and nurses in starched white outfits passed him, but no one said anything. The small hospital did not have strict visiting hours. His eyes scanned the name plaques outside closed doors, MRS. P. GUHA, MRS. NIRMAL SINHA, MRS. JYOTI KISHAN and so on, and one that read FAMILY SINGHAL.

Madan walked out, waving to the clerk behind the desk, who gave him a confused look, waving back politely as though he remembered him. Madan took up his post at the dhaba again until the gate shut in the evening, and then caught the bus to the youth hostel, to the one bed that he could afford. He had saved money doing odd jobs when he was not helping Harbans at the carpet shop, though it was not much.

His duffel bag was stowed under the bed; it still held the few clothes that Jaggu had packed for him when he'd left. He supposed he should find a safer place for it. This was a common dormitory with over twenty beds, but right now he did not have the energy to care.

When Trilok-bhai's car drove up the next morning, he recognized it at once. Madan watched from near the gate. The driver, Bhola, emerged first and, after retrieving a wheelchair from the reception area, opened the car door. Neeta memsaab got out, leaning in and offering her hand to the person inside. Neha stepped out and, except for the drawn look on her face, she seemed the same. She glanced about indifferently as her mother talked to her. When Neha turned toward the wheelchair, Madan made out the unfamiliar shape of her body under the loose shirt of her salwar. Bhola wheeled her in before coming back outside to park the car.

Madan waited. He couldn't go up to the front with the driver parked right there, sitting in the car and listening to the radio. He wanted to run in, shout her name till it echoed down the sterile hallways. He fought with the insistence inside him, holding himself back. He had waited this long, he could wait a short while more.

Resuming his surveillance from the nearby dhaba, he was on his third cup of tea when he saw the car drive away, Neeta memsaab in the back. He was not sure how long she would be gone, but this was his chance. As soon as the car was at the end of the road, he was inside. The reception clerk seemed unsure when he saw him; it could have been his faded, scruffy jeans or his T-shirt pockmarked with holes, but Madan strode with confidence to the desk.

"I'm here to see Mrs. Jyoti Kishan," he

said, recalling a name from one of the plaques on the rooms from the day before. The clerk nodded and turned the register toward him.

"Sign here, please."

Madan signed, *Ram Kishan,* and said, "Room twenty-three, right?" The clerk checked his book and smiled. "Yes," he said.

Madan retraced his steps through the double doors, following the arrow pointing toward the patients' rooms, again scanning the names. He nearly walked past the room for FAMILY THAKAR before realizing that it was Trilok-bhai's last name. He could hear the sound of the TV.

He pushed the handle down slowly and stepped into the room. She was in bed, the blanket covering her waist, and her back against the raised top of the bed. At the sound of the door, she opened her eyes and sighed, turning her head and staring vacantly at him. Then she gave a small cry, her hand flying to her mouth. She tried to push herself up, to sit straighter, but failed; she gulped for air, looking around frantically.

He rushed to the small side table and filled a glass with water. "Drink this," he said, placing the glass in her hand. Of all the words he imagined he would first say to her, these were not them. She took a couple of fast sips.

"I'm fine," he said, "I escaped. I've been waiting, trying to find a way to see you." He smiled, wanting to take her face in his hands, to kiss her, but she still took sips of water. Her hair came loose, hiding her face.

"I know we didn't have time to think," he continued. "But we can work this out. If we face them together, we can tell them that we want this. Then how can they say no?"

She did not respond. "I know you're surprised," he said, and moved in closer, but she shifted slightly. The covers tightened around her swollen middle, halting him. He pushed away the sudden feeling of awkwardness. "But I'm here now. I can take you right away. We don't need them. We can go wherever you want. Back to Mussoorie, or down south — to our town like we'd planned. Live there without worry or fear. I can take care of you . . . of both of you . . ." He stumbled over his words; talking of the baby was confusing. "We can go anywhere . . ."

Her face crumpled, and she covered it with the sheet. Her shoulders shook.

"Please, don't cry," he said. "Let's leave right now."

She looked up at him. Her cheeks flushed,

and she spoke softly, as if with great effort. "Madan, Madan, always so confident. You thought you'd inherit the kingdom, and now you want to live in castles of air with your princess." She took a long, shuddering breath. "Even if I wanted to get out, there's no way out."

"Of course there is. Listen to me."

"I've had time to think too, Madan, lots of time. Time was all I had while I was locked away, confined by my father to my room at home. Only allowed out for short walks in our garden with my mother, or with one of my brothers. None of them talking to me. I've had plenty of time, and I realized that in trying to get away from one prison . . ." — her hand swept her stomach — "I locked myself in another. It's useless to fight them, men like my father, like Avtaar Singh, because either way, they always win."

"Don't say that. We've talked about this, we know what to do. Come with me and it'll be okay. I promise."

"It was all talk, Madan. Why did we only talk? Why didn't we leave when we could? Because we knew. In our hearts, we knew there was no escape. But we didn't want to admit it to each other. They have us when they want us, and they discard us when we're of no use. Look at you. Look at what they've done to you." She slumped down with despair, as if unable to bear the sight of his tattered clothes or the weight of his empty pockets.

"The baby —"

"Don't worry. They have an answer to this problem too." She smoothed her hand over the hump of her stomach. "It'll be over soon. Tomorrow. Pandit Bansi Lal is taking care of it."

Pandit Bansi Lal? Madan's mind was reeling. How had Pandit Bansi Lal come into the conversation? Had he missed something she'd said?

He hadn't realized he'd stepped back until she spoke. "Yes," she said dully. "Run, get out of here. If they catch you this time, they won't leave the job half done."

She laid her head down, turning back to the window, shutting her eyes once again. "Go," she commanded. But Madan stood there, unable to peel his eyes away from what he had desired for so long. He stood there like his mother did in front of Minnu memsaab and his father had in front of Avtaar Singh, head bowed, eyes wanting, forever the servant.

At the hostel, everything was as he had left

286

it; no cyclone had come to sweep away the remnants of his life. He got into bed. He would sleep now. All he need do was make time pass. That would take care of the pain, until he couldn't easily remember what had caused it, or who. He closed his eyes, forcing himself to sleep.

His body, however, took only so much rest, and by the early hours of the morning, while it was still dark, he awoke with a rage he had not felt for so long. He wanted to hurt someone, see the blood flow, and feel the familiar yielding of skin and bone as it surrendered to his fist.

He grabbed the sides of the bed's smooth wooden frame and squeezed it hard. He squeezed until he was out of breath, and then, when he sensed the scream about to rip from him, he let go. His breathing slowed, and soon it matched the measured breaths of the person in the bed across from him.

He would go to Gorapur and collect his mother, grandfather and Swati. His mother may not have forgiven him, but she had come to terms with him before. She always frightened them into thinking that there was no other place for them but Gorapur. That was no longer the case. He could take care of them, and to hell with everyone else:

Minnu memsaab, Trilok-bhai, Rimpy, Dimpy. To hell with Avtaar Singh.

He felt the wet trickle on the side of his face. He wiped the tears away angrily, refusing to let any more fall.

When the tea stall opened, he got a cup, sipping the foamy top, savoring the strong cardamom aroma. The market was beginning to stir. He would grab something to eat and go to the bus stand. Should he wait for evening before he caught the bus to Gorapur so no one would see him? No, he was going to go now. He couldn't wait any longer.

He downed the last sip and saw a bus pull into the stop. The bus that went to the hospital. Before he considered further, he was on the bus, on his way to Sheetal Family Hospital. He wouldn't go inside. Just take a walk around and get the next bus back. When he disembarked, a car pulled up, and through the window he recognized the pugnacious face of Pandit Bansi Lal.

What was he doing here? He waited, giving the pandit time to go inside. Then he followed. At the reception area, there was someone else at the desk.

"I'm here to see Mrs. Jyoti Kishan," he said.

The lady looked puzzled but checked the

register. "She's checked out."

"Oh," he said. "I'm sorry. I meant Family Singhal."

The lady looked down at her register again and he began to walk toward the double doors.

"Wait —" he heard her say, and he turned, giving her a reassuring smile. When he turned around again, Pandit Bansi Lal was standing in front of him, the double doors swinging slowly shut.

For someone who looked like he saw a ghost, Pandit Bansi Lal recovered quickly. "You! You. Like a cockroach you appear in every crack in the wall. I thought we saw the end of you. I should have known Avtaar Singh would not go through with it."

Madan started with surprise. Pandit Bansi Lal assumed Avtaar Singh knew he was alive. But the pandit caught on. "Oh! So Avtaar Singh does not know. So he thinks that you're already food for the crows. We can take care of that right now."

He opened his mouth as if to give a shout. The gesture propelled Madan forward. He was going to gouge the man's eyes out; he would cut him into little pieces and feed him to the stray dogs outside.

But Pandit Bansi Lal halted him with his walking stick, thrusting its tip into Madan's chest like a sword. "What're you going to do? Attack me? Here? An old pandit?" His mouth dropped as he made a sorry face. "Wait — I shouldn't have stopped you. It would've been such fun to see what they'd do to you, but we'll see soon enough."

Madan flicked the walking stick off his chest.

Pandit Bansi Lal's voice dropped to a harsh whisper. "Not even God can save you now, not even God. You have done something that exceeded even the reach of Lord Yama." He thrust his other arm forward, and in its crook Madan noticed a small bundle trussed up in a light blue cotton fabric. Pandit Bansi Lal shoved it under Madan's nose.

"What?" Madan stepped back. Was Pandit Bansi Lal handing him something? What did he want him to do?

Pandit Bansi Lal cast his walking stick aside with impatience and peeled back the corner of the cloth.

Tiny and scrunched, fingers like toothpicks, hands fluttering near its mouth, a small round face lay within the folds of the fabric, whispers of hair swept over the top of its head and arched over its closed eyes.

"Is this . . . ?" whispered Madan.

"The wages of your sin, boy, the wages of

your sin."

A long, satisfied smile curved up Pandit Bansi Lal's face and the baby opened its mouth, letting out a shrill howl. Pandit Bansi Lal shouted, "Help! Help! Trilok-bhai! Get an orderly." He shouted to the lady at the desk, "Call the police! This boy's wanted . . . Help! Help!"

The sound of racing feet thudding heavily on the linoleum floor goaded Madan into action. For now, he had to run. He ran through the parking lot, out the gate and to the bus waiting at the stop. He jumped on, not caring where it took him. As the bus pulled away, he saw two orderlies rush out, scanning the road up and down. He found a seat and sat shivering, unable to think.

The bus lurched over a pothole, jolting him back to the present. Soon everyone would know he was alive, even Avtaar Singh. He had to find a phone as soon as possible. He got off at the next stop, found a PCO booth and called Jaggu at the mechanics garage.

As soon as Jaggu picked up he said, "It's me."

"What happened? Why're you calling?" Jaggu was alarmed.

"I don't have time to explain, but they know I'm alive."

291

"What? How? You went there, didn't you? You're in Karnal."

"Jaggu, what d'you want me to say? You're right. I can't come back. Please, I need you to get my mother to call me. I have to talk to her."

"She won't —"

"Tell her anything," Madan said. "Just make sure I can talk to her. I will call back in an hour."

Madan returned to the hostel to collect his duffel bag. He would tell his mother to pack up what she needed and take the bus to Karnal. He returned to the PCO and called again.

"Ma?" he said into the phone.

After a moment she spoke. "What do you want?"

"Ma, I know you're angry with me, but please, listen." He spoke quickly but firmly, telling her his plans, feeling that if she heard how he would take care of everything, she would relent. What was her alternative? "You can't stay there, Ma. Avtaar Singh will never allow it. We'll go someplace safe, where we can all be together. Ma?"

"I can't believe you came from me," she said, no hint of expression in her voice. "You have caused me nothing but grief."

"Ma, but Avtaar Singh —"

"Avtaar Singh! Avtaar Singh! If he wanted to do something to us, he would have done so by now. Even then, I'll take my chances with him. Swati already owes him her life. But you. Listen carefully. Get away from us. Get so far away that we can't hear you or smell you or ever see you. You are dead to him. And as for me, I'm really cursed now because I never had a son."

Silence, and then the crackle and hum of the phone connection, and over the static Jaggu was saying, "Madan? Are you there? Give her time. She's still upset. Madan? Madan, are you there? At least call and tell me what you're going to do . . ." Madan barely heard Jaggu's fading plea before he placed the phone back on its rest.

He paid the telephone operator, but stood uncertainly around. "You need something else?" asked the operator.

"I need to get out of town," said Madan.

"Number five bus, goes straight to the train station," mumbled the man into his cash register.

There was not much of a line at the station's ticket booth.

"Where to?" asked the man behind the iron bars, impatient when Madan did not answer. "Come on," he said. "Amritsar, Delhi, Meerut, Lucknow, Patiala, all these trains are leaving soon. Where to?"

"Delhi," said Madan, "third-class seat."

"One-way or return?"

He slipped the money under the bars. "One-way."

Madan found a seat by the window. By the time they left, several men fresh from the fields and at least two noisy families crowded into the remaining space in the compartment big enough for six. The train pulled away with a high whistle and soon the fields of sugarcane and wheat were rushing by him. An hour later, people started opening up their tiffin-boxes of food, families settling around each other for dinner.

Madan concentrated on the disappearing landscape outside his window. Released by Avtaar Singh's impervious order, death was everywhere in Gorapur, its distinct, rancid smell tracking him down, seeking him out. When he had shaken hands with Avtaar Singh for Swati's life that first time, it was Madan who had stipulated the conditions of the exchange. This time, Avtaar Singh had set the terms of the bargain, leaving Madan with no options, no means or ruses to tip the deal in his favor. He had to run if he wanted to survive Avtaar Singh and his thugs.

The shadow of the train moved alongside

like a dark, gloomy twin. The swaying silhouettes of people sitting atop the train eerily changed the train's elongated, reflected shape. Unable to afford a ticket, they'd scampered onto its roof for a free ride. He counted at least twelve people above his train car.

He'd seen this before, read about them in the newspapers when there was an accident, when they had failed to duck low enough for an oncoming tunnel or failed to see it altogether because their eyes were shut against the strong winds, or it was too dark, or . . . who knows? No one could ask them. Swept off into the rivers below, their mangled bodies washed up quickly, as though even the waters were eager to get rid of them.

"There's always someone worse off than you," he remembered hearing in those early years when he returned from school feeling sorry for himself because of someone's hurtful transgressions. Who had said that? He couldn't recall now.

He leaned his head against the glass of the window. The shadows on the roof rocked back and forth with the motion of the train. As the train shuddered and clanged, changing tracks, he saw an indistinct hand reach out and grab the slightly raised edge of the roof, and there it stayed, holding on tight, struggling to stay on, trying not to fall.

CHAPTER 13

New Delhi, 1993

One of the kids wore nothing but a faded button-down sweater, his small, drab penis peeking out from under the sweater's frayed edge. He looked no more than a toddler in stature, especially compared to the two other boys standing over Madan in ragged T-shirts and shorts, their hair afros of dirt and dust.

"He's here," one of them shouted to someone outside. "We told you. He always comes here."

The half-dressed kid dug his fingers into Madan's jeans pocket, deftly searching around inside, checking for any loot before Madan came to full consciousness. The kid came up empty. Someone else had already cleaned out Madan's pockets.

"Fucker," Madan swiped his hand away. "Get off me."

They laughed at him as he raised himself

up groggily, his back stiff from the hours passed out on the rough concrete floor of the sewer pipe. The taste in Madan's mouth was bloody and foul. The pipes were not yet in the ground and already the bulbous gray rats had taken up residence. The kids scrambled out ahead of him and scooted into the gaping round opening of a neighboring pipe, where their mother fanned a cooking fire. Stacked up in mounds at the side of roads and near construction projects, the long tunnels of rough cement flushed out migrant laborers, homeless derelicts, drunks and drug addicts, before they were buried deep underground to continue to drain the shit and piss of the city.

Madan's new friend, Tahir, idled on a rusted-out scooter by the roadside. "I was sure this time you'd have caught the train and disappeared," Tahir said. "I don't remember seeing you after three o'clock this morning."

He handed Madan the cigarette dangling from his lips. Madan took a grateful drag, closing his eyes against the hurtful glare of daylight and the pressure in his bladder competing with the dissonant honk from cars, auto-rickshaws and taxis streaming in and out of the nearby train station. How easily everyone clambered on the trains and left the mad city.

After stepping off the train nearly three years ago, he stayed in the station for a few weeks, sleeping on the platform, foraging for leftover food dumped out of the first-class cabins, dodging the police clearing the station of detritus and people like him. Every day he saw the Gorapur train come and go with its shrieking whistle.

"Seet!" Tahir said, searching his pants pockets, his Bihari accent eating up the *h* sound of *shit.*

"Seet! Where's that paper? This guy told me about a job at a garment factory near Naraina."

Before Tahir there had been Manoj, and before that Sunjay, and before that some other boy. He met them at the train station, where he earned a few rupees cleaning bogies, doing odd jobs sorting garbage, slapping political posters on city walls in the middle of the night or hauling construction debris. They were all more or less his age, and whether it was Bihar or Odisha, Rajasthan or Uttar Pradesh, he made sure he knew no more than the rudimentary facts of where they were from or why they were in the city. He was afraid to learn that he was no different than the whole miserable lot of them.

Smoke from the cooking fire wafted toward Tahir balancing on the scooter and pricked Madan's eyes. In the deep loneliness of his days, he could imagine himself stepping out of the train in Gorapur, walking past tender shimmering fields to the timber factory, sharing a beedi down to its burning end with his grandfather, watching Swati mumble as she sewed or Jaggu singing along to the sound track of the radio. But as the days of piecemeal work and hard labor turned into nights of oblivion, return seemed more distant, more an imagined suitcase of riches at the end of the line. His mother's harsh edict had been his final shove out, but the sharp, savage truth was that the man who had sent him into exile was the only one who possessed the power to grant him permission to return home.

A couple of times he built up the nerve to call Jaggu at the auto garage where he worked, but put down the phone before anyone picked up. If word reached Avtaar Singh or he had an inkling of Madan's call . . . Madan couldn't bear to think about what would happen to Swati, and Jaggu, even his captious mother, if Avtaar Singh learned that Madan had been in touch or they had any idea of his whereabouts. He had evaded Avtaar Singh's final and deathly decree once, and he was no fool. Avtaar Singh had made sure of that much, at least.

Tahir finally extricated a torn corner of a restaurant menu and flashed it in triumph at Madan, and then touched his breast pocket where a bottle of typewriter correction fluid nestled in the folds. The white, pasty fluid was Tahir's own train station to nowhere. A few sniffs and the gray cast descending over his eyes took him away from this broken-down scooter, the rawness of his bitten-down nails and whatever had caused the puckered scars laced across his jaw. The same kind of bottle sat by the typewriter in Mr. D'Silva's office in Gorapur. Madan could see it clearly. Every rattle of the door or wobble of the desk knocked the tiny bottle over, and each time it aimlessly rolled about until someone righted it.

Madan ground his cigarette butt into the pavement, surprised to see it didn't go up in flames. The midmorning sun baked the concrete pavers. He could feel the heat burning the soles of his feet through his flimsy canvas shoes. A dip in the cool, flowing waters of the canal would soothe the web of mosquito bites drilled across his back and arms and wash away the sticky layer of dirt welded to him. But a bucket of tepid water back at his rented room would have to suffice, if the room was still his. With Tahir there was only money for today and none for tomorrow. It was not a bad way to survive when who knew if the light of the morning would be yours to enjoy.

A flock of pigeons landed in a feathery jumble in the median of the road, as if the few scraggly trees around them were not worth their while. To their credit, the only real green was the slash of jade-green uniformly adorning the blaring three-wheeled auto-rickshaws. They pecked between the pavement cracks, and the sewer pipe boys waited for a break in the traffic before running across the road to shoo and chase the birds back into the air for the fun of it.

What did they think, these sewer boys, about what this day or the next would hold for them? Life would not allow them to spend it chasing pigeons. They weaved through the traffic, joining the other beggars knocking on car windows, pleading and lamenting their situations for some change. What had the boys been told when they fought off the night's cold wrapped up in day-old newspapers or went another day without a dry chappati in their bloated bellies? He watched the old man dragging his wooden plank for legs from car window to car window, and the lady with the baby disintegrating in her arms, and the water seller breaking his back pushing his heavy cart to sell a glass of cold water for a measly five paisa, and felt that they must know something that eluded him. If this was all there was to life, why did they cling to it so desperately, insisting on living when there seemed no need for them to do so?

Tahir was trying to read the information on the scrap of paper. He claimed he had completed elementary school, but it was probably a lie. Madan whipped his arm around Tahir's neck in a headlock, twisting tighter as Tahir choked and flailed about, pulling at Madan's vise-like grip.

"Garment factory?" Madan spat out. "What do we know about making clothes, you idiot?"

Tahir had been living off the streets much longer than Madan, and with a forceful grunt he leaned into Madan and propelled himself off the scooter, which listed to the side as he toppled them both over with a thump. They tussled and jabbed. Pedestrians hustled by without the time or inclination to interrupt or get involved. Just as quickly as they had started, the two of them stopped. Madan was the first to jump up. He noticed Tahir flinch as he thought

Madan was going to come back at him. Putting his hand out, Madan helped Tahir up, and they dusted themselves off. Tahir straightened the scooter and Madan vaulted onto the backseat.

"Motherfucker," Tahir said. "Can't even help this guy without a fight."

The deep, sonorous gong delineated the day workers from the night, and caused a commotion among the labor as they gulped their morning tea from the stall outside the metal factory gate. The smog suffocating the sun turned the sky a pallid white, but the good thing about factory work was there was no time to look up and contemplate the color of the sky. Madan streamed in with the morning shift, skirting the throng of laborers gathered outside the small temple beside the gate. At his annual Diwali address, the pot-bellied proprietor of Choice Leather Works had encouraged everyone to start their day's labor by remembering God, and on the days he appeared with the morning gong instead of after lunch, he stood up front and led the morning prayers. For most of the laborers, it was a good way to put off work for five minutes.

In the honeycomb of garment factories along the unpaved roads in this industrial pocket of the city, work was constant if temporary. When there was a big order and the machines were at full charge and trucks needed loading and unloading, there was work. But when the orders were scant, the factory took a large chunk of the workforce off their books until the next time. Madan had become used to being let go and re-hired. There was always the next factory close by, and if there was a skill he could claim to have — it was factory work.

Tahir chafed against the routine of the work, the strictures of labor. "It's not my style," he said, and left. If Madan knew where to go, he would have left too. Tahir's solace was in the streets at night, smoking under overpasses, sleeping the afternoons away in a haze of ganja, earning enough to eat and buy a couple of bottles of something to help him forget. Fine for Tahir, but Madan had lost the ability to forget.

"Wait for me!" Dinesh pumped his thick-set arms to keep up with Madan, his shirt stretched taut by the speed bumps of muscles across his chest. When not hauling skins off the tannery truck, Dinesh spent his time at the bodybuilding gym. The red smear on his forehead told Madan he had come from the temple.

"What are you doing after work?" Dinesh asked.

"Busy."

"Doing what? I want to tell you about —"

"Not interested," Madan interrupted.

"It'll take a minute. One minute, and your life will be different! Let me help you."

"I've already told you how you can help. You said you'd speak to the supervisor to make me permanent. After this week I'll be on the streets again, and you'll be scratching your ass in here."

"What're you saying?" Dinesh said. "I've spoken to Ketan-bhai. I swear. He said when a space opens up he'll talk to us. Just listen to me for a minute." Dinesh tried to reach for Madan's arm, but Madan was going too fast. Dinesh always had some hustle going.

"You won't be able to say no to this," Dinesh said. "I swear."

Madan shook him away and loped off to work. He didn't care if he made it onto the full-time roster, but it had been the only thing he could think of when Dinesh had asked for help with some bank paperwork and Madan wasn't about to do the work for free or it would be a never-ending list of requests. Though it would be a nice change to have a regular place to come to every morning, and not have to scrounge around for his next job. And he was grateful for the bone-deep exhaustion that came with the grind and toil of manual labor, so he could collapse into a dreamless sleep every night, keeping off the streets and away from the temptations of the train station.

It was after one in the afternoon when Madan stepped out of the factory gate. The lunch-crowd rush was huddled around the lunch vendor's wooden cart. Workers sat on concrete slabs, eating, smoking or dozing against the sun-warmed wall spattered orange and brown with tobacco spittle and mud. Madan bought a dried-leaf plate of beans and rice and found a spot to read his newspaper while he ate, tuning out the drone of the numerous conversations swirling around him.

"All I'm saying is this is a chance, not a small chance, not a big chance, but an enormous chance to set yourself up for life." Dinesh was talking loud enough for the whole group to hear.

"But I don't understand," said a worker.

"I know these things can seem complicated on the surface, but really it's very simple." Dinesh stood up to make his point and to make sure that more people could hear him. It worked. Men turned to listen to him as they smoked their last beedi before going back to work.

"Vladimir, who runs the gym I go to, was with the Russian heavyweight Olympic team. He's an expert in body and health. He's developed this powder. You suffer from tiredness, your joints ache, you catch a cold easily, your skin is dull — this powder can fix all these things and more. Mix one spoon in your dal or your beans, in your curd, or make your rotis with it, and you'll get all the health benefits, all the vitamins you need to have a long and healthy life."

"But how'll we make money from the powder?"

"He's going to sell this powder in shops everywhere, in gyms, in chemist shops. Even your vegetable seller will carry it." Dinesh put up his hand as someone tried to ask a question, not letting them speak. "Listen carefully, because you're getting in from the start. You contribute to the starting fund, say five percent of your salary. He's going to use this fund to manufacture and distribute the powder. Not only will he give you this powder free every month, but every time you bring in another person, you will get two percent from their five percent and one percent from everyone your investor brings in."

The man who handled the account books lit a cigarette, puffing a stream of smoke in their general direction. He stood with Ketan-bhai, the general supervisor, who sniffed disapprovingly at the cigarette smoke. Ketan-bhai's neatly pressed safari suit and polite, firm manner of talking distinguished him from most of the workforce, and Madan had often seen him walking the floor fiddling with the reading glasses folded away in his breast pocket.

"All of you are out here," said the accountant. "And who is going to do the work?"

"Listen to Dinesh, Accountant-saab. He's telling us something very interesting."

Dinesh repeated his pitch to the accountant and Ketan-bhai. "Bring in your brother, your neighbor, your uncle, already you have three contacts and have made a six percent return on your investment. But don't stop there. What about your in-laws, and your friends? Now you've eight, ten, twelve percent return. Money from all directions. You only have to look."

"What's in this powder?" Ketan-bhai asked.

"A good question," Dinesh said, removing a glass jar from his bag that was filled with a grainy brown powder. "I can't tell you everything that it's made of. That's secret. Some of the main ingredients are fenugreek and almond powder."

There was a groan from the crowd, and Dinesh looked offended.

"Madan," Dinesh said. "Come on, my friend. At least you try it, and tell them."

Madan turned his face away and tried to shrug off Dinesh's hand.

"Just give it a try," Dinesh insisted.

"Who is this?" Ketan-bhai asked. "I think I've seen you before."

"Remember, Ketan-bhai?" Dinesh said. "This is the boy who I was telling you about." Ketan-bhai looked puzzled. Clearly, in spite of swearing up and down that he had, Dinesh had never spoken to Ketan-bhai as he'd claimed.

"You worked at Forex Garments, I think," Ketan-bhai said.

"He's worked here previously as well," said the accountant.

"Where're you from?" Ketan-bhai asked.

"Looks like he's from this side," said the accountant. "Haryana? Punjab?"

"What do you think, Madan?" asked one of the workers. "You're always reading those big books and these newspapers. I have to get my sister married soon. I need to make some extra money fast."

"Our fund is just the way. Vladimir won a gold medal. He knows what he is doing," Dinesh said. "Take it from me in writing, you'll be giving your sister a wedding so grand we'll all be talking about it."

The man looked dubious. "Would you do it?" he asked Madan again.

"I'm not interested," Madan said.

"Don't listen to him. He's not interested in changing his life. Do you ever hear him complain? He likes this dog's life we lead here."

Madan had had enough. "It's an interesting proposition," he said to the worker, and a few curious ones turned to listen to him and sat back down.

Dinesh smiled and said, "See? Now he's making sense."

"But if I were you, I wouldn't give my hard-earned money to some guy who could disappear tomorrow. If you ever want your money back, where will this Vladimir be? Laughing at you all the way from Russia. And I'd ask what proof is there that this powder is good for health. If I don't know what's in it, why would I eat it? Why would I give it to my family and friends?"

Dinesh's face turned red, and he laughed and frowned and laughed again. "What do you know?" he shouted at Madan. "Bloody rogue." He addressed the group. "Are you going to trust this motherfucker who came into our midst yesterday? You know me. I tell you, Vladimir is a trustworthy man. Not like this one. Who the hell is he? Does anyone know?"

Ignoring Dinesh's bluster, they turned to Ketan-bhai for his advice. Ketan-bhai looked like he found the whole exchange distasteful, but he answered with tact. "This is not the place for your schemes, Dinesh," he said. "It's time for all of you to go back to work," he told the workers. "You're better off putting your money in a fixed-deposit account with a bank. Your return may be less, but at least your money is safe."

"That's what we thought," the workers murmured.

"Can't believe Dinesh is such a fucking cunt. I was ready to bring the cash tomorrow."

"Has anyone even seen Vladimir's gold medal?"

They disappeared inside the gate, and Madan, released from Dinesh's grip, got up to follow them.

"You bastard, why don't you mind your own business?" Dinesh snarled.

"I was trying to," Madan said, tossing his lunch plate and newspaper in the pile of trash by the electricity pole. All at once he was furious. How dare Dinesh force him to get involved in a scheme so ridiculous? He wasn't beholden to anybody, not anymore, and certainly he wasn't about to let a slimy idiot like Dinesh jerk him around. Madan whipped back around and grabbed Dinesh's waist. Using the force of his body, he took Dinesh down. Dinesh's head caught on the edge of the concrete slab but it did not knock him out.

Madan flipped Dinesh onto his back and held him in place with a knee on his chest. Blood trickled out of the gash on Dinesh's forehead.

He slammed his head down into Dinesh's face. It should have been Dinesh screaming in pain, but Madan heard his own scream of rage.

He looked up into the void before him. Where was he and how had he gotten here? He stared blearily at Ketan-bhai, standing straight, rooted tightly in place. The accountant's cigarette hung loosely from his lips.

Madan let go of Dinesh and straightened up, leaving Dinesh writhing on the ground.

"He's broken my arm," Dinesh screamed. "Motherfucker, asshole. I can't feel my hand. I am dying."

Madan raised his arm to wipe the sweat and blood off his forehead. Ketan-bhai and the accountant reflexively took a step back. Only a few people remained around them. They kept their distance.

Madan was suddenly sorry. Dinesh was a chump and a moron, but these shortcomings were no reason to attack him. Madan was becoming what Pandit Bansi Lal had prophesized, was turning into the uncouth goon his mother had accused him of being with her silences. He was Avtaar Singh's domesticated dog set free, not knowing how to behave without its master. He wished he could have reacted differently, shaken Dinesh off and walked away, but he seemed not to know how to control himself. Madan knelt down next to Dinesh and tried to work his arm under Dinesh's back. He tried to get Dinesh to sit up.

"Don't touch me! Stop him!" Dinesh bellowed.

His last plea moved Ketan-bhai, who had not taken his eyes off Madan. Surely Ketan-bhai was going to fire Madan for this outburst, or worse. "What are you doing to him?"

Ignoring Dinesh's whimpering and wailing, Madan continued to try and lift Dinesh up. "I'm taking him to the doctor," Madan said.

"The doctor?" Ketan-bhai repeated. He exchanged a baffled glance with the accountant. "You're taking him to the doctor?"

Madan didn't have time for their waffling. "I need help," he said.

"You broke his arm," Ketan-bhai stated, as if filling Madan in on something he had missed.

"I think it's his wrist."

"And now you're taking him to the doctor?" Ketan-bhai turned disbelievingly again to the accountant.

Together, Madan and Ketan-bhai maneuvered Dinesh into an auto-rickshaw. All the way to the hospital, Madan propped Dinesh up while Ketan-bhai kept his injured arm steady, the older man's eyes wide with confusion and a grudging respect.

"What is your full name? Kumar?" he repeated when Madan told him. "A common enough name that tells me nothing about you."

"I am what you see," Madan said.

The smell coming from the toilet was sharpest in the morning, when the hole in the ground was in most demand. It would be overflowing and unusable if he didn't hurry. His room was a recess in the wall of a building, its threshold crossed in two steps. Rolling up his sleeping mat, he collected the bucket sitting by the door for his wash. The plastic bag slouching against the bucket tipped over, spilling out pieces of leather and bits of crepe, chenille, cotton, georgette and velvet. The day before, in the garbage bin at the back of the factory, he'd come across a jagged piece of goat hide which he could not leave behind even though his bag of discarded cuttings was almost full to bursting. The star-shaped piece would delight Swati. Stuffing the scraps back into the bag, he secured the top with a tight knot.

From the narrow ledge out his door, he descended the steep spiral staircase to a long lane of crumbling plaster. Out of corroded grilled windows on either side poured sounds of babies crying, bells tinkling in morning prayer and hymns sung in stilted voices, muffled shouts of argument and calls for cups of tea. Skittish goats with matchstick legs and jute sacks slung over their backs for warmth bleated and tugged at the ropes leashing them to doorways and window bars. He washed up quickly under the broken pipe protruding from the wall, the cool water from the municipality spurting out with a pounding force at this time of the morning. A gurgle of soap suds from the previous bather oozed around his feet, flowing down along the sloping gradient of the street. After his quick bath, he filled his bucket to take back to the room. By the time he returned in the evening the copious flow from the pipe would be down to a trickle, and he could do with one less inconvenience. He should be used to the shrill noises, the mordant smells, the slimy concrete blocks beneath his wet feet, but every small vexation, every tiresome moment, counted toward the drip of hurt and bitterness slowly filling his heart.

He remembered making Swati laugh when, after a bath, he'd chase her around the compound vigorously shaking his wet head, spraying her with droplets of water as she ran, giggling and yelling, "Stop! Stop!" He did it to hear her laugh. He did it to hear his mother say, "Wear some clothes, you'll catch a cold." She would say it with her usual brusqueness, as she had since his father's death, but he felt for a moment in those few words that she still worried about him, cared about him in some way.

On his way to his room, he rapped on the open door of a room below his staircase. He owed money to the lady who prepared evening meals for him. Her cross-eyed husband would appropriate the payment if he was around, so Madan waited for when he knew the husband was out, to pay her directly.

"I'm coming," she said.

Madan waited by the doorway, his eyes adjusting to the dimness of the interior. A baby lolled on a mat, plump and naked, with a black string tied around his middle, his tiny eyes lined with a dark smudge of kohl. Another baby hung off the lady's hip. She bent over the stove, lighting a burner and stirring a deep pot on the ring of blue flames. Her other children were playing in the web of alleyways somewhere.

Madan felt something run over his foot, and looking down he saw the plump baby crawl out the open door and into the street.

"Behn-ji," he said, "your baby."

"Get him," she said, unruffled. "My hands are full."

The child sat in the middle of the lane and raised his arms up and down as if hailing a rickshaw.

"Come on," she hollered, "he won't bite you."

"You're making me late," he said. Another tiny face, bundled tight, prickled his memory. "Get him," she said again. "I'll be

318

there in a second."

The baby would drown with the trash in the drainage ditch by the time she turned around. Madan didn't see why he had to make the effort when she didn't seem worried about a bicycle or tonga running him over as he sat cackling in the lane, his bottom covered in gravel. He stepped out and, picking the baby up by the waist, deposited him back down on the mat.

She came to the door to collect the money from Madan. "Such a big man, scared of a small person like this." She laughed. The baby jiggling at her side sucked on a piece of carrot.

"Don't need any food tonight," Madan said, irritated by her amusement. She had five needy children and a husband who barely managed to play the trumpet in a wedding marching band, and she laughed at Madan as if he were the one who was a joke. He would eat near the factory; perhaps go out with one of the other boys. He deserved a night with a half bottle or more of someone's homemade mind-numbing brew. He checked the pocket of his pants for his stash of notes. It wasn't much, but whatever he had, he always kept it on himself.

Still seething, he jumped on the bus, and

if there hadn't been an empty seat he would have thrown someone off and taken their seat. He plunked down, shifting closer against the window as another passenger took the seat beside him. The bus jerked along from stop to stop. At the hospital with Dinesh, Madan had asked Ketan-bhai to add him to the permanent roster.

"You now have an opening for a full-time worker," Madan said. "I can start right away."

Ketan-bhai smiled thinly, thinking Madan was joking, and then realized he was not. "You're serious?"

"Yes, of course. The position is open now."

"So let me see. You beat Dinesh up, break his arm —"

"Dislocated his wrist," Madan corrected.

"Pay all his hospital fees, and now you want his job."

"You heard the doctor. Dinesh won't be able to use his hand for some time."

"And what if I don't? Will I have to look over my shoulder from now on, worrying that you'll be waiting to break my legs?

"If I wanted to break your legs I would have done it by now. But you haven't given me any reason."

Ketan-bhai had rocked back and forth on his heels, his arms folded at his chest, almost laughing, but he had gone ahead and taken Madan up on his proposition. Madan had a full-time job again, and his life was beginning to settle.

He had thought at one time that there could be no other factory as big as the timber mill, but most of these factories surpassed it in size, and he'd heard of far larger ones coming up on the outskirts of the city. He wished he could take the bus and go straight to Avtaar Singh, not to complain or rant, but just to be with him for a while. Madan knew exactly what stories he would tell about this place to make Avtaar Singh laugh in his big, booming way, or say, *Really? We should think about doing that,* or shake his head and affirm, *That's why we're happy here in Gorapur.*

He played out again the memories of those last days, before he arrived in Delhi. He should have taken the baby from Pandit Bansi Lal and run. Why hadn't he? It was his as much as it was Neha's. Instead of languishing here all alone, he would have had someone. Confusion, fear and the shock of the preceding events had not let him think clearly. He could have grabbed the baby out of Pandit Bansi Lal's arms, he thought. Pandit Bansi Lal was no match for

321

him. Madan could have been out of the hospital and on his way before the pandit opened his wretched mouth.

As far as he could see, children didn't need much more than what he already had — a place to live and a job to bring in some money. Out of his bus window, he could see kids on the streets everywhere, learning, growing, living, surviving. It wasn't that hard, if they could all do it. And Avtaar Singh would have understood why he took his baby. *Yours is yours,* he'd have said.

He lost track of time as he wandered down the road of possibilities, getting off at his stop and entering the factory without paying much attention to the predictable surroundings. Avoiding the temple, he made his way to sign in. He caught Ketan-bhai looking at him hawkeyed from the fringes of the crowd of worshippers.

"Madan." Ketan-bhai broke away from the group, calling out to him. When Madan slowed down, Ketan-bhai handed him a roll of newspapers.

Madan took it with a nod of his head in thanks. He had quit trying to dissuade Ketan-bhai from passing on his morning's newspapers, which would include *Dainik Jagran, Navbharat Times* and an English-language paper. He could always find a discarded one lying about. But Ketan-bhai insisted and it gave them things to talk about when they had lunch together most afternoons, a routine they had fallen into that Madan had come to enjoy.

"Ketan-bhai," the workers said. "How come you don't sit and talk with us?"

"All you buggers do is bore me by complaining about your wives, your children, your jobs," Ketan-bhai said. "Madan can tell me ten interesting things in the same time."

There was an air about Ketan-bhai that made him seem older than the decade or so he had over Madan, and his plain-dealing ways elicited a deference from everyone, adding to his aura of sagacity. In the quick glimpse Madan once had of Ketan-bhai's office, he'd seen files lined up in clinical order, pens separated by color in different cups on an uncluttered desk and tagged leather jacket samples methodically hung up on garment rods. Everything, even the charts on the wall, displayed Ketan-bhai's penchant for order and harmony. "It makes my wife crazy, but I can't sleep if I know something is not where it should be," Ketan-bhai had said. "Bothers me to no end when anything is out of place."

Madan tucked the newspapers under his

arm and slowed his pace to match Ketan-bhai's. He didn't mind these friendly discussions on wars in the Gulf and beyond, or debating economic reforms brought about by the budget payment crisis, or the latest cricket scores. Ketan-bhai would try to dig deeper, but it was no use trying to explain why it didn't matter that he was not working behind a desk in an office or doing productive work with his mind rather than his hands. When a man has no beginning to his life and the end is a question mark, then what he does in the middle becomes irrelevant.

Ketan-bhai's disappointment at Madan's reticence was clear, as Ketan-bhai was a man who couldn't hide his feelings behind stoic expressions or polite chitchat. Madan had seen Ketan-bhai's young son waiting for him by the gate on his way back from school. Ketan-bhai would hurry out and throw his arm around the boy's shoulder and pull him close, bending his head to ask a question, and he would smile at whatever the answer, and they would talk and forget everything around them as they made their way to Ketan-bhai's scooter.

All at once the weight of his jumbled, distracted thoughts when jumping off the bus drained out of Madan. It was a sign of madness to think that he could have taken the child and fled. Dreaming about how he would feed it, and clothe it and have the lady downstairs look after it for a few rupees. What did he know about taking care of a baby? Madan was useless to that child, as it was to him. From its inception, the small, crying creature had come along and ruined everything. No one wanted it; even its own mother had sought her emancipation.

Perhaps realizing Madan's inattention, Ketan-bhai meandered off, and Madan entered the workroom. A man on a rickety ladder was replacing a faulty tube light and it flickered on, flooding the room with artificial brightness, and illuminating brown-and-black-mottled goatskins splayed out on worn wooden worktables. Before starting, the men hung around exchanging morning pleasantries. Most would collect their monthly pay and send some of it to wives and children, old parents and younger siblings, hoping in the end to make enough money to one day return to their waiting homes dotting the countryside all the way to the Bay of Bengal, in villages where goats ran amok on dusty roads, and men tilled the land with oxen, and electricity was a luxury of an hour a day.

With a sheet of emery, Madan began to slough off the top grain of the goatskins with a steady back-and-forth motion, buffing away the cuts and scratches, the bites and horn marks and imperfections. It would take all morning to get through this first pile, but soon the upper crust of the skin would be powdered grit at his feet, and the smooth nap underneath would then be ready to be embossed with a pattern, dyed to an unnatural color, cut up and sewed back together to become something it was never meant to be.

CHAPTER 14

The worktable began to tremble. Madan lifted his head to look around and heard a burst of explosions like the rattle of gunshots somewhere below. Others began to ask, "What was that?" or "What's happening?" And then someone said, "Run."

The doorway was at once blocked, everyone fighting to get out, scrambling up and over each other. "Keep calm," someone said above the din. "You'll kill us all here." When one person managed to break free from the gridlock, the others spilled out, and Madan streamed out with them into the murky hallway filling with dark, gathering clouds of smoke. The back of his throat burned and his eyes began to water. He could hear the pounding of footsteps but they seemed to be coming from all directions. He made out vague shapes and felt the air move when someone passed by. The doorway disappeared behind him. He was unsure if he had turned left or right.

Eyes squeezed shut against the heat and ash in the air, he moved along the wall. At its end, he came upon another room and stumbled inside, taking stock of his surroundings. Upturned tables and chairs and boxes of thread rolls littered the room. He closed his eyes against the onslaught. A few more steps, surely, and he would be out in the open and able to take a deep, cleansing breath. "We need help!" he heard a holler from the basement stairs behind him. It was Jairam, from the packing room. Jairam shouted into the emptying hall, "Help!" before running back down.

There was no one to follow him but Madan. The basement was a warren of illegal rooms dug out to accommodate different parts of the factory process. Madan kept an eye on Jairam's blue shirt. There was ash in the air along with gritty cement dust. The walls had crumbled in piles of rubble.

"Where to? Where to?" Madan huffed to Jairam. The heat was unbearable. Behind an accordion iron gate, three women peered out though the slanted bars, their saris covering their mouths to sieve the acrid air, their eyes wide with hopelessness. Rubble from the collapsed ceiling filled the gate's tracks, jamming the folds of the gate shut.

There was another scream when a block of cement fell and shattered to pieces on impact.

"Leave us, son," said the woman closest to the gate. "Save yourself."

"Are you mad?" cried another one. "Help us, help us," she shouted to Madan and Jairam.

Jairam began to clear the area in and around the tracks, and Madan crouched down to help. Pieces of brick and cement ripped the skin off their hands, dirt grinding into the wounds. The ladies chanted softy, "Jai Mata Di, Jai Mata Di." When the tracks seemed cleared enough, Madan pulled at the handle of the gate to test if it would move, but drew back at once. The iron bars were hot. He removed his T-shirt and wrapped it around his hand. He pulled on the opening of the gate but couldn't hold on for long before the heat came through the thin cloth, adding to the fiery pain of his cut-up hands. He stripped off his pants and used both garments to hold on to the bars.

Jairam did the same. "Move back," he shouted to the ladies.

In their grubby, loose shorts, they jiggled and tugged at the gate stuck in its tracks while around them chunks of mortar fell in unnerving thumps at their feet. "We have to hurry," said Jairam.

Madan strained harder and harder against the twisted iron until he heard Jairam grunt, "A little more."

The gate gave way, rolling back in the track with a short, unassuming squeak. One of the women squeezed out and then turned to help the others as Madan and Jairam held the gate open. Jairam led them away, with Madan following at the rear. The women trembled with shock and relief, crying and praying as they climbed back up the stairs.

At last Madan collapsed on the steps outside. They were wet and cool against his bare back and legs. A van pulled up, and there was a commotion as they loaded up the injured and took them away. A few men continued to hasten about with metal pails filled to the brim with water, and khaki police uniforms appeared in Madan's line of sight. His first impulse was to run to escape the whack of their lathis, but then he laughed at himself. He was not lying drunk on the footpath at some odd hour. It was daytime, he was in the factory, and if they wanted to clear him out, they would have to put down their batons and scrape his charred remains off this step. He stretched out and looked up at the bright sky. The sloshing of the water in the buckets pained him above all else. "Give me some," he said, but nobody heard his whispered plea.

Ketan-bhai sat on a metal chair next to the hospital bed in a starched safari suit, his prematurely gray hair slicked down heavily with hair cream, holding the open newspaper up to Madan's face. "We were in the news," Ketan-bhai said grimly. "Second page."

"Two Dead in Factory Blaze" read the headline, followed by a few long paragraphs.

The words swam before Madan. He rested his head back down. The sheets were a jumbled mess beneath him. He tried to cough but it hurt his throat and his head, and nausea came like a crashing wave. He retched into the steel pan at the side of the bed.

"It will take time for your hands to heal." Ketan-bhai gently patted Madan's heavily bandaged hand. "You took in a lot of smoke, so your mouth and throat are going to be sore for some time. Doctors were surprised you didn't pass out."

There were other patients in the ward on dinged and corroded metal beds like his, and Madan could see legs and arms flung listlessly out on white sheets.

"Jairam?" Madan asked. "Is he here?"

"He's home now," Ketan-bhai said. "He wasn't as bad as you."

"Who was it?" Madan rasped, pointing to the headline announcing the dead.

"Did you know Govindraja from Chhattisgarh? Uttam from Badarpur?" Madan hadn't heard of them.

"Govindraja, I knew him from some years ago. How afraid he used to be of these government hospitals. He'd heard that when the wards filled up, they would get rid of the excess population by attaching an empty IV bottle and pumping air into their veins. A killer air bubble would travel to the heart or lungs and the hospital would claim 'natural death.' I guess it is good Govindraja found a way out without stopping here."

Ketan-bhai's gaze traveled up the IV line inserted into Madan's hand, to the plastic bottle hanging from a hook.

"Yours is full of medicine," he told Madan reassuringly. "Yours too," he added to the worried patient in the next bed listening in to their conversation. Ketan-bhai probably knew all their names and where they were from by now.

"Didn't know Uttam very well," Ketan-bhai continued. "There was some trouble with his brother back in his hometown, but I heard he was a solid, hardworking fellow. Once you're gone, what else is anyone going to say about you? But why am I talking of Govindraja and Uttam? Our pasts have no meaning in this city, where everyone has a story. That's why we all land up here. To change how the story ends."

A nurse moved from bed to bed checking blood pressure, handing out medications and making notations on her sheaf of papers. "Hello, sister," Ketan-bhai said when she came to Madan. "Where is the patient's lunch? My friend needs some nourishment to regain his strength."

"Visiting time is ending," she said, sticking a thermometer into Madan's armpit.

"Of course, of course." Ketan-bhai solicitously picked up his chair, placing it flush against the wall, out of the way. He came and stood by the bed, and waited for the nurse to finish with Madan.

"Is there anyone I can call?" Ketan-bhai asked. "I can send a message to your family, to anyone."

The nurse took a reading of Madan's temperature. "Let the patient rest," she said, noting the information on her chart. Ketan-bhai dithered for a moment but it was not in his nature to overlook the rules. "You are sure?" he said to Madan. "It's no problem."

"I've told you before," Madan said. "I have no one."

The pants the hospital charity gave him were too loose. They dragged on the ground and caught under the soles of his rubber slippers. He took care not to trip and hurt himself further. His hands itched and throbbed under the tight bandages. The clarity in his voice came and went. Before discharging him from the hospital, they had admonished him to rest his vocal cords, and given him a brown paper bag filled with a strip of medication and a tube of salve.

He made his way through the tapering lanes, muddy with overflowing drain water, to his room. Overcome by a bout of dizziness, he leaned against the wall of the curving stairway, daunted by the steep climb ahead.

"You! You!" a woman's voice called to him. She stepped out from her doorway, blinding Madan in her bright green sari and clinking red bangles. "Where have you been? You haven't ordered food from me for so long." She took in his stubby beard, sunken cheeks and the pallor of his eyes. "What happened to you?"

Too tired to elaborate, he waved his

bandaged hand, keeping his balance by concentrating on the big red bindi on the middle of her forehead.

"Where are you going?" she asked.

"Up. To my room."

"It's not your room, silly boy! You didn't pay rent for these days, and he's given it to someone else," she said about the landlord. "Come with me." She bustled off, waving for Madan to follow her to her place. She was holding his white plastic bag when he caught up with her. "He was throwing your things out. I wasn't sure you would be back, but I kept this for you." She passed the bag into his stiff grasp.

He opened the bag. Inside were his extra set of shirt and jeans. Gone were the arduously collected bits of fabric, the soft velvet and silky chenille, the patterned cotton and scraps of leather.

"There was some junk in the bag. I threw it out," she said. "But I saved your clothes."

She was waiting for him to leave. He stood there swaying on his feet, staring stupidly into the emptied bag. "Are you hungry?" she said, and, not waiting for his answer, she brought out a roll of raw onions and chapatti. Opening the bag, she placed the food on his clothes, and gently hooked the handle around his fist.

"Okay," she said. "Now you can go."

He wandered back down the lane and sat at a bus stop. On his lap, the bag was a deflated lump. The chappati was soft and warm against the crunchiness of the raw onions. He ate much too fast and the pungent onions irritated his throat and nose. A fit of coughing shook his bones. When it passed, he found that he was ravenous and unsatisfied despite the burning of his throat. He tried picking at the crumbs in his lap, and realized that the bandages would have to go. He needed his hands for work, and no one would give him a job with bandages impeding his range of motion. What's more, he needed water and something else to eat. It was too late for langar at the gurdwara, but he could make his way to the Sai Temple and join the other needy in the food line. Hungry as he was, the thought of going to the temple did not appeal to him. He unwound the bandages, letting them fall to the ground by the bench, and wiggled his stiffened fingers. Ignoring passersby, he changed into his jeans and stuffed his pockets with his medicine and the money he had received for his injuries. It was a token gesture from the factory. He would need to earn something to supplement it, but he would have enough to eat for a few good days. On a sagging clothesline strung between two light poles in the middle of the road, trousers, frocks and underwear snapped in the wind. Cars whizzed by on either side. He stepped into the traffic and held his hand out as he crossed to the median, making the cars and scooters slow down for him. The drivers honked their horns in frustration and gesticulated with annoyance. Jumping onto the median, he added the oversized hospital shirt and pants to the pile on the line, and crossed back to the bus stop. The cars protested again but he paid them no mind. Let them try to run him over and crush him under their dusty wheels.

"Seems like you're getting bolder by the day." Ketan-bhai was at the bus stop on his shiny blue scooter. The helmet cradled in his arm had flattened his peppery hair, and he'd forgone his usual safari suit for a plain starched shirt tucked carefully in his belted trousers.

"What are you doing here?"

"You weren't at the hospital and you'd given this basti as your address." Madan waited for more of an explanation, but instead Ketan-bhai asked, "Are you hungry?"

They found a corner stall in the market.

337

Ketan-bhai insisted on paying for the plate-fuls of rice covered with creamy yellow curry, and soft pakoras, a sprinkling of crunchy pappad on top, and mango pickle on the side. Madan gave his spicy pickle to Ketan-bhai. He didn't want to start cough-ing again. They rested against the scooter, and in a few silent minutes he cleared his plate, and waited while Ketan-bhai chewed thoughtfully.

"What? You're done? Take something else," Ketan-bhai said.

"I'm fine," Madan said, though he could eat another plateful. He didn't understand why he was so hungry all of a sudden.

"So what're you going to do now?"

"I was thinking of going back to the fac-tory."

Ketan-bhai stared plainly at Madan's scarred hands. "Why don't you try some-thing else for a change?"

"I don't know anything else."

Ketan-bhai raised his brow. "Do you take me for a fool?" he said. "You think I'm fol-lowing you around for your friendly person-ality?"

Ketan-bhai gestured angrily as if he was going to toss away his half-eaten meal, but stopped midway when he saw Madan's focus locked on the unfinished rice and curry.

"Here. You have it," he said. "I'm full."

Madan ate slowly this time, savoring each bite and washing it down with the cool, milky lassi he'd bought for each of them with some of his restitution money.

"Not as good as my wife's," said Ketan-bhai with a big gulp. "You must come to my house, meet my family."

Madan laughed.

"What's so funny?" asked Ketan-bhai.

"Why would you want me to meet your family? You don't know me."

"By the way, how old are you?"

"Twenty-three."

"That's very young," he said, and looked taken aback, as if he would have to rethink his opinion of Madan.

After Madan returned the empty glasses, he watched Ketan-bhai remove a cloth from his scooter's storage compartment and begin to polish the chrome, dust the seats, and wipe down the handlebars. He could tell Ketan-bhai was in deep contemplation as he went through his well-practiced cleaning routine. Maybe Ketan-bhai would put in a good word for Madan at another place. But he hesitated to ask Ketan-bhai for any favors. He had lied about his personal details without any compunction to police investigating the factory fire; he couldn't allow the slightest chance of them asking questions about him in Gorapur. Yet Ketanbhai, with his gracious smiles and his affable inquisitiveness, seemed even more of a threat to Madan.

The sun was lazily slinking down and Madan would have to find somewhere to sleep soon. He began to take his leave, but Keten-bahi, having wiped off his spotless scooter, stopped him.

"I want to show you something," Ketanbhai said, a cloth bag in his hand.

From out of the bag he pulled out a wire hanger, from which hung a supple leather jacket with big pockets and black buttons. Ketan-bhai looked excited and nervous, as if he were uncovering a thousand-kilogram stash of hashish.

"I've had this sample made," said Ketanbhai, proffering the jacket for Madan to feel the fabric. "This is the best quality. Look at the lining and at the stitching. Small and indistinguishable, except here and here" — he pointed to the arm seams — "where it is part of the design."

"It's very nice," Madan said politely.

"Nice? It's more than nice. You know what they say about me? There is God that gets

340

things done, and then there is Ketan-bhai." He folded the jacket and delicately placed it back in the bag. Ketan-bhai lowered his voice as if afraid the office workers slurping down their kadhi chawal or the shopkeepers behind their counters would overhear. "There is a buyer here, these days," he said. "From America. He is looking to place an order. There are many factories that want this order, but they are small. It will take five or six of them to make the number of pieces this buyer needs." Ketan-bhai smiled. "I, on the other hand, know each and every factory. I can coordinate, and I have experience to know how to make the garment to the buyer's specifications."

"That's good, Ketan-bhai, but I have to go if I'm going to get a bed in the temple's dormitory tonight. Or I'll be sleeping right here."

"You can't tell anyone. This is my idea and there are those who will try to wrangle in and do the same. But I wanted to ask you —"

"Is someone troubling you, Ketan-bhai? Do you want me to make sure they leave you alone?" He hadn't had a good jaw-snapping, head-punching, arm-twisting, bloody rout for some time, and perhaps that was what he needed.

"No, no," Ketan-bhai said. "What are you talking about, and what am I talking about? You do not understand." He held on to Madan's arm as if he were afraid Madan was going to level the evening rush of commuters with one fell swoop. "Madan, I am a simple man. There are no twists and turns with me, only straight lines. If we're to go forward, you must know that."

If only Ketan-bhai would go on with whatever he was trying to say. Madan was beginning to feel woozy again. The spurt of adrenaline that had kept him on his feet for this long was draining away along with his patience.

"This opportunity with the buyer has come about suddenly. I've been hoping for a chance like this for some time. I've lived all my life first on my father's farm in Punjab, near Abohar, and then working in factories. I am not confident in other situations. I've gotten to know you in the last year. I've seen you help others, whether it's with their pension papers or to move to a new house. You ran behind Jairam without hesitation. What I want to know is if you are interested. To do this with me."

"Such a venture requires money, Ketan-bhai. And as you can see, I'm going to be sleeping on the footpath tonight."

"I had some land back in my village, in Abohar. It was of no use to me sitting there unattended. I recently sold it. I have capital, but I need support. I know where to get the leather, the materials and I can get a good price for the production. I need someone who is confident speaking to these buyers, negotiating with them. I've talked to my wife about you and she agrees with me that you would be a helpful partner. We can set up a company. We need one room for an office, and a letter of credit. We will be in the middle, take the American order, give it to the local manufacturers and take our cut. It's a good deal for you. How long can you be a laborer like this?"

"You're going to trust me with your money?" Maybe it was Ketan-bhai who had suffered oxygen deprivation during the fire.

"You know how often I argued with them about the way the factory was set up. I warned them that something could happen, but they didn't listen. The police let me go this time, but what about the next time? Who are they going to catch when they can't get the owners? The supervisor. That's who. How long can I work in these places, at the mercy of people like these? I have to take this chance to do something on my own," he said. "Look, I have a young son.

There is a different life I see for him, different from mine. And I can see that someone has taken a lot of effort with you, educated you, taught you how to think and reason, how to evaluate and get things done. Someone must have cared about you very much to do this. Don't let it go to waste."

It was the end of the day. The men accumulated outside the factory gates, smoking and chatting. Spying Madan's approach, they called him to join them. "Arre, Madan-bhai!" "There's our hero!"

The men began to quiz him about his restitution money.

"Where did it go, Madan-bhai? Women? No, you are too uptight. Drink? Must be drink. He is the type to have many sorrows to drown."

Madan allowed the men to rib him. Of course the money would be of primary interest to them. How shocked they would be to learn how little of it remained. He had left Ketan-bhai, with his scooter full of dreams, to find a place to sleep. He ended up roaming from neighborhood to neighborhood like a nomad.

At midnight, a reluctant silence descended on the city. The jagged concentric circles of the ring roads took him to shuttered markets glowing with dirty yellow lights. He walked with the stray dogs, pausing for warmth by roadside fires, where the men huddling around the flames shared their beedis and gave him space in their cozy cabals, but soon he moved on, wandering in circles until the sun broke over the sign for the New Delhi Railway Station. He had more than enough money. He could get on the train and tomorrow no one would remember him or wonder where he was.

He did not need permission or an invitation to return to Gorapur, after all. Home was a birthright, like freedom. Why shouldn't he get on a train? Was it because, after all this time, perhaps he would not remember their faces, or they, his? His mother's, Swati's, Jaggu's? No, the reason he hesitated each time was not because of his mother or sister or anyone else. It was because he could not bring himself to face Avtaar Singh like this. With nothing to his name but a set of torn clothes and a body scarred and broken.

The ticket counter opened up and people jostled Madan, but the trains would all have to leave without him. When he did show up in Gorapur someday, he would not be in the same sorry shape as when he left.

He called Ketan-bhai at the factory after

the morning bell sounded and told him he would meet him that evening. With a few passport photos and no proof of residence, no electricity bill or tax receipt, the tout at the food office exchanged the chunk of notes for a forged ration card.

"Do you have a preference for "father's name"? the tout asked.

Avtaar Singh, Madan was about to say. *Avtaar Singh is my father.* He had known no other.

"I have a list." The tout showed Madan a typed list of names, more added by pen at the bottom. A generic list for people like him with no connections in the world and with no one to claim as their own. He gave the list back without reading it. "Prabhu Kumar," Madan said. "My father's name is Prabhu Kumar." There were some things that could not be changed or taken away, regardless of how much anyone, even Avtaar Singh, desired it.

He hoped that Ketan-bhai had not reconsidered his offer or had a change of heart. To sign contracts and other official papers he needed the card for proof of identity, but more than that, he could sense its counterweight, giving him equilibrium and mooring him.

Ketan-bhai came out of the factory. He

didn't show any surprise or interest when he saw Madan waiting. They walked to his scooter and as Madan hopped onto the backseat, the men shouted, "Don't grovel too much to get your job back!"

At the notary office, Madan drew up the papers, stating clearly that though Ketan-bhai was putting up the capital, the business would be an equal partnership. Ketan-bhai was about to sign when Madan asked, "Aren't you going to read it?"

"No, no," said Ketan-bhai. "You're like my son. I trust you."

Madan snatched the paper away. "I am not your son. You have a child already, am I right?" Ketan-bhai nodded. "Never," said Madan firmly, "call me son."

"Okay, okay," said Ketan-bhai, holding up his hands as though the paper were a gun pointed at him. "I won't call you son — happy? Now," he said with exaggerated exasperation, "can I please sign the paper? My wife is waiting for me for dinner and, son or not, you'll be eating with us tonight." He motioned to Madan to place the paper back down.

Looking down on Ketan-bhai's prematurely graying hair and his hand crawling over the dotted line, Madan had to stop

himself from telling Ketan-bhai to hurry
up.

CHAPTER 15

The guests under the sweeping white tent were getting restless. The wedding ceremony was over. The pandit went on long enough with his incantations and lecturing, and the bride and groom had walked around the fire and been showered by rose petals. It was nearly one in the morning and everyone was eager to get to the buffet table.

Madan was anxious to leave, but Ketan-bhai and his wife, Nalini, continued to mingle with friends and didn't seem in any rush to go. The wedding was of the daughter of a fellow garment exporter, and Madan had driven with them in Ketan-bhai's car, his shiny blue scooter replaced by an equally spiffy blue Toyota.

"Have some sweets," said Nalini, noticing Madan's impatience. "We'll go in a bit."

"Tomorrow is a holiday," Ketan-bhai said to Madan. "Don't be in such a rush. Go, enjoy. Meet some people."

If Avtaar Singh had been sitting at this party, Madan thought, there would be a bevy of boisterous guests surrounding the table, his presence enough to draw all eyes to him. While he was tall and imposing, directing the tone and matter of the conversation, one could go by and never notice Ketan-bhai, sitting in his chair, enjoying his drink, conversing with one or two people, an eye on his wife to make sure she had all she needed, swooping in now and then to ask her opinion on the subject at hand. The two men were alike, though, in that neither ever seemed to see the need for a day of festivities to end. Why stop living when work was over?

"I'll get some dessert," Madan said. He slipped outside to where the food tables were set up. The dessert station, he knew, would be full of creamy pineapple pastries, layers of cherry-studded Black Forest cake and spirals of orange gooey jalebis. Always there were the jalebis bobbing merrily on the surface of the hot oil. He got himself a coffee and walked out into the hotel's gardens. Away from the hotel building and the humming tent, there was a pleasant gust of air and calming, muted light.

The century had turned, and that in itself felt momentous. Ketan-bhai and Madan had started their leather business at an opportune time, in the boom of the nineties when the overseas demand had surged. Their first order from the American buyer gave them a taste of their partnership and its possibilities, and they hadn't remained middlemen for long. They were exporters themselves now, with their own factories manufacturing shoes, jackets, handbags, belts and wallets. They had recently ventured into real estate and had been discussing their project in the car on their way to the wedding when Nalini said, "Can you men talk of something besides work? Madan should be thinking of settling down, starting a family. Who are you doing all this for, anyhow, Madan?"

Contemplating that question, Madan veered off the garden path and into the deep shadows of the hotel's lawn, where hidden lights illuminated clumps of champa trees encircled in stone. He loosened his tie, undoing the top button of his shirt. Immediately he felt more relaxed. Slipping off his shoe, he placed his foot on the lawn. Through his sock, the grass was cold and wet with dew. Like the grasses of Gorapur. It was as if a century had passed since he had left. Seeing the bride, her head bent with the weight of the flower garlands, her small smile peeking out from under her lashes, her brother by her side, a hand on her elbow guiding her, he thought of his mother. This wedding was what his mother had wanted for Swati. He could give her that now. He could give his mother the home she dreamed of and the wedding she wanted for her daughter, but the longer he was here and the harder he worked, the further away they both seemed. He wanted to pick up the phone or send a letter. He thought about sending them money. But he never did.

"Hey! Hello!" A girlish voice intruded on his silence. Madan slipped his foot back in his shoe.

"Do you have a flashlight?"

The girl had come from the wedding with her heavily embroidered pink lehenga and the glittering necklace around her delicate throat.

"No," he said.

"I lost my earring by the bench," she said. "My mother's going to kill me."

"I have this." He took out his cell phone from his pocket. It was a new model and the reception was erratic but he had felt the need to splurge on it.

"Wow," she grabbed the phone from his hand. "Is it a Nokia?"

The small screen glowed as she pressed the buttons. Without asking Madan, she headed back to the bench stationed at an angle under an arbor of jasmine. Madan followed her. He didn't want to let the phone out of his sight and she seemed to have a penchant for losing valuable things.

"My ear was hurting, so I took the earring off for a minute, but it slipped out of my hand when I was putting it back on."

She crouched down, the skirt of her lehenga billowing around her, and scanned the ground with the light from his phone. "My mother took it out from her bank locker just today, and made me promise to take care of it."

Madan got down too and felt around with his hand. Abruptly she got up and sat on the bench, leaving him to hunt alone. "What will I say to her? I tell my kids to be careful with their belongings, and here I can't take care of a small earring."

She seemed too young to have children but here in the fuzzy light it was hard to see clearly.

"Wear artificial, my mother told me. These days everybody wears artificial and keeps the real jewelry in the locker. But of course I didn't listen."

Madan felt she really should be looking

353

instead of talking. He was about to interrupt her when he brushed against a nubby, hard shape in the dust.

"I got it," he said.

"Thank god! You saved my life." She leapt off the bench and exchanged Madan's phone for the earring. A life delivered from harm, just like that, Madan thought. By the finding of a trinket. No fury or rage, no treachery or carnage needed.

"Preeti, I got a flashlight." A young woman carrying a hefty black flashlight joined them, and a pack of finely dressed men and women trailing behind her descended upon them, swirling around Preeti like rings of gold.

"No need," Preeti said. She flashed her bejeweled ear. "Found it." There were exclamations of relief. "Guys, this is Madan," she said to her friends. They said hello, and then Preeti and her group turned and went back to the party.

"Wait," Madan said. "How do you know my name?" But she was gone.

He stood still for a moment, surprised and confused. Sometimes he couldn't shake the feeling that Avtaar-Singh knew where he was. Did this pretty girl somehow know Avtaar-Singh? The tranquillity of the garden vanished with the disturbing thought. He went back to the party, finding Nalini and Ketan-bhai at the table where he had left them. They were ready to leave.

"What happened to you?" Ketan-bhai asked, noticing Madan's strained expression.

"Just something . . . strange," Madan said.

"We are at a wedding," Ketan-bhai affirmed, helping his wife up. "And marriage is the strangest business of all."

The land before them was an unceasing stretch of untilled field taken over by scrub and a withered tree. Tractors were driving over the hillocks of dirt, and rolls of chain-link fencing lay about in disarray.

"This is gold, I tell you. Gold!" The real estate developer flapped his arms up and down to underscore the desirability of the barren land on the outskirts of Delhi. "It does not matter what you have on the land, a small hut or a mansion. The real value is the land."

"You don't have to convince us, Sourav," Ketan-bhai said. "We are with you already."

Sourav came from a town in Punjab half a day's journey from Gorapur. With his similar background and hardscrabble success, Madan felt an affinity with Sourav that Ketan-bhai failed to see. Sourav had grown up watching his father's small cement factory start and fail many times. When he came to Delhi he was a nobody, but in the years that followed he used a few remaining family connections to ingratiate himself with every politician controlling state construction projects, ensuring through any means that his company would be the sole supplier of cement for the large, unwieldy projects. His family business went from a small, puttering establishment to a recognizable name on every sack of construction gravel. Once Sourav had shown Madan an AK-47 clumsily wrapped in a towel in the backseat of his jeep. He had brandished it about but claimed it wasn't his and that he was keeping it for someone. Madan knew better than to mention the incident to Ketan-bhai, who was already disturbed by Sourav's bragging tales of violent altercations and dirty deals.

Sourav's assistant unfurled a roll of sketches on the hood of the jeep. It was the second multistory apartment project they had invested in with Sourav, and the drawings laid out the plans for the complex of high-rise buildings with ample parking, power backup, and access to the megalith malls sprouting along the high-way out of Delhi.

"So much expansion going on, so much

demand for this type of housing," Sourav said. "How many people can really afford to buy and live in Delhi anymore? And all these multinational companies opening here. These suburbs are where they are finding the best of both worlds. But first, we start with the land."

"Someone once told me that land is like a pot in which there is always food," Madan said. "It can feed you forever. If you lose the land, you lose yourself."

"Whoever said that is right," said Sourav. "And there's enough to keep us busy for some time. Next, people are talking about developing Manesar, and then onwards. The way things are going, soon you will be able to go from Connaught Place all the way to Pakistan, and it'll all be a suburb of Delhi."

"And where will our farmers go?" argued Ketan-bhai. "My family used to be farmers. Had land in Abohar."

Sourav and Ketan-bhai continued to discuss the changing landscape. The land they were discussing included Gorapur as well, and Madan couldn't tell yet if the thought of turning the farmland of his hometown into a modern suburb filled him more with excitement or with dread. Madan couldn't imagine Avtaar Singh relinquishing the soul of his beloved Gorapur to such change. When Avtaar Singh talked about land, he talked about Gorapur. If he lost Gorapur, he would lose himself. And Avtaar Singh had never lost anything that was dear to him.

"This is just the beginning," Sourav said. "By your next visit you'll not recognize this land."

The driver opened the car door, and Madan and Ketan-bhai slid inside. "That man can talk. And why he insists on bringing those goons with him, I don't understand," said Ketan-bhai of Sourav's two bodyguards, who had stood in the shadows throughout their meeting. "As if you or I would ever hurt him. We wouldn't know which side is the trigger and which side the barrel."

"Where I grew up I was taught to shoot when I was thirteen." Madan rarely talked of his past, but he was fixated on the idea of Gorapur gone, covered over with shopping centers and modern houses.

"You? No. I can't believe it," Ketan-bhai said. "You're not like these thugs. You don't even raise your voice when things get rough." He paused to give Madan a chance to elaborate, but Madan said nothing more.

Ketan-bhai turned thoughtful, changing tack as if he did not want to think about

358

what Madan had revealed. "This land has withstood so many invasions," he said. "The Greeks, the Turks, the Mongols and the Musalmans, the British, all wanted to rule it. Now we are left, but in the process of making ourselves kings, what damage will we do?"

"You can leave me at the office, if you're going home," Madan said to Ketan-bhai as the car approached the city. It was the end of a long day but he could fit a few hours more in.

"You are coming with me to my friend Dilip's house," Ketan-bhai said. "Remember, I told you about it last week."

Madan remembered the invitation, but he could not recall agreeing to go. Dilip belonged to Ketan-bhai's chess club, and though Madan had met him a few times, he could not think why Dilip would have invited him. Madan had neither the time nor the inclination to go.

"Drop me off at the office," Madan repeated to the driver.

"Madan, please," Ketan-bhai said in his dogged way. Madan shot him a shrewd look, and Ketan-bhai sighed. "I want you to meet Dilip's daughter. Nalini thinks it's a good idea too. Now the business is growing, you must take care of other aspects of your life before it becomes too late. Very decent family." Ketan-bhai was adamant. "She will suit you. You are coming with me to have a look."

Reluctantly, Madan gave in. Driving through the hamlet-like neighborhoods, the air thick with the carbon fumes of rush hour and his mind overflowing with work, he resigned himself to a few wasted hours. They pulled up in front of the nondescript two-story house.

Dilip and his wife Sarla welcomed them in. He saw that Nalini was already sitting in the living room. "I have new respect for your Ketan-bhai," Nalini said to Madan, when Madan sat down next to her. "I never thought he'd be able to get you here."

The door opened, and Madan first saw the wide serving tray wobbling with the weight of its contents. Sarla grabbed the tray before it tilted over, and helped her daughter place it on the table.

It was the girl from the wedding. She was dressed in a simple churidar suit, her hair casually tied back, with small gold studs in her ears. There was a flutter of a smile behind her sober expression. Preeti said her hellos and served everyone before sitting down quietly with her mother, while the conversation skipped from the traffic on the way over, to their business expansion into retail outlets. "It's keeping us very busy these days," Ketan-bhai said proudly.

After tea, they sent Preeti and Madan for a stroll and she led him to the park in front of the house. "Thanks for not mentioning the lost earring," she said. "I was sure you'd blurt something out."

"I am good at keeping secrets."

Gentrified bungalows peered down into the park, and in their balconies old couples rested on wicker chairs with their own cups of evening tea. Preeti and Madan strolled along the stone pathway encircling the park's manicured grass center. Groups of ladies in salwars and sneakers passed them by at a clip, having deep, animated conversations. Children swung from the monkey bars, their maids standing nonchalantly by, warning them now and then to be careful.

"I wondered how you knew my name," he said.

"My dad had pointed you out before. You think I'll allow my parents to call anyone home without having a look first? I am not a handbag for sale in a shop window that you check out and then move on. I look, then you look."

"So I passed the 'looking' test?" Madan

grinned, charmed by the unintended compliment, and she seemed embarrassed that she had revealed something she had not intended. Ketan-bhai would have a good laugh to see him joking and flirting with a girl.

She had a degree in education and was working as a kindergarten teacher, an only child, born and brought up in Delhi. "Never missed having a brother or sister," she said. "I've lots of close friends who keep me so busy. That's why I don't read as much as I like to, maybe some magazines," she said. "Ketan-bhai said you enjoy reading."

"I don't get as much time as I used to either," he said.

"You and Ketan-bhai have worked very hard. We've heard how you made your business over the last eight years."

Madan lost count of the many times they circled around the park, and when he found he had run out of questions to ask, she chatted on, filling his silences. He could have continued walking with her, but the park was emptying and her parents were awaiting their return. They stepped out of the revolving gate and headed to her house.

The next morning, in his top-floor apartment, he watched the sun crest over the water tanks and the crenellated brick terraces lined with pots of bougainvillea. Besides the bed, there was a desk and chair, a bookcase and a sofa handed down from Ketan-bhai and Nalini. "Is this a home or a cell in Tihar Jail?" Ketan-bhai would never fail to comment when he stopped by. "Put up a picture, at least."

Madan was never home, so he didn't see the need to decorate, but now he was irritated with the sparseness, and with the spreading water stain on the living room wall that had appeared during the monsoons. The seepage was causing the paint and plaster to blister and flake. There were doors that would not shut properly, and because he would either eat out or at Ketan-bhai's, he never got around to applying for a gas cylinder and the kitchen remained unused. How long could he go on living this half life? But weddings and relationships were for other people, not for him.

If the buildings were cleared north of his window, he would see all the way to Gorapur. Sometimes he wondered if it had actually been him on those well-trodden byways, his arm flung around Jaggu's shoulders, their faces turned to the sun, laughing, their hair soaked from a dip in the river, where the fish in those murky depths darted in surprise from the boys who knew no fear.

He would tell Ketan-bhai to give up the whole matchmaking business. He had blundered grievously once, and because of his mistake, there was a child somewhere going to school, or begging on the street, or more likely dead.

Yet she was suitable, as Ketan-bhai had said. Well-educated, well-spoken and attractive in a way that was not too disarming. And if she called now, he would forget the nonsense troubling his head and would be at her house, ready to walk with her in the park again, and for a few moments he would know what it was like not to be so alone.

He collected his briefcase and grabbed a cold slice of bread from the fridge for breakfast. He chewed slowly as he went down the stairs to the street. The driver opened the door for him, and he settled in, the street-sweeper wishing him salaam as he cleared the fallen leaves into piles with his long-handled broom.

Their courtship began with a series of long phone calls each evening after work. Soon, every Saturday he would turn up at her doorstep and they would go out for dinner or a movie or a drive around town, meeting up sometimes with people she knew. With Preeti, suddenly everything in the city that

hc had found mundanc or ridiculous became alluring and fun. He discovered a city
full of lively establishments where the
revelry continued into the early hours of the
morning. He and Preeti slurped bowls of
hakka noodles, shared wood-fired pizzas
and watched late-night shows. Where he was
quiet, she was full of chatter. She possessed
a certain type of equanimity that reminded
him of a young Swati, before their father
had destroyed her. But Preeti's imperturb-
ability came from a different source. Preeti
had never hungered or truly despaired or
felt any hurt beyond minor transgressions.
Her largest fears were abstract and far removed.

"When my dog Candy died, it was the
worst day of my life," she said. "She was a
dachshund mix, so cute, and I can't think
of getting another dog now. Did you have a
pet?"

He thought about Prince, and how he had
carried the squirming Pomeranian in his
arms up and down the back streets of Gorapur, afraid all the while of getting a speck of
dirt on his white fur, the dog's continuous
yapping giving him a blasting headache.

"No," he said. "Never liked animals
much."

A month after submitting their registration forms, Madan and Preeti were married in court, as Madan wanted. When her parents wanted a religious ceremony as well, Madan refused. There would be no temples and pandits. Her parents were stricken at the thought of forgoing God's blessing for the union, and Ketan-bhai tried to smooth things over, but it was Preeti who took Madan's side. "I know it's unusual," she said to her parents. "But it's like you both always say: we're blessed enough already." She was firm in her position, but gracious and respectful, bringing them around without rancor. If he had any doubts about her, or marriage or the step he was taking, they were gone in that instant.

After their wedding, Madan would rush home, paying no mind to Ketan-bhai's teasing, knowing that when he entered he would be greeted not with silence, but with laughter, as Preeti's friends were always dropping by, staying for dinner, playing silly pop songs, sharing opinions and raucous tales over bottles of gin and single-malt, and at night, with her next to him, her arm flung across his chest, with his every robust breath he could slowly, surely, feel himself getting stronger.

CHAPTER 16

The gate swung open, and the driver pulled the black Mercedes into its usual spot by the steps leading up to the entrance of a stout, glass-faced building. Madan stepped out of the car, glancing up at the sign spread over the entrance, MERIDIAN INDUSTRIES. The guard jumped up and saluted before pulling open the heavy glass door, releasing a blast of air-conditioning. The tapping of heels on parquet floors accompanied the soft hum of conversation as managers and assistants made their way to their desks with cups of steaming tea or files and papers. They greeted Madan when he came in, nodding their heads and murmuring good morning as he strode past the leather sofas in the visitors' lounge, and past the glass cases along the wall displaying a sampling of their wares — smooth and supple leather jackets, calfskin gloves, embossed belts, pebbled leather handbags, luggage and briefcases of every shape and size.

He took the stairs to the top floor, to his office: a functional, carpeted room with a long hand-hewn desk of dark walnut, a matching credenza, an oval conference table and art worth over a million rupees on the walls. He thought, always, of the other office he had known so well, Avtaar Singh's room with its yellowing walls and sagging sofa, the scratched desk and the rickety metal filing cabinet. How well he remembered the mingled scents of incense, motor oil and Avtaar Singh's cologne, the air outside heavy with sawdust and black smoke.

His past was still unknown to Ketan-bhai or Preeti. He told them enough to satisfy their initial curiosity. He had a family once, he said. "What happened?" Ketan-bhai prodded. "Where are they now?" Madan found he could not say. Anytime he tried to put the story together, to take Ketan-bhai in his confidence, he was filled with unease and a certain fear. He had taken succor from his memories. They were his, and he recoiled from sharing them, as if, once he did so, they would become diluted or unreal. Already, with time, everyone seemed to be getting more distant, as if they were part of a folktale he'd heard.

In the end, he had said to Ketan-bhai, "Sometimes a storm comes and knocks just one tree down, and sometimes the same storm lifts away your house and takes everything with it." It was as close to the truth as he could get.

He had moved on. Any day now, Preeti was going to have a baby, a thought that filled him with as much anxiety as excitement. In Gorapur, they would have moved on too. There would have been changes. Avtaar Singh was still there, he was sure. Avtaar Singh's soul was so entrenched in Gorapur that to separate one from the other would kill them both.

Meridian Industries, meanwhile, was growing from leather-goods manufacturing into a multifaceted organization with concerns in many sectors of industry, such as telecommunications and wind energy initiatives, and they had recently partnered with a luxury hotel group to open five resorts in India. When Sourav approached Madan with the idea of building a township, Madan had been as skeptical as Ketan-bhai still was today. It would be a massive project, bringing them great acclaim, yet Madan was hesitant to tie up their company's time and resources. But Sourav had found a way to persuade him. When Madan entered his office, the two men were already there, Sourav speaking animatedly, making the same arguments that he had to Madan.

"This will not be the same old townships we're seeing everywhere," Sourav was saying. "It'll be a world-class town, accessible to Delhi but far enough away from the crowded city. A lot of these international conglomerates are moving their back-office work from Gurgaon and Manesar. We will make it a green city, use technology in ways that will make everyone hold it up as an example. It will change the landscape wherever we decide to build it. Out with the old, in with the new. And, make no mistake, everyone will know your name because of it."

Madan could envision it now, this new city drawn from scratch, built to specifications, built with intention instead of whim. Not like the metropolis of Delhi, where the old constantly battled with the new, and modern, cookie-cutter apartments worth crores of rupees were superseding crumbling colonial bungalows, and everywhere people squeezed in and fought for space, while the everyday conveniences of water and electricity and drainage struggled to keep up with their burgeoning demands. Nor would it be like Gorapur, which started as an afterthought, a place to store the refugees streaming in at the time of India's partition, and then never growing, never flourishing beyond the control of men like Avtaar Singh.

No one appreciated a novel idea, a grand plan, a triumph of ambition more than Avtaar Singh. It would be exactly what Madan would give him. And the township would make way for his return to Gorapur, proud and unafraid.

"Your recent wedding has had a good effect on you," Ketan-bhai said to Sourav now. "We don't want anything to do with the old Sourav, you understand? No dirty business. Madan brought to my attention that with the current rate of attrition from rural to urban areas, India will need a slew of new cities to accommodate the migration. Our current cities won't be able to handle the load for much longer. If we're building planned, sustainable cities, then perhaps we're doing the best we can in the situation." He picked up Sourav's proposal and shook it at him. "But, for what you suggest, we're going to need land, and plenty of it."

Land. Even a small patch could make you a king. Madan could see in his mind the land stretching so far and flat one could forget that beyond it there were the deepest, darkest oceans and mountains of unscalable height.

"Leave that to me," Madan said.

They were wrapping up, discussing specifics when the call came, at last, from Preeti's mother that Preeti had checked into the hospital. "No need to rush," Ketan-bhai said. "These things take their own time." So after he and Sourav left the room, Madan, telling them he wanted a moment alone, returned to work. He had promised to see to the land for the project. It felt important to him, all of a sudden, to begin the progress on the township before the birth of his child.

They could spend years buying small parcels from this person and that, but he had a quicker way in mind. Within the space of a phone call to their detective agency, his messenger was on the way with their retainer and starting expenses. With the two nuggets of information Madan had provided — jewelry shop in Mumbai — they shouldn't find it hard to locate the man who, Madan hoped, had outlived the death sentence bestowed on him by Avtaar Singh nearly a quarter century ago. Having set this first surge in motion, he was ready to go and see Preeti.

Madan did not notice the entrance to the hospital, or the way to Preeti's room when he got there. Preeti glowed through her exhaustion, and he sat with her before being relegated to pace in the waiting room, while Ketan-bhai and Dilip flipped lazily through magazines and talked into their cell phones. Every time the elevator doors swished open he snapped to attention, not knowing whether to be excited or terrified, swinging between relief and anxiety, until the doors revealed Sarla, walking toward them, beaming, her open arms enveloping them all. She said something to them but Madan could not comprehend a word.

Sarla took him to Preeti's room, and when the nurse moved toward Madan, he planted his feet as if to block her in case she whisked away the bundle in her possession. She did not notice, placing the tightly wrapped bundle in his arms. "Congratulations, sir," she said. "It's a boy."

He glanced down. This time he did not let go. This time, he held on.

"Looks like his father," Ketan-bhai said, coming in behind them, but Madan barely heard him. He eased away the wrap, and the baby squirmed in protest. Madan tightened his grip. How could he have known that everything he had endured was to bring him to this moment? To this bundle in his arms?

A second chance yawned and raised his tiny fist in greeting.

CHAPTER 17

Madan tried to pay attention to the detective on the line but his baby son was playing in his bassinet, distracting him.

"I'm sorry," Madan said. "Give me the particulars again. You said where in Mumbai?" He took down the details quickly so he could get off the phone. He pulled Arnav's bassinet closer. "Look," he said, after hanging up the phone, "Papa has to go to Mumbai. For a short time. For this," Madan unrolled a swath of waxy, opaque paper. Arnav gurgled when he heard the rustling, and smacked his lips.

"This, my son, is Jeet Megacity," Madan said, presenting the rendering of the township.

Preeti came in, the maid trailing behind her with Arnav's bottles. "Time to eat," she said.

"Feed him here," Madan said.

"Your father is crazy," Preeti said, cradling

Arnav in her arms and settling down on the study's couch. "It's a good thing he can't take you with him to the office or to meetings or on business trips, or Mama would get no time with you."

The maid smiled too. "Memsaab, you're right. Saab would put him in his briefcase and take him if he could," she said.

"We have to enroll him in a school. There are such long waiting lists," Preeti said to Madan. To Arnav she added, "And what will your papa do when you start school? Poor Papa won't be able to drop in and see you anytime then."

"Which schools?" Madan said, already worried as well. His son would have the best of schools. "Give me a list. I'll start on it right away."

"I can do it," Preeti said with a laugh.

Arnav could not fight off his sleep any longer and the maid took him up to his room. Preeti had chosen the name Arnav after an intense search, and though she had consulted Madan about a host of baby names, he never felt any particular affinity for any of her suggestions, until she said Arnav, and it fit. Ketan-bhai rocked him in his arms and agreed, "Yes, he is Arnav, the vast ocean, and like his name he will immerse you in waves of his love." It was the truest thing Madan had ever heard.

Landing in Mumbai always made Madan glad he had ended up in Delhi, and not this sludgy seaside city. The information Madan had shared with the detective agency proved invaluable. It hadn't taken them long to locate Dhiru Sood, now a prosperous dealer of diamonds and semiprecious stones in Mumbai's Zaveri Bazaar. Shortly after Arnav's birth, Madan had called Dhiru Sood to remind him of who Madan was. Dhiru Sood, whose skin had slackened and belly had grown, had not forgotten. He came to the airport to pick Madan up, taking him to his house for lunch.

"Forgive me," Dhiru Sood said, when Madan caught him staring at him yet again. "It's hard for me to believe you're the same boy from Gorapur."

Madan indulged Dhiru Sood's reminisces, bringing him up to speed as to Madan's reasons for seeking him out. He was here for Dhiru Sood's vast tracts of ancestral land on the outskirts of Gorapur. Though Avtaar Singh had claimed the land for his own, for all intents and purposes the land still belonged to Dhiru Sood. The township of Jeet Megacity would rise from this land.

Dhiru Sood was cautious at first, becoming more intrigued as the scope of the project sank in. "Will Avtaar Singh allow it? If this big city comes up next to his, what will happen to Gorapur? The influx of people from the outside who don't give a damn who Avtaar Singh is will bring big changes to the area. These new people will have their own ideas and ways of doing things, and will not give him or his town the importance he's used to. And who will want to live in Gorapur with Jeet Megacity offering jobs, and security, and a life where they don't have to be beholden to Avtaar Singh? Gorapur will be reduced to a dusty village, sucked dry of its people and its influences."

"He can't stop us," Madan assured him. "We have the political will on our side, we have the financial backing, we have re-sources and we have the manpower to get it done."

"You don't need to give me this salesman-ship talk," Dhiru Sood said. "I understand what you're doing. Avtaar Singh is Gora-pur, and Gorapur is Avataar Singh. You destroy one, it's the same as getting them both."

Dhiru Sood wasted little time accepting Madan's offer. "Of course," said Dhiru Sood, nervously touching the spot where the bullet had struck him. "A shot to the heart would be quicker. But you've decided to give him a long, slow death." Dhiru Sood signed and transferred the yellowing title papers to the Jeet Megacity project. Madan promised Dhiru Sood a share in the township project for his children. He shook Madan's hand and folded Madan into a tight embrace as he took his leave.

That was seven years ago now. Avtaar Singh did not give up Dhiru Sood's land easily. Assuming that Dhiru Sood was fodder for the field rats, Avtaar Singh hadn't bothered to issue another title, but had paid revenues on the land, which he believed made him the de facto owner after all these years. He was angry and stupefied to find himself fighting for what he had thought was his. With revenue records in hand, Avtaar Singh's lawyers swept into court to contest the title, but the lawyers for Jeet Megacity, with the original title papers, fought back.

Madan spent his days plotting with the lawyers, and lying in bed at night he wondered if Avtaar Singh was up as well, gazing unseeing into the dark fields, puzzling out Dhiru Sood's reappearance. When Avtaar Singh realized that the only way Jeet Megacity Enterprises could have got the title papers was from Dhiru Sood himself, did he question who had let him down so long ago? Did he think back, and recall who had sauntered into his office to assure him that Dhiru Sood would never trouble Avtaar Singh again, that he was no more than a corpse rotting under the cornstalks? It should not take Avtaar Singh long to recall. It had been Madan.

It was a late Delhi afternoon, heavy clouds and the monsoon breezes tempering the heat of a particularly scorching summer, when Madan heard Avtaar Singh had withdrawn his case. Perhaps he realized a corporation of the size of Jeet Megacity would not give up easily and there was no point in paying lawyers to drag out the case in court for years to come. Or perhaps it may have been the additional pressure by Jeet Megacity lawyers who threatened to lodge other cases against Avtaar Singh for fraud and criminal intimidation. Dhiru Sood, they told Avtaar Singh, was willing to appear in court to give witness. Avtaar Singh capitulated, postulating that he had better things to do with his time than argue over an inconsequential piece of land. The team celebrated the news in Madan's office. Madan wanted to warn the revelers to remain vigilant. This was but the first skirmish. Avtaar Singh would not disappear so easily.

Finally they began laying ground. As Madan had planned, Ketan-bhai became the public face of the Jeet Megacity project, talking to the press and overcoming hurdles on the ground. "Why don't you do it?" he said once to Madan. "Didn't you say you spent some time in your childhood in this area?"

Madan had deflected, saying that Ketan-bhai was much better at dealing with such matters than himself. He had done his utmost to ensure that when Avtaar Singh dug deeper into the provenance of Jeet Megacity, he would not find any connection to the Madan he had known over two decades ago. He had listed Preeti as a major shareholder instead of himself.

Going over the progress a few months after construction began, Madan noticed the first real casualty of the behemoth that would be Jeet Megacity. Guru Gianchand's akhara had disappeared from the map, demolished, the land cleared for what would take its place.

Avtaar Singh's response came swiftly, beginning with a project manager pulled out of his car and roughed up enough for him to quit while recovering in the hospital.

The harassment continued. Equipment vandalized while guards or workers who were supposed to be on the lookout made themselves scarce, allowing property damage, labor strikes, work stoppages and financial losses. Then reports came of a large fire that consumed two godowns, one on the north side of the construction site and the other on the west. Both contained large quantities of construction material. Madan could not stand any more delays. He waited for the time when Jeet Megacity would be ready. He could feel Avtaar Singh urging him on, pushing him for completion so they could face one another again. Yet, perversely, it was Avtaar Singh who stood in the way, causing problems.

And so, unbeknownst to Ketan-bhai, Madan met up with Sourav in a hotel bar. Ketan-bhai would not approve of what Madan was going to ask of Sourav, who was on his second martini, olives tossed aside in disgust, when Madan brought up Jeet Megacity.

"I understand this is a big problem," Sourav said. "For someone like Avtaar Singh, this is war. We are threatening his domain, and he'll do all he can to disrupt us. There are no rules in a battle like this. One way or another, Avtaar Singh wants to

382

win. Ketan-bhai is well meaning, but his ways will have no effect on Avtaar Singh."

Ketan-bhai had wanted to buy Sourav out some time ago, but Madan resisted cutting Sourav loose. He and Sourav shared more than their recent affiliation. Sourav could have grown up in Gorapur. Madan could see Sourav hanging out with Jaggu and the rest of the boys, playing truant from school, living for the next cricket match, ending up every evening in Avtaar Singh's office, grateful for any word, any sentiment Avtaar Singh deigned to bestow.

Madan said, "I need someone to show Avtaar Singh that we'll reply in kind to any nuisance he creates for us. Show him in a way that he'll understand that any losses on our side will mean losses for him. Don't get us any undue attention, but you know what needs to be done."

Sourav nodded. "I see what you're getting at. I'll have my nephews send their people. They've been helping me take care of my concerns in Punjab." Madan had scant knowledge of Sourav's large clan, spread over Haryana and Punjab. Sourav, as the most ambitious and educated of the lot, headed their family business, and one could forget the web of brothers and uncles and cousins running and helping with the different arms of his organization. "My nephews, they're young guys, in their early twenties, full of action, running around town with their guns and cars. Better they make trouble where I tell them to, than cause me trouble."

"Make sure they understand my concerns. These young boys can be quite hotheaded, and I don't want any more problems than we already have," said Madan.

Sourav finished his drink and signaled for another. "You worry too much," he said.

CHAPTER 18

"Papa?" Madan heard as he slipped on his jacket. "Papa?" He turned to see Arnav peering around the dressing room door.

"What are you doing up?" Madan asked. "You're supposed to be in bed."

Arnav grinned. "I'm hungry."

Madan shook his head ruefully and tousled his son's hair. Arnav would be turning nine in a few months and Madan could no longer lift him up into his arms with one big sweep. Even now Arnav protested when anyone hugged him tight or treated him like a baby.

"Your mother is going to be upset to see you out of bed," said Madan.

"Why can't I come to your party, Papa?" asked the boy.

Indeed, Madan himself would have preferred to spend the evening with Arnav instead of half of Delhi. He didn't think it appropriate for a forty-two-year-old man to have a birthday party, but Preeti, who couldn't let the chance for any celebration slip by, had insisted. "A small party," she'd promised. "Eighty people at the most." From the preparations outside, he could see that the guest list would far exceed that number.

"I want that cake," Arnav said, pointing to the sheet of frosted cake sitting on a separate table. His entreaty caught at Madan's heart. Madan thought of Swati, with her swinging braids and incessant demands. If she could see Arnav now. His heavily fringed eyes were Preeti's, but in other mannerisms and features, he was all Madan. Swati would have lost her girlish braids by now, but whatever the changes that had come with age, he would know her instantly, he was sure of it. Would she recognize Madan if she saw him? Would she see Madan in her nephew's features, if she knew him?

Madan laughed, slinging the boy over his shoulder like a sack of wheat. Arnav giggled as he bumped along upside down on the way back to his room, forgetting the cake entirely. Madan helped his son back into bed. "Stay," Arnav ordered, and so Madan lay down as well.

"Do you want me to read this book?" Madan said, picking up a Hardy Boys novel from the pile on the bedside table.

"It's so boring," Arnav said with hesitation, knowing how that attitude exasperated his father.

"How about this one?" Madan asked, but Arnav was shaking his head and reaching over to remove a coffee-table book on Formula One race cars.

When Madan was Arnav's age he recalled the sense of wonder he had felt when putting letters and words together, and his amazement at how a few systematic rules could make numbers work magic on a page. That his son had no regard for the marks he got in school and the books and the learning so freely thrown at him baffled Madan. Preeti had stopped working soon after their marriage, but she was still a teacher and she drilled and pushed Arnav to achieve decent marks at school. "He lacks interest, not aptitude," she would say, trying to comfort Madan.

On the bed near Arnav was a red racing car with a knobby remote control panel, a recent gift from his parents. Arnav always got a gift on Madan's birthday. It was more fun for Madan that way. Madan and Arnav had spent all evening until the sun went down racing the car around the swimming pool perimeter, making it flip back and forth and screech around corners as if they were tearing around the Monza racetrack. After, they had jumped into the pool with their clothes on, and he had thrown Arnav in the air as the boy shrieked with delight.

Some hours later, Madan held the cake knife aloft, its sharp blade glowing in the candlelight. The buzz of conversation was dying down and he could sense the guests waiting for his move, rows of white teeth gleaming at him expectantly. Smiling gamely, he slid the knife through the rectangular sheet of cake, through the delicate roses piped around its border and through the scrawling script *Happy Birthday.* Clapping broke out, someone started singing "Happy Birthday" and others joined in, but the song petered out as Preeti sliced off a sliver of cake and brought it to his lips. He took a bite. A melody from the baby grand piano wafted out from the house, and their guests converged on him, men shaking his hand, ladies kissing his cheek.

Back in Madan's study, Ketan-bhai raised his glass to Madan in salute, and Madan raised his in return. On the table next to Madan was what appeared to be Lego pieces from Arnav's playroom. But this was no toy. It was the first model of Jeet Megacity, created by their architectural firm, and depicting what was turning out to be the largest solar city in northern India. Just above Jeet Megacity, a blue dot, labeled *Gorapur,* cowered in the shadow of his glitzy new development.

It galled Ketan-bhai that Madan had never been to see the Jeet Megacity site. "How can you stay away?" he asked. It was not easy. Madan wondered if Avtaar Singh, out of anger, pride or churlishness, kept away as well. Or had his curiosity led him there? Madan held off Ketan-bhai, saying truthfully he was waiting to see the finished city in all its brilliance. Until then, he had plenty to do here in Delhi.

His birthday was not the occasion he was waiting for. No, his daydreams were of the opening ceremony that would mark the official start of Jeet Megacity, now less than a year away — unless, of course, Avtaar Singh caused further delays. With the assistance of one of Preeti's event planners, Madan had laid out every detail to ensure the occasion would amaze and impress the locals. A Bollywood dance troupe and a well-known playback singer would entertain the crowds, while schoolchildren sang nationalistic songs and politicians talked about job creation and how every corner of India was becoming part of the twenty-first century. There would be free food and soft drinks and, at nightfall, fireworks.

Madan knew he was overdoing it, but he wanted the world's attention to be on Jeet Megacity during the speeches and ribbon-cutting, so that even those who didn't attend would learn about Madan Kumar's triumphant return, standing there on the stage with his wife and son, his influential friends and allies praising him for creating the city of the future.

"Did you see the message from Ghosh?" Ketan-bhai called out to Madan as Madan passed by his office the day after the party. Ghosh was the current project manager of the site. "We have a problem at Jeet Industrial."

Turning his laptop toward Madan, he clicked the tab. Pixel by pixel the images uploaded.

The sister project to Jeet Megacity and a largely classified venture, Jeet Industrial City was to be the commercial hub of the development. There would be no place here for smoky, decrepit factories. Instead, industries of information technology research and the manufacturing of silicon chips were going to provide jobs for Jeet

Megacity's population for years to come. The process of acquiring land for construction would begin soon.

Ketan-bhai began scrolling through image after grainy image of growing and angrier crowds of men in loose white turbans and women in bright saris. Landowners and farmers, furious that their land was being taken over. Madan was sure Avtaar-Singh had stirred them up. "My God," said Ketan-bhai at the parade of images.

At the end of the row of pictures was a short, fuzzy clip taken from a mobile phone. Ketan-bhai pressed play. "I'm not sure I want to see this," he said. In the video, a man, a native of Gorapur by the look of him, was standing tall above the others, shouting and whipping up the mob. "Who will reimburse you for the investments you made in your land? Your livestock? Your house?" the man was shouting to the mob, who echoed him. Madan couldn't make out all the words, but he watched and listened as, all of a sudden, a short, deafening bang drowned out the man's words. The camera angle swung to the right. Two cars had driven up. Young men sprang out holding shotguns. "I wonder who they are," Ketan-bhai said. Madan's stomach clenched. He was pretty sure he knew who they were.

The video turned scratchy with the sounds of running and shouting and gunshots. The images became dirt and grass, the ground appearing to move as the videographer retreated quickly. Ketan-bhai and Madan watched as the video blurred. But then the camera regained focus and zoomed in. Madan could make out a young man, one of the ones who had arrived in the cars, being dragged away, a large dark area above his eye at his temple as if there were a dent in the side of his head. They watched as his companions lifted him into a car and both vehicles screeched off, chased all the while by Avtaar Singh's men, who did not let up.

Madan heard the beeps of a phone ringing. Ketan-bhai was calling the project manager, Ghosh.

"Who was the young man? The one who was hurt?" he asked when Ghosh picked up. His gaze met Madan's with surprise, and he repeated, to confirm what he had heard, "Sourav's nephew?

"What was he doing there?" Ketan-bhai asked. "What do you mean, he's been assisting us? Did Sourav send him?"

Madan watched Ketan-bhai's frown grow deeper as he listened to the voice at the other end. "On whose authority?" Ketan-bhai asked Ghosh. "And why didn't you tell me?"

There was only one answer to both of Ketan-bhai's questions: Madan.

"I see." Ketan-bhai finished his conversation. He had grown still, the usual animation of his expressions drained away. He told Ghosh to remain available and they would get back to him.

"You must think me a fool," Ketan-bhai said when he disconnected.

"Something had to be done," Madan said. "The holdups were costing us, and —"

"Sourav's a scourge. People like him don't live by a code or have any regard for anyone but themselves. Whatever the change in his circumstances, he'll always be a provincial gangster at heart. So will his family. It's why I didn't want to get involved with him. Nothing good comes of it." He considered Madan without anger or condemnation, but he could not hide his distress. "No, you must think me a fool for believing you were different."

Stung, Madan stood up, his chair sliding backward. "This is who I am. You know it. You may have shut your eyes and ears to it, but you knew from the first day you met me. I haven't changed."

"You are mistaken. I saw a different man.

393

A man who chose to help others even when his own life was in danger. A man who saw his wrongdoing for what it was, and rectified his mistake regardless of his pride. A man who I learned was a true brother by my side when we faced our biggest challenges. That was the man I saw, and the man I know. And I'll go to my death believing so."

"I'll speak to Sourav to see what happened," Madan said. "You're giving this incident more importance than it deserves. By tomorrow we'll make sure everyone would've forgotten about it."

"Ghosh says the protesters will be back for the opening ceremony. You'll be in the news then, but not how you intended."

When Madan first came to Delhi, he hadn't known if he was going to stay or move on, and there were days when he didn't know where he would sleep or what he would eat. What he knew beyond doubt was one day he would find a way to return to Gorapur. The big announcement for Jeet Industrial City, along with the ceremonial laying of the first brick, was on the agenda during the opening ceremonies for Jeet Megacity. He could not allow any detours or disturbances to stop Jeet Industrial City from rising up from those fields and forever changing the landscape of Avtaar Singh's world.

"I will take care of it," Madan assured Ketan-bhai again. Madan got ready to leave his office.

"It's true we've staked a lot on Jeet Megacity," Ketan-bhai said. "But your partnership, your friendship, means more to me than any damn piece of land or investment. Is there anything else you're keeping from me?"

Madan shook his head without hesistation.

"Look who's here." Madan's assistant ushered Arnav in and, dropping his school bag by the door, the boy clambered onto the chair next to him. There was a half day at school, and as Arnav had no tennis lessons or playdates, he was going to spend the afternoon with Madan.

All morning Madan had tried to contact Sourav, but he did not pick up his phone, so Madan dispatched a couple of the office drivers to track Sourav down at one of his various places of business. He was glad for the distraction Arnav offered, as he waited to hear back about what had happened to Sourav's nephew and if there was any fallout from the protests.

Arnav launched into a tale of some boys

from school, and Madan listened with half an ear, his attention on the emails popping up on his screen. His phone rang and, seeing it was Ghosh from the Jeet Industrial project, he lifted his finger to his lips, cutting off Arnav midstory. It was a long phone conversation, followed immediately by another one, and many minutes later he glanced around to see Arnav absentmindedly kicking his chair.

"What is it?" Madan asked.

"Will I have to do this?" Arnav asked. "When I grow up? Talk on the phone, read files all the time? Mama says this is going to be mine."

Yes, Madan wanted to say. *I am doing this for you.* But that was not the answer Arnav was looking for. It was a hard notion for a boy who knew nothing, after all, of the darkness in Madan's past and who lacked the slow, burning patience Madan had needed to build this future. A boy who longed for nothing more than to hurtle down the track of life like one of those race cars he loved.

Madan said, "All this is for you someday, but only if you want it."

Madan went back to his work, but Arnav piped up again. "What did your papa give you?"

"What?" Madan thought he had misunderstood or misheard.

"What did your papa give you?" Arnav repeated.

What could he tell Arnav about Avtaar Singh, the man who had given Madan his own life, taught him right from wrong, lies from truth, failure from success? Shown him how to live, how to act, how to breathe? To fight till you win? What had he bequeathed Madan upon which he could build a life and a future?

"An education," Madan said.

When they managed to locate Sourav, he was at one of his work sites a short distance away.

Madan told Arnav they were going to stop at the construction site first before going home. As always, Madan was thankful for Arnav's easygoing nature. Arnav never complained too strongly, was ready to accommodate a change of plans, could keep himself busy when needed. Madan's conversation with Sourav should be simple enough, and then he and his son would be on their way.

The construction site was off the highway. Nothing but a board with Sourav's company name marked the general location of the site. The sign had been knocked to the side as if someone had tried to bulldoze it to the ground. Madan's driver turned into the lot, slowing down as the car shuddered over the rutted land.

"This won't take long," Madan said to Arnav. "You can stay in the car." He handed Arnav his phone so the boy could play one of his many downloaded games, but Arnav said he didn't need it and instead sent the driver out of the car and moved into the driver's seat to play with the steering wheel.

The construction site was a mess of building materials and twisted barbed wire. Cleared in parts, the land undulated freely until pockmarked by old broken structures and half a wall of an abandoned store. Piles of gravel, burst bags of sand and cement and broken red bricks littered the ground. It was quiet. A buzzard circled in the aluminum sky. Sourav was in deep conversation with his site manager, who spied Madan making his way toward them.

Sourav turned. He didn't look happy to see Madan.

"I've been trying to call you," Madan said. He noticed Sourav's men lolling around his Jeep.

Sourav would not meet his eye. "Everything is getting a little crazy," he said. "You shouldn't have come here. You heard what happened to my older nephew?"

"Yes," Madan said. "I saw a video. I never thought he'd rush into a mob like that. I should never have asked for your help. How is he?"

"Not good. In a coma. I'm frantic, but what I can do? You know how these boys are. Sitting idle, money coming in, but no real work to do. And these days, heroin is flowing like a river from Afghanistan, Pakistan, straight into their veins. These boys pop balls of afeem in their mouth, and it's like their battery's overcharged. They got it into their head to go there. And when they saw that crowd, everything got out of control."

A rumbling sound filled the air, reminding Madan of the thunderclouds rolling over the fields of Gorapur. Madan turned and saw an Audi sedan drive onto the site, wheels crunching over broken rocks and stones.

"It's my brother, Surjit," Sourav said, sounding panicked. "Damn it."

Sourav's men whipped out their revolvers. Alarmed, Madan thought of his boy in the car. Sourav ignored them and took Madan by the elbow. "You better go." But before he and Madan could move, a large man came barging at them.

"Sisterfucking son of a whore pig!" the man shouted, towering over Sourav. Spittle flew off his mealy lips. His eyes sank in bags of flesh, and his skin was black, scorched and lined as if he'd stuck his head in a tandoor clay oven. The buttons on his shirt strained to keep together.

"Bhai-saab!" Sourav said. "I was on my way to you."

Surjit lifted a meaty palm and smacked Sourav, who tottered and regained his balance. "You did this," Surjit said. "What is this work you gave them? I told you to keep them busy, not to cost me a fucking son."

Surjit's eyes fell on Madan, who was trying to make his way back to the car, to Arnav.

"Which whore's son are you?"

"Bhai-saab, calm down," Sourav pleaded, quickly explaining who Madan was.

"You?" he said. "You're the one?" A fat finger poked Madan in the chest. "Bastard, dressed up like some five-star dandy in your tie and suit. This is how we're to be treated? Like garbage. You think we're here to do your dirty work? You can use us, and then throw us away like we're chewed-up bones. Is that what your father taught you?"

"If there's anything I can do —" Madan said, making to get away from Sourav and his oaf of a brother, and back to his son in the car.

What an idiot Madan had been. A reckless, vengeful idiot. Madan couldn't believe he'd thought Sourav was in any way like him just because they grew up a short distance from each other in kindred towns. Nostalgia had blinded him. Avtaar Singh would never have recruited a gutless ass like Sourav.

"Look at me!" Surjit said. He brought his face close to Madan. The stink of his sour breath made Madan hold his own. "You can't even breathe near me, and you want to do me a favor. What can you do for me? That's my son, my heir, lying in the hospital."

There was no reasoning with the man. Madan's hand itched to pound the bastard's already pudgy face to pulp, but he thought of Arnav. He needed to get back to Arnav. How could he have been so stupid as to bring him here? And, he needed to calm the man. "It was not meant to happen like this," he said.

"Not meant to happen?" Surjit mocked. "I'll go to your house and fuck your wife red, then I'll do your sister. And if you don't have one, I'll fuck your mother. Then I'll say it wasn't meant to happen."

Madan's fist shot out and Surjit staggered backward. Blood spurted from his nose. It was rote instinct. At Sourav's shout, his men came forward to help him. Righting himself, Surjit threw them off. He blew his nose like he was clearing the mucus from a cold, and cleaned his bloodied fingers on his shirt. Madan turned away in disgust. Through the rolled-up window he could see Arnav, up front in the driver's seat.

Surjit followed Madan's gaze. Both men watched for a long moment as Arnav, unaware of what was going on around him, turned the steering wheel of the stationary car left and right, the soft curve of his cheek rising with his smile, his tongue sticking out in concentration, still absorbed in his pretend game of driving the car.

Madan began to make his way back. He was almost at the car when, from the corner of his eye, he saw Surjit grab a revolver from one of Sourav's men and come after him.

"I'll show you hell," Surjit screeched at him. "You think you can cause this mess and walk away? Someone has to pay."

Madan turned to face him. A smear of blood shone greasily on Surjit's chin. Farther back, there was only Sourav and his henchmen, unmoving against the background of construction rubble. Madan looked at the gun pointing to his heart. He tensed, quickly assessing his next move.

The gun swung away from Madan, the aim readjusting to a target behind him.

"Now you'll feel what I feel," Surjit said.

Madan threw himself at the car. He heard the gun discharge.

He felt the whiz of the bullet, and was thankful he was in the way. But he had turned porous, become nothing but air. He landed hard, shattered glass pouring over him.

Madan reached for the car window, debris burning his eyes. He pulled himself up by the door handle, but he couldn't see Arnav. He saw only the splatter of blood dripping slowly onto his outstretched hand.

CHAPTER 19

In an unoccupied hospital room, two somber policemen stood before Madan. He could hear voices and footsteps from the other side of the closed door, and could feel Ketan-bhai's supporting hand on his elbow as he grimly accepted the policeman's condolences. Madan stared blankly at the insignia on the policeman's sleeve. His shirt was stiff with blood where Arnav's head had rested just a short while ago. He had rinsed his hands but they still felt wet and sticky from trying to stanch the blood flowing from his son's chest.

The creak of the ceiling fan slicing through the air caught Madan's attention. When he was four, Arnav had developed a fear of ceiling fans. He believed that if the fan rotated too fast it would spin off the ceiling and whiz through the room, chopping off ears and noses as it flew through the air. "Turn it off, Papa, turn it off!" he would yell, and

Madan would quickly flip the switch. Papa had always saved him.

After the policemen finished with their questions, Ketan-bhai led the senior of the two officers to the corner and handed him a wad of notes "We want to take our child home," Ketan-bhai said. "If the paperwork is completed soon, we'd be thankful."

"We'll be in touch," the lead inspector said with a nod.

"I want those bastards," Madan said abruptly, as if waking from a stupor. The policemen looked alarmed as he moved toward them, blood in his hair, his arms and face scarred from the broken glass. "I want every one of them. I am going to kill —"

"Madan," Ketan-bhai interrupted, laying an arm on his. "The inspector will do all he can." He glanced apologetically at the officer. "You understand that he is very distressed right now, otherwise he never talks like this."

Madan shook Ketan-bhai off him. "Do you know me?" he asked Ketan-bhai. "You don't know me; don't know what I've done or what I am capable of."

"We are all upset," Ketan-bhai said again to the officer.

"We'll open the case and get the warrants going," the inspector assured him.

Madan's hands suddenly were on the man's throat. "No. You don't understand," he shouted. He could hear Sourav's brother's words echoing back at him: *Someone has to pay.* He slammed the inspector's head against the wall. He felt the man's Adam's apple, his struggling breath on his face. He squeezed harder, droplets of spit spraying onto the inspector's face.

"Madan!"

"Someone has to pay, Ketan-bhai," Madan roared, as Ketan-bhai and the other policeman pulled him off.

Ketan-bhai clasped Madan tight. "You are paying," Ketan-bhai said in his ear.

When the light broke though the space between the curtains, Madan had to remind himself that he was in his bedroom. He could hear Preeti through the walls. She was with her mother. Her keening had filled the house throughout the night. When he had returned from the hospital with the news, she had launched at him, her mouth open grotesque and wide, shrieking. Unable to hold her up, he let her crumple to the floor. She had clawed at his shirt, the last vestiges of her child now flakes of blood stuck under her nails.

He forced himself to move his limbs and

get out of bed. Every part of him was a numbing ache. He had been unspeakably reckless. He had thought that all he had created and achieved and built from the ground up made him untouchable and invincible. He had thought his boy would be by his side always. He had been wrong. "Every move has a consequence," Avtaar Singh had told him as they had watched the wrestlers in the pit.

Downstairs everyone was up and about. Nalini was organizing breakfast. Ketan-bhai was on the phone taking care of the final preparations, and Dilip was overseeing the rearrangement of the drawing room, helping to move sofas to the side, laying white sheets over the carpets for the prayers that would go on for the next thirteen days. The pandits would be here soon. Had he agreed to all this, pandits and praying? He couldn't remember.

"Sit and eat something," said Nalini. She pushed him into a chair at the dining table, placing a pile of toast before him. Madan stared at the charred bread and pushed it away. Preeti sat at the other end of the table, her hair a disheveled pile atop her head, wearing the same clothes from the day before. Her eyes followed Madan as he moved around the room.

Her teacup hurtled across the table and grazed his head, breaking into jagged pieces of rosy pink china, cutting his scalp.

"Why did you take him with you? What were you doing there? How could you bring Arnav someplace where there were guns?" she asked. "Always, 'I'll take Arnav. Let Arnav come with me.' Now who'll bring him back to me? Where is he? Where is my son? Bring him back to me. I want my baby back," she howled.

Preeti pulled at her hair, swaying and shouting. Her mother led Preeti back to her room, and Ketan-bhai came in. "She does not know what she is saying," said Ketan-bhai. "She's distraught." Tenderly, he dabbed at the drops of tea and flecks of blood on Madan's cheek with a napkin. "How could you have known?" He placed his hand on Madan's. "Don't blame yourself. It won't change anything and will only make it worse for you and her."

What did Ketan-bhai know about blame and responsibility?

Arnav lay on the drawing room floor on a bamboo stretcher, his body wrapped in thick white cotton cloth brightened by garlands of marigolds. An oil lamp burned nearby, casting flickering shadows on his still form. The pandit murmured a chant, asking Madan to repeat it. Madan almost refused but then found that he didn't have the energy.

At the crematorium, funeral pyres burned in various spots for those sharing this day with them. Madan looked up at the blue sky and the circling carrion birds and at all the faces around him. Faces with eyes that saw and mouths that breathed and hearts that beat, while on a burning bed of sandal-wood his boy went up in a rush of flames.

Tomorrow, they would return to collect the bones and the cooled ashes. In a few days, Madan, Ketan-bhai and Preeti's father would leave for Haridwar. All that Madan had left of his son he would scatter in the Ganges.

Days later, Madan found himself alone in the house. Ketan-bhai and Nalini had finally gone home, returning to their lives. The servants were gone for the day, and Preeti was, he assumed, with her parents. Even when she was in the house, in the days after Arnav's death she moved past Madan as if he were invisible.

Madan retired to Arnav's room. A musty dampness permeated the air. He had drawn all the curtains shut. There was no need for sunlight. His head hurt. Sleep had become an erratic friend.

Since Arnav's death Madan had called Sourav repeatedly, but he had only once answered the phone, saying, "Shit, I'm sorry." From then on, a robotic message informed him that the number was unavailable. Surjit claimed he had been nowhere near Delhi at the time of the shooting. The police had lodged a case and gone to bring him in, but he had filed anticipatory bail and was out free until it was time to come to court. The goons had disappeared, as had the gun, and the police wondered how they could prove the brother's presence in Delhi when there was only Madan's word. The story disappeared from the news.

He opened the drawer of the bedside table and removed his son's old shirt. The stripe pattern was coming through the splotchy bloodstain on the front, which had turned brown. He sat on the bed and studied the variegated lines of the splatter, a familiar rosette of blood. In his boy's bed, his shirt clutched in Madan's arms, he did not notice when he fell asleep.

Pandit Bansi Lal leaned on his cane. Madan peered at him in the dimly lit hallway. Suddenly the pandit thrust his cane aside, shoving his arm under Madan's nose. A baby lay there, cozy and asleep. Pandit Bansi Lal began to hobble away. *Go after him, Madan,* he heard someone shout, *he has Arnav.*

Madan ran but could not catch up, and soon the pandit's figure faded in the distance. Madan spun around; he was in a grove of trees. Again, he saw the pandit's retreating figure and ran after him. *Not that way,* he heard. He twisted and turned in the thicket of swaying trees, trying to decide which clearing to take. In the dusky light, a dhoti-clad figure shuffled away.

He heard laughter and the screech of tires and abruptly the pandit appeared in front of him. Madan raised his hand to grab him, but the pandit was out of his reach. A baby's cry pierced the air. *Don't hurt him,* Madan shouted. Pandit Bansi Lal shimmied before him, sweeping the cloth off the bundle in his arms.

He gave a lopsided grin, presenting the bundle to Madan like a waiter proffering a tray of pastries. Madan leaned in, peering closely.

"Very sorry," said Pandit Bansi Lal.

The baby wasn't Arnav.

Madan's eyes fluttered open to the sound of his voice. He did not start or sit up, but lay calmly in bed, the covers smoothed over

411

him. It was the same strange dream that often disturbed his sleep, though sometimes instead of through the trees he would chase Pandit Bansi Lal over the brown, muddy waters of the canal, the pandit skimming easily away over the water's surface.

"I thought I heard you call for me." Preeti stood silhouetted against the corridor's night-light.

His heart pounded. He shivered.

"Madan?"

He shook his head to clear it, but she thought he was telling her to go and she returned to her room.

Wait, he tried to say, but his mouth was dry, and the plea stayed glued to his tongue.

CHAPTER 20

The landfill was a mountain of white. There was so much garbage that as he drove by, his eyes, unable to distinguish shapes, colors and sizes in the undulating landscape of waste, washed the entire spectrum in a milky bright light. From the cocooned hush of the car, Madan couldn't hear the squawks of the circling buzzards above or the scavenging boys calling to each other as they weaved between the stoic cows determinedly chewing on peaks of trash and lazily taking in the plentiful landscape.

The outskirts of Delhi fell away. Behind him lay the keyhole ramparts of Red Fort and the call of the muezzin from the minarets of Jama Masjid.

There had been no one up when he'd left early that morning, the driveway gravel slick with dew, his breath visible in the crisp air. He hadn't told Preeti where he was going, or that he was going at all. Nor had he told

Ketan-bhai.

Dusty faces peered down at him from the bus windows, villagers and townspeople returning home. On the far side of the road, two plodding elephants with smears of red on their foreheads flapped their ears. Loaded trucks lined the highway.

The car sped north along Grand Trunk Road. Gone was the narrow, two-lane, pot-holed road. With this new highway, it would take him half the time to reach Gorapur than it would have twenty years ago.

Towns and villages appeared and then disappeared in his rearview mirror. He looked for signs heralding his approach to Gorapur, but on either side of the highway massive billboards sprang up relentlessly before his eyes, the artwork in bold colors conveying as much as the written messages:

Dream no more . . . It is here. The City of Tomorrow. Jeet Megacity.
You are thirty kilometers away from Jeet Megacity . . . come see the home of your future generations.
Jeet Megacity . . . A luxurious oasis of peace and prosperity.
Vastu-friendly apartments and villas. World-class facilities.

Live green. Love green. Be green. Dream green. Jeet Megacity.

He forced himself to ignore the signs. He drove straight on, slowing down when the billboards petered out. Water-drenched paddy fields rippled out on either side of the highway, dissolving into swaths of maize, their broad leaves flowering open in supplication to the sun. In the distance, a lookout tower stood in solitary contemplation.

At last a broad, metal sign, GORAPUR WELCOMES YOU, arched across the road. He drove under it, and after a few kilometers the surroundings began to look familiar. The roads crisscrossing the center of town were as before. It was everything that stood around them that had shifted and changed.

Now that he had his bearings, Madan felt the town reaching out, drawing him in. He drove on, the singular action of moving forward taking full possession of him. He knew where to turn, when to cross and where, finally, to stop.

He was at the corner. The road straight ahead led to the main house, and to the left was the turn into the narrower street of the servants' quarters. He parked to one side and got out of the car. A slow-moving bicycle rickshaw trundled past.

He had been twelve when he stood at this corner after having just met Avtaar Singh for the first time. "How old are you, boy?" He could hear that voice boom in his head. "How old are you?"

Very old now, saab.

He couldn't see any obvious changes to the main house. Long and broad, as he remembered it, a row of windows peeking out from behind the pointed tips of the Ashoka trees. The gate was shut. How many times had he driven in and out of it, or stood outside frittering away the time with Jaggu, or stepped out through it to take Prince on his daily walks?

Back in his car, he turned onto the road to the servants' quarters, then got out and walked to the rusted gate. He peeked in. The courtyard was empty. Strokes of a broom scored the dust on the recently swept cement floor, and a puddle of water lay at the base of the water pump. The doors of all three rooms were closed. There was no rope bed outside by the wall.

The middle door swung open and a man emerged, wringing a cloth and wiping his face. He quickly recovered from his surprise at seeing a well-dressed man at the entrance.

"This is the back way," he said, waving his

cloth at Madan. "The front is from the main road."

"I'm looking for Durga," Madan said. "She works in the main house?"

"Durga?" the man repeated.

"This house belongs to Avtaar Singh?" Madan asked, realizing he shouldn't assume that nothing had changed.

The man nodded. "I don't know of a Durga, but I've not been here long." He knocked on the adjoining door and another man came out. They walked to Madan and the first man said, "He's looking for someone called Durga, says she works here."

"Durga?" The man spat a glob of phlegm into the street's drain. "Durga? Oh, yes, a few years ago. She's not here anymore." The men looked at Madan curiously.

"Do you know where she is?"

"No." The man shook his head. "She moved away after her father-in-law died. I heard she went to live with her daughter."

Madan stepped back, surprised. "Gone to live with her daughter? Are you sure we're talking about the same Durga? Her daughter lived with her."

"No." The man was quite firm now. "The daughter would visit but she didn't live here, not since I've been here."

Madan took this in. "Thank you," he said,

and they turned away. Madan took one last look around the barren compound. He was not sure what to do now. "Wait," he said. "Is there a hotel around here?"

"You can check Hotel Emerald," one said. "It opened a few years ago." They gave him directions. "But if you come back next year, there'll be a grand hotel in the new town, in Jeet Megacity."

Startled by the sudden reference to the township he had conceived and created, Madan paused and murmured, "Yes, I saw the billboards . . . on my way here."

"We'll all have to live there soon," said the man. "There'll be nothing left for us here."

Madan drove away slowly, passing by Prem Dhaba still serving customers steaming-hot tea, but a vending cart occupied the tiny square of land on which Bittu's Paan Stand once stood.

He checked into his room, tossing aside his phone full of missed calls from Ketanbhai. Nothing from Preeti. Tired, he lay down, letting all that he had learned sink in. His grandfather, gone. On that last day, had he spoken to his grandfather? Had he paused in all the crying and shouting to light him a beedi or rub down one of his spasms? No, he had not spared the old man a thought.

And what about his mother? He never thought his mother would move away. Hadn't she chosen to stay in Gorapur over him? He would drive to Jaggu's place tomorrow, though he harbored little hope of finding him in the small room he and his mother used to rent. At this rate, he might be back in Delhi sooner than expected.

That evening he walked the main market, noticing the many changes, every recognizable step bringing him to something new and different. He deliberated getting a bite to eat when his eyes fell upon a bright neon sign, SUNRISE GENERAL GOODS.

Sharma-ji's shop. He walked up the two steps to the double glass doors, stepping into the brightly lit store, looking around in amazement. No shelves filled with mismatched foreign foodstuffs lined the walls, and no glass case filled with biscuits and soap ran the length of the once-narrow store. A huge showroom lay before him, goods piled department-store-style in islands, while shoppers browsed in the aisles, baskets in hand. By a far wall, an arrow pointed to the upper floor, LADIES, MENS AND CHILDRENS GARMENTS. Two ladies dressed in spiffily pleated saris helped customers.

"Can I help you, sir?" one of the ladies asked.

"Uh . . . yes." He hesitated. "Is Mr. Sharma here?"

She looked nonplussed and said, "Do you have an appointment?" At the same time a door near the staircase opened. "Oh, wait, here he is," she said, as a young man in jeans and a button-down shirt rushed out holding a sheaf of papers.

"No, that's not —"

But she had already called out, "Mr. Sharma, this gentleman is here to see you."

The young man stopped and came toward them, but Madan was already apologizing. "I'm sorry," he said. "I used to know an elderly man —"

"Oh, you must mean my father."

"Yes," he said, relieved, seeing it all clearly. "I didn't know . . . well, I knew he had children, but I never met you. I remember when this place was a quarter of this size. You are running the store now?"

"Yes, my brother and I took it over. Did you know my father well?"

"Sort of," said Madan, holding out his hand and introducing himself.

"Do you want to say hello to him? He's here in the back office. He still likes to come in when he can."

"Yes," said Madan. "Yes, of course. I hope he'll remember me." He followed the young Mr. Sharma into a hallway behind the stairs.

"We are hoping to expand further," said young Mr. Sharma. "There's going to be a big mall near here soon . . ."

"I heard," Madan said dryly. "In Jeet Megacity."

"We're leasing some space there. We hope to build a chain of Sunrise General Stores. It's an exciting time."

There were a few people in the office, but he brought Madan to the desk where old Sharma-ji sat, a walker by his chair, his wizened face barely visible under the large, square-framed spectacles on his nose.

"Papa," said the younger man. "This gentleman says he used to know you. His name is Madan."

Sharma-ji peered out of his thick glasses. "I don't know any Madan," he barked.

The young man gave a small, embarrassed smile. "His memory tends to come and go."

Madan was about to tell him not to worry and take his leave, but Sharma-ji spoke up again.

"Has he come for his collections? Look in the cash register, under the drawer."

His son looked mystified. "No, Papa, what collections? He knows you."

421

Madan put a hand on the young man's arm to stop him. He went up to the old man. "Sharma-ji, it is me, but I haven't come for any collections today. I came to say hello. And I came to ask you —" Madan was not sure if this would work, but he thought he'd give it a try. "Sharma-ji, do you remember another boy who sometimes was with me . . . Jaggu? Joginder? He would come with me for my collections?"

Mr. Sharma harrumphed. "I don't know any Madan," he said.

Madan straightened up and said to the younger Mr. Sharma, "Well, thank you."

But he wasn't listening. "Do you mean Joginder who runs Manika Multiplex? I've heard people call him Jaggu. Thin chap, very peppy."

"Yes, that sounds like him," said Madan. "Runs Manika Multiplex? That old cinema hall down the road?"

"He owns it," said young Mr. Sharma. "But it still has one screen. He swears it's going to be a two-screen theater soon. At least that's what he's been saying for the last few years."

"Yes," said Madan, smiling, relief and excitement coursing through him. "That would be Jaggu."

Madan walked back past his hotel to

Manika Cinema Hall. *Multiplex,* he corrected himself. He stood in front of the soaring building, wondering where Jaggu would find a space to fit in another screen, sandwiched as it was between a store and a restaurant. On either side of the entrance hung a NOW SHOWING movie poster. Madan recognized the actor Shah Rukh Khan but not the pretty actress.

He walked to the ticket booth. "Is Mr. Joginder in?" he asked.

"No," the ticket man said. "Jaggu-saab has gone home. He'll be back tomorrow."

Madan stood rooted to the spot for a second. "His office is on the second floor," the ticket seller said, indicating Madan should move to make room for the paying customer waiting behind him.

That night he looked out of his hotel room window, and the streets of Gorapur bustled. A tonga pulled by a roughened horse clopped down the road, a crowd of youngsters gathered outside a café. He could make out the BHARAT PETROLEUM sign beaming its yellow and blue light from the end of the road. A flock of pigeons lit out across the sky, landing on the statue planted in the center of the roundabout, children in ragged shorts dodged traffic, cars honked and food carts trundled by, and mottled mutts with their lopsided ears and severed tails curled up before storefronts. The sky was dusky blue. He could have been looking out at a vista of Delhi. Was there no difference between this place and that? Perhaps the only difference all along had been him.

The next morning, Madan waited in the hallway for over an hour. The peon told him that Jaggu-saab was meeting with some distributors and he would have to wait. Madan's gaze traveled down the wall lined with glass-encased posters of upcoming movies. It made sense that this was where Jaggu ended up. Doing something he loved.

"Is Jaggu-saab married?" he asked the peon.

The man nodded. "Three children."

Madan laughed. Jaggu had been busy since he'd last seen him. The man looked offended, thinking Madan had laughed at him. The door opened, spewing out a stream of people. Madan wiped his damp hands on his jeans. What if Jaggu refused to see him?

"Can I see him now?" he asked. The peon went in to check.

"Saab, there's a man outside to meet you," he heard.

Madan leapt up and followed the peon.

Madan saw Jaggu standing by the doorway

of his office, one hand on the doorknob, the other gesticulating in the air. His eyes fell on Madan and widened in horror. Before Madan knew it, he had slammed the door. The slam reverberated through the room.

Madan pounded on the door. "Let me say sorry, Jaggu, let me at least say sorry — to your face."

After a moment the door opened and Jaggu stood there, his face scrunched up, his lips trembling and tears running down his face. He took a deep breath and wiped his face on his sleeve. The peon looked unsure what to do.

"It's okay," Jaggu said to the peon. "He's my friend."

Madan sat in the chair across from his old friend and looked around the office. Old film reels lined the walls, framed posters leaned against the furniture in the room.

"So, you own this place," Madan said.

Jaggu nodded. They sat in silence for a while, Madan waiting for Jaggu to say something, and then Madan finally said, "I should've called you. I thought about it many times. I was never as good a friend to you as you were to me."

Still Jaggu did not say anything, but stared at him. Madan could not keep his eyes off

Jaggu either, taking in the changes wrought on his face, the fine lines etched around his eyes, the deeply grooved laugh lines around his mouth.

"You can't have come back for the heck of it. Just to say sorry to me."

Madan gave a short laugh. "No," he admitted. "But it's a long story. I'm not sure if you want to hear it."

Jaggu fixed his gaze on one of the posters. "No," he agreed. "Not yet."

"I went to the compound," said Madan. "They aren't there."

"No. They moved some time ago."

"Jaggu —"

Jaggu looked at his watch. "How about lunch?" he asked. "Are you free for lunch?"

Relieved that Jaggu was willing to spend time with him, he said, "Yes, yes, anything you say."

They left the cinema hall and walked down to a nearby Chinese restaurant. After they ordered, Jaggu looked directly at him. "Lots of changes?"

"Yes," agreed Madan. "Some better than others — like seeing what you've done, with the cinema hall."

"We'll see how long the cinema lasts for me," said Jaggu.

"What d'you mean?"

"There's this new development, you must've seen the billboards. Jeet Megactiy. It's going to have a modern multitheater complex. I'll be left to show C-grade movies to villagers and old people. The younger generation, they're thrilled with the new opportunities. Now they don't have to be stuck doing the same thing their fathers did. But for the rest of us . . ." Jaggu shrugged philosophically. "Maybe I can begin showing art-house movies."

The sweet-and-sour chicken turned bland on Madan's tongue, the noodles slick and soggy. He stared down at his plate, knowing he would have to say something soon.

Jaggu fiddled with his fork, inclining his head. "He helped me, you know. I started working in the cinema hall right after you left, and then the Marwaris, who owned it, looked to sell. I got a loan from the bank for part of the payment and he gave me the rest. There was not a lot remaining, but one of his men came to the door and handed me an envelope. I had not heard from him since you left. And even then, I never saw him. He never spoke to me or sent me a message. I paid it back in full, though, as soon as I could, even before the bank loan. Went and gave an envelope to Mr. D'Silva at the factory."

427

"Why?" asked Madan. "Why would he do that?"

Jaggu put down his fork. He calmed his fiddling and held Madan's gaze. "Because of you, Madan. It was always because of you."

Jaggu dug into his lunch with gusto, silencing with a quick jab the constant beeping of his cell phone.

"I'm keeping you from your work," said Madan.

Jaggu finished his last bite and pushed his plate away. "What are your plans for the day?" he asked.

Madan had none. He went back to the cinema hall with Jaggu and sat in his office while Jaggu handled the business of the day. In between, he told Jaggu about his other business interests, about Ketan-bhai and their partnership.

"You own factories, a big business," said Jaggu. "It's hard for me to imagine, but you were always good at organizing things, looking at numbers and making them work for you. What about family? You're married?"

"Yes," he said. "I hear you are too."

"Many years now," said Jaggu, smiling. "Any children?"

How to answer a question like that? Yes,

he did have a child. Arnav was and would always be his child. And no, he didn't. Arnav was not here to slip his small hand in his, or to call for his father when he awoke at night. And what about the child who came before Arnav?

Jaggu's sudden look of consternation suggested his last question must have turned his own thoughts to that other child as well. Madan kept his answer as simple as he could. "I had a son," he said. "Arnav. He was nearly nine. There was an accident; we lost him recently."

"Aaah," Jaggu said, shaking head, like the pain was his. "That should never happen to anyone." He paused. "Is that why you're here?"

"Partly," said Madan, and he was grateful that Jaggu didn't press him for more.

At the end of the day, Jaggu, locking the drawers of his desk, said, "Let's get you out of your hotel. You're coming to stay with me."

Jaggu lived in one of the old neighborhoods. Low-slung houses lined the streets, some updated, but the framework remained, each house presenting a veranda and good-sized lawn in front, a short driveway to the side.

They stopped in front of a white gate.

"Madan," said Jaggu. "Give me a minute, let me explain inside."

"Of course." Madan stood by the car as Jaggu walked through the gate and up and across the veranda, disappearing inside the square house. Madan heard voices, and two children ran out to play on the front lawn of the neighboring house.

It was taking Jaggu a long time, and he felt bad for causing Jaggu any problems with his wife. But then the front door of Jaggu's house swung open, and he waved Madan in. Madan climbed the veranda steps, noticing that Jaggu was talking to someone behind the front door. "It's okay," Jaggu said when Madan reached them. A woman stepped out. She looked familiar, yet he could not place her. She held on to to Jaggu's hand, trembling, tears brimming in her eyes, and turned to face Madan.

"Swati?" Madan said.

She looked up at him, and Jaggu said to her, "See, I told you. I told you one day your Madan-bhaiya would come back."

Swati's eyes darted across Madan and back to Jaggu.

"Let's go inside," Jaggu said, breaking the shocked silence.

Madan couldn't hear a thing, like someone had rung a bell near his ear, leaving the sound to reverberate incessantly. He followed them into a spacious living room. A large jhula swung from the ceiling in the corner, and there were low sofas and chairs upholstered in a colorful patterned fabric, and small side tables of handcrafted walnut.

"What should I get?" Swati asked Jaggu, her brow furrowing. "Nimbu pani, Coke, tea?"

"Wait . . . Swati. You live here?" Both of them stared at Madan from the doorway. "What's going on?" he asked.

Jaggu came and put and a hand on his arm, guiding him to one of the sofas. "You are not the only one who can keep a secret," he said.

Swati bent her head shyly. "Are you surprised, bhaiya?" she said, acknowledging him at last. "Jaggu said you'd be surprised. We've been married over fifteen years now."

"Why don't you get us some tea?" Jaggu said, and she nodded and went out.

"She seems . . ." Madan struggled for the word. "Not like how she used to be."

"She has good days and bad days," Jaggu said. "After you left, I missed you so much I spent a lot of time at the compound. I started taking her out, to cheer her up, to distract her. She asked about you constantly. Took her to lots of movies, especially since I

431

worked there. We saw a show together nearly every day. They were singing about love on the screen and we found love sitting in the balcony section. As soon as I could . . ." He tapped a picture on the side table, Swati dressed in a red and gold lehenga, he in a cream kurta, garlands of flowers hanging from their necks.

Madan shook his head in wonder. "My mother?"

"She lives here. She has a room in the back, that's how she likes it. She retired a few years ago. She's at the temple for the evening aarti. She'll be back soon."

"Has she . . . is she still angry?"

"Who knows? You know it's hard to tell what your mother's feeling."

"But she must be happy about you and Swati."

"Oh, yes," Jaggu said, grinning. "I can do no wrong."

There was a commotion, and Swati came in, followed by a boy and a girl. She placed the tray on a table. "This is your Madan-mamu," Jaggu said. "He's come to see us after a long time." The girl hid behind Swati, but the boy looked boldly at Madan.

"This one's Nima," said Jaggu, pulling the girl forward. "She's six. And that one" — he nodded toward the boy — "is Vikas. He's eleven, our oldest. Say hello to your mamu." They both murmured something and the maid came in with a two-year-old riding on her hip. "And the baby is Vipul."

Madan sat back, confounded. He had missed so much.

"When I was at the market," he said to no one in particular, "I saw that Sunrise General has a whole toy section now." Vikas, playing with a fighter jet, stopped, trying not to show his increasing interest. Madan hid his grin. "Tomorrow, that's where we'll go after school," he said to Swati.

"They have enough toys, bhaiya," she said. She looked worriedly at Jaggu, and he gave her hand a squeeze and she relaxed.

"She's right," Jaggu said. "I'm always saying there are too many toys in this house."

"No, I insist. No matter what your parents say," he said to Vikas directly. Vikas couldn't stop the smile that broke across his face. How Arnav would have loved having an older cousin, Madan thought.

He heard movement in the hallway and everyone stopped talking. He knew who it was.

Her hair was more white than gray and she stooped a little. She was heavier.

"Ma," he said, and then he choked. "Ma." She shuffled slowly toward him. Nima bounced on the sofa, the thumps and creaks of the cushion springs filling the room. Swati caught her, stopping her mid-jump.

Madan's mother put her hand to her chest. It looked like she was going to collapse in a heap, and Jaggu rushed to her side, clutching her arm, trying to make her sit in a chair.

"Jaggu," Madan's mother said, leaning on him but refusing to sit down, "is that your friend?"

"It's your son, Ma," Jaggu said.

She pushed Jaggu away, pulling her sari tighter around her shoulders. Her befuddlement cleared, replaced by the cold intensity of nothingness. "I have no son," she said to Jaggu.

Swati began to sob and say, "Don't say that, Ma. Don't say that. It's Madan-bhaiya."

"My poor girl, still so simple. When will you learn? If you had a brother, he would never have neglected his duty to you, or to his mother. He wouldn't have been so foolish as to see beyond his status, never would have thought himself so high and mighty that he could follow the stars in his eyes and put us all in jeopardy. And you . . ." She twisted back to Jaggu. "It's your business if you bring people from the street into the house, but either he goes or I go."

"It's my house," Jaggu said.

"You're right," she said, and they watched her stiffened back retreat out the door, Nima trailing after her grandmother and asking for a snack.

That night, Madan finally returned Ketan-bhai's calls, the rising and rolling hum of Jaggu's argument with Madan's mother vibrating through the walls. His mother had threatened to return to the temple, spend the night in the streets if she had to, but Jaggu firmly and unequivocally had insisted that no one was going anywhere. "We are all finally together," he said. "For now, no one is leaving this house." Madan stayed in his room, grateful for Jaggu's unfaltering hospitality.

Ketan-bhai answered at the first ring, shouting into the handset, "Where the hell are you?" Not waiting for a reply, he continued, "Going off like that? What's wrong with you?"

"I had to leave for a few days."

"Tell me where you are. I'll come get you."

"I'm not in Delhi," he said. "I have something to attend to."

There was silence on the other end. "Madan," Ketan-bhai said at last. "To disappear like this on Preeti? To leave her, after Arnav? Madan, there is only so much she can take."

"I know," he said. "I need a little time to sort out a few things."

"I've said what I want to say. When can we expect you back?" When Madan was noncommittal, he hung up with a long, resigned sigh, saying, "Call her."

Madan tried to call Preeti but she didn't answer.

When he woke the next morning, the sky was bright, and outside on the lawns there were women everywhere. Squatting, sitting cross-legged, standing, the ends of their saris covering their heads or tucked into their sides. And from what he could make out, they were all sewing. Cloth of different shapes, sizes and colors lay strewn around, bits of thread hanging off everything, measuring tapes and chalk littering the ground. His mother sat on a wicker chair in one corner of the veranda.

"What's going on?" he asked.

"It's what she does," said his mother, nodding toward Swati, barely visible in the milieu of women, giving orders and instructions. His mother's pinched expression and the hostility of her tone and carriage made it clear that she was anwering him unwillingly. She removed a package wrapped in plastic from a pile next to her and tossed it to him. Inside, he could make out a cream-colored table mat set, beautifully embroidered with a red paisley pattern. On the outer package, a green sticker with a flower logo in the corner read *Gorapur Mahila Co-operative.*

"They're from the slums around town or they're farm laborers' wives," his mother said, sticking to the matter at hand. "She teaches them to sew and embroider. They make all sorts of things: tea-cozy sets, table mats, tablecloths, bedding sets, quilts. They sell them at the tourist rest stops and home stores. One lady from Delhi buys a lot and sells them in her boutique." She paused as the maid brought Madan his tea. "Swati sets a quota for them to complete every month and what profit they make is divided equally among all the women in the cooperative. It supplements their income, helps feed the children when the men have drunk away the money, and helps send their children to school."

"How did it happen, Ma?"

His mother's voice thickened. "We didn't stop living because you decided you didn't want anything to do with us."

"I didn't mean that —"

But she held up her hand to stop him. "I have put a stone on my heart all these years not knowing if you are alive or dead, and now you reappear like you just went out for lunch."

"You talk as if it was all my doing," he said. Had she forgotten the choice she had made, how she'd cast him off with her piercing denouncement? "I asked you to come with me. I could have taken care of you both."

He stood in anger as if to leave, but his mother said, "Sit. Jaggu told me a little about what happened to you, with your son."

Madan noticed Swati glance at them, her smile faltering, and he took a seat. They both watched her move through the throng of women. She still walked with an odd, rolling gait.

Madan said, "You were telling me about her."

"Something in her snapped back after you left. She kept waiting for you to reappear, kept asking for you. It brought her out of the trance she was in."

"I can't believe Jaggu is my brother-in-law. How could I have missed that?"

"I didn't think much of all their meetings

at first. I thought it was good for both of them. Then all of a sudden he's saying he wants to marry her. You can't miss your friend that much, I said to him. I mean, Swati has her problems; they never went away. But he got help for her. It took many years, but he didn't give up.

"Your bapu was a difficult man, but he was my husband. There's always someone we can't imagine our lives without. I feared that man alive, and I feared what would happen when he was dead. And it terrified me more than anything that you had no such confusion."

"Ma —"

"I know why. You had Avtaar Singh. You recognized something in Avtaar Singh's soul, a kindness, a gentleness, that no one else could see. And this connection bound you both, leaving all of us out." Her gaze bore into Madan. "Avtaar Singh never spoke of you. Never asked if we had seen or heard from you. Acted like you were never there. Like you never walked with him, or stood with him, or lived for him."

Madan watched the tea leaves swirl a slow and sleepy dance to the bottom of his teacup. "For him, the dead are better left that way," he said.

Chapter 21

"Bhaiya, do you have any pictures?" Swati asked. They were sitting on the veranda later that afternoon, after the trip to the toy store that Madan had insisted on. Her children were running around them, toy airplane and dolls in hand.

It hadn't occurred to him to bring photos along. He was not sure where the photo albums were anyway; Preeti handled the picture-taking and cataloging. He was about to shake his head, but in a burst of inspiration reached in his jeans and took out his cell phone. "Maybe . . ." he said, pressing buttons, scrolling through the options. "There may be something in here. Let me check."

He had not gone through the pictures in his phone for some time. The screen blinked as the photos changed, and then it blinked again and Arnav stared back at him. Madan still couldn't look without that excruciating stab to his heart.

He had taken Arnav to the children's play area at the City Club. Preeti had insisted they become members, but the only part of the club Madan ever visited was the playground. While Madan was on the phone, Arnav had run from swing to merry-go-round, and finally at the slide he said, "Look, Papa, look at me!"

He had been at the top of the slide, arms triumphantly up in the air, when Madan had snapped the first shot. The next picture of Arnav's was of him at the bottom of the slide, rosy cheeks flushed with energy and excitement.

Madan handed the phone to Swati. "This is —" It was hard to say his name. "This is Arnav."

She took the phone and turned it toward the light, his mother peering over her shoulder. Swati scrolled backward and forward. Arnav at the top of the slide, Arnav at the bottom. "Bhaiya," she said. "He looks like you."

Jaggu came around and looked over Swati's shoulder as well. Quiet tears ran down Madan's mother's face and she dabbed her eyes with her sari. Swati scrolled down further.

"The others are from work," Madan said,

but she angled the phone to him.

"Is this . . . ?" she asked, holding the screen up so he could see.

It was a picture of Preeti, from the shoulders up. Madan was sure he hadn't taken it. She was dressed in a glittering outfit, the kind she used to wear when they went out for the evening. Now their lives were all "before" and "after."

He nodded. "That's Preeti. My wife."

"She's beautiful," Swati said. His mother took the phone and examined the picture of her daughter-in-law.

"Why didn't she come with you?" Her eyes were dry now, her voice back to its strong and sharp tenor.

"I wasn't sure what I would find here, if there was anyone still around." He left it at that, but his mother seemed dissatisfied with the explanation. "So," she said, "why did you come back?"

"Ma!" reproved Swati.

"No, no. It's all right," Madan said. "But first, there is something else I need to tell you all." He was going to say it straight, but yet he took a moment to bolster his resolve. "The new township, Jeet Megacity . . ." He turned to Jaggu. "I'm responsible for the project. I have a major stake in it."

They stared back at him, as if he had

shouted at the top of his voice but they had not heard.

"Jeet Megacity is your doing?" asked Jaggu.

Madan nodded. "Mine and a number of other people's."

"You fucker," said Jaggu, forgetting about the presence of his wife and mother-in-law in his astonishment.

"What's he talking about?" Ma asked. "That place you took us to see, Jaggu? With the tall buildings and those workers?"

"Jaggu took us for a drive around there," Swati said. "Everyone is talking about it, so we wanted to see it for ourselves."

"I haven't seen it," said Madan to his stunned audience. "The opening ceremony was due to take place soon. I had planned to come then."

"Back in Delhi, my family and friends — they know nothing of you and of my life here. I've told them nothing," he admitted.

"What?" Jaggu exclaimed.

As the last of the sun's rays faded and people retreated into their homes, drew their curtains, turned down their lamps and tuned to the night's news on their televisions, Madan talked without disruption. Even if they wanted to interrupt, they did not know what to say.

When he wound down, Swati said softly, "I wish we could have met him. I wish we could have seen Arnav."

Madan glanced at his mother. She was quiet, listening carefully, but not showing any reaction. "You've not finished," she said.

Jaggu and Swati turned to him again. "No," Madan said. "I need to tell you the real reason I'm here. The other reason. I wanted so much to see you all again. But there's something else. Since my son, there's something I keep thinking about." He hadn't fully known that that was what he was after in Gorapur until he heard himself say the words.

"You don't know of this, but on the morning of the day I left Karnal, I ran into Pandit Bansi Lal at the hospital. He had the baby in his arms." He did not pause for long because he could see they were anxious for him to continue. "Do you ever wonder what happened to the baby?" When no one answered, he continued, "I want to know. I want to find out what happened to him or her."

His mother looked stunned. "You came back for this?" She stood up, vibrating with anger. "You need to go back to your wife and get on with life. How long are you going to hang on to the past? What is the use of uncovering all that mess? Didn't it cause us enough trouble the first time around?"

She shuffled away, and Swati went after her. Jaggu glanced uncomfortably at him.

"You really want to do this? Look for this child?" Jaggu asked.

"I know now that I have to, Jaggu."

"Then I'll help you," his friend answered, ready at Madan's side, as always.

Madan's plan had been to go first to the old pandit in search of the baby he had taken, but Jaggu explained that Pandit Bansi Lal had died some years before. There had been only a handful of people who knew about the baby. If Pandit Bansi Lal was not around, who else would be able to give him information? Was this other child lost forever too? Madan considered his options. No, he realized. There was someone else he could try.

In the car the next day, Madan looked out the window at the blurring landscape. Jaggu had easily tracked down Neha's address. Her husband owned a string of petrol stations along the highway, and was well known in the Ambala area. He listened as Jaggu told him about Neha's wedding, which had taken place shortly after Madan left.

"You should've seen Gorapur," said Jaggu, "it was like the President was coming to visit. Trilok-bhai spared no expense. I guess he had to prove something to the world, and himself, that his money could still get him what he wanted." Jaggu gave a cynical snort. "Pandit Bansi Lal did the ceremony, can you imagine? What were they all thinking while Neha walked around the fire?

"We never went anywhere near it, not your mother or me, but for the rest of the town it was a good time. When it was Rimpy and Dimpy's turn to get married, Avtaar Singh, of course, outdid his old friend, and we went around holding our full stomachs for days."

Hearing the names of the two constant companions of his childhood startled Madan. While everyone else had crossed his mind at some point, he had not thought about Rimpy and Dimpy in years. "Where are they?" he asked.

"Dimpy lives nearby, in Chandigarh. Her husband is the regional bank manager of some American chain of banks. Rimpy got married right after Neha, to an investment banker. They settled in Singapore."

"They're not together?" Madan asked. "They live so far away from each other?"

Jaggu nodded. "It was never the same

between them after that Karva Chauth evening. I think Dimpy never understood why Rimpy spoke up like that and behaved the way she did." He sighed. "I see her sometimes — Dimpy. She comes with her family to see a movie. I make sure she gets the VIP box. She always stops to say hello and to ask about Ma and Swati."

A herd of bleating goats circled their car. They were passing through a town no bigger than a thumbprint, the traffic choking the main road slowing them to a crawl. Everyone honked, yet no one moved. The goatherd swung his stick at his confused animals as they trotted away, swarming around lorries, horse carts and motorcycles. Jaggu inched the car forward into the emptied space, bursting free at the end of the thoroughfare.

"How strange," said Madan, "that Rimpy, Dimpy, you, Ma, even Preeti, all your lives, changed because of me. Do you remember me then, Jaggu, at that time, at that age?"

"That's the Madan I do remember," said Jaggu. "This new Madan is the one I have to get used to."

Madan let a small smile escape. "I was a simple boy."

"You were an atom bomb," said Jaggu, not unkindly.

"Are you still angry with me?"

Jaggu took a moment to answer. "No," he said. "I can't be. You're the one still hurting. The only one still in pain."

They found the house easily. High gates corralled large houses all the way down to the end.

Madan sat in the car and looked up at number 22. Jaggu took a swig of water from the plastic bottle at his side. He didn't utter a word. Madan continued to sit, looking up at the house.

"I'll wait here," said Jaggu after a while.

Madan nodded, wiping his palms on his jeans. "I don't know what to say," he finally admitted.

Jaggu put a hand on his arm. "Remember why you're here. If Neha has any information, something we can use, you need to know. Keep that in mind."

Jaggu was right. Finding his child was the most important thing right now. He walked down a short path with green lawn on either side.

He had barely stepped up to knock on the door when the gate opened. A sleek gray sedan rolled up beside Jaggu's car. Two girls and a boy tumbled out, tall and gangly in their teenage awkwardness, swinging their backpacks playfully at each other. They looked to be no more than sixteen.

Madan watched as their mother emerged from the car, hands full of books and lunch boxes. Her hair was untied and long, straight and thick as he remembered it. She flipped her head back, adjusting the dupatta around her shoulders. She looked up, her gaze following her children's to Madan on her doorstep.

Her arms gave way. The servant girl ran to pick up the books and pencils and pens on the ground. She ignored her, nearly stepping on her as she walked toward the front.

The lines on her face mirrored his. She was not the same girl who had met him when night fell on those mountain peaks so high they speared the clouds in the sky. Age, children, time, had thickened her middle and her arms. The salwar stretched across her, too tight in some places. Her face was heavy, but her eyes . . . her eyes, he saw, still glinted with copper.

"Neha," he said. The children started at the sound of their mother's name, so intimately whispered from the mouth of this strange man. No *Mrs. so and so*. He couldn't even remember what Jaggu said was her married name. "I have to talk to you."

Three pairs of inquisitive eyes swung to their mother.

She snapped at the children, suddenly aware of their presence. "Go inside," she ordered. They turned, filing reluctantly away, her tone forbidding argument.

"You haven't changed much," she said when they were gone. "You look older, of course, a little gray here." She touched her own temples to indicate. "But otherwise . . ."

He looked away from her self-consciously.

She looked down at her hands, the skin swollen around her diamond rings. "Are you married?" she asked.

"Yes."

"Children?"

He paused, that tricky question again. For now, he settled on saying, "No."

"I heard you got married . . . soon after," he said.

"My father didn't let me continue with college. There was no more fight left in me. I decided to make do with what I had," she said. "But I don't understand. Why are you here?"

"Talking about children —" he said.

"Oh!" Her hand flew to her mouth.

"Neha." He spoke fast. "My life has gone in so many different directions, it's impossible to untangle most of them. But there is one thing I have to settle before I can go on with my life; one thing I've realized I have to know is . . . about . . ."

"You can't be serious."

"When I said I didn't have any children, I meant that I have none I know of. I had a son. I lost him in an accident recently. It made me rethink everything in my life. It made me think . . . it made me want to know about . . . about our child."

She gave a sharp cry, looking around as though someone may have heard him.

"I don't want to cause any trouble," he said. "I came to see if you have any idea, if you can give me any information about what happened. That's all I want, and then I'll go away. You'll never see me again. I promise."

She didn't answer, kept shaking her head.

"Neha, haven't you ever wondered? Haven't you ever thought?"

"I never even saw the baby," she said. "They took it right away. I asked, but both my mother and father refused. My mother said it's better that way. I'm sorry." Her gaze softened as she looked into the distance. "I made myself forget. It was the hardest thing I ever had to do."

Forget me or forget what we made together?

451

The query darted in his mind, but at the same time, as if to calm his thoughts, he realized her response did not matter. It had ceased to matter a long time ago. Their fleeting storm of passion had shattered with the first assault, and would never have lasted beyond the artless summers of their youth. If not for this child, he would have gone on with his life, never needing to seek her out.

He had wished differently for her, he realized as she walked him back to the car, the sound of her children babbling through an open window. When he thought of her, he'd always imagined that she'd found a way out. That she'd fled into the rest of her life, and was somewhere protesting environmental catastrophes, fighting for farmers' rights, against police brutality and misogynistic edicts. He'd hoped she was leading the charge, penning manifestos. He thought she would have found a way to live by no one's dictates but her own. But she was right here, not far from where he'd left her. Life had twisted them around since they had parted. They were both destined to live with their regrets. Or perhaps this was always how it was going to turn out. Perhaps there was less fight in her than he'd thought.

Jaggu got out of the car as they approached. "Is that your old friend?" she asked.

"Yes, it's Jaggu."

Acknowledging Jaggu's greeting, she turned to Madan. "You were always lucky in the people who loved you." She stood close now, not as aloof, more friendly, her eyes lost in her sad smile.

"Yes," he agreed. His thoughts flew to Preeti, Ketan-bhai. "I still am," he said.

CHAPTER 22

They rode home in silence, and when they got back to the house it was dark. A car sat in Jaggu and Swati's driveway, a black SUV. "Who could that be?" Jaggu asked. Madan was silent, though he felt he already knew. When they pulled up, a man got out of the front passenger side. "Saab wants to see you," the man said to Madan.

"No," Jaggu said. "Tell your saab he won't come —"

"Jaggu," Madan said. "It's all right."

"But you can't —"

"You've spent enough of your life worrying about me." He embraced Jaggu and, keeping his voice low and even-keeled said, "I knew I couldn't come back without the news reaching him." Before Jaggu could protest, he got in the waiting car.

As they drove away, he kept his gaze out the window at the houses flying past. They drove through town, and presently Madan noticed they were not heading toward the timber factory as he had expected. He began to pay more attention to the scenery. Somnolent fields glowed in the moonlight behind the town, and the car lurched over potholes before joining a smoother roadway. Madan's stomach turned as he realized the direction of their journey. The car picked up speed on the deserted highway, and twenty minutes later he was standing at the entrance to Jeet Megacity.

Security guards manned the barricades at the entrance, and barbed wire surrounded the development. Floodlights blazed from above, spotlighting the temporary barracks that ringed a large dirt lot and housed the offices of the project managers. The guards watched him step out of the car and look around. This was a strange place to bring him. What could they do to him here?

He waited for one of the men to say something, tell him what to do. The driver was on a cell phone, and, clicking the phone shut, he told Madan to look back.

A long sedan maneuvered in behind them. The driver jumped out and opened the back passenger door.

Madan held still. Avtaar Singh emerged from the car, a walking stick in his hand.

Madan took a few automatic steps toward

him, and then stopped. If Avtaar Singh wanted to talk to him, he would have to come to Madan.

Avtaar Singh dug the end of the cane into the dust, grasped the molded silver handle and adjusted the shawl draped lightly over his shoulders. He straightened up and looked around. Avtaar Singh didn't hesitate. He made his way to Madan, the high-pitched buzzing of the floodlights drowning out the scrape of his cane on the dusty ground. There were the usual markers of time on his face, his jowls looser, his dark eyes cocooned deeper into the folds of skin, his thick hair and mustache turned ashy white, but the confidence of his lean, trim bearing remained untouched by the years. The gleaming wooden cane, it seemed, was no more than a stylish accessory.

At Madan's side, he extended his hand. But Madan didn't reciprocate, and Avtaar Singh let his hand drop. Together they turned and regarded Jeet Megacity, bright and pulsating like a giant interloping space-ship, the creak and groan of timber and steel drowning out what they could have said or what they wanted to say.

"Is it you who is responsible for this monstrosity?" The cane twirled a depression into the ground. "If you wanted to kill me, there were easier ways. But I should have known. No one else could do this."

The guards talked into their radios and kept a watchful eye. Madan wondered how Avtaar Singh had found out. Had the news of Madan's arrival juxtaposed two opposing thoughts and jolted Avtaar Singh into making an accurate guess? Standing next to Avtaar Singh, he was finding it impossible to get a fix on his own thoughts.

"You know who this is?" Avtaar Singh said to his men standing a few feet away.

They regarded Madan without interest.

"He is a son of Gorapur, you useless sons of bitches," he shouted. "And see what he has done —" Avtaar Singh swept his cane up and around to encompass the whole city, his shawl slipping off his shoulders and into the dust. "See what he has done to you, to Gorapur and to . . . me."

The squealing of the walkie-talkies filled the quiet following Avtaar Singh's outburst. No one moved. "You have nothing to say to me?" Avtaar Singh huffed.

Madan bent down and picked up the shawl, his earlier dread and anxiety dissolved into numbness. Anything this bickering, aging man said no longer had the power to scare or cow him. He shook out the shawl and folded it into a neat square. Taking

Avtaar Singh by the elbow, he guided him back to the car. Avtaar Sigh sank down into the seat with relief, jerking his arm out of Madan's grasp.

"Gorapur is not my home," Madan said. "You took that away from me."

Avtaar Singh's knuckles gleamed white against the dark polished wood of his cane. He stared straight ahead to the cranes and bulldozers parked alongside the road.

"Get in," he said finally to Madan.

The guards looked relieved when they saw the cars pull out. In the backseat with Avtaar Singh, Madan watched as Jeet Megacity dimmed to a point as they drove away.

"This may not be your home, but it is mine," said Avtaar Singh. He fidgeted with the cane resting between his legs and, seeming bothered by it, tapped the shoulder of the man in front. When he turned around, Madan realized it was the man who had been rallying the farmers in the cell phone clip. Avtaar Singh passed his cane to the man, and sat back comfortably.

"We can't stop progress," said Avtaar Singh. "The whole country is in a rush. They're not waiting for this century to finish, they're already propelling us into the next. I myself have had to diversify. Can't count on these boys anymore," he said about the men in front. "They want to be waiters in the fancy hotel and photocopy boys in big offices. Idiots, all of them."

He scrutinized Madan, as if compelling him to speak or offer some rebuttal. When Madan didn't, Avtaar Singh charged on. "I may not like the changes, but I understand. . This will be the new Gorapur. A reincarnation, a rebirth. You have your money and your reputation on the line, and as you know, I can make things easy, or I can make them difficult."

A week ago, if a massive flood had swept over Jeet Megacity, wiping it off the face of the earth, Madan, bereft of spirit and strength, would not have cared. With Arnav gone, he'd found it hard to understand how the whole world could go on, yet Jeet Megacity had forged ahead unfaltering.

Avtaar Singh could sit here and choose to forget how he'd betrayed the promises he had made, spoken and unspoken. He could forget how he had repaid Madan's devotion with his blood-thirsty demands. Avtaar Singh could forget. Madan could not. He thought he'd lost the will to go on, but he vibrated now with a rare possessiveness at the thought of this man getting anywhere near Jeet Megacity.

"No," Madan said. "I'll never allow it."

"It seems you haven't changed that much," said Avtaar Singh. "Still as stubborn as ever. How it irritated Pandit Bansi Lal. He said you were spiteful, difficult, but I knew it was merely your firmness of mind. When you knew what you wanted, nothing would deter you.

"But you must remember how Pandit-ji thrived in his discourses?" Avtaar Singh rolled along with his memories, taking everyone in the car with him. "He was very fond of the story of King Hiranyakashipu. Have you boys heard it?" There were some noncommittal noises from up front. "In his quest to become invincible, the king prayed and sacrificed to Lord Brahma, and was granted a boon that he could not be killed indoors or outdoors, at daytime or night, neither on the ground nor in the sky, nor by human being or animal."

The boon had indeed made the tyrannical king undefeatable, but when the time came, his nemesis, Lord Vishnu, took the form of half lion, half man and, by placing Hiranyakashipu on his lap so he was not on the ground or in the sky, struck the fatal blow in that in-between time of twilight, when it was not day or night, in the courtyard of his palace so they were neither indoors nor out, thus circumventing the parameters of the boon.

"You think you've covered all the possible angles, shielded yourself from every possibility, made sure you're unbeatable." Avtaar Singh laughed derisively. "But there is always that one small opening, one possibility you haven't considered, and in that unguarded space the dagger darts in and slays you."

The car came to a stop outside Jaggu's home. He clicked the door open, eager to put some distance between himself and Avtaar Singh.

"I took a tour of Jeet Megacity a short while ago," Avtaar Singh said as Madan exited. "Actually, it is truly stunning."

Madan stood flabbergasted at the gate as the car skidded away. Avtaar Singh had seen Jeet Megacity, walked up and down, admired every corner, when Madan had not even entered the place yet.

His immediate instinct was to run behind the car and flag it down. He wanted to hear more. Soak up what Avtaar Singh had seen as he gazed up at the tall towers; bask in his impressions as he considered the land, altered beyond recognition. Madan gave himself a mental shake, and wondered how Avtaar Singh had gained access to Jeet

461

Megacity. Regardless of all the safeguards and barriers he'd put up, Avtaar Singh had found a way in.

"Are you okay?" Jaggu hurriedly undid the latch of the gate. "What did he want?"

"What he always wants," Madan said, re-assuring Jaggu that he was fine. "More than he deserves."

"Forget him for now," Jaggu said. "I thought of someone who might know something about the baby."

Kasturba Gandhi Hope and Healing Center was a boxy building with high walls as long as its name. Jaggu turned into a parking spot near the entry gate. They were going to see Feroze, Avtaar Singh's old goon with the eyes that missed nothing. Feroze, whose name was known to every prostitute at Champa's and who had arranged the same for Jaggu and Madan that first time. Feroze, thought Madan soberly, who had beat him up and left him for dead.

"Because if Pandit Bansi Lal needed help getting the child out of Karnal," Jaggu had explained, "he would have asked someone he knew, who would do it for money but keep his mouth shut. That's Feroze. I've seen him off and on over the years, we've greeted each other from afar. But I heard recently that he's moved into an ashram."

"He's found God?" Madan had asked, disbelieving

"No, not that sort of ashram. It's the type of place you go when you're sick and you have no one. They give you a bed and take care of you until the end."

In the car all the way to the ashram, they'd tried to recall Feroze's last name, but it did not come to them.

"More than his name, first we'll have to see if he's alive," Jaggu had pointed out when they arrived.

They walked now into the deserted foyer, where informational posters on AIDS and hepatitis B lined the walls. There was no one by the desk in the corner, and they walked through to the central courtyard, visible on the other side of the inner doors.

Outside, people in white kurtas milled about, some playing a game of cards under the shade of a large tree. Madan and Jaggu spotted a nurse standing off to the side. "Excuse me," Madan said, "we're looking for a friend of ours, Feroze —"

Before he'd completed his sentence, she bellowed out, "Feroze, visitors!"

Jaggu and Madan's gazes snapped in the direction she had shouted. A man sitting cross-legged on a cane chair, a newspaper in his lap, looked up at her call. Slowly he uncrossed his legs and stood up. His skeletal face peered vacantly ahead as he shambled toward them.

Madan and Jaggu met him halfway. "Jaggu?" he said, his pale eyes cloudier with age.

"Feroze!" Jaggu embraced him eagerly, caught up in the relief of finding him.

Feroze began to cough, and Jaggu stepped back. "Sorry," Jaggu said.

"No, no it's okay." Feroze waved his hand. "I've become too fragile, as you can see." He studied Madan curiously, but said to Jaggu, "How come you remembered me after such a long time? I used to see you running in and out of your cinema. You forgot your old friend then, ha?"

Jaggu fidgeted uncomfortably and moved back, nearly stepping into Madan. "We've come for some information," Jaggu said.

Again Feroze peered unsurely at Madan, trying to place him.

"Okay," said Feroze. "Let's go to my room. This is the first time anyone has come to see me."

They followed him to a small room in the east wing of the building. A metal bed, a cupboard and a wooden writing desk and chair were the few fixtures in the sparely furnished room. Madan pulled out the chair and Jaggu and Feroze sat on the bed.

"Nice place," said Jaggu, looking around.

Feroze laughed bitterly. "Yes," he said. "It's the fucking Oberoi Hotel. So what do you want?"

"You still haven't recognized him, have you?" asked Jaggu.

"Who?" Feroze said. "Your friend?" He turned to look at Madan again.

"My very good friend," Jaggu affirmed. "From many years ago, when we all used to roam the streets together. He was our leader, though you fancied that you were."

But Feroze wasn't listening. "No," he whispered in disbelief, leaning forward, looking closely at Madan.

"Hello, Feroze," said Madan. Feroze fell back as though Madan had hit him. "Don't worry, I'm not here for revenge. I need to know something."

"Madan," Feroze squeaked out. "Madan, Madan, Madan. You're harder to get rid of than this disease that's eating me alive." He shook his head, incredulous. "I can't believe I'm here to see this."

He leaned toward Madan again as if to ascertain Madan's undeniable presence. "When you turned up alive in Karnal, I got into so much trouble. I thought those were my last days. Now I wish they were." He dabbed the beads of sweat on his upper lip with his kurta sleeve. "Sorry," he said, "with this sickness my body temperature goes up and down." He took in a ragged breath, but couldn't seem to stop talking.

"When we got back to Gorapur, Pandit-ji was going on about your appearance in the hospital, your clothes all dirty and torn, like a tramp off the streets. 'But where is he?' Avtaar Singh kept asking like a child. 'Why didn't you bring him to me?' We didn't know what to tell him. All we could say is, you ran off. Suddenly Avtaar Singh got up and walked out. Like he'd had enough. He just went. Left us both in the office with our mouths open. And no one saw him for a few weeks after that. Sick, Minnu memsaab said. Can you believe it?" He shook his head, knowing only they would understand the improbability of this. "Even a cold first asks permission from Avtaar Singh to visit him. When has Avtaar Singh ever been sick?

"But maybe he was sick," Feroze reconsidered. "After he came back, it was like he'd become an old man. He would forget things; he would look at you but not see you. With you gone, everything changed with him. We'd come to his office in the evening, but he never talked and debated like before.

466

Soon he only called us for work, and that too didn't have the same masala. Just business-type work. My shiv was used solely to peel apples."

Madan felt Jaggu's worried gaze on him, but he kept his face blank. He ignored the roiling beginning inside him, brought on by Feroze's accounts, and forced himself to concentrate on Feroze, who enjoyed having an audience.

"Pandit Bansi Lal did manage to take his cane to me, though, but that was nothing compared to what I was expecting. And here you are again. Why?"

Jaggu and Madan looked at each other. Would they really get a name, an address, an actual spot on the map of the world?

"I saw Pandit Bansi Lal in Karnal the day I disappeared," Madan said. "Did you by any chance — were you helping Pandit Bansi Lal that day? Did you know anything? About a baby?"

Feroze smiled. "I had a feeling my long memory would pay off someday. How, I was not sure, but I had a feeling."

Jaggu put his head in his hands and gave a frustrated roar. Madan almost mimicked him.

"You know something?" asked Madan.

"What do you want?" asked Jaggu. "We'll

467

give you anything."

Feroze pursed his thin lips. "Look," he said. "I may live a year, maybe two, but not longer than that, I'm told." He paused, and, when he saw no sympathy forthcoming, went on. "Sometimes families of people who are here, they make a donation for a better room, one with a TV." He pointed to the floors above.

"You want us to get you a better room?" asked Madan.

Feroze nodded. "You look like you can."

"Feroze, Feroze, Feroze," said Jaggu, imitating him from a short while ago. "You tried to kill this man, beat him and left him for dead. I think you owe him, rather than the other way round."

Feroze refused to meet their eyes, saying stubbornly, "I want a better room."

Madan and Jaggu stepped outside his room to talk. "He did try to kill me," Madan whispered.

"Yes," agreed Jaggu. "On the other hand, if he has any bit of information —"

"I know," Madan said. "Good thing I brought my checkbook."

An hour later Madan signed the final papers in the accounting office, and they helped Feroze move his few things to his new room. It was a better room; there was a rug on the floor and a tray with a jug of water on the table and, of course, the TV. Feroze was ecstatic.

Jaggu scowled at him. "Your information better be good," he said, irritated that Feroze had managed to weasel the money out of Madan.

Feroze sat down on his new bed and began to laugh. "You motherfuckers are still so stupid."

"Feroze —" Jaggu warned.

"You think such important things would ever be shared with me? There are only two people on earth who know where that baby is: that ass Pandit Bansi Lal, and the man who knows everything . . . Avtaar Singh."

"I'm going to finish you right now," said Jaggu, lunging at Feroze. "Do you think this is some kind of joke?"

"Wait . . . wait," said Feroze, throwing his hands up, his bravado gone. "Look, my job was to take Pandit Bansi Lal to the hospital in Karnal and bring him back. In between, he told me to make myself scarce. I know that Avtaar Singh told Trilok-bhai he would take care of the baby, it would be Avtaar Singh's responsibility to clean up the mess. It was the last conversation between them. What Avtaar Singh and Pandit Bansi Lal did with the baby . . ." Feroze shrugged.

Madan poured himself a glass of water. He ached for both of his lost children. For his child bartered from hand to hand, an inconvenience cast away into the arms of strangers. And Avtaar Singh had sat there wasting Madan's time rambling on about progress, growth and fables about kings. What future had Avtaar Singh consigned to his child?

He knew there was no other way to find out. He would have to ask the man himself, and he knew now what Avtaar Singh would ask in return. How much was Jeet Megacity worth to Madan? What could it give him, now that he had nothing?

CHAPTER 23

Slowly, Madan slipped the last bolt out and the front door creaked open. Out on the veranda the lights were on, and the grass of the front lawn glowed with a pearly sheen. The downy grass was cold against his bare soles and cushioned his tired feet. Stars dotted the sky and he watched the dawn take its time, turning the sky orange, and then cream. The shredded leaves of the palm trees shivered in the high breeze, but the ferns stood unmoving against the wall as he walked the length of the lawn. A dog yowled at the fading of the moon, and footsteps shuffled by beyond the wall, morning walks in progress, neighbors hailing neighbors, "Ram, Ram."

He heard the squeak of the door and Swati came out, but she did not disturb him. She watched him for a while, then went to sit on one of the wicker chairs and, taking some of her sewing from a plastic box, turned toward the light and began to work.

Madan joined her, taking a seat on the stool at the sewing machine. "Let me show you something," he said. Deftly, he slipped the fabric between the needle and the raised base plate of the sewing machine. He adjusted the hand wheel until the needle pierced the fabric, and firmly pressed the foot pedal, guiding the cloth on as a row of stitches appeared along the hem. Madan raised the needle when he came to the end and then, raising the presser foot, pulled the neatly sewn edge out with a flourish. Swati put her hand to her mouth, gasping in awe, and she clapped.

"One of my first real jobs was in a factory where they made clothes," he said. "I learned to sew."

She let him talk, telling her about those first years, the length and breadth of the loneliness, the adventures and heartaches, until the children woke and Swati went to attend to them. Madan went to his room to pack his clothes and wash up for his return journey. It was time to go back.

Swati, of course, had understood, but Jaggu was aghast when Madan told him in the morning of the bargain he planned to make with Avtaar Singh. "You can't just hand it to him. Forget Avtaar Singh, you can't give that much away," he had said.

"I need to know about my child," Madan had said. "I didn't know Arnav nine years ago, and now I'd give away the whole lot to have him with me. Wouldn't you, for this one?" Madan reached out and caressed Vipul's round cheek. He craved only the right of every parent, the chance to know: Are you okay? Are you happy?

He said his goodbyes. Jaggu, Swati and the children waved to him until he could not see them in his rearview mirror. The real problem with forfeiting Jeet Megacity was practical, not emotional, he told Jaggu. Everything was in Preeti's name. He couldn't give Avtaar Singh his share of Jeet Megacity, simply because it was hers, and only hers to give. There was no fine print or hidden loophole. He had made certain of that when drawing up the ownership. Preeti still hadn't spoken to him, or answered any of his calls. She could refuse to part with Jeet Megacity, leaving him with no bargaining chip with which to approach Avtaar Singh. He turned onto the highway, and the billboards of Jeet Megacity assaulted his views once again. She could leave him bereft of her as well.

The house was immaculate. Madan surveyed the spotless room, the polished tables, the shiny cabinets. Perhaps the house always looked like this, only now coming to his attention after the cluttered, overflowing rooms of Gorapur. And it was so quiet. Where had everyone gone? In quick alarm, he stepped back into the foyer, relieved when the door slammed and a servant came running out, apologizing for not hearing him drive up. Where was Preeti? he asked, but the boy only said memsaab was out. Is she coming back? But the boy had already gone about his work.

Madan wandered through the house, making his way to Arnav's room. Though confused and distracted when he stepped into the house, he had not paused at the entryway, his eyes desperately searching the empty hallways, his ears attuned in futile hope for the shout of, *Papa!* He came home knowing not to look up, not to seek out, not to cling to useless hope.

His dropped his bag by Arnav's bed. The closet door creaked when he pulled it open. Arnav's clothes hung from the rod in a straight line, his sweaters and T-shirts in neatly folded piles on the shelf. Madan gathered the ends of the hanging shirts and pants, burying his face in them. There was a whiff of faded detergent and the woodsy odor of the closet. He hugged the clothes to him. *Sorry,* he said to the angled pocket of the jeans in his hand. *Papa is so sorry.*

He had thought to lie down for a minute but tiredness had hammered his eyes shut, and it was early evening when he woke. Was Preeti back home? He splashed water on his face. In the drawing room he heard voices. To his surprise, he saw Ketan-bhai. He was talking to Preeti. Tea steamed in their cups, and the biscuits on the plate lay untouched.

"Madan." Ketan-bhai came up to greet him but retained a wary look, his smile forced and fading away quickly. Madan tried to pat his back, but Ketan-bhai returned to his chair.

Madan made a move toward Preeti, but she kept her gaze firmly trained away and looked like she was here under duress.

"Sit down. Have some tea," Ketan-bhai said. "How're you feeling now? Your holiday was good?"

Madan nodded, trying to figure out their intentions, sure Ketan-bhai was leading him somewhere. Preeti and Ketan-bhai exchanged glances.

"Madan," Ketan-bhai said. "Don't be angry, but we consulted a psychiatrist." He held up his hand when Madan was about to speak. "Hear me through," he said. "His name is Dr. Mitra, he comes highly recommended. He says your sleeping problems, this disappearing act, are all signs of post-traumatic stress. You know, after Arnav you've never really . . . never really had an outlet. Dr. Mitra can help you, if you allow him. He can help you find your old self again."

Madan took in his wife's swollen, red-rimmed eyes, the concerned lines around his friend's face.

"Find my old self?" It was a frightening thought. "How far back is the highly recommended doctor willing to go, Ketan-bhai?"

He picked up Arnav's picture from the table. The sweetness of his son's face pierced his heart. "You don't know me."

They began to protest but he shook his head to stop them. He began to pace back and forth. "I have something to tell you," he said. "It doesn't seem like it now, but you're going to find it very hard to believe what I'm going to say. It's going to change everything. I've told so many lies that I have to tell you everything from the beginning,

476

so nothing is left out. So you know it all at the end."

Both Preeti's and Ketan-bhai's expressions dissolved into confusion and doubt. Ketan-bhai gave a short, sharp laugh, and Preeti turned away as if what he was going to say were of no accord. Madan didn't hesitate, didn't let himself think about what this would mean once said, or how it would be received, or of wounded feelings and broken loyalties.

"When I was twelve," Madan said, "I went to live in the town of Gorapur. My father worked for a man who owned a timber factory there, but more than that, he owned most of the town. Not only real estate and property — but people. He had a way of owning you without you minding. No one sneezed without him knowing. He was the most powerful man I ever knew. I thought him more powerful than any god. His name . . ." Madan sat down. "His name," he said, "is . . . Avtaar Singh."

"Avtaar Singh?" Ketan-bhai latched onto the familiar name. "You mean . . . What d'you mean? You didn't tell me . . ."

There was no way to spare Ketan-bhai the anguish of what he was about to learn. "Yes," said Madan, "the same."

"Who's Avtaar Singh?" Preeti asked.

"What are you talking about?"

A dumbfounded Ketan-bhai turned to Preeti. "From the township project . . ." he said, confusing her further.

"That is where I was these last few days — in Gorapur. I have a mother there, a sister." As Madan spoke, Ketan-bhai stood and paced back and forth. The phone rang, Nalini probably wondering where her husband was, but they did not pick up. Madan didn't stop until the end.

"What was clear in my mind a short while ago feels meaningless now," he said. He'd thought he was invulnerable with his new self, his new life, with no possibility of loss or defeat. As if he could use what Avtaar Singh had taught him and turn it against Avtaar Singh. But an arrow shot into the sky can fall anywhere.

"What glorious plans I had, what I envisioned. It was all I could think about. Jeet Megacity. What it would take away from Avtaar Singh. I thought I knew how it felt to lose everything when I left Gorapur, but no. I had no idea."

Ketan-bhai and Preeti exchanged glances, at a loss for words. "You didn't know?" asked Preeti.

Ketan-bhai shook his head. "I can't, I didn't . . ." He couldn't go on.

"A mother, a sister?" Preeti kept her gaze on Ketan-bhai, did not look at Madan.

Again, Ketan-bhai shook his head in disbelief. "But why now, Madan? Why tell us now?"

"Ketan-bhai, I've been thinking about all I've done in my life so far, all that has happened. Perhaps I shouldn't have had Arnav. There's no grief when you lose what you don't have, but to imagine my life without him seems a much bigger loss. I wished many times I'd gone with Arnav. Why am I still here? What else am I supposed to do? What else is left?"

He turned to Preeti. "I have failed many people in my life, but there is one person out there, someone I turned my back on and walked away from."

"Madan —" He heard the warning in her voice and saw her recoil, but the time to reconsider was long gone, and he would not allow anyone to stop him now. She must understand. If it had been Arnav, she would never have walked away, never have abandoned her child to the vagaries of this chaotic world. And if he, at that time, had had but a morsel of the understanding he held within him now, he would have slain anyone who stood in his way.

"All I want to do is make sure that this

child has a good, decent life, that —"

Preeti shot out of her chair like he had taken a whip to her. "You had a child," she said. "Or is Arnav so easy to forget? Is he so easy to replace?" She stopped to catch her breath. "Arnav never even knew his father." She pointed her finger at him. "All he knew was a lie."

Madan turned pleadingly to Ketan-bhai, who slumped on the sofa, tears in his eyes. "I made you part of my family. Morning, noon and night we talked. And not once, not once could I ever think or imagine what you were keeping from me." Ketan-bhai blew his nose and dabbed his watery eyes.

"I have got some good leads . . ." he began to tell Ketan-bhai, but his friend was pulling himself up and muttering about going home.

"I'm sorry," he said to Preeti, who had followed Ketan-bhai to the door. She stopped and turned at his apology.

"I'm sorry," he said again. "You never asked for any of this. Even when I think about it, I find it hard to understand. So for you — I can't imagine. I'll do whatever you want. You want the house, the factories, the business. I'll make sure you'll never want for anything, ever. But there is one thing."

She could call him selfish, reprehensible,

a lunatic, callous and deplorable. She could call him whatever names she liked; whatever would ease her shock, he was ready to accept it all.

"It is about Jeet Megacity," he said.

"You'll make your name with that place."

Not my name, he thought. He explained what he wanted her to do.

"All it'll take is a few signatures," he said. "Twenty minutes of your time. All I need is your assent. You can have anything in exchange."

"Answer me one thing," she said. "Can you give me Arnav?"

She left Madan alone with the blazing lights shining solely on him.

Madan glanced impatiently at his silent phone. Ketan-bhai sat across from him and, clearing his throat, he pensively contemplated the edge of the desk. An office boy entered, letting in the hum of the busy office floor. He gathered the emptied coffee cups off the desk, wiped down the surface and left, closing the door behind him, and leaving Madan and Ketan-bhai alone once again.

Ketan-bhai had stewed for a while, then succumbed to his fondness for Madan, unable to resist Madan's relentless calls of apology and self-reproof. Madan knew now that he could have trusted his friend. Ketan-bhai's sentimental heart would have taken him in and understood, regardless.

"It's foolishness," Ketan-bhai said, searching again for a reason to dissuade Madan, but it was too late. Ketan-bhai would soon be partners with Avtaar Singh in Jeet Megacity.

To Madan's surprise and relief, Preeti had agreed to sign the papers the morning after their conversation, simply saying to inform her where and when, demanding nothing in return. He dared not question her decision, and later, sitting by her side as she signed and initialed, he searched for some way to convey the depth of his gratitude. Returning home at the end of the day, he learned from one of the servants that Preeti had left for her parents' house with a suitcase. She had rebuffed all his attempts to talk to or see her since then.

It had taken a few weeks to get everything in order, to explain to the investors, to get everyone on board, to draw up contracts, sign and send the documents to Avtaar Singh. Madan had promised there would be no other major changes. He would see Jeet Megacity to its completion. The opening ceremony would go as planned, but without

Madan and Preeti.

Before these transitions, Madan purchased three apartments in the names of Jaggu's children, and a villa for Swati and Jaggu. The value of these bits of real estate along with the rental income from the properties should cover the losses Jaggu would incur from the opening of the movie theater in Jeet Megacity. The owner of the movie theater chain had promised Madan that Jaggu could have the job of managing the multiplex theater, if he wanted it.

Madan's cell phone beeped. Ketan-bhai and Madan sat up straighter. It was Jaggu.

"Your people have just left," Jaggu said. Madan could hear the nervousness in his voice. Jaggu was at the timber factory after many years. "He says he wants to talk to you first."

There was the scrape of chairs and the fuss of the phone changing hands. "Leave me," Madan heard a gruff voice say. Avtaar Singh was sending Jaggu and whoever else was there out of the room.

He heard Avtaar Singh's heavy, deliberate inhale. "You should've brought me the papers yourself," Avtaar Singh said.

"They told you what I want in return," Madan said.

This was his final handshake with Avtaar

Singh. Never again did he want to hear the name or squander another moment of his life on the conceits of this man.

"Why do we have to fight?" Avtaar Singh said.

"Fight?" He was fast losing patience. "I'm not fighting. This is a business transaction."

"You can come back, you can help me." His voice lowered as if he if didn't want anyone to overhear. "I have no one." The complaint was soft, but the words were clear with yearning. "I'm surrounded by buffoons, there's no one I can trust. Who'll follow me when I'm gone? What's done is done. Come back to where you belong. It'll be like before, you and me —"

"You have your daughters," Madan interrupted.

"Daughters?" He was abrupt again, angry. "Girls . . . they get married and leave, they go to their own families. But, my son. I need my son —"

Madan disconnected the phone.

"What happened?" asked Ketan-bhai "Did he tell you? He signed the papers; he can't go back on his word."

Madan couldn't speak. He was at a loss, his agitated heart dragging against the currents of time. *I need my son.* The words fell gently and landed with a thousand pinpricks. His cell phone rang and Madan stared at it, unhearing. The rustle of Avtaar Singh's voice filled his ear as he battled the potency of those words, and from some long-unheeded place a quiet wail arose, decrying the infallible power they possessed to undo him. The phone rang on insistently, but his every breath dueled against the wrenching need to run to Avtaar Singh, to be in his presence, to walk alongside him again.

"Madan?" Ketan-bhai prompted.

Madan picked up the phone. It was Jaggu.

"Have you got a pen?" Jaggu sounded excited. "I have an address."

Madan trod softly around his room, collecting his things, the morning sunlight still weak and undecided. There was much that refused to let him rest. He contemplated the address on the square of paper before slipping it into his pocket. "Avtaar Singh said Pandit Bansi Lal made all the arrangements," Jaggu had said. "The address is for a lawyer, an Advocate Naresh Ganguli. But listen to this, his office is near Lajpat Nagar. In Delhi."

Delhi? How could it be? The city that gave him shelter, concealing him even from himself, allowing him to rise from his

485

despair, and sending him fleeing back into those very depths again? He'd sped toward it on that clattering train. Had the baby, his child, been on a parallel journey at the same time as Madan back then? Had Delhi hidden them both, even from each other?

Before following the trail of the address, he needed to make one quick stop. He had driven past the Hanuman Mandir near his house many times, barely noticing the temple's small white dome and walls decorated with strings of marigolds. The bell rang frequently as the morning worshippers came in, and tendrils of heavy, smoky incense tickled his throat. Madan removed his shoes and bought a cane bowl filled with flowers and prasad from the outside stall before joining the queue of worshippers waiting in line for their blessings.

What would he have done if Preeti were not there when he had returned from Gorapur? Would he have given up this search and gone after her, or would he have accepted her decision to leave? Either way seemed impossible to contemplate. No longer would he let fate flip his life like a coin, forcing him to choose one side or the other.

No, now was the time to demand from fate or from himself, or whoever was listening, that he wanted both — heads and tails,

486

before and after, all together and all forever. And he hoped he had the time. Time enough to finish what he was looking for. And time enough to make her understand that if she was not with him, the rest could not exist because it would not matter. One could not be without the other.

He reached the head of the line. The pandit continued his chanting as he took the flowers and prasad from Madan, placing the offerings before the statue of Hanuman. Madan cupped his hands for the tiny spoon of holy water, sipping it and spreading the rest over the top of his head. The pandit dotted the vermilion tikka, cold and wet, on his forehead. Madan joined his hands and bowed his head, squeezing his eyes shut. But nothing came to him; he could not think what exactly to ask for. "God bless you, son," he heard the pandit say, and then it was time to move out of the way for the next person in line.

The drive to Lajpat Nagar was like every other drive in the city, with its amalgamation of fits and starts, crowded red lights and traffic jams. Hopping out to ask a auto-rickshaw driver for directions, the driver turned the car into a drowsy street, inching along, peering at the numbers and pulling up in front of a building with a tempered glass door.

Madan peered at the name printed in gold lettering on the door: NARESH GANGULI, ADVOCATE. He took out the paper from his pocket to make sure, but he did not need it. This was the place.

He looked around. There were a few cars parked up and down the road, and a hawker rattled by with a covered cart. He pushed open the doors and walked into the carpeted waiting room, well-furnished with potted plants and comfortable chairs. A lady in a heavily starched sari was at the desk.

"I would like to see Mr. Naresh Ganguli," Madan said.

"Mr. Ganguli is in court. Do you have an appointment?"

"No. When will he be back?"

"I'm not sure, but if you want to see him you must make an appointment."

Madan pinched the bridge of his nose to stop himself from shaking the woman and demanding she call Naresh Ganguli to appear right now. Her phone rang and he took the opportunity to take a deep breath, wresting his temper under control.

"Oh, Mr. Ganguli," he heard her say. "Yes, sir. Okay, sir. There's a client to see you, sir. No, no appointment." She listened and then placed the receiver against her shoulder. "What's this about?" she asked Madan. "Did someone send you?"

"It's a personal matter. And I'll wait," he said, taking a seat. Looking at the messages on his phone, he thought about returning the calls, but was too restless. The hours passed slowly, and Madan nearly nodded off when the door swung open, sending the papers on the secretary's desk flying.

"I tell you, Saloni," said the man who walked in, placing a stack of files on her desk, "one stay order after the other; it's a wonder any work gets done in this country."

Saloni settled her desk and said, "Mr. Ganguli, this is the gentleman waiting for you."

"Yes, yes." He turned around.

Naresh Ganguli shook Madan's hand, his head of thick white hair shaking with him. He carefully studied the business card Madan handed him.

"Come in, please," he said. "I have a few minutes and we can talk. These days property issues are the number one cases for me. I have come across them all."

Naresh Ganguli indicated the chair across from his desk as he took off his black robe and hung it behind the door.

"It's not a property issue, Mr. Ganguli,"

Madan said.

"Oh," said Mr. Ganguli. "You said personal, so I assumed it was property. I do not deal with family law, you see, I can refer you to someone —"

"No, no, it's nothing like that," said Madan. "It's . . ." He stopped to get his thoughts in order. What should he say to assure Mr. Ganguli's cooperation? Maybe he should have brought his own lawyer along. A lawyer knows how to talk to a lawyer.

Madan took a deep breath. "Mr. Ganguli, it's about a child, a baby. Over twenty years ago a Pandit Bansi Lal from Gorapur —" Madan broke off.

Naresh Ganguli went as pale as his hair. He jumped up and shut the half-open door. Back at his desk, he removed a handkerchief from his pocket and dabbed his forehead.

"Who are you?" Mr. Ganguli whispered.

"Please, Mr. Ganguli, don't be alarmed. I only want information. I want to know where the child went, who took it. I used to know Pandit Bansi Lal. I know most of his dealings were not so black-and-white, but I'm not here because of that. I just want to know about the baby."

"Why?" he asked harshly, a stubborn tone in his voice.

"Mr. Ganguli," said Madan. "I am that

child's father."

They stared at each other across the desk, each refusing to look away. Naresh Ganguli wiped his brow again. "Look, Mr. Ganguli," Madan said. "We can be civil about this or not, it's up to you, but I've come a long, long way, and gone through hell to be here. If it's proof you want, I can go back to Gorapur and bring half the town. All I want is my question answered."

"Let me think." Rising up, Mr. Ganguli paced back and forth. "Once we tried to get in touch, find out if we could meet with the mother or father. We were rebuffed badly, threatened and told it would not be good for us if we tried to look for the parents. It scared everyone."

"You tried to find us?" Staggered by the disclosure, Madan stood up.

"But why now? Why after all this time?" asked Mr. Ganguli, wringing his hands. "The child is an adult."

"I know more than anyone how much time has passed," Madan said. "I mean no harm. Mr. Ganguli, please understand." His voice choked. "I want to know what happened. I can go on my knees and beg if you want, I can pay you, but I need to find my child."

Naresh Ganguli looked like he was going

491

to throw up.

"You look like you have children of your own, you look like a father, Mr. Ganguli," said Madan. Mr. Ganguli reluctantly nodded. "Then you understand."

Mr. Ganguli stared at him, his eyes buried in a layer of crinkles, a frown cutting his forehead in half. He laid his hand on Madan's shoulder. "Sit," he said. "Sit." He guided Madan down to the chair and took a seat again.

"It's quite a shock . . . after all these years . . . hearing the name of Pandit Bansi Lal, Karnal . . . I put it all out of my mind."

"You have the information I need?" asked Madan.

"Yes," said Naresh Ganguli. "I do. But what about the child's mother?"

"She's not in the picture," Madan said. "It's only me."

Mr. Ganguli absorbed this and said, "You'll have to come to my house." He wrote down the address, handing it to Madan.

He didn't take it. "Mr. Ganguli, I really have no intention of leaving without the information I came for."

"And you will have it," he said. "But not here, not in my office. This is a real address, you can check with the receptionist outside.

I've been in this office for many years. I'm not going anywhere. Come to my house at six o'clock this evening and we can talk more then."

Still Madan stubbornly refused to take the card.

"You have waited this long," said Mr. Ganguli. "What are a few hours more?" Again he held out the card to Madan.

Madan finally took it, glancing at the address scribbled on the back of the business card. "Six o'clock," he said, "but you better have it then."

"I will," said Mr. Ganguli.

Madan lay atop Arnav's bed, staring up at the ceiling. There was no more comfortable place in the world. He heard the swish of the bedroom door. Preeti came in, startled to find him at home in the middle of the day instead of at the office.

"What are you doing here?" she asked. In her hand was a nylon bag. She had come to collect some more of her things. Bit by bit she was disappearing from the house, and from his life.

He sat up and smoothed the rumpled bed-covers. "I went to see that lawyer, from the address given by Avtaar Singh."

She stiffened. "And?"

"He says he can tell me what I need to know. He wants me to meet him at his house this evening."

She was silent, and he willed her not to move. "Preeti," he said. "After Arnav, it was hard for both of us to understand why we were still alive. How we could still be breathing when he wasn't."

She nodded. "I still don't know why," he said. "It seems a miracle, inexplicable, that we are. Such pain should've taken us too."

Whatever he said next, he wanted to get right. "Pandit Bansi Lal," he said, "gave me a lot of reasons to be angry with him. But I think the worst thing was he made me question what need or purpose there was to any kind of faith, in God or any other divinity beyond our understanding. So without faith, I did not know . . . could not recognize . . . the blessings that came my way. Without faith, I didn't need to thank anyone for the miracles in my life. I took for granted that you should happen to me, Arnav should happen to me.

"But Pandit Bansi Lal also used to say that faith doesn't come to a man from thin air. It has to have a starting point, a reason to come into existence. My beginning is you. I don't want you to ever think, to ever feel, that finding my family in Gorapur, and finding my child, will deny you any part of me, this person who is lucky to have you."

She leaned against the wall, looking off to the side, but he knew she had heard him. He waited while she wiped her eyes. "Since when have you started talking so much?" she said.

The strained tightrope he balanced on was unsteady, but he managed a small smile. It was true — in all the years they had been married, he'd probably never said so many words to her in one stretch.

"Preeti, before I shut up and go back to being my silent self, I want to ask — will you come with me?"

"Where?"

"To the lawyer's place, this evening. Whatever I find out, whatever happens, I want you to be with me."

She left the room without a word, but as he collected the car keys from the drawer of the foyer table, he heard her heels tapping on the stairway. She was rummaging through her purse as she descended, in a fresh, simple salwar, her face scrubbed and bright.

He had never turned to look up at her before. He had been too busy on the phone or he just never noticed. But Arnav had always turned and looked up at his descending mother, scrutinizing her carefully as if committing to memory the effortless joy with which she lived, recognizing what had drawn his father when they'd walked in the park in front of her house before he was born, what had made Madan say to Ketanbhai, "Yes, why not?" Arnav had done that for him, lest his father should ever forget.

As they made their way to Alaknanda he glanced at Preeti, her puffy eyelids the only hint of what had taken place that afternoon.

"Have you brought any cash with you?" she asked.

"Some," Madan said. "He did not ask for anything, but I brought some, in case."

Turning into the gated colony, they drove past the central park surrounded by apartment complexes. "It's Phase III B," he said.

"There." Preeti pointed, reading the painted numbers on the wall. Madan parked and they entered the building, climbing the switchback staircase to Apartment 4B. Mr. Ganguli opened the door at the first ring, inviting them in.

Preeti and Naresh Ganguli said their namastes as Mr. Ganguli indicated the sitting room off to the side. A glass coffee table separated two sofas in the long room.

"Please sit," said Mr. Ganguli. Madan and

Preeti sat beside each other, exchanging a confused glance. The coffee table held a veritable spread of food. There were all sorts of crunchy namkeens in silver bowls, biscuits and pastries, rasgullas floating in heavy syrup.

"My wife will be right out," said Mr. Ganguli. A woman appeared from the inside of their apartment, followed by a servant holding a server heaped with fresh pakoras.

Madan did not know what to make of this, and he saw the bewilderment on Preeti's face as well. They rose to greet Mrs. Ganguli. She stared hard at Madan, but her tone was polite when she said, "Can I get you something? Tea? Or something cold?"

"No, that's all right," Preeti stammered, Madan nodding in agreement.

"No, please," she insisted. "You have to have something." She gave the retreating servant some instructions.

"We do not want to take up too much of your time," said Madan. "As you're expecting guests. If you have the information for us . . ."

"No we're not expecting anyone but you. And we're glad you brought your wife," said Mr. Ganguli.

Mrs. Ganguli handed out the snack plates, insisting over their protestations that they take something, and she poured the tea, asking for their preferences in sugar and milk.

With everyone served, Mr. Ganguli sat back and took a long sip.

"Mr. Ganguli?" Madan said.

"Yes, I know," he said. "I wanted you to come here, to my home, because I wanted Bhavna to be here too. I will start at the beginning," he said, when he saw they were at a loss for words. "You're upset with Pandit Bansi Lal, and he was a shady character, I give you that, but he also gave us our greatest happiness."

As Naresh Ganguli spoke, Preeti moved closer to Madan as if to shield him. Madan was thankful she was there so she could witness what Mr. Ganguli said, assure him later of what he had heard.

Naresh Ganguli took frequent sips of his tea to get his thoughts in order, and began his story. Blessed with one beautiful child a few years after their marriage, they were unable to have another. For a long while, they tried a variety of treatments — allopathic, homeopathic, pujas, yatras — refusing to give up hope even when the doctors did. At the time, in Naresh Ganguli's practice, he used to spend many hours under the creaky fans at Tis Hazari court, swatting at flies and waiting for rulings. Another lawyer whom he knew reasonably well noticed his worry and Mr. Ganguli confided in him.

"It didn't take much for me to tell him. Somewhere in the back of my mind I recalled hearing that he could help couples like us," said Mr. Ganguli. "And I was right."

The lawyer had helped Pandit Bansi Lal place a child a year before. From the adoption agencies, one was never sure what child from what poor family one would get, and the lawyer assured Mr. Ganguli that Pandit Bansi Lal only dealt with babies from good families. The pandit had contacted him recently. A baby would soon be available.

"After everything, we didn't need much time to think about it," Mr. Ganguli said, as his wife dabbed her eyes with her dupatta. "Pandit Bansi Lal wanted money, of course. I borrowed from my brother, we sold some of Bhavna's jewelry, but it was all worth it when that night he put the baby in my arms —"

"The child was ours from then on," his wife interrupted, a little defensively, unable to stanch the flow of tears streaming down her face.

Mr. Ganguli patted her hand. "Pandit Bansi Lal told us that an underage girl from a rich family had the baby, and would never look for it. He never said anything about the father. And since it was all under the table, we did not ask many questions. All we wanted was a healthy baby. We didn't care about anything else."

Madan was glad Preeti spoke up, because he could not get the words out. "You . . . you both? You're the people who took the baby?"

Mr. Ganguli nodded. "I filed the birth certificate papers, after paying off the filing clerk, with our names as parents."

Preeti turned to Madan, her face wet with tears, and he wondered when he would cease giving her reasons to cry. Bhavna Ganguli reached over to the side table and placed a mahogany photo frame in Madan's hands. Preeti leaned in to look.

A young man and woman stood next to each other, smiling. A curve of a beach, a few palm trees, a white building in the background. The clean-cut young man had his arm over the woman's shoulder.

"That's in Goa, last year," Mrs. Ganguli murmured.

Madan touched the glass reverently, his finger tracing the outline of the taller figure. "Is this . . . ?" the words could barely escape his lips. They dried on his tongue and clung to his heart and the roof of his mouth.

"Is this him?" Preeti asked.

Mrs. Ganguli leaned over too. "Oh, no, that's our son Naveen. This" — her finger tapped the young woman grinning through the glass at Preeti and Madan — "is Nitasha," she said. "This is — she is who was given to us — who came to complete our family."

Madan felt the gentle weight of Preeti's hand on his. "It's the girl, Madan," she said. "A girl."

Madan looked at the picture of the girl in a blue T-shirt and white shorts, a tanned, pretty face, her hair hanging loosely over one shoulder.

"Is she here?" asked Preeti, looking around the place.

"Not at the moment," said Mr. Ganguli. He traded glances with his wife. "She knows she is not ours by birth. We've told her."

"Though she's so smart she would've figured it out herself anyway." Husband and wife shook their heads and shared a small private laugh, as only parents who recognized the specialness of their child could.

Mr. Ganguli said, "Look, you said this morning that all you wanted to do was make sure she's all right. As you can see, she's everything to us, to her brother. It was never a question with us; no matter how she came to us, she could never be more ours than if we . . ."

"Yes, I understand," said Madan, but he sounded befuddled, as if he couldn't comprehend what they were saying.

Then he heard Preeti's voice, strong and clear. "We are grateful," she said. "We are grateful for all you've done, and yes, Madan wanted to make sure that she was all right. But Mr. Ganguli, Bhavna-ji, we've gone through a . . . a very bad time recently and it made Madan look for . . . Nitasha."

A name, thought Madan . . . Nitasha. He held the picture frame in his hands, seeking it out again and again, his reflection superimposed on the smiling girl's.

"But if Madan could meet her — he won't say what you don't want him to say — but, we would be so thankful."

Madan looked at her. How was she able to articulate his thoughts when he himself did not know what was going through his own wandering, agonized mind?

"Please," Preeti said.

"We told her you were coming here today. Her brother took her out so we could meet you first," Mrs. Ganguli said. "She'll be going back soon to school in Boston. She's at MIT, doing her master's in chemical engineering."

"She's old enough. The decision is hers," Mr. Ganguli said.

They all turned as the lock on the front door clicked open. A young man stepped into the room. He was nearly as tall as the doorway and they could see the resemblance to the Gangulis.

"Dad?"

Mr. Ganguli rose up hurriedly. "Naveen, come in," he said. To Madan and Preeti he said, "This is my son."

Naveen continued to look questioningly at his father, and when Mr. Ganguli gave him a small, firm nod, he moved aside. "She was impatient," Naveen said to his father.

Madan should have been looking at the door but it was too much, and he turned to Preeti, and saw her smile, rise up and walk toward the door with her arms stretched out. His gaze trailed Preeti to the girl who had jumped out of the picture frame and into the doorway. Mr. and Mrs. Ganguli stood on each side, and her brother behind her, protecting her, but Preeti broke in and gave her a loose hug. "We're very glad to see you," she said. And Madan stood up and made himself put one foot before another. He wondered why he was moving so slow, when he should be running, flying, but he kept on until he was beside Preeti.

The girl put her hand out, and they shook.

"I've been waiting for a long time," Nitasha said.

"Not as long as me," he said.

Mrs. Ganguli broke the ensuing hush that fell between them by urging everyone to sit down. Preeti sat on another chair, giving Nitasha room next to Madan. There were things he knew in life he would never forget, whether it was the gleam infusing Arnav's being as he trained his eyes on the checkered flag at the end of the raceway, or the comfort of Preeti's head on his shoulder, or the way Nitasha sat angled on the sofa, the poise with which she sized him up, her parents in her line of sight behind Madan, her loose hair falling around her shoulders, her eyes dotted with sparkling copper.

"Dad and I were discussing what I should call you," she said, and her tone was city-girl strong, the bonds anchoring every corner of her life never in doubt. Her family was here, she was in her home and who was Madan? Someone to whom she could give no name.

"Whatever you want," he said. "I'll answer to whatever you call me."

He would forever remember this conversation, he thought, awkward at times, the silences filled by the Gangulis or Preeti. He would have liked to stay on, ask her about things — he knew not what — but how could he not know what was her favorite color, and did she like tennis or cricket, and who were her best friends, and did she prefer Italian food or Chinese?

But she was meeting up with some friends for dinner. Though Madan was reluctant to leave, he understood from the look Preeti gave him that it was best to let them be, best to give everyone a chance to catch their breath.

"These youngsters," Mr. Ganguli said, "always so busy. She has so many friends she has to see before she returns. No time for her old parents."

Nitasha hugged Mr. Ganguli, and said with a smile, "Please, Dad. Stop with your emotional blackmail."

Before they left, Preeti insisted that the Gangulis come for dinner at their house. They looked hesitant, even a little uncomfortable at her suggestion, but she did not let them think it over, continuing to insist, taking down phone numbers, saying she would call to confirm. "My parents would like to meet you both," she said. "My chacha was a high court judge, recently retired," she said to Mr. Ganguli. "And you will meet our friend Ketan-bhai and his family."

She chatted on until they were unable to refuse. They saw Madan and Preeti off, seeming more than a little stunned by what they had let her talk them into. Even Madan was not sure why she was being so insistent.

Their car was boxed in between two others, and once they managed to squeeze out and get back onto the main road, he asked, "Are you sure about inviting them over?"

She stared straight ahead into the swallowing darkness and said with her usual firmness, "Let them come to the house and see where we live. And you must invite Mr. Ganguli to see the offices. Let them see we are decent, solid people. They will see what is past is past, and we must make sure they're comfortable with us."

He should have realized that the Gangulis didn't have a chance once Preeti unleashed her complex social skills on them. And in this matter, she was right. They had to show them there was nothing to fear from Madan meeting their child. His last glimpse of Nitasha was of her standing at the top of the stairs, saying good evening before she turned to answer her cell phone.

"If I'd known going to the temple could make a day turn out like this, I would've gone much earlier," he said, more to himself than to Preeti.

"You went to the temple?" Her voice was sharp with surprise.

"Yes, this morning, to the Hanuman Mandir near the house."

He waited for her to comment. When she didn't, he tried to get a good look at her, but it was dark, and she was facing away from him, looking out the window, her arms crossed around her middle, shivering as though cold. He reached out to turn up the heat, but an unsettling thought came to him that it was not the temperature causing her to shake. In fact, the more he thought about it, the more certain he became that his wife was silently, and heartily, laughing.

CHAPTER 24

The small mosquito is a big monster. Warnings about dengue virus were appearing on billboards across every bus stop, signaling the start of summer, but already the air was so thick and viscous that standing outside for even a minute was akin to walking through a heavy brush of glue. Madan waited in the cooler confines of his car, while Preeti stepped into the bakery to pick up something to take to the Gangulis'.

Tonight they were attending a jagrata at the Gangulis' place, a night of continuous worship devoted to Durga Mata. He glanced up from his phone to see Preeti talking to a couple of ladies outside the bakery doors, and went back to reading the Internet article he had pulled up on his phone.

All these years Nitasha was so close, less than an hour, yet more than the breadth of his life away. Maybe they walked the same markets, visited the same restaurants, stood next to each other somewhere, all the while unaware of the other cutting across their path.

The many images he formed and re-formed of her were like a string of paper dolls. Questions swarmed through him, like what attracted her to this stream of academia — chemical engineering — and he tried to imagine if this mix of science and industry would have caught his interest if he had gone on with his education.

She was to leave for school in a few days. How quickly the time had flown. They had met the Gangulis for dinners as Preeti had planned, Mr. Ganguli duly visiting the factories and offices. So far, Nitasha had never shown anything but eagerness to see Madan, yet he could sense she was maintaining a safety zone, taking full stock of him before committing fully to his re-appearance.

A luncheon had taken place in a small French restaurant a few days ago, just Madan and Nitasha, and he had waited then for the inevitable questions. "I know I should ask why," she had said. "Why you didn't keep me and all that, why you came looking for me now, but . . ." She paused, as if not wanting to hurt his feelings. "Is my mother, the one who gave birth to me, is she around, alive?"

"You were born when we were younger than you are now," he said. "In a place where some lines could not be crossed, and the repercussions for any breach was not affected by birth, or life or death."

"She does not want to see me," she said. Nitasha's frank look belied the disappointment he knew she must feel.

"Neha" — and Madan said her name so Nitasha would have some part of her — "was ready to break the system, start a revolution, when I knew her. She knew what she wanted to fight against, but she stumbled, because she did not know what she was fighting for." Nitasha gave him a quizzical look, and he said, "It's something I was told once. What I'm saying is she tried, but the fight crushed her. She has had to forget what defiance is to live in peace."

Nitasha turned her gaze to the window, the white glazed glass blurring out the shrubs and asphalt, the humans and animals choking the lane on the other side, her casually tied ponytail brushing the collar of her shirt. He had no sixth sense, but he knew she filled in the empty spaces, coloring in the broken lines to create a picture that resembled a truth she could live with.

"One day I'll show you Gorapur, and

when you see it you'll understand."

"I would like that," she said.

"I understand that you tried to find us as well. Why did you look?" he asked.

She sipped her Coke and looked as if she were too embarrassed to answer. "I wish I could say it was some amazing reason," she said. "I mean, I love Mom and Dad. But look at me. I don't look anything like them. I was on a school trip with my friends and someone asked if I look like my mom more or my dad, and I said neither. They joked and said, 'So do you look like the milkman?' and for a while they called me Dhoodhwali, you know, Milk-Delivery-Girl. Very amusing. And it just got me thinking, where did all this come from?" She pointed at her face, circling a few times. "Of course, when we couldn't find anyone, and Dad told me to let it go, I did, but it didn't stop bugging me."

Dad. The way she said it, with a sense of possession. It reflected the same tone with which he would address Avtaar Singh, and people would turn and look and understand the sense of belonging that existed between the two individuals, of which no one else was a part.

Avtaar Singh would say everyone began life with a finite number of breaths, a certain

511

number of heartbeats, and when your quota was over, it was the end. What struck Madan, sitting with Nitasha, noticing their physical similarities, was that the two of them were raised by men who had no say in their births. By men who, nonetheless, had invested devotedly in their breaths, and in their heartbeats. Who passed on their convictions and their presumptions without fanfare, but with care and effort, and who had seen in them a way to assuage their own demons. They were the master builders, defining to them their value to the world.

It seemed to Madan that each child and parent were predestined to be bound to one another, each offspring ending up with the person fated to be the architect of their life. Some children, he supposed, landed straightaway in the arms meant for them. Some, like Nitasha, like him, took a more circuitous route.

He had watched her cut into her grilled chicken and spear a baby carrot as she hopped from topic to topic, saying she was considering turning vegetarian but did not want to give up fish, "So I may become a fisheterian," she had said. "Wait until I confuse every auntie in the colony with that word." And she had grinned at herself and her mangled word, and he had felt proud of her. Though he had nothing to do with how she spoke or how she thought, or how she turned out, he saw that if he had taken her and run, or she ended up with some other lucky man she called "Dad," it didn't matter how they got her here, only that she was.

Madan continued now to study his phone, waiting for Preeti, thinking that he should remember to ask Nitasha for her email address before she left. If she would like, that is, to keep in touch. He was about to click on another article when Preeti returned, slipping into the air-conditioned coolness of the car.

"Who were they?" he asked, starting the car back up. Usually he didn't ask, but she looked upset.

"Kiran Bajaj and Mira Mittal. Their sons go to his school . . . used to go to his school . . . I mean, they still go —" She gave up, impatiently snapping her seatbelt. "It's not the same," she said.

He didn't know what to say. It was not the same to mingle with Mrs. Bajaj and Mrs. Mittal, or Mrs. Khanna or Mrs. Sidhwani. There was no foothold, no reason to linger and murmur with this one and that, irrevocably yanked, as she was, from discussions centering on school and homework and birthday parties, and where Rohit was going for skating lessons, and whom Chetan was seeing for extra tutoring. Where before the ladies' conversations circulated round and round like water going down the drain, all that remained now were forced pleasantries. No, it was not the same.

The sky curved pink with the setting sun. They waited in a line of cars for the traffic light to change. The honking began when the light turned green and no one could move. Once again, the carefully planned boulevards of the city were defeated, this time by a car at a standstill in the middle of the road, its occupant busy feeding a stray cow his leftover lunch through the window. When the other drivers collectively tried to surge forward and go around the vehicle and cow, they blocked each other and were now stalled crisscross all over the road. The driver of a two-wheeled scooter, attempting a U-turn to get out of the mess, found himself tangled in the oleander bushes of the center divider. Finally, a rickshaw driver decided to be traffic cop and stood in the middle of the road, shouting, swearing and directing cars out of their conundrum and around the oblivious bovine pleasurably masticating on cold chapattis.

"This is Delhi," Madan said. "In its order there's chaos, and within this chaos there's order — much like life."

"You've become such a philosopher in your old age," Preeti said.

Nitasha, sitting with Mrs. Ganguli in the pressing crowd under the awning that stretched over the central park of the Gangulis' apartment complex, gave a friendly wave, still treating him like an uncle who has come for a brief visit. Mrs. Ganguli, unable to make herself heard over the timbre of the loudspeaker blaring music and prayers, pointed Madan in the direction of the men's seating area.

He found Mr. Ganguli, shaking his hand before sitting down cross-legged on the white sheet. Naveen, sitting with his father, smiled in greeting at Madan. He was a reserved young man who, like his father, was a lawyer, though he worked for an international conglomerate's local office.

Madan felt a pat on his knee. Mr. Ganguli rose, indicating that Madan should follow him. He got up and filed out behind Mr. Ganguli and Naveen. "I'm not one for such long-winded things," said Mr. Ganguli as they emerged under the stars, the warm air refreshing after the cloistered tents. "And you don't seem the jagrata kind. Our association insists on this once a year. Bhavna

515

is more involved, but I tell her to keep me out of it."

Back in the apartment, they sat in the drawing room and Naveen poured drinks, serving his father and Madan a whiskey and getting a beer for himself. They talked about politics and business and the surprising efficiency of the subway system.

Madan asked Naveen about his work and as Naveen answered, Mr. Ganguli interjected. "These children, Madan, wonderful opportunities for them these days. Not like us sweating in the dusty courts. All they do is write briefs all day. What a life!"

Madan laughed and Naveen said, "Dad, it's not like we don't work hard." Mr. Ganguli fondly slapped his son's back to show it was in jest.

"Yes, Madan," Mr. Ganguli went on, fully immersed in praise of his children. "I never had to worry with these two. I knew they would do well, never had to worry about their studies, whatever my income. Naveen didn't want to go abroad; he studied law here. And when Nitasha wanted to study in America, the money from the trust was very helpful with her tuition and other fees."

"Trust?" said Madan, picking up on the word like it was gold among the grit. "What trust?"

Mr. Ganguli clammed up, looking dumb-founded, as if some other person had spoken. Naveen glanced at his father in exasperation.

"It's okay," said Mr. Ganguli to Naveen. "So what if he knows?" He reached into his pocket and handed Naveen some keys. "Get the file from the Godrej almirah," he said.

Naveen disappeared into the apartment. "This sometimes makes me talk too much," Mr. Ganguli said, shaking his glass. "But really, what is there to hide?"

Naveen returned and Madan forced himself to keep sitting, to ignore his growing trepidation, his clammy back, the urge to grab Preeti and run. Run out of the room and away from the red file folder, and from Mr. Ganguli unwinding the string sealing the file closed.

"Nitasha had been with us for about a year at the time," he said, opening the file and laying it on the coffee table. "We were living in another place then. We were so happy; Naveen here was excited to have a sister. Then one day this man showed up at the door.

"At first we didn't let him in. He looked quite frightening, didn't he?" Mr. Ganguli turned to Naveen, who nodded, even though he was probably too young to remember, but he'd heard the story often enough.

"He said he was from Gorapur and he was here about the child. The papers were not fully filed by then, so we were afraid he was here to take her away, that someone changed their mind. We wouldn't let him in." Mr. Ganguli paused. "When you came to my office that first day, it was almost a repeat of what I went through then. But he said he wanted a few minutes of our time and he wasn't there to cause trouble."

Mr. Ganguli began to rifle through the papers in the file. "He had a fancy car; not many people had a car like that at the time. In fact, it's not manufactured anymore. What was it?" He tapped his forehead, trying to recall.

"A white Contessa," Naveen supplied. Madan almost leapt up, but the pressure building in his head kept him down.

"Yes," said Narash Ganguli. "Anyway, he came in; he had this file in his hand." He held up the file.

"What did he say?" Madan managed.

"He said he knew the child's father and he wanted to see the baby. He wanted to see that she was healthy and happy, and well settled in our home. He wanted to meet us. Bhavna was hesitant — we both were — but

518

those eyes . . . those eyes could convince you of anything. So she brought Nitasha out. He held her in his arms, it wasn't for long, but he stared at Nitasha like he was ready to eat her up. Then he gave her back and said, 'Yes, she looks so much like him.'

"He set up a trust, he said, a trust she would get at eighteen that was for her education. He was adamant. Not for her wedding, or for her other needs as she grew. He could help with those things if we needed, but this was solely for her education. Her father had so much promise, he said, and she will too. I wanted to ask how he was so sure, but he wasn't the type of man you questioned. Bhavna and I hardly said a word, and it happened very quickly. He handed this to us and left."

Naresh Ganguli removed a sheet of paper and, placing it on top, slipped the file onto Madan's lap. Madan stared down at the official-looking sheet, yellowed with age, the stamp of the notary public a faded inky swirl of blue.

His finger reached out to trace the familiar signature, one he could still replicate exactly as it was here, the sweeping *A* and the resolute *r* and the demanding, mercurial *S*.

Avtaar Singh.

"Nitasha doesn't know much about this,"

Mr. Ganguli said. "Naveen helped me open the trust for her America studies. I can picture Avtaar Singh to this day sitting on our sofa, holding Nitasha in his arms. Who was this Avtaar Singh to you?"

Madan stared at the flood tide of printed words, but understanding eluded him. He placed the file and papers on the desk and, rising up, hastily stepped away.

"Please," he said, "I must go."

Taken aback, they tried to follow him to the door, but he was wishing them good night, saying he would speak to them soon, and then he was gone, taking the stairs two steps at a time.

He signaled to Preeti in the mass of women. Nitasha was not with them, and though Preeti looked strangely at him, she bade Mrs. Ganguli a hurried goodbye and emerged from the crowd.

He grabbed her hand. "We have to go," he said.

"What is it?" Clutching her purse, she adjusted her dupatta, tripping over her own feet as he pulled her along. "Madan, what's the matter?" She was barely in the car before he reversed and then sped down the street.

"What is it, Madan? Slow down. What happened?"

He pulled over to the side and got out of the car. Though it was late, the market beside which he parked was lively. Lights streamed out of the row of shops and lean-tos, and music blared. Under the canopy of an eatery, people stood by their motorcycles and scooters, eating fish tikkas and mutton kebabs off paper plates, chutneys of mint and coriander dripping down their fingers. The air smelled of grilled meat and rising bread.

In a barren park behind a chain-link fence, teenage boys played cricket by the light of the street and passing cars. Preeti came out to stand by Madan. They leaned against the car, and the boys played, the bowler's momentum lifting him off the packed dirt, his feet cycling in the air as if attempting to cross a great divide, the released ball hurtling to the waiting batter, the thwack of bat and ball, and the fielders scattering, their eyes on their moving target.

Of all the things Avtaar Singh could have done for his child, he bestowed on her the gift of education. Madan wished he could feel indignant, swear at him, curse him out. He wanted to burn with the familiar anger that kept him warm these many years. But instead he took Preeti's hand and held it to his heart. He tried to imagine Avtaar Singh stirring from Gorapur, making the long journey to hold his daughter in his arms, to see her, to cradle her and to give her his blessings. Yet as he puzzled over these images, struggling to gain momentum against the turbulence of emotions pounding through him, he could feel Avtaar Singh's reach, firm and enduring, over land and river. He told Preeti then, the truth becoming plainer to him in his retelling. The sharp ax of regret had long ago brought down the tallest, strongest, most unconquerable tree.

Madan glanced at his watch. Preeti stretched in the seat beside him, her limbs cramped from the car journey. They would be reaching Jaggu's house soon, and so he waited patiently for the Kanwariyas, the pilgrims swathed in bright saffron dhotis, shorts and T-shirts, to walk on ahead, while he slowly trailed in his car behind them.

Madan pointed out the train station to Preeti, unchanged since he had first arrived as a child. Two platforms sandwiched the twin tracks, and when a train pulled in, people grabbed their children and bundles of belongings, spilling out on either side, some onto the platform, others onto the train tracks.

On the long benches of an outdoor restaurant, a group of men sat talking and eating their lunch, looking out of place on the fraying edges of Gorapur. They were the last batch of project managers from Jeet Megacity, and soon they would be gone. Jeet Megacity would be up and running. Families had begun moving in, streetlights flickering on, stores opening, fountains sputtering to life. The last of the cranes were moving out and on to Jeet Industrial City, which would begin construction shortly. Madan was overseeing Jeet Megacity to the end, but would not be involved with Jeet Industrial City. And, though when the time came there would be one last wistful pang, he knew he would gladly let Jeet Megacity go. It belonged to everyone but him now — to the Avtaar Singhs, and the Jaggus and Swatis and their children, and to their children after them.

Nitasha had returned to school, and he mirrored the Gangulis' sadness at her departure. He would have felt the same way if it were Arnav. If he could, he would hold on to his children, these beings fashioned equally with joy and heartache, and never let them go. Never let them be farther away than the reach of his hand or the roof of his house.

The road widened and Madan was able to

drive around the Kanwariyas. They walked barefoot, these pilgrims, from their villages to the town of Hardiwar and back, for some a journey of a thousand kilometers or more. In Hardiwar they collected water from the Ganges River for consecration in the Lord Shiva temples of their villages. The Kanwariyas dotted the roadways all the way from Delhi to Gorapur as he and Preeti had driven here, visible from afar by the poles they carried on their backs, festooned with brightly colored scarves, from which hung the pots brimming with Ganges' holy water.

The Kanwariyas surrounding his car were mostly young men, and even a boy not more than fourteen. With no harvest work during the monsoon months, some of these young men were on pilgrimage to keep themselves busy, while others wanted Lord Shiva's blessings, or a wish granted, or the respect of their community when they returned with the holy water for their hometown's temple.

Yet whatever the reason, like all pilgrims they walked on with the knowledge that no matter how rutted the road or hot the sun, how heavy the load or how distant the holiest point of their journey may be, it was only when they returned home that their pilgrimage was truly over.

When they got to Jaggu's house, the family was waiting for them. The kids and Swati flitted around Preeti, exclaiming at the gifts Madan had remembered to bring with him this time around. His mother had left for a pilgrimage to Vaishno Devi with her temple group. "She spends most of her time at the temple now," Jaggu said with a shrug.

Madan dropped off their bags and made sure Preeti was settled in. "You're sure you don't want me to come inside with you?" Jaggu asked, car keys jiggling in his hand.

"Yes," said Madan. "Just drop me off." He didn't want to have a car waiting outside for him, his own or Jaggu's. He wanted no temptation, no means of ready escape at hand.

They drove silently through town, past maize stalks and white egrets, past the lanky eucalyptus trees lining the roadways and the hunched women in the rice fields. One day, he'd told Nitasha, I'll show you Gorapur. And he longed for the time when he would take her wading between the rice fields, and they would see the dabchicks skittering across the ponds, and gnaw on sugarcane straight from the field, fish in the canal and climb the lookout towers from which every horizon was visible. They would thread their way through markets lined with wooden carts heaped high with puffed rice and fresh fruit, where storefronts spilled out onto the sidewalks and makeshift temples grew under the shade of the banyan trees.

But where would he take her first?

"We're here," Jaggu said, as though Madan were not already aware of the sign soaring above the iron gate.

He didn't hear Jaggu drive off. He stepped through the iron gate and over the chasm of the intervening years. The factory was as he had left it, buzzing with activity, as if carrying on wholly for him.

Above him, the ceiling of sugar-brown dragonflies pulsed and shifted. The pitch of their humming picked up as he walked under the hundred rolling eyes. The ground was soft with layers of sawdust. Somewhere under these long-standing layers there must be a network of his old footsteps, fossilized in their various stages of growth, like a yardstick of years gone by. He took a few steps farther in. The imprint of his shoes remained for a moment before the breeze coming off the rice fields blew sawdust over them once again.

A truck trundled through the gate, the driver calling for help with the unloading. The sharp smell of wood glue rose from the vats at the far end of the factory. The workers paused in their labor, watching as he lingered every few steps over this and that, staring off into the distance and nodding to himself as if checking off a list in his head.

He picked his way through the hillocks of logs and wound around the machines and piles of finished boards. There wasn't anyone around the giant steel furnace, yet from behind its closed door he heard the flames roar like a muffled creature, its waves of heat causing the surrounding air to bend and flicker hypnotically.

There was a crunch of footsteps behind him. He turned. Mr. D'Silva peered at him through the dappled sunshine.

"Madan?" The old accountant held a ledger to his chest. "Madan?"

"Mr. D'Silva!" He took Mr. D'Silva's hand, frail and soft; all that remained of his full head of hair was a thin edge of gray. "You're still here?"

Mr. D'Silva clutched Madan's hand. Through his glasses, his eyes raked over Madan's face. "For a moment I thought my failing eyes were deceiving me . . ." He looked up at Madan, shaking his head. "I stepped out for a minute, and you're standing here like you never left."

"In some way, that's what it feels like. It's very good to see you."

"And I never thought I'd see . . ." He stopped and collected himself. "I'm officially retired, but since I'm the only one left from the old days, he likes me to come around. Look over everything." He smiled and patted Madan's hand. "You're seeing the changes?"

Madan nodded. "That's new." He pointed to a long green metal contraption.

"It has a conveyor system that dries the boards in about ten minutes flat. We still pile them in the heating rooms, the old way, but we try these modern things as well."

"And what about the new factory? It must have all the latest stuff."

Mr. D'Silva laughed. "Those blueprints have probably turned to dust in some corner of the office," he said. "No one has spoken of them for over twenty years now."

He took Madan's arm as they walked away from the roughened brick walls and into the open. "He busied himself with other things."

Back out in the yard, the chalky yellow walls of Avtaar Singh's office stood before them, the same door, part wood, part glass, closed to the noise and activity.

"Go to him," said Mr. D'Silva, nudging him on. "He waits and he waits."

In Gorapur, Madan would tell Nitasha,

There is one place we go first before all others, to the one man with whom, as we all do with the great cosmic giver-and-taker above, I bargained three times — once for my family, once for my life and then for you. He is the beginning of your story and mine.

It may not be the story she would want to hear, but it was the only story he had to tell.

Madan went toward the door without hesitation or fear or sadness. He forgot Mr. D'Silva, and the clanking machines, the trucks rumbling in belching black smoke, the prying dragonflies and the brick walls that bore witness, of what came before and what was yet to be.

Through the half window in the door, he could see the light shining through.

ACKNOWLEDGMENTS

Eternal thanks to my editor Jill Bialosky for shaping and infusing *Three Bargains* with her excellent insights, perception, and kind regard. Thank you as well to everyone at W. W. Norton.

I am indebted to my agent Emma Sweeney for her guidance, support, and commitment, and to everyone at ESA who helped along the way.

Thank you to my writing partners Maya Creedman and Dr. Jennifer Gunter, for their generosity of time and spirit, for reviewing draft after draft, and for their wise counsel, motivation, unwavering faith, and encouragement throughout the years.

To Nikki Marchesiello for painstakingly reading, critiquing, polishing, and honing every single word of the manuscript time after time. Thanks for the innumerable cups of fortifying tea (and sometimes shots of Limoncello!) at her kitchen table, for giving me courage and inspiration when I most needed it, for never allowing me to give up on myself, and mostly for exhorting me to face it all with, "head up, shoulders back, and tits out."

To my brother Sameer Gambhir, who puts life in perspective and makes me laugh like no one else, and his wife Nikita, for the many nights of brainstorming and deliberations over different aspects of the plot.

An immense debt of gratitude to Annie Yearout, Anjie Seewer Reynolds, Tina Bournazos, Cathy Petrick, and Jennifer Bell, for reading and providing invaluable feedback on various versions of the manuscript.

Special thanks to my cousin Puneet Gambhir, and to my family and friends for information and advice, especially: Kusum Malik, Dr. Manish Malik, Dr. Rashmi Malik, Advocate Sachit Setia, and Arti Setia (constant and forever friend).

To my dog Deuce for his companionship, and for ensuring I went for a walk every morning and evening to stretch my legs and think.

To Rajiv, for his steadfast strength, for keeping me sane, and for paving my way with his love and humor. And finally, to Samara, for the joy she brings to my every moment, for making life worth living, and for allowing me an understanding of myself I never thought possible. You are my one and only bargain.